FIRE of HEAVEN

Also by Bill Myers
Blood of Heaven
Threshold

FIRE of HEAVEN

BILL MYERS

ZondervanPublishingHouse
Grand Rapids, Michigan

A Division of HarperCollinsPublishers

We want to hear from you. Please send your comments about this book to us in care of the address below. Thank you.

ZondervanPublishingHouse
Grand Rapids, Michigan
http://www.zondervan.com

Fire of Heaven
Copyright © 1999 by Bill Myers

Requests for information should be addressed to:

ZondervanPublishingHouse
Grand Rapids, Michigan 49530

Library of Congress Cataloging-in-Publication Data

Myers, Bill, 1953–
    Fire of Heaven / Bill Myers.
        p. cm.
    ISBN: 0-310-21738-5
    I. Title.
PS3563.Y36F57   1999
813'.54--dc21   99-15207
                                                        CIP

Published in association with the literary agency of Alive Communications, Inc., 1465 Kelly Johnson Blvd., Suite 320, Colorado Springs, CO 80920

Interior design by Sue Vandenberg Koppenol

Printed in the United States of America

00 01 02 03 04 05 /❖ DC/ 10 9 8 7 6 5

For the Bride,
that she may be presented
without spot, blemish, or wrinkle

PREFACE

I wanted to try something different with this book. And I figured I should warn you up front so if you're reading this in a store you can slip it back on the shelf before it's too late, or if you're already at home you can race back and get a refund before the pages get bent.

My point is . . . this book is not for everybody.

First of all, I wanted to try to write Christian fiction. Not just entertainment that you expect to be moral or that has a Christian theme. I wanted to write a piece of Christian fiction for Christians. Something that begins with what we already believe about God and explores Him from there. Something for the disciples after the crowds have been entertained and gone home. Something that assumes exploring God's truths (some may call these portions preachy) can be just as engaging as the fastest car chase or steamy romance scene. So if you're looking for some good, old-fashioned, escapist entertainment, go ahead and slip this back on the shelf, no hard feelings. Maybe we'll connect the next time around.

Also, despite what you may have thought, this is not an end-times prophecy book. My purpose is *not* to expound upon end-time events. Lots of other books out there claim to have those answers. This isn't one of them. In fact, I'd be surprised if *any* end-times happenings unfolded the way they're depicted here. That wasn't my purpose. I wanted to explore end-times themes, not events. I wanted to touch upon end-times teaching as Christ might have when talking to his disciples. It seems nearly every time they asked him for the ear-tickling details, he gave a few generalities and then used the opportunity to springboard into a deeper truth. Instead of getting their flesh worked up and excited about the mark of the beast, or the timing of the

Rapture, or who the Antichrist will be, he usually went for a deeper, spiritual truth ... like encouraging them to be ready.

That's what I've tried to do here. The rest is just backdrop, a little scenery that we may or may not see along the way to his Second Coming. As I've said, if you want a clearly marked road map, hundreds of other books claim to know the way. All I want to do with this one is to challenge us to examine our hearts as we make that journey.

As I did in *Threshold* I need to briefly mention the gender of the two end-times witnesses. According to the Greek experts, if these two witnesses are actually people, then one definitely must be male. However, there is nothing in the original language that prevents the other from being female.

And now finally, to the thanks ...

First of all my deepest appreciation goes to a friend who wishes to remain anonymous. She prayed every day for the book, from its research, through the outlining, and during the actual writing. There were days she fasted, and nearly every day my e-mail had an encouraging word of Scripture from her. No writer could have been more blessed, and in many ways this book is as much the fruit of her labor as it is mine.

There was also that woman from Ohio (I don't think she ever told me her name) who, on the most critical day of the book, tracked my phone number down and called up to say she'd been led to pray and fast for me.

Special thanks also to Dale Brown who made this book much better; as well as to Rolland and Rena Petrello; Dr. Craig Cameron and his wife, Sue; Geog Pflueger for his hospitality in Jerusalem; Oswald Chambers for the "powder of contriteness" quote; Tina Schuman; Scott and Rebecca Janney; my research assistant, Doug McIntosh; James Riordan; John Tolle; Gary Smith; the incredible folks at Zondervan; Susan Richardson and the staff at For Heaven's Sake; Lissa Halls Johnson; Vince Crunk; Erdogan, my guide in Turkey; Carla Williams; Diane Komp, M.D.; Tony Myles; Francine Rivers; Lyn Marzulli; Greg Johnson; and always to Brenda, Nicole, and Mackenzie.

"And I will grant authority to my two witnesses, and they will prophesy for twelve hundred and sixty days, clothed in sackcloth." These are the two olive trees and the two lampstands that stand before the Lord of the earth. And if anyone desires to harm them, fire proceeds out of their mouth and devours their enemies; and if anyone would desire to harm them, in this manner he must be killed. These have the power to shut up the sky, in order that rain may not fall during the days of their prophesying; and they have power over the waters to turn them into blood, and to smite the earth with every plague, as often as they desire. And when they have finished their testimony, the beast that comes up out of the abyss will make war with them, and overcome them and kill them. And their dead bodies will lie in the street of the great city which mystically is called Sodom and Egypt, where also their Lord was crucified. And those from the peoples and tribes and tongues and nations will look at their dead bodies for three and a half days, and will not permit their dead bodies to be laid in a tomb. And those who dwell on earth will rejoice over them and make merry; and they will send gifts to one another, because these two prophets tormented those who dwell on the earth. And after the three and a half days the breath of life from God came into them, and they stood on their feet; and great fear fell upon those who were beholding them. And they heard a loud voice from heaven saying to them, "Come up here." And they went up into heaven in the cloud, and their enemies beheld them. And in that hour there was a great earthquake, and a tenth of the city fell; and seven thousand people were killed in the earthquake, and the rest were terrified and gave glory to the God of heaven.

Revelation 11:3–13 NASB

PROLOGUE

Katherine Lyon wasn't sure if she'd heard her son scream or if she'd dreamed it. It didn't matter. She flung off the coarse wool blankets and hit the cold stones of the floor running.

There it was again. Faint, distant, but impossible to miss. It *was* her son and he *was* screaming.

Katherine grabbed her robe, raced to the wooden plank door, and threw it open. The first traces of pink reflected off the snow-covered mountaintops and filtered into the courtyard. Dawn was about to break, but she barely noticed. She turned left and ran across the second-story balcony toward the men's quarters. Once again she cursed the fact that they were separated. But

Eric was thirteen now. The thickening fuzz on his face and his unsteady voice made it clear he was entering manhood. And segregation in the compound was expected, demanded.

Then there was the other matter . . . the growing number of devotees who insisted upon calling him Master, or in some cases, God. Somehow it didn't seem fitting for God to continue rooming with his mother.

The two of them had been on their own for eleven years now. The first seven after Gary, her husband, was shot in the line of duty. The rest after Michael Coleman, a close friend, had laid down his life for them—but not before accidentally infecting Eric with a special DNA.

A DNA that many believed to come from the blood of Christ.

Katherine passed two young women wearing sandals and loose colorful pants called *punjabis*. As disciples who were privileged to live within the compound, their joy, their pleasure, was to serve Eric and members of the Cartel. And they did so with unwavering devotion. Even now they carried *pujaas*, plates of colored rice and flowers, as an offering that would soon find its way outside Eric's quarters.

Initially, she and Eric had tried to shun the adoration. But their attempts were only mistaken as humility, which only offered more proof of his godhood. This along with his uncanny insight into other people's thoughts continued to deepen his followers' reverence. People talked, rumors spread, and the harder Katherine tried to clear the record, the greater the worship grew.

Breathing heavily, she reached the men's section. She rounded the corner and nearly ran into an armed guard stationed outside Eric's door. He was military but not from Nepal. No surprise there. More and more countries were offering their services in order to court the Cartel's favor. The soldier was simply one of a rotating group of international representatives. Southeast Asian, the best she could tell.

"What do you want?" His accent was thick. He was new and obviously unnerved from the screaming inside.

"I am the boy's mother," Katherine said, trying to catch her breath. Despite the number of months living here in the Himalayas, she had never entirely adjusted to the thinness of the air. She started for the door, but he blocked her path. She looked up, glaring at him. "My son is having a nightmare. If you don't let me in, you may bring his displeasure upon you." She took another gulp of air. "And I'm sure neither of us wants that, do we?"

It was a ploy she used more and more often. And, given Eric's recent outbursts of anger, it usually worked. Changes were happening with her son just as they had with their friend Michael Coleman. Although Eric's supernatural powers continued to grow, the tender mercy and compassion he'd once exhibited had begun to die. The deterioration that Coleman had fought in himself was now happening to her son. It was all Eric could do to control his hostility . . . an unfortunate reversal and not-so-minor side effect of man trying to reproduce the genes of God.

There was another scream. Muffled this time, almost whimpering. Katherine's gaze remained fixed on the guard. She would not back down.

He shifted again, glancing around the courtyard, obviously hoping for someone to rescue him. But there was only Katherine. He took another breath, swallowed, then finally nodded and stepped aside.

Katherine brushed past him and threw open the door.

The room was several times larger than hers—an eclectic mixture of East meets West. Saffron silk drapes here, the latest computers and monitors stacked over there. A giant, blue-skinned Krishna statue leaned against one plastered wall, while posters of the latest rock idols were taped on another. And there, writhing and tossing in the giant four-poster bed, was young Eric.

Katherine raced to him, scooping him into her arms. He was still asleep and whimpered slightly until she began to rock him.

"Shh, now, shhh . . ."

Instinctively, he wrapped his arms around her, clinging to her as he had when he was a baby. Emotion rose deep within Katherine, tightening her throat and making it ache. She'd read once that there was no love more pure than a mother for her child. She agreed. Despite his outbursts, despite the embarrassments he caused, he was her son. He would always be her son.

"It's okay," she whispered hoarsely as they continued to rock. "It's just a dream, it's okay."

He stirred, then opened his eyes.

She kissed the top of his head. "Was it Heylel?" she whispered. "Did he show you something scary again?"

Eric gave no response but turned his head and continued to cling.

Katherine had her answer. Originally, she had been wary of Heylel's appearances to her son. But after listening to half a dozen experts on the subject who insisted Eric was communicating with his guardian angel or a spirit guide, and after reading another dozen books extolling the benefits of such communication, Katherine had begun to relax . . . a little. As an embittered preacher's kid who was toying with returning to the faith, she could find nothing wrong with her son's experiences. Wasn't the Bible chock-full of angels speaking and directing people? Why should Eric, with his heightened sensitivity to the supernatural, experience anything less?

Heylel was careful never to reveal his exact identity. But, because of his piercing insight into political situations and the absolute accuracy of his predictions—which he communicated to the Cartel through Eric—several thought he might be the departed spirit of some military genius, perhaps Napoleon or Alexander the Great. Those with a vivid imagination suggested Eric could be channeling some wise and benevolent alien from another planet, while many with a more scientific bent suggested that Heylel was merely a subconscious extension of Eric's own supernatural giftedness.

It made no difference. The point is, everyone was positive Heylel was good—the books, the counselors, Eric, the specialists Katherine had insisted be flown in to examine him, the Cartel, everyone. Everyone . . . except Katherine. Because, despite the overwhelming evidence, she still found something unsettling about the times Eric would give up control of his voice and become a channel for this entity to speak through.

Still, Heylel was always courteous, never abusive, and he always offered brilliant counsel. A counsel that the Cartel had grown more and more dependent upon. A counsel that this semisecret organization of international bankers, politicians, and world leaders was using for the betterment of all.

And yet . . .

Katherine pushed back her son's damp hair and kissed him on the forehead. He did not pull away. She tried to lift him from the bed, but those days had long passed. He was far too heavy. Instead, she helped him to his feet and gently guided him toward the door.

"Come stay with me," she said softly. "Just for a while."

She was pleased Eric didn't resist as they headed for the door. God or no god, this frightened boy was going to spend the rest of the early morning hours with his mother.

Brandon bolted up in bed. He sat there for several seconds, catching his breath, waiting for the last of the nightmare to fade. It was always the same one. The one where he stood before the altar of his father's church confronting a giant serpent head. As always the vaporous specter had floated above the aisle, just a few feet before him. As always, it had opened its tremendous mouth in preparation to devour him. And, as always, Brandon stood terrified, staring helplessly into its throat, seeing a whirling vortex of human faces, fiery apparitions that twisted and distorted, faces screaming in agony as they swirled around and around, spiraling down into an endless abyss.

The vision was horrifying. It always was.

So was the wind. The fierce, screaming wind that tugged at him, trying to draw him into the mouth. As in the other dreams he had spun around to grab hold of the altar, hoping his grip would somehow prevent him from being sucked into the throat, from joining those thousands of tortured, screaming faces.

The nightmare didn't come often, but when it did, it always left him cold and shaken. The reason was simple. It was identical to the confrontation he had actually had in his father's church over a year ago. Only, in that confrontation, his grip on the altar did not hold. The encounter had been fierce and excruciating. It had taken his father's life, and it had nearly destroyed his own.

But tonight, there had been another difference. As he clung to the altar, he had noticed some sort of crescent moon and five-pointed star carved into the wood. The image seemed vaguely familiar, but he couldn't place it. And, even now, as the last of the nightmare faded, the moon and star continued to linger in his mind.

He turned to the clock radio on his nightstand. It read 2:39. He wouldn't be able to go back to sleep, he was certain of that. He pulled off the damp sheet that still clung to his body, snapped on the light, and sat on the edge of the bed. Scattered on the floor around his feet were the remains of yesterday's newspaper. There were the usual headlines about the recent crash of the Tokyo stock exchange and fears that Wall Street and NASDAQ were following. Another article spoke of the masses of people starving from the drought. There was also something about the rapid spread of a new virus they'd nicknamed "Scorpion." Latest estimates were that 1.3 million of the world's Semite population, mostly Jews and Arabs, were already infected, and it was going to get a lot worse before it got better. Finally, there was another article on the progress Lucas Ponte and the Cartel were making toward world peace.

But yesterday's headlines were of little interest to Brandon now. Now, his eyes were drawn to a pile of sketches on the dresser across the room. Sketches made by Gerty Morrison before she'd died. No one had taken the old woman seriously when she lived, but the prophecies she had given regarding Brandon and Dr. Sarah Weintraub had proven eerily correct, down to the tiniest detail. Still, the past prophecies were nothing compared to the ones she claimed were yet to be fulfilled. The ones insisting that both he and Sarah were the two endtime prophets mentioned in the Bible.

Of course, it took more than one woman's predictions to get them to take such a claim seriously, no matter how accurate those predictions had proven in the past. And God seemed only too happy to oblige with further evidence . . . such as the words of other so-called prophets spoken over his mother when she was pregnant with him . . . and the demoniacs who always screamed whenever he or Sarah entered their presence . . . and the results of the paranormal tests Sarah had run on him when they'd first met . . . and the showdown between heaven and hell that had killed his father and nearly taken his own life.

There was, however, one further piece of evidence, perhaps stronger than all of the others combined: the emergence of Brandon's own prophetic gifts. And, just as importantly, his newfound ability to heal the sick.

If God was trying to make a point, he'd certainly gone out of his way to do so. Yet, at the same time, he was frustratingly silent when it came to any details on the how or the when.

With a heavy sigh, Brandon rose from the bed and shuffled toward the pile of sketches. Many of them were detailed drawings Gerty had made of him at pivotal moments in his childhood. The fact that she had never seen him during this time made them even more compelling. But the last sketch was the one he and Sarah had found the most unsettling. He riffled through the pile until he found it. It was a sketch that featured both of them together. Their hair was cut short and they stood side by side in an ancient walled city. And hovering directly in front of them was the vaporous snake head of his dream. Its mouth was opened wide, and it was poised to devour them. But equally disquieting was that the serpent was held at bay by what looked like flames of fire ... spewing from Brandon's mouth.

Brandon stared at the sketch a long time before setting it back down on the dresser. Then, taking a deep breath and slowly letting it out, he glanced back at the time.

It was now 2:43.

He headed back to bed. He shut off the light and stared up at the ceiling. It was doubtful he'd be able to sleep, but he needed to try. After all, today was going to be a busy day. Busier than most.

Today, in just eleven hours and seventeen minutes, he and Dr. Sarah Weintraub were to become husband and wife.

PART
ONE

CHAPTER 1

*S*arah, your veil, it's all—here, let me straighten it. Sarah, tilt your head this way. Sarah!"

Dr. Sarah Weintraub obeyed and leaned forward.

"A little more. Now please, *please* pay attention."

She stood just outside the sanctuary doors as the wedding coordinator flitted about making last-minute adjustments to her gown, her veil, or anything else that the poor lady could fixate over. But Sarah didn't mind. The elaborate wedding had mostly been for Brandon's mother. Which was okay. It seemed a small price to pay to comfort a woman who had lost her daughter, her husband, and was now about to lose her only son. Of course they would stay in touch with her, try to meet her needs. But as the clinic continued to grow and word of Brandon's healing ministry continued to spread, time for any personal life was becoming less and less of a reality.

Some thought the wedding came too quickly. Others were sure it wouldn't last. It would be hard enough to begin a life amidst the growing famine, the panic sweeping the world over this new virus, and the current financial calamities. But add to that the fact that Brandon was four years her junior, and many were certain that the couple was asking for marital disaster.

Although the other issues were of concern, the age difference was inconsequential. It didn't bother Brandon and it certainly didn't bother her. In fact, Sarah found him less self-absorbed and ego-driven than most men twice his age. Not that he didn't have his moments, but over the past year Brandon Martus had become the most compassionate and sensitive man she had ever met. And, best of all, much of that compassion and sensitivity was directed toward her.

There were other differences, such as their backgrounds and their education. Brandon grew up in this Indiana farm community and was lucky to finish high school. Sarah was West Coast born and bred and held her doctorate in neurobiology. If ever the term "opposites attract" applied, it would have to be to these two.

But there was that prophecy in Revelation ... and the mound of evidence that indicated they just might be the two end-time prophets who would prepare the world for the return of Jesus Christ much as John the Baptist had prepared it for his first coming. Of course most of that was subject to interpretation, which proved to be a major source of disagreement between the two of them. She never understood why Brandon insisted upon taking every word so literally, while she, although admitting that the two of them might somehow be used, saw the prophecies as more spiritual and symbolic. The truth of the matter was, nobody knew for certain. Not even Gerty. But, at the very least, from what they could tell, the two of them were to work together as a team. And what better way to be a team than to be husband and wife?

Oh, and there was one other detail that carried weight in their decision for matrimony . . .

They loved each other. Fiercely. They were absolutely committed to one another, regardless of the odds.

Sarah peeked through the glass in the sanctuary door. She could see Brandon standing before the altar, incredibly handsome in his tuxedo.

For her, the attraction had been instant, love at first sight. Yes, there was his long black hair and those muscular shoulders. And yes, there were those killer gray eyes which could still make her stomach do little flip-flops. But that was just the wrapping. Because inside, inside was a heart not only full of kindness, but a heart full of her. What had he said the night he'd proposed? "You're the missing piece I've been looking for all of my life . . . you're what fills my hollowness." The words had made her cry then and they almost did now. She knew that whatever the future held, despite graying hair, wrinkled skin, or sagging body, he would always be there for her. Always. And she would be there for him.

Of course there were a few other obstacles to overcome . . . like the forces of hell trying to destroy both of their lives. For Brandon it had been a showdown in this very church, a confrontation with what they believed to be a manifestation of Satan himself. For Sarah it had been a violent collision that sent her flying through a pickup's windshield. If it hadn't been for Brandon's intervention at the hospital, one of the first times he'd put his healing powers to use, she would not be standing here today. And, except for a nasty scar running across her forehead and down to her right jaw, she was as good as new.

Actually, better. Because, in the process of praying to heal her body, Brandon had healed her soul.

"Get ready, Sarah. The prelude is almost done . . ."

Sarah glanced up at the wedding coordinator who was pulling open the doors in preparation for the wedding party processional. She gathered herself together and threw a look at her father. The poor guy appeared more nervous than she was. She leaned over and whispered, "It's okay, Dad—everything will be all right."

He gave what was supposed to be a reassuring smile and patted her arm with his cold, damp hand.

As a little girl she had never seen much of her father. But she did inherit his love for medicine, and even more importantly, she inherited his drive to be the best. If Sarah had learned one thing from her father, it was that success had little to do with brains or beauty and everything to do with ambition and hard work. Although it could be a plus, the ambition had created terrible problems for her in the past, and on more than one occasion it had proven to be her Achilles' heel. Still, as time passed and her love for God increased, she had learned how to deal with it and for the most part kept it under control.

She looked back at her father. He was a good man, full of understanding. Despite their Jewish roots, he made little protest over her conversion to Christianity. "If it's what you want, if it's really what makes you happy, then it's fine by me," he had said. But there was no missing his resigned shrug and quiet afterthought. "Still, I suppose it's best your mother isn't alive to see it."

If he was tolerant about his daughter's change of faith, the good doctor was anything but pleased over his future son-in-law's disposition toward miracles. He did not spend all of that money sending his baby to graduate school to have her marry some backwoods faith healer. That's why he had come a week early. And that's why after several days of carefully examining the clinic's work—both Brandon's healing of the sick, as well as Sarah's medical evaluations of those cases—he grudgingly admitted that there was something going on. Of course Sarah had tried to explain that "something" in terms of her new faith, but the subject fell on impatient and increasingly hostile ears.

The wedding party was in place, and the music began for Sarah's entrance. She stepped up to the doors. Now she was able to look over the entire church. More accurately, as they rose to their feet, the entire church was able to look over her. She felt her face growing warm. Some of it was from excitement, some of it was her self-consciousness over the scar. Funny, Brandon had tried repeatedly to erase the scar, but had never succeeded. Neither of them was sure why. And, oddly enough, it was the only thing that made the normally self-confident Dr. Sarah Weintraub just the slightest bit insecure.

Still, this was their day and she would not be intimidated. As her father escorted her into the sanctuary, Sarah cranked up a smile and made a point to look as many people in the eye as possible. Most were friends and family of Brandon—a definite hometown advantage. Only a few belonged to her. But there were also dozens of patients who had become friends—men, women, children who had entered the clinic doors with severe injury or disease, some diagnosed as terminal, but who now stood perfectly healthy, anxious to share this day with them.

Of course, there were the others. The skeptics, the stone throwers . . . and the media. These were the people on the clinic's "Win Over" list. The list had been Sarah's idea, and she kept it regularly updated. She loved Brandon and respected him more than any person alive. And as his gifts increased, his mercy and compassion followed suit. But it took more than mercy and compassion to run the clinic. With the addition of three full-time staff members and the purchase and leasing of medical equipment, along with Brandon's insistence that they only accept donations—"It's God's work, Sarah, we can't charge them for what God is doing"—it was all they could do to keep their heads above financial water.

Common sense dictated that they had to increase their donor base by increasing their exposure. The more people they won over, especially the skeptical and influential members of the media, the greater their exposure, and the greater their exposure, the greater their chances of avoiding fiscal suicide.

And they were making progress. In fact, just yesterday, Sarah had been contacted by Jimmy Tyler Ministries. They had invited the two of them to fly out to L.A. and sit on the platform during some upcoming, nationally televised event. Because Tyler was one of the leading televangelists in the country, and owner of GBN, the Gospel Broadcasting Network, his endorsement alone could make or break the clinic. Sarah had worked long and hard courting their interest, and now they were finally coming around. But what type of event was it, and how could they best utilize it to fit their—

Stop it, Sarah chided herself. *Stop working. This is your wedding day, for crying out loud.*

But old habits are hard to break. Before she knew it, she was again scanning the crowd, making mental notes of those who had shown up for the event and those who—

"You!" A wizened old man suddenly leaped in front of her, bringing her to an abrupt stop. As he pointed at her, he turned to the crowd and shouted, "Behold . . . the whore of Babylon!"

Murmurs rippled through the congregation as the organ music came to a halting stop.

Sarah stood paralyzed, unsure of what was happening, what to do. She threw a helpless look at Brandon, who stood equally as shocked.

The old man continued. "She who shows her ankles to foreigners."

The murmuring increased. Suddenly, the man's hand shot up to Sarah's veil. Before she could stop him, he'd grabbed the lace and ripped it aside. She gasped along with the rest of the church as he tore it away.

"Behold!" He jabbed his finger at her scar. "The mark of the beast! Proof of her iniquity—"

"That's enough!" Brandon's voice cut through the air with authority. He'd recovered from the initial shock and moved toward them.

The old man spun to him and practically hissed. "What have you to do with us, servant of the Most High?"

A cold chill rippled across Sarah's shoulders. She'd seen this type of confrontation before, at the clinic, and she knew what was about to happen. But before Brandon could respond, her father moved in. He reached for the man's shoulder, trying to grab his arm.

But the old-timer spun around, driving his elbow deep into her father's belly. He gasped and doubled over.

"Daddy!"

"That's enough!" Brandon repeated. His voice brought silence to the commotion. "Leave us."

The old man seemed to hesitate.

"I order you to go."

At last he found his voice. But it was smaller now, a false bravado of what it had been. "You may think you have authority . . . but not forever. Your day will come." He pointed back to Sarah. "The day of destruction will come for you and your harlot. Very soon, victory will be ours."

"Go!"

"Our business is not yet—"

That's when Brandon's two friends, Frank and Tom Henderson, suddenly appeared, each grabbing one of the fellow's arms. And that's when Frank deftly landed two lightning quick blows to a kidney, making sure it would be a while before the old codger interrupted any more weddings.

The man coughed and gasped.

"Guys," Brandon protested, "be careful."

Frank broke into his famous smirk then turned to Tom and nodded. Immediately they half-dragged, half-walked the coughing man up the aisle toward the exit.

Sarah turned back to her father. He was still bent over, clinging to the edge of a pew. "Dad? Daddy, are you all right?"

"I'm okay," he said, coughing slightly and trying to rise.

She wasn't convinced. "Are you sure?"

"I said I'm okay." He righted himself and carefully tested a rib or two. She glanced at Brandon, who nodded to her that he thought the man was all right. "Just tell me where . . ." Her father coughed again. "Just tell me where I'm supposed to sit."

"Over there." Sarah motioned toward the front pew. "But if you're not—"

"I said I'm okay. Let's just get on with this thing, shall we?" He started for the front pew and was immediately joined by the pastor, who had stepped down to assist him.

Meanwhile, Brandon's aunt had risen to help replace Sarah's veil. Another woman began smoothing her dress. For the briefest moment Sarah stood disoriented, unsure of what to do . . . until she saw Brandon reaching out and taking her hand.

She looked up at him. There were those riveting eyes. She felt them looking inside of her again, probing her heart the way they did when he wanted to know what she was really thinking. Sometimes she found the look frustrating, knowing there was nothing she could hide from him. Other times their intensity made her knees the slightest bit weak. This time she knew he was making sure she was okay and that she really wanted to continue.

She swallowed hard and forced a smile.

But Brandon still didn't have his answer. He asked again, this time in a language only she understood—a language they'd first used in the hospital when he'd stayed all those nights at her side, praying for her recovery, when her face was bandaged so completely that she could barely utter a sound. More recently it had been his method to see if she'd fallen asleep as they watched old movies on late-night TV. It was a simple code. Childish, really. But it was theirs.

He gave her hand two gentle squeezes.

Sarah's heart swelled. She swallowed again and then gave one simple squeeze back. That was the signal. It was going to be okay. Things were going to be all right.

They turned and headed for the altar.

Katherine was not fond of these afternoon sessions. Come to think of it, she was growing less and less fond of any of the sessions involving the Cartel. These were the times when Eric was the most vulnerable, when he made himself available for Heylel to speak through him and give them counsel. These were also the times Katherine wandered the adjacent hallway, visited nearly every secretary whose office was in the vicinity of the meeting room, and put down more than her fair share of coffee. Sometimes the meetings would go on for an hour, sometimes several. It all depended upon what international fire had to be put out. The current meeting had just begun its third hour.

She sat in an armchair inside a lobby of one of the offices and idly flipped through another magazine. She didn't mind the Cartel members themselves. In fact she almost liked a couple of them. Even though they were some of the most influential people in the world—international bankers, business moguls, past and present politicians—as human beings, they weren't half bad.

For Katherine and most of the world, the Cartel's history was murky at best. Until they officially acknowledged their presence less than a year ago, many people weren't even sure they existed. And that invisibility, according to the experts, was their greatest strength. Some insisted the group had roots as far back as the Knights of the Temple, or more recently, the Illuminati. Others insisted they were a major force behind the creation of the United Nations, the Trilateral Commission, and the European Union. Whatever rumor you cared to believe, the point was they were heavy hitters who had finally come out of seclusion for one purpose and one purpose only: "To assist global powers in bringing about permanent world peace." That was it. Despite the conspiracy rumors and paranoid hearsay, they insisted they were not interested in "world domination." They didn't want to run the show, merely save it.

And what better man to become their spokesperson than Lucas Ponte? Twice elected president of the United States, he had quickly earned a reputation not only for his compassion, but for his commitment to world peace. In the first term he had become a national hero. By the second, his admirers and followers were international. If anyone had the golden touch for peace, Ponte did. First there was the miracle of bringing fruitful dialogue to the Balkans, a region which except for Soviet domination had not known rest for over a century. Next came his peace brokering amongst the warring republics of central and western Africa. And finally there was his success in easing tensions between India and Pakistan. As his tenure in office drew to a close, many feared the world would become a less kind place with his absence. Fortunately, the Cartel would not let that happen. Instead, they stepped out of seclusion and asked Lucas Ponte to become their chairman—giving him the opportunity to complete the job he had so successfully begun.

Still, even at that, Katherine didn't entirely trust them. Not at first. After all, this was the organization that had bankrolled the research of the GOD gene. They were the ones who tried to have portions of Christ's genetic code reproduced in Michael Coleman and who inadvertently infected her son. In short, they were the ones who had ruined Eric's life.

Of course that hadn't been their intention. They were simply exploring the possibility of gene therapy to curb man's tendency toward violence. And what better DNA to attempt to duplicate than that belonging to the Man of Peace?

It was an intriguing theory. Until it backfired. Until a few greedy individuals tried to reverse the process, attempting to create conscienceless killing machines. Need some general to press the nuke button? Some infantryman to fight without fear or mercy? Just inject the reverse gene, something called *antisense,* into them for a period of time and stand back. Such a drug would prove invaluable to any nation or military with the money to buy it.

Invaluable? Yes.

Unconscionable? Absolutely.

That's why, after Coleman's death, she and Eric did their best to avoid the Cartel . . . until the group's clout and unlimited financial power finally flushed them out. Yes, the Cartel admitted, there had been a handful of "loose and very greedy cannons" in the program. But they had been discovered and promptly disposed of. The Cartel's purpose was the same as it always had been, to promote world peace. And Eric, with his newly acquired powers and, more recently, with his ability for allowing Heylel to speak through him, could become an invaluable player in that process.

But Katherine was not terribly interested in world peace. And, despite all the books she'd been reading and the counsel she'd received, she was becoming less and less excited about her son's channeling abilities. No, it was the other carrot they offered that brought the two of them to the compound and persuaded her to endure these sessions. It was the Cartel's offer to do everything in their power to find a cure for Eric—to stop the degeneration that had begun as a result of their own experimentation. Not a bad promise considering they were major stockholders in some of the largest genetic laboratories of the world . . . considering Eric's condition had taken a turn for the worse . . . considering they were the only hope she had to stop her little boy from turning into some sort of antisocial psychopath.

So, here Katherine sat, flipping through magazines in a plush office amidst the mountains of Nepal while her son met with and offered counsel to some of the most powerful men in the world. Then again, it really wasn't her son. It was somebody or something else. And it was that somebody or something else that was making the Cartel's offer less and less appealing, that was making Katherine think more and more seriously about getting out.

"Only, the Arab Coalition will not call for a cease-fire until Israel agrees to return to the negotiating table . . . and, of course, Israel will not negotiate until there's a cease-fire."

"What about a nuclear threat?"

"Lots of saber rattling. But with the right guarantees, the Jews won't go nuclear if the Arabs don't go biological."

"Guarantees provided by . . . us?"

"Who else."

The group sat quietly around the table as the former NATO secretary general finished his report. He gathered his papers, leaned back, and resumed chewing a cigar almost as big as his ego.

Eric didn't like the man, never had. Even his voice irritated him. In fact, it was all he could do not to shout the pompous old windbag into silence. But Chairman Lucas Ponte hated it when Eric did that sort of thing, especially at these briefings. It not only disrupted them, but it embarrassed Lucas.

And Eric didn't want to do that. After all, Lucas was his friend. In many ways he'd become the father Eric never had. And Eric was becoming the son Lucas had always wanted.

Now, if he could just get his mother to go a little easier on the guy . . .

"Mr. Chairman, once again I must insist that we delay the groundbreaking and that we seriously consider moving your installation into office to another location." It was one of the bankers. The woman from South Africa. Eric hated her almost as much as the secretary general. So did the other nine members of the Cartel gathered around the table. At least that was Eric's impression. "To stage such events at this time in Jerusalem will not only exacerbate the situation, but it will prove dangerously reckless to your own safety."

"I disagree." It was another banker, this one from Germany. "An action like this will only show our resolve. It will underscore our strength and our insistence that world peace will not be held hostage to fragmentary elements."

Some around the table agreed, others did not. But it was the South African's voice that rose above the din. "One can hardly call these Middle East outbreaks fragmentary!"

More comments flew back and forth. But Eric barely noticed. He pushed up his glasses with his little finger and returned to work. At the moment he was secretly carving his initials into the side of the mahogany table with a $750 Mont Blanc pen. Like all the other meetings that were supposed to be so important, this one was going nowhere fast.

A scientist spoke up. Swiss, if Eric guessed right. "One would think Scorpion should make them sit up and take notice. The disease has reached pandemic proportions. Every continent reels under its impact." He turned to Aaron Stoltz, head of media. "A virus of unknown origin striking primarily the Semitic races, the Jews and Arabs ... I am not convinced we are taking full advantage of this situation."

Aaron Stoltz nodded. "We're continually flooding news services with the latest death toll. We're playing the 'judgment of God' angle to the max, with the hopes that they'll start cooperating with each other, but—"

The secretary general interrupted, "—but everyone is listening except the Jews and Arabs."

Ironic chuckles circled the table. But Eric had had enough. "I say we just nuke 'em!" The words came louder than he had anticipated and the laughter quickly faded. Some glanced around the table; others shifted uncomfortably. Except Lucas. Lucas was cool. Even when Eric had his outbursts, Lucas Ponte always showed him the respect he deserved.

"So tell me, Eric, do you think that would be a solution?"

"It'd sure stop them from wasting all our time at these stupid meetings."

Lucas smiled. "You may have a point. And with all the other issues to cover it's certainly—"

"Eric ..." It was Heylel. Eric could sense his approach as much as he could hear it.

Lucas continued. "But I'm not sure nuking the entire Middle East will exactly solve the unrest or that it will stop this new disease."

"Eric ..." Heylel's voice was louder now, so loud that it had started to drown out Lucas's. Eric shifted in his seat, pretending to ignore it.

Lucas turned back to the scientist and asked, "What progress are we making toward a vaccine?"

"*Eric* . . ."

Not now, Eric thought back.

"*I have something very important to share with the group.*"

Lucas turned back to Eric. He was speaking to him, but Eric could barely hear now. The man's lips moved but he sounded muffled, growing fainter and farther away. Despite Eric's resistance, Heylel was taking over.

"*Eric* . . ."

It's not that Eric resented Heylel. He'd shown him lots of neat stuff—astral projection, telepathy, bilocation. And the little mind game he'd played with Dr. Reichner, that psychic scientist in the States, was especially exciting. But there was a price: Whenever Heylel wanted to speak, he spoke. Whenever Heylel wanted to use his body, he did. Oh sure, Eric could resist, but lately it was getting harder and harder to say no.

"*I have another movie to show you, Eric.*"

But, things are just getting—

"*It's another war.*"

But I . . . Eric hesitated. *What type of war?*

"*Oh, you'll like this one. It's much better than the last. All sorts of soldiers are stabbed and killed. Some even get blown up. And, if you watch carefully, you'll get to see a decapitation.*"

Eric felt himself weakening. *Really?*

The voice chuckled. "*Child, have I ever lied to you?*"

Of course, he never had. From the moment he'd first appeared to Eric, Heylel had never lied. Granted, only a few of the promises had been fulfilled, but the bigger ones, the ones Heylel had made about worldwide fame and popularity, were definitely on their way. All Eric had to do was keep cooperating.

"*Here, just take a little peek* . . ."

Before Eric could respond, sound and images flooded his brain. It was like a movie, only a hundred times better. It was as if he was really there. Men in bright blue uniforms running, shouting. Cannons exploding, swords stabbing and skewering. Sometimes a person would explode and fly through the air screaming in agony. It was everything Heylel had promised and more.

And, as Eric gave himself over to the images, he began to sink deeper and deeper—falling from his own mind, falling someplace very, very special. Soon he felt his throat being cleared, his vocal chords vibrating, and his mouth begin to move. But he could not hear what he was saying. It would be hard to come back up and take control. Each time it got a little harder. But that was okay. At least for now. Because right now the gore and killing that surrounded Eric was a thousand times better than sitting in some boring old meeting listening to a bunch of boring old-timers talk about controlling the world.

Brandon sat with his shirt off on the hotel bed, as nervous as a schoolboy. For the second time he clicked on the TV and for the second time he clicked it off. He didn't know much about romance but somehow he figured CNN was not the appropriate background for his wedding night.

He threw another look at the bathroom door. What on earth was taking her so long?

He shook his head, musing at the depth of his feelings. How was it possible? How could one person bring out such tenderness in him, such caring? He once considered himself the most selfish human on the planet . . . and now, in less than a year, he'd become so committed that he would do anything for her, give anything to her, be anything for her.

He rose, crossed over to the twenty-fourth-story window, and pulled back the sheers. It was the same view he'd seen thirty seconds earlier—the Chicago River, the Navy Pier, and beyond that Lake Michigan. It was still just as impressive and still just as intimidating. He'd never been in a hotel, at least not like this. Sure, he'd seen the Hyatt Regency whenever he came up here to Chicago. But he never gave it a second thought. That's where the rich and famous stayed. The hotshots. Not people like him. No way. Well, *no way* had come and gone. Now he was here, with his bride, spending their first night together.

The room was Frank's idea. Brandon had made it clear that neither he nor Sarah had the time or money for a honeymoon. But Frank and the guys at the plant insisted upon pitching in for at least one night. And when Frank made up his mind it was pretty hard to change it.

So here they were.

Brandon gave another look at the bathroom door. He wasn't entirely sure what she was doing, but he had his ideas. Ever since the accident Sarah had spent an inordinate amount of time on her looks—brushing her hair, checking her makeup, that sort of thing. He knew it was because of the scar. Before the accident, her beauty came naturally, something she took for granted. Now it was something she felt a constant need to work on. He sadly remembered her excitement the day she discovered her hair had finally grown out enough to start covering the scar.

Brandon wasn't crazy about the thing, either. But he hated it more for what it did to her on the inside than what he saw on the outside. He hated the way it made the once-confident woman suddenly insecure and self-conscious. And the closer their wedding approached, the more insecure she became, and the more she needed to be reassured of her beauty. Of course he did this gladly, but he also made it clear that there was an even greater beauty inside. Not that he had always been so sensitive. After all, it was her good looks that had originally taken his breath away. But that had been a long, long time ago. A different lifetime, a different Brandon. A Brandon who had been lost, searching for meaning and purpose. A Brandon who—like many of his fellow Generation Xers—had lived aimlessly for the moment and only for himself.

Not that he'd completely changed. He'd be the first to admit that there were still plenty of rough edges to work on. But gradually, day by day, as he and Sarah studied the Scriptures, and as they poured themselves into people at the clinic and into each other, he saw the shift in both of their lives. Why hadn't anyone told him how exhilarating it could be? How liberating? By taking his eyes off of himself and focusing upon others he was becoming a different person. And that was fine with him. It was fine with both of them. The sooner the better. Because from what they'd read in the Bible, it appeared that their role in the end times would be crucial. Very crucial.

But when? And how?

God had spared no effort in making it clear they were to be participants, but when it came to the details, He remained aloof, completely silent. With no course to follow but their own, they put their heads together and came up with the clinic. It seemed the best way of combining their talents ... his gifts of faith and healing and her background in science and medicine.

Granted, this didn't exactly make them the fire-breathing, turning-water-to-blood prophets spoken of in Revelation. But, as Sarah had always argued, there were other interpretations of this Scripture than just the literal. Those who believed Revelation to be a book covering the entire span of the church age looked upon the witnesses as symbols of devout Christians who, throughout the centuries, had turned the waters red with their martyred blood. Those who believed Revelation applied strictly to the times of Roman persecution immediately following the writing of the book and that the number 666 was a secret code for Nero, believed the two witnesses to be historical individuals such as Peter and James. And those who believed it was completely spiritual and symbolic, believed the two witnesses represented the old and new covenants, or Jews and Christians, or the civil and religious law. There seemed to be endless possibilities in interpreting who they were and what they would be doing. And, although

Brandon still leaned toward the literal approach, Sarah's arguments certainly made more and more sense.

Yet they had to do something. The world was unraveling at an alarming pace. Crashing stock markets, worldwide famine, spreading disease—all within the past twelve months. If anyone needed proof we'd entered the end times, all they had to do was read a newspaper. Things were rapidly coming to a head, and the sooner the two of them were ready the better.

But ready to do what? And how? If only God would stop being so mysterious.

There was a gentle rap on the hallway door and a voice calling, "Room service."

Brandon looked up. Room service? They hadn't ordered room service. They couldn't afford it even if they had. Unless . . . maybe this was more of Frank's doing.

"Mr. Martus?"

Brandon rose. Although the voice was muffled, there was something about it. Something nervous. He grabbed his shirt, threw it on, and crossed to the door. When he opened it he saw a young girl, probably high school age. She stood beside a silver cart that was draped in white cloth and held a sweating silver ice bucket. Inside the bucket was a bottle wrapped in more white linen.

"I'm sorry," Brandon said. "We didn't order any, uh . . ."

"Champagne," she said, just a trace too cheerily. "Compliments of the hotel."

"Oh, um . . ." He opened the door for her to enter. She rolled the cart into the room.

"Are you finding everything satisfactory?"

Instantly, he knew. The girl had lied. He wasn't sure how he knew. He was never sure how he knew these things. Some called it clairvoyance, others insisted it was God's gift of discernment. Brandon wasn't sure. All he knew was that as he grew less self-absorbed and freer of himself, he could listen to others more deeply and hear them more clearly. It was the little signs that spoke the loudest . . . a self-conscious glance, a nervous swallow, the slightest increase of pitch in the voice. The signs had always been there, but before, Brandon had been so full of himself that he hadn't noticed.

He leveled his gaze toward the girl and quietly asked, "What would you like from me?"

She glanced up, a little surprised. "I'm sorry, what?"

"Why did you come here? What do you want from me?"

She tried holding his look, but her eyes wavered then glanced away.

Brandon continued, gentle but firm. "Why are you here?"

But she could not answer.

He tried an easier question. "The champagne wasn't the hotel's idea, was it?"

Her eyes dropped to the floor. Her breathing grew more labored. He waited patiently. Finally, she shook her head. As she did, tears fell from her lashes. She reached up to wipe them, and that's when Brandon saw it. Her hand. It was crippled. It twisted inward, turning upon her like a self-accusing claw. It might have been an accident, a birth defect, even polio. Brandon didn't know and it really didn't matter.

The tears came faster. He took her arm and helped her to a chair. "Here." He grabbed a tissue from the counter. Several tissues. By now tiny rivulets streamed down her cheeks. But that was okay. Crying was good. In the beginning, he used to try and stop it, but not anymore. Sometimes the tears cleaned and washed parts of the soul that he could never see.

He handed her the tissues and kneeled down in front of her. "Have you had that all of your life?"

She nodded.

He waited for more.

She gave a loud sniff and continued. "Since I was a baby."

He looked back at the hand and saw two, maybe three, sets of scars running from the knuckles to her wrist. "How many operations?" he asked.

"Three." She sniffed again. "We've been to specialists and surgeons and tons of healing services." She wiped her nose. "But nothin' ever happens. It never gets better."

Brandon nodded. Again, the details really weren't important. They were only a way of helping her relax, of getting her used to her surroundings before he asked the hard question. But she wasn't ready for that. Not yet.

"What's your name?"

"Latisha. Latisha Cooper."

"Hello, Latisha. My name's Brandon."

She nodded at the obvious and didn't look up.

"You go to school around here?"

She shook her head. "Used to. But then I—" She caught herself and started again. "But not anymore."

"Not since you had the baby."

Her eyes shot up to him.

"It's okay," he said softly. "It's all right."

A new wave of tears streamed down her cheeks. And for one brief moment Brandon thought his own heart would break. He understood now. The hand had ruled her entire life. It was the reason behind her pretended indifference to school. It was the reason she hung out with gang members and why she slept around. It was also the reason that she'd finally gotten herself pregnant.

He cleared his throat, trying to hide the emotion in his own voice. "How old is your child now, Latisha?"

"She'll be eighteen months next Thursday."

"Is she as pretty as you?"

She gave a little shrug and pulled her claw in closer. Before she could withdraw it any further he asked, "May I hold your hand?" There was a moment's hesitation. He started reaching for it. "Is that okay? May I hold your hand?"

She watched as he took it. When they first touched he felt the tiniest flinch. But it wasn't fear. It was deeper than that. It was guilt. And shame. And anger. The poor child was consumed by them. They were the real sickness, her real disease. And they were the reason she'd come to him. Of course she didn't know it, probably never would. But he did.

At last, the time had come. He had to ask the question. "Latisha, tell me . . . do you really want to be healed?"

Her eyes widened in surprise then narrowed in anger. Was he mocking her?

Brandon held her gaze, waiting for an answer. It was an absurd question, he knew. But on more than one occasion he discovered people really didn't want to be healed. Oh sure, they said they wanted help, but those were merely words. In reality, their crippledness had become their identity, the trademark of who they were. And for those afraid of losing their identity, who in their heart of hearts really didn't want to be changed, the infirmity would not leave. Sometimes, even more tragically, if it left it would return.

Suddenly, he heard the bathroom door open behind him, and he saw Latisha look up.

"What on earth . . ." It was Sarah's voice. She no doubt looked more lovely than he'd ever seen her. And probably more surprised.

"Sarah." He cleared his throat. "This is, uh, Latisha. Latisha . . . Sarah." He'd been in more awkward situations, but at the moment he couldn't remember when.

The girl started to rise and pull her hand away.

Brandon's grip tightened. "No, please, it's okay."

She looked at him doubtfully.

"No, really." Then, over his shoulder, he called, "She wanted me to take a look at her hand, to see if there was something we can do for her."

He knew Sarah had been caught off guard and was definitely miffed. He also knew she would see the girl's desperation and would understand. After all, they encountered this type of need a dozen times a week at the clinic . . . although, not exactly in these circumstances.

Once again, Latisha started to pull back her hand and rise, but this time Sarah spoke. "No, please, sit. It's okay, please." Brandon heard the strain in her voice, but he also heard the compassion.

Still unable to see her, he called over his shoulder. "Would you like to join us?" He knew she would refuse. She was aware of the procedure and the need to create a bond of trust. If she were to barge in now, they'd have to start over, and that would slow things down.

"No, I've got some work to do over at the desk. You two go ahead."

He nodded and watched Latisha's eyes follow Sarah back into the bathroom. He winced slightly, realizing she'd probably gone back to grab a robe. Yes sir, things couldn't have been any more awkward. When he heard Sarah re-enter he asked again, "Are you sure you don't want to join us?"

"No, that's okay," she said as she crossed to the desk behind him. "You two go ahead." She still didn't sound convincing, but she was trying. A moment later he heard the familiar sound of her laptop opening and the faint whir of a hard disk starting up. He almost smiled. It had been nearly ten hours since she'd checked her e-mail. No doubt some kind of record for his bride, the information junkie.

He turned back to Latisha. It was time to re-ask the question: "Do you really want to be healed?"

This time she was able to hold his look. And this time she nodded.

"Good," he half-whispered. "Good." He wrapped both of his hands around hers. Then, closing his eyes, he started to pray. With lips barely moving, he silently thanked the Lord, expressing his gratitude for Latisha and his gratitude for the opportunity to help her. Then he began seeking God's will, making certain this was the time and place, that the Lord didn't have some greater plan which did not include a healing.

As he continued to pray, he began to feel the heat. It started in his palms, then spread out to his fingertips. Soon, both of his hands were on fire, their warmth encircling hers. He knew it took all of her will not to panic and pull away, but he also knew she was a strong girl.

Nearly a minute passed before he reached for the fingers of the hand. Then, kneading her hand as if it were soft, malleable clay, he began opening the claw. Latisha stifled a gasp, but he kept his eyes closed. From time to time he would release the pressure to feel if the hand would twist back into itself.

It did not.

Another minute passed before it was entirely straight and the healing was complete. At last Brandon opened his eyes and looked up at the girl. Her face was as wet with tears as his own. She held up the hand, astonished. She turned it, staring at it as if it belonged to someone else. Ever so carefully, she closed it. Then opened it. She repeated the process, faster. She grabbed it with her other hand, squeezing it, testing it. Everything worked perfectly.

Suddenly she threw her arms around Brandon—clinging to him tightly, burying her wet face into his shirt. "Thank you," she whispered fiercely. "Thank you, thank you, thank you." Brandon said nothing, holding her for as long as she needed, silently thanking the Lord.

At last they separated. She struggled to her feet and started talking excitedly. They were the usual promises—she'd live a better life, go back to church, get right with God. Brandon listened and smiled. He knew she meant well. They always did.

Finally, she gathered herself and started toward the door, practically skipping. "Thank you, Mrs. Martus," she called over to the desk. "Thanks so much!"

"You're welcome" was all Sarah said.

Her response surprised Brandon. Normally Sarah would be excited, sharing in the patient's joy and offering plenty of hugs of her own. But this time, though she smiled and was pleasant, she remained in front of the computer, very much preoccupied.

After a few more thank-yous and more promises to live better, Latisha finally stepped out into the hallway. Not, of course, without giving Brandon one more hug. He returned it, wished her the best, and after another set of good-byes, was finally able to close the door. He leaned against it silently. Some healings were harder than others, depending upon the emotional baggage attached. This one had been exhausting.

At last, he turned to Sarah. She was still staring at the computer. Even in the screen's blue-green glow she was beautiful . . . her graceful neck rising from the top of the white cotton robe, that rich auburn hair grazing her delicate shoulders. There were times, like now, that he found her presence absolutely intoxicating. It took a moment before he could find his voice. "Sarah?"

She gave no response.

"Sarah?" Still nothing. "Is everything all right?"

She finally turned to him, her face a mixture of concern and confusion.

He started toward her. "What's wrong?

"We have some very strange e-mail."

He arrived at her side and looked at the screen. "From who? What's it say?"

"It's from . . . Gerty Morrison."

"Gerty Morrison? No way."

She motioned toward the screen. "See for yourself."

He leaned in beside her for a better look. "That's impossible. Gerty's been dead for over a year."

Sarah looked up at him and slowly nodded. "I know."

CHAPTER 2

Help me! Somebod—" The cry was interrupted by an unearthly scream. Part animal, part little boy. "Help me!"

Katherine exploded into the room. She pushed her way past the Cartel members who hovered over her son. Those who didn't have the foresight to step back were shoved aside. "Excuse me! Excuse me, please!"

She'd been milling around the hallway all afternoon and into the evening, just in case this sort of thing happened. It didn't happen often, but it happened enough—whenever Eric wanted to regain control of his body before Heylel was done using it.

"Help . . . me!"

She pushed aside the last Cartel member and saw her son convulsing on the floor. To the untrained it looked like a seizure, but she could see his eyes were opened, and although they were wild, she could tell he knew exactly what was going on. More importantly, she knew he would continue to fight until he got his way. He always did.

Of course Lucas was already at his side, Lucas was always at his side. He was trying to hold the boy's head, trying to comfort him and convince him to relax. "Take it easy, sport. Take it—"

"Stop it!" Eric shrieked. "Let go of me! Let go!" But he wasn't screaming at Lucas, he was screaming at Heylel. "Let go!"

Katherine arrived at his side. She took his hand and reached over to his sweaty face. "Shh . . ."

"Mom . . ."

"It's okay, sweetheart, I'm here. It'll be over in a minute."

"He won't . . . let . . ."

"It's okay, darling . . ."

"Let go of me! Let—"

"It's okay—"

". . . gooo!" The last word was a wrenching cry from the boy's gut. As it faded the writhing stopped. Eric had resurfaced. Heylel was gone. The room grew quiet, its silence broken only by the boy's heavy panting.

"Sweetheart, are you okay? Sweetheart?"

He didn't answer.

Katherine tried to move closer, but Lucas was in the way.

"Sweetheart, here." She reached in toward him. "Let Mom—"

But Lucas was already helping him sit up. Katherine watched with resentment as the boy clung to him and the man began stroking his hair. "You all right, sport?"

Eric may have given the slightest nod, she wasn't sure. But it was enough. That was her son and she was going to hold him. "Excuse me," she said, reaching past Lucas. "Excuse me . . ."

And then Eric did something that broke her heart. Something that made her all the more resolved to end these sessions. As she reached toward her son, Eric turned to Lucas as if asking for permission.

Her son! Asking for permission? Outrageous!

"It's okay." Lucas nodded encouragingly. "Go ahead."

Incensed, Katherine moved in and pulled him away from the man. Eric didn't resist. "It's okay, baby," she said as she began stroking his damp hair. "It's over. It's okay, it's all over."

"You said the seizures would stop! You gave me your word!"

Katherine and Lucas were alone in his office. A year ago she'd been intimidated by his fame and popularity. Like droves of other women, she was physically drawn to his good looks and emotionally moved by his charm and sensitivity. Add to that the sympathy factor of losing his wife to cancer the last year he was in office, and you pretty much had every woman's dream. But Katherine soon learned that when it came to sex Lucas Ponte's feet were made of the same clay as the next man's. And after he made several smooth but failed attempts to bed her, it was safe to say her first blush of reverence and timidity toward him were gone. Long gone.

Lucas shook his head. "I said *Heylel* promised they would stop."

"Well, Heylel is a liar!"

Lucas remained silent, letting her words reverberate against the rich mahogany walls. He was known for his compassion and for being calm under pressure. Calm and compassionate. She had never seen him otherwise. Another reason she disliked him.

"Katherine . . . I can appreciate your feelings—"

"You know nothing about my feelings!"

He paused then nodded slowly. "You are correct. I'm sorry, I've never had the opportunity of experiencing a parent's heart."

"You've got that right."

"But Heylel has never lied before."

"I don't care what—"

"Once he gives his counsel to the Cartel he leaves. He always has. It's only when Eric insists on interrupting and fighting for control before Heylel finishes that we have these problems."

"It's Eric's body; he's got a right to do what he wants with it."

Lucas nodded, thinking. "It should also be his right to decide on whether or not to continue hosting Heylel. As far as I can tell the dangers are minimal, and Eric's certainly been more than willing."

"He's only a kid."

"He's a young man, Katherine. And he has a will of his own. He's always had the ability to say no. No one is forcing him to cooperate with Heylel."

Katherine's anger rose. Not over what he'd said, but over her inability to refute it. How she loathed this man.

"You know how important Heylel's counsel is to us."

"Not as important as Eric is to me!"

He nodded. "Once again, you are correct. But without his advice, without his insight . . ." Lucas paused, pretending to gather his thoughts, but she knew he already had them. He always did. "Katherine, for the first time in history, we are on the brink of world peace. I know it doesn't look like it now, but deals are being made, bargains are being struck. And much of it, dare I say a greater degree of it, is due to Heylel's counsel . . . and to your son's willingness to facilitate that counsel."

Katherine started to object but wasn't sure how.

He continued. "Nearly every country is supporting us now. In just a few weeks we will hold the groundbreaking in Jerusalem, followed by my installation into office. For the first time in history, the entire world will know peace. Think of it. People from every nation working together for a common good. And your son's participation will be one of the primary factors. In many ways his contribution is greater than mine, greater than any of ours. And perhaps, in the grand design of things, this is a token payment for all of the suffering you two have been forced to endure."

"If it doesn't destroy him first."

Lucas frowned. "He's been in no real danger. I'm not sure exactly what you mean."

Katherine wasn't sure either, which only added to her frustration.

Before she could answer, Lucas continued. "You have paid an incredible price, Katherine. To ask you to do more would be terribly unfair." He took a deep breath and slowly let it out. "But, to deprive Eric of this opportunity, especially if the risks appear to be minimal, would it not be even more unfair?"

She started to answer, but he wasn't finished.

"Especially if it's what he wants? He's not a little boy, Katherine. And if he chooses to be a major historical figure in bringing about the peace of the world, shouldn't he have that right?"

Katherine felt her argument slipping through her fingers and fought to hang on. "*If* he knows the consequences."

"Then explain to him these perceived fears of yours. But be fair, Katherine. Be certain he understands both the risks . . . and the rewards."

"And if he chooses to quit?"

"Then it will be his choice. Of course it may be difficult for me to convince our labs to find incentive to continue searching for a cure to his genetic problem, but at least it will be his choice. You owe him that, Katherine. We all owe him that." He held her gaze, making perfectly sure she understood.

Almost against her wishes, Katherine began to nod. As always Lucas made perfect sense, and as much as she wanted to stay angry at him, she had lost the reason. Still, there was the other issue. "What about this doctor, this neurobiologist that used to be on your payroll?"

Lucas frowned.

"The one who worked for that institute you guys sponsored in the States."

"Oh, yes. Sarah Weintraub?"

"Yeah."

"We've tried contacting her. We've explained both Eric's deteriorating self-control as well as this situation with Heylel. We've asked that she come to observe him and to make an evaluation."

"And?"

"At the moment she's preoccupied with a new clinic she has started . . . and a new husband."

Katherine felt her anger returning. "I want somebody to tell us what's happening to my son. You said she's good—"

"I said she is the best. She's one of the few neurobiologists in the world who also specializes in paranormal research. It's a rare combination."

"Then you get her here."

"Katherine . . ."

"If you want to keep using my boy as your cosmic communication center, then you get her here to tell me what's going on." Katherine was grateful to have found another reason for anger, and she knew it was time to leave before he found another way to diffuse it. She turned and started for the door.

"And if we can't convince her to come?" he asked.

She turned back to him. "I've seen what your resources can accomplish, Lucas. When you boys set off to do something it gets done. If you can't bring one little doctor here to look after my boy, then it only proves to me how unconcerned you are for his welfare. And if that's the case, then you'd better start looking for someone else to help you save the world, because we won't be sticking around."

She turned and stormed out of the office, pleased with her performance and with her terms.

She just hoped he wouldn't call her bluff.

Dearest Brandon and Sarah:

By the time you get to reading this I'll be home with the Lord. I've asked a young man to be sending this note along with a few others at different times to help guide you through your treacherous course.

"Is this for real?" Brandon asked.

Sarah glanced up from the screen. "From what I've read of her other letters, it sounds like the same woman."

"You don't think it's a forgery?"

"There's always that possibility, but how many people knew she even existed?"

Brandon nodded and they turned back to the screen.

I know the following words will be hard. But as His two witnesses He'll be requiring a lot more from you than most.

Like others from Scripture, you will be made an example for folks to see. Trust Him. The cost is great, but you must remain faithful. You've read 'bout your deaths in Scripture. Don't let it worry you. Death comes in many forms. Fact, it was the good Lord Himself who said, "Unless a kernel of wheat falls to the ground and dies, it remains only a single seed. But if it dies, it produces many seeds."

As you're about to read, the call upon your lives is very real and very great. But He must take you through several steps. Each one requires faith, and they won't always be making sense. But you've already taken His hand. Now for your sakes and the sake of the world, don't be letting go until all is complete.

Your sister in Christ,
GM

"Where's the rest?" Brandon asked.

"In an attached file."

"Have you read it?"

Sarah shook her head and doubled clicked the mouse, bringing a new document up onto the screen. This one was much different in both tone and content:

My Children:

Before I formed you in the womb, I knew you; before you were born I sanctified you; I ordained you as prophets to the nations. Only be strong and courageous. Do not tremble and be afraid.

Sarah took a breath to steady herself.

My heart is heavy, to the point of breaking. For as a harlot looks to many lovers, so my bride has turned her eyes from Me.

As a wife treacherously departs from her husband, so she has dealt with Me. With her mouth she says, "Come, My Beloved, I eagerly await," but with the fruit of her thoughts she pleads for My absence.

Listen carefully, My children. I have paid a great and terrible price for my bride, and I will not be denied. She is Mine and no one may have her. Yet she is neither willing nor ready for My return. And I will not approach her chamber until I am her sole desire.

Warn her, my children. Warn her of her lustful neighings, of the lewdness of her harlotry. This is My decree to you.

This is how she will hear My voice. Though you are wed and your covenant made, your relationship must not be consummated.

You must neither lie together nor become intimate with one another.

"What?" The word escaped before Sarah could catch it. She threw a look to Brandon. He was also scowling. She turned back to the screen and continued:

For just as my bride and I are legally wed, just as I love and long for her, I will not consummate our relationship until she is cleansed. She must put aside her harlotries and be purified for the arrival of her Bridegroom.

Sarah had reached the end of the screen and scrolled down to read more. But that was all, there was no more. She turned to Brandon. "Did I read what I thought I read?"

The pain and confusion in his eyes made it clear she had.

"But that's ... that's not possible," she said. "It's a joke, right? Some sick, practical joke."

Brandon said nothing. He reached down and scrolled back to reread the message.

But Sarah had seen enough. She scooted back her chair and rose. "This can't be real." She headed toward the window then back toward the desk. "You're the one who said wait until we were married. You're the one who said sex was so precious it was only to be shared by husband and wife."

He nodded. "That's what the Bible says."

She crossed back to the window, continuing to pace. "And we obeyed. Lord knows it was hard, but we obeyed." She spun back to him, jabbing her finger at the screen. "And this is our reward? Not to 'lie together,' not to 'consummate' our relationship?"

Brandon had no answer.

"No, no, this isn't the God we've been reading about. This isn't the God of love and mercy. No way. This is some sicko God, some sexually repressed—"

"Sarah."

"Brandon ..." Her voice revealed the hurt. "This is our wedding night."

"I know," he said sadly, "I know."

"And you really think that this could be His will? Weren't you the one who kept telling me how God was the one who created sex, how it was supposed to be the deepest communication between two people? Isn't that what you said?"

"He's not saying sex is dirty—"

"No. He's saying *I'm* dirty!" She felt her throat tightening with emotion. The words on the screen had hurt more than she thought. "Don't you see it? I'm the 'bride.' I'm the dirty one, I'm the filthy one."

Once again the years of guilt and condemnation began welling up inside of her—the ambition, the using of people, the abortion. Of everything Christianity had to offer, this had been the most beautiful and hardest to accept—that Christ had taken the punishment for all of her failures, that her past was completely forgiven, that he saw her as pure and holy . . .

Until now, until this pronouncement that she wasn't even fit to sleep with her own husband.

"Sarah . . ." He held out his arms to her. "That's not what he—"

"Of course it is! It's right there, see for yourself!"

"He's using us as examples," Brandon said, "as symbols. You think this is any easier for me?"

"I don't know why not. After all, you're the good guy. You get to be the bridegroom, you get to play Jesus Christ. While I get the role of some cheap, two-bit prostitute. Fitting, don't you think?"

"Sarah . . ." He reached out to her. She turned away as hot tears spilled onto her cheeks. She gave them an angry swipe, but they kept coming, which only made her more angry.

"Sarah." He wrapped his arms around her from behind. "Sarah . . ."

At first she resisted until finally she turned and pressed her face into his chest. "This isn't the program I signed up for," she said. "It's not fair."

"I know." She couldn't see his face but heard his heart pounding, felt his labored breathing. "You're right," he said. "It's not fair. It's not fair at all." She remained in his arms, feeling his strength, grateful for it. She wished they could stay like that, just like that, forever. He continued. "But . . ."

She closed her eyes, knowing there was more.

"I know you're having a hard time accepting a lot of this end-times stuff—especially when it comes to taking it literally. And, to be honest, so am I. But this . . . I mean, you can't get much clearer than this, can you?"

She gave no answer.

"If we're agreed that Gerty's never been wrong . . . along with all of the other Scriptures and prophecies and things that have been happening to us . . . if we can agree on that much, that she's never been wrong . . ." He took a deep breath and let it out with heavy resignation. "Then what other choice do we have? What else can we do but obey?"

She said nothing. It wasn't the answer she wanted, but it was the one she'd expected—at least from Brandon.

"Sarah?"

She still would not speak. If that's what he wanted, if that's what God wanted, okay, she'd comply. But that didn't mean she had to approve it, it didn't mean she had to gleefully accept it.

"Sarah, please . . . say something."

Still, Brandon shouldn't have to bear the entire burden of making the decision. After all, this was the man she loved. And they were a team.

"Sarah?"

At last, she gave a grudging nod. She could feel relief spread through his body. Although the decision was far more his than hers, they'd made it together. At least that's what he'd think. He tenderly kissed the top of her head. She pressed deeper into him, feeling his warmth and strength and love.

"Hold me," she whispered. "Please . . . just hold me."

CHAPTER 3

Eric! Eric, lunch is ready!" Katherine rose and shaded her eyes from the blinding snow above. Behind her, terrace after terrace of young grain-fields descended like emerald steps until they reached the small village below. A handful of peasants were hunched over, working the fields, as a distant water buffalo pulled a wooden plow through one of the plots.

"Eric?" She scanned an outcropping of rock. That's where she'd last seen him playing with Deepak, his bodyguard. "Eric?"

The picnic had been her idea. To get him away from the compound and its influences. To get him back into the Nepal countryside with its violet blue sky and dazzling white mountains. Later, when the time was right, she'd ask him what he thought about moving on. There were some powerful pros and cons, and she wanted to know his opinion.

"Eric!" With a heavy sigh, she started up the steep slope after him.

Of course the biggest reason for staying was for the help the Cartel continued to offer. Their genetic scientists had already come up with some drugs that had drastically slowed down his progression toward violence. It had been entirely different for Michael Coleman, their original guinea pig. His moral disintegration had taken only a few weeks. For Eric they'd slowed it down to many, many months.

Still, slowing it down was not the same as stopping it. And, as Eric's interest in the supernatural increased, his moral conscience and concern for others seemed to decrease. Not that he didn't try to be good. There were many times Katherine saw his face scrunched into a frown as he struggled to make the right decision. But as the impulses toward evil increased, it became more and more difficult for him to resist. And nothing pierced Katherine's heart deeper than to discover her son off by himself, full of remorse over some recent outburst of violence.

Another plus was his attachment to Lucas. Of course she was jealous, she knew that. Truth be told, she should be honored that such a man had taken an interest in her son. And it wasn't just because he was powerful. Except for his womanizing, you couldn't ask for a better male role model. Everybody loved Lucas Ponte—an acclaimed international leader, respected by men, adored by women. And, although the wheels of power had positioned him as the figurehead to bring the nations together, he always maintained a certain humility, a grace, and compassion.

Against those two strong pluses for staying was the only minus . . . Heylel. No one knew what the name meant, though from time to time he also referred to himself as Light Bearer. Whatever he was, he continued to make Katherine more and more uneasy.

The initial contact with him had come simply enough. One of the compound's Tibetan monks had suggested they turn to meditation as a cure for Eric's violence. If he could successfully empty his mind and enter that quiet place deep inside of himself he would find his guardian angel or perhaps a spirit guide who could help. It didn't take Eric long to master the process, and he said there were lots of guides wanting to assist ... until Heylel came along. Then everyone stepped aside and allowed him to come forward.

"He's like the head honcho," Eric had explained. "Everyone's afraid of him."

Heylel had never spoken directly to Katherine, but he had been providing invaluable counsel to the Cartel. Lucas was right. Heylel's knowledge and insight into other leaders' thinking, as well as upcoming world affairs, was as helpful in bringing them toward world peace as all of the other Cartel resources combined. Normally, Katherine might even consider this a plus, if it weren't for the power struggles that were starting to end the sessions.

Katherine was breathing hard by the time she rounded the cleft of rocks. "Eric? Eric, where are—" She came to a stop. He sat high atop another group of rocks, some thirty feet away. His legs were crossed and his hands rested on his knees in the lotus position. Several feet below, Deepak lay stretched out, sound asleep in the afternoon sun. But it wasn't the bodyguard's fault. Eric liked his privacy, and entering weaker minds and coaxing them to sleep had become child's play for him.

Now, however, Eric was playing another game ...

Two large, gray-back shrikes sat perched on the stones in front of him. They had the typical black masks around their eyes and beautiful yellow-gold breasts. Katherine was surprised to see two such perfect specimens side by side, much less so close to Eric. Normally they were cautious of each other and of humans. But not today. Today they were all friends. Today they sat on the rocks staring at Eric, calmly tilting their heads as if listening. Maybe they were. From time to time, one or the other would preen himself then hop a little closer.

It was a touching moment, and Katherine was grateful to see her son enjoying the peace—something that, because of the genetic deterioration, was coming less and less frequently. Figuring lunch could wait, she dropped back behind the rocks to watch, unnoticed. A birch prayer pole rose from the outcropping above her, its hundreds of Buddhist prayer flags snapping and fluttering in the wind.

As Eric continued focusing upon the birds, they began to preen themselves more vigorously. At least Katherine thought they were preening . . . until they began pulling out feathers. At first it was just one or two. But as seconds passed they began tearing out clumps of white down, then some of the larger, blue-gray feathers.

Eric shifted, pushing up his glasses and concentrating more intently.

The more he concentrated, the more violent their actions became. Beakfuls of down and feathers flew as the birds pecked at themselves more and more furiously. Then came the first sign of blood. Bright red against their golden breasts. And still they tore into themselves. Brutally. Insanely. Self-inflicted wounds that grew deeper and more bloody.

Katherine's hand rose to her mouth.

The poor creatures began to stagger under their own blows. But even that wasn't enough. Not for Eric. He focused more intensely until, suddenly, the helpless birds turned against each other with a vengeance. The fight lasted several more moments as beaks and talons ripped and tore, as blood and feathers flew. It was all Katherine could do not to cry out.

And then, at last, the battle came to an end.Both birds lay on their sides, heaving bodies gasping for final breaths. Eric's private cockfight was over.

Katherine turned away as a half-cry, half-groan escaped from her throat. She looked back, hoping he hadn't heard. But she was wrong. The boy's head swiveled in her direction. She pulled further into the rocks. And there, hidden by the boulders, with the flapping prayer flags above her, Katherine began to cry. She'd suspected this behavior before, had done her best to deny it.

But now . . .

She closed her eyes and swallowed back a sob. This monster was not her son. Not her baby boy. Where was the child whose heart broke the time a sparrow hit their picture window? Where was the little boy who wanted to raise ladybugs for a living? What of the toddler who padded into her bedroom at night just to cuddle? Where was he now?

And . . . what would he be tomorrow?

They were trapped, she knew that now. Despite her fears, despite her rantings at Ponte and her objections to Heylel, there was no alternative. They had to stay. The Cartel and their genetic research to reverse the deterioration of her little boy . . . it was his only hope.

It was her only hope.

Brandon had just finished his last session for the day. It had been a grueling one with a mentally disabled girl and her mother. The children always took the most out of him. Their sessions were the most rewarding when the time was right and the healings were successful, but they could also be the most painful when God, for whatever His reasons, said no.

And this time, He'd said no.

Brandon escorted them out of the examination room and into the dimly lit hallway. Of course there were plenty of tears and he did his best to console them, encouraging them to return in a few months to try again. They'd nodded, and after the good-byes and obligatory hugs, he turned wearily into the room to begin filling out the girl's chart.

The paperwork had been Sarah's idea. And she was right. There was no reason why they couldn't run the clinic like any other medical facility—recording each patient's malady, carefully documenting the healing, or the lack of it, as well as the number of sessions necessary before it was finally complete. In short, they were simply removing the superstitious elements from God's work and evaluating it rationally and scientifically.

"Science and religion don't have to be enemies," Sarah had said. "Not if we look upon science as just another means of studying God and His work."

Of course the clinic wasn't the first of its kind. There had been others ... like the one founded in the early part of the twentieth century in Spokane, Washington, by John G. Lake. Records indicate that up to two hundred people a day were treated at this facility, often with some sort of medical follow-up or scientific verification. Now, Brandon and Sarah were doing much the same, though with their slower style of care and compassion they were lucky to squeeze in ten people a day. And since their success rate hovered between seventy and eighty percent, word was quickly spreading and appointments were having to be made weeks in advance.

All of this was good. Now if they could just reach an agreement on the finances. If he could just get Sarah to see that you don't charge money for God's free gift. The subject was coming up more and more frequently, as were other major and minor disagreements in their marriage. But didn't newlyweds always have problems and rough edges to smooth out? At least that's what he'd heard.

Brandon finally finished the chart and gathered his papers. He crossed to the door and snapped off the lights. But he'd barely stepped into the hallway before Salman Kilyos grabbed his arm.

"Mr. Brandon ... please!" He was a young man, no older than Brandon. His grip was weak, but desperate. "Help me, you must." His wrists were so skinny that the fake Rolex slid up and down his left arm like an oversized bracelet. The translucent skin on his arms showed three purplish bruises—sickly looking things, Kaposi's sarcoma, a frequent symptom of those in the final stages of AIDS. Brandon's first instinct was to pull back and break the hold. But then he looked into the man's hollow face and pleading eyes.

"I beg you, Mr. Brandon . . ." He began to cough and quickly pulled out a soggy handkerchief, shoving it to his mouth. Brandon's revulsion did not lessen. Salman continued coughing, each spasm wracking his frail body. "Please . . . for the love of God!"

Brandon watched with compassion. On the man's left forearm he saw the tattoo of a crescent moon with a star hovering over it. They'd talked about it during an earlier visit. It was the symbol of Salman Kilyos's homeland, Turkey. But it was more than that. Because as Brandon stared at it, he realized it was the same symbol he'd seen in his last dream, carved into the altar. What did it mean? A coincidence? He doubted it. If there was one thing he'd learned in the past year it was that coincidences like these were never a coincidence—especially when connected to the dream.

Then what was it?

Salman had originally come to America looking for a remedy to his disease. "God's curse for liking the ladies too much," he had joked, making sure the emphasis was on *ladies*. Although many clinics were experimenting with possible breakthrough drugs and procedures, none was either willing or able to help him. And, now, in his final days, nearly all hope had run out.

All hope but in Brandon . . . and his God.

As the coughing subsided, Brandon gently admonished him. "Salman, what are you doing here? You should be in bed."

"In bed? In bed? What am I going to do in—?" The anger sent his body into another coughing fit, and he had to lean against Brandon for support.

"Here." Brandon gently took his arm and eased him into the chair next to an old metal desk. He glanced up and down the hall for one of the staff members. But they were either up front in the reception area or down the hall helping Sarah. That's when he saw the open window to the fire escape. "Did you break in again, Salman?"

The young man fought back the coughing long enough to gasp, "It is the only way I can get in to see you."

Brandon sighed. This had been typical of his entire day. Better make that the last couple weeks—ever since he and Sarah had received their little edict from the Lord. Although they'd moved into their new apartment, and although it had two bedrooms, they'd decided it was best for him to continue sleeping at his mother's. They may be end-time prophets, but they weren't fools. Of course they still had a thousand and one questions to ask, but there had been no further word and no further answers. Nothing. Now, all they could do was obey and wait. As frustrating and, at times, as angry as it made them, there was no other alternative but to obey and wait.

Tensions were no better at work. Brandon had learned to smile and laugh at the newlywed jokes, but each one felt like a blow driving in deeper the unreasonable demand God had made and—although he constantly pushed the word out of his mind—the *cruelty*.

Finally, there was Sarah. As painful as it was for him, there was no telling what it was doing to her. Being told she represented a harlot, an adulterous bride, that she wasn't even worthy enough to sleep with her husband? When she'd first become a Christian, it had been all she could do to grasp the concept of God's unconditional love. And now . . . who knew how all of this was tearing her up inside?

He directed his attention back to Salman, kneeling down before him as the man continued to shudder with each wracking cough. The poor fellow didn't have enough strength to be out of bed, let alone out in public. He'd been to the clinic a dozen times. And each time Brandon had turned him away.

Not because he wanted to, but because he had to. Because every time that he prayed, seeking the Lord's will, he had the clear and unmistakable impression: *Healing is not yet permitted for him, not at this time.*

The response always troubled Brandon. He'd healed several AIDS patients in the past, so why not Salman? Every time he'd turned him away his heart grew heavier. And every time the man walked out the doors of the clinic he looked like he'd received his death sentence. Perhaps he had.

The coughing became more violent.

"Salman . . . Salman, are you all right?"

Salman tried to respond, but it was impossible for him to answer.

"Salman?"

His grip tightened on Brandon's arm.

"Salman!"

The man gestured frantically but could not speak. He wasn't getting enough air. With his free hand, Brandon reached toward the phone on the desk. He grabbed the receiver and pressed 306, Sarah's extension. The line began to ring.

Salman's coughing grew more frightening, his wheezing and gasping more desperate.

The phone continued to ring, but no one answered. Brandon turned and shouted down the hall, "Sarah!"

No response.

"Somebody! We need some help here!"

The door to the reception area flew open and Ruth Dressler, a young part-timer, ran in.

"Where's Sarah?" Brandon yelled.

"She's picking up supplies. Is that Salman Kilyos?"

Brandon nodded.

"Mr. Bran . . ." That was all Salman could wheeze. It was barely a whisper. But his eyes had connected with Brandon, and they cried volumes. *Why? Why won't you do something? Why would God allow this?*

Of course, Brandon had asked the same question. Hundreds of times. Not only about Salman, but about the others. About the thousands of drought victims he saw dying of hunger every day on TV, about those bodies ravaged and destroyed by the Scorpion virus, about the innocent war casualties, about the mentally tormented like that little girl he'd just refused, about the endless stream of humanity whose emotional and physical misery would never come to an end.

But Salman's could ...

The thought surprised him, yet it made sense. Salman was right there, right in front of him. And it's not like he'd be disobeying God. After all, God had never said, "Never." He'd simply said, "Not yet, not at this time." Well, "not at this time" meant there had to be *some* time. And, by the looks of things, this was about the only time Salman had left. If it didn't happen now, it was doubtful it would ever happen. And since there was so much pain and fear, and since God was a God of love and mercy, and since Brandon had the power to at least end this person's suffering ...

He reached back up to Salman and placed both of his hands on the man's chest. Silently, he began to pray. Without waiting for confirmation from the Lord, he quietly but firmly began speaking healing into the man's body. It wasn't disobedience. How could it be? After all, God was doing the healing. And if He didn't want to heal, He didn't have to heal. It was as simple as that.

Luckily for Salman Kilyos, it appeared, God did.

Brandon felt the heat begin in his palms, then spread out to his fingertips.

Salman felt it too. His gasps grew more panicked.

"Just relax," Brandon said. "Just relax."

Salman nodded. Soon his breathing started to come easier. In a matter of seconds, the wheezing had all but vanished. But the healing wasn't complete, and Brandon continued to pray. The heat in his hands gradually spread to his arms and then up into his shoulders. He began breaking out into a sweat. But this had happened before. With the more severe cases it happened.

"It is so warm," Salman whispered.

Brandon nodded and glanced up to him. For the first time that he could remember, he saw Salman smiling. Brandon smiled back. "How do you feel?"

"The pain . . ." Salman sat up in the chair. "I can feel no pain."

Brandon shifted his weight, but kept his hands on the man.

"Praise God." It was Ruth behind him. He'd almost forgotten she was there. "After all this time, praise God."

"Yes." Salman nodded. "Praise God." He reached up and took Brandon's arms. His grip was much stronger. "Praise God. Praise the Lord!"

Brandon smiled again and continued to pray.

A moment later Salman rose unsteadily from the chair.

"Easy . . ." Brandon warned.

"Praise God!" he shouted. "Praise the Lord!" Although he was still weak, Salman was now on his feet.

"Be careful . . ."

The man barely heard. He began dancing a little jig. "Praise God!" He reached down, urging Brandon to his feet. Brandon cooperated, but for some reason, the sudden rise made him a little light-headed. For a moment it was Salman's turn to steady him.

"Thank you, Lord!" Salman shouted. "Thank you, God!"

Brandon looked on, smiling. He, too, was thankful. But instead of feeling the warm afterglow that so often accompanied the healings, he felt nothing. Heaven had grown strangely quiet. He frowned slightly, wondering. But only for a moment, because Salman had suddenly discovered something else about his healing.

"Look!" He'd pulled up his sleeves, showing his arms. Then he reached for his shirt and unbuttoned the top three buttons until he could look down at his chest. "They're gone!

My spots. They are all gone!" He pulled out his shirt to check his stomach. "All of them. They are gone!"

He reached out and took Brandon's hands, pulling him into the dance. "Praise God! Thank you, my friend. Thank you from my heart's bottom. Thank you!"

Brandon had to grin. Salman's joy was contagious. But only to a point. Because there was something else. Something that felt no joy or excitement. Something that felt the slightest bit uneasy.

Katherine finished her e-mail to Dr. Sarah Weintraub and hit the spell checker. It had been her second mailing to the neurobiologist in almost as many weeks. Once again she had urged the woman to come see her son, and once again she had promised "very substantial" compensation . . . including the power and prestige involved in working with the Cartel. During the upcoming months that sort of connection should prove very valuable. These were the same points she had used in her first mailing, but in this one Katherine had included a slightly different approach.

Instead of facts and figures, with which she always felt the most comfortable, she took a chance and tried speaking from her heart. She tried reasoning with Sarah, woman to woman, pointing out how Eric was her only child, how she loved him more than her own life, and if Sarah had or ever would have children of her own, she would know exactly how she felt. The tone made Katherine uneasy. She hated sounding needy to anyone. But this was her little boy she was battling for, and she'd do whatever it took.

After catching a few typos, Katherine hit *send,* and the mail was on its way.

She never knew if Sarah had read the other e-mail or not. It had been answered, but by a staff member who explained how incredibly swamped Sarah was, and how, at least for now, she had to stay near the clinic. However, the answer had included an invitation for Katherine and her son to come to the clinic for an examination and consultation anytime they wanted.

The naiveté of the offer angered Katherine. They couldn't fly back to the States. Not now. Didn't these people read the news? The Cartel was in the final stages of negotiation. Eric's input was needed now more than ever. Katherine had included this in her latest mailing, but again wondered if Sarah would ever see it. Still, between her mailings and the promised communiqué coming from Lucas's office, something should shake loose.

Katherine keyed back into the main menu. Computers had been a part of her life ever since her Omaha days, way back when she'd worked for the Department of Defense. But after the murder of her police officer husband, and the next eighteen months of blur lost in the bottom of a bottle, she had decided it was time to make a new start. That was when she packed up little Eric, headed west, and tried to forget everything about her past. Well, everything but her expertise in computers.

She'd opened a small computer store in Everett, Washington. Unfortunately, it had set a record for the most amount of money lost by any company in its first year of business. And that was her good year. From then on things got worse. She may have been a whiz at computers, but she was clueless about business.

When the Cartel had first approached them about staying at the compound, Katherine had insisted she have access to a computer and the Internet. She'd also insisted upon being able to read all files on any DNA research their main lab in Belgium was conducting. After all, it was the Cartel's genetic engineers that had gotten Eric into this mess in the first place. It was only fair she be allowed to check on their progress as they tried to get him out.

She scrolled down to the genetic file named "Antisense." This was the area of most importance to Eric. By inverting specific segments of any genetic code, molecular biologists are able to create characteristics 180 degrees opposite of the original piece of DNA. As best as anyone could figure, that's what had happened to Eric with the genetic code they had replicated from what they believed to be Christ's blood. At first, Eric had exhibited strong, Christlike characteristics— mercy, compassion, a knowing beyond what his five senses could detect, even the performing of some miracles. But the process had eventually reversed itself. And instead of creating a loving, self-sacrificing savior of the world, the Cartel's scientists had created a—

Katherine refused to think the thought. Whatever Eric's problem, it was only temporary. They'd find a way to reverse the process. They'd find a cure. She just hoped it would be soon.

Up on the screen she noticed there had been only one new report filed since the last time she checked—a minor breakthrough in cancer research utilizing antisense to replace deactivated tumor suppressor genes. Not exactly what she was looking for.

Katherine sighed and prepared to shut down the computer. She glanced down at the screen's clock. Dinner was in less than an hour. She turned to look outside. The late spring blizzard continued to rage. And, over there, across the room in his bed, Eric was enjoying a peaceful afternoon nap. She decided to stay.

Turning back to the computer, she scrolled through some of the other genetic research files. Earlier, when she and Eric had first arrived, she'd tried reading everything she could find on the subject. But it was overwhelming; the Cartel was involved in far too many aspects of research on the topic. Eventually she had learned to focus only on the areas that applied to Eric.

As she continued to scroll, the file labeled "Scorpion" caught her eye. That was the street name for the virus that had been attacking the world's Semite population. For the most part other races were immune to it, but there was something about the DNA makeup of Jews and Arabs that made them vulnerable to the virus's fury. A fury that attacked internal organs, eating them up and turning them to jelly. A fury that, like its cousin Ebola and other Class 5 viruses, seemed to come from the very pit of hell.

The disease got its name from its scorpionlike tail that could be seen under an electron microscope. No one was sure where it came from or how to stop its spread, and every continent was reeling under its impact. Latest death tolls were pushing two million. Of course all of the top labs and humanitarian organizations in the world were focused upon the problem, and the Cartel was no different, utilizing a sizable portion of its influence and funding. But, so far, success had been elusive.

With nothing else to do, Katherine opened the Scorpion file and scanned down its subfiles. She'd been here once or twice before but had never gone all the way through. She doubted she would this time. She did, however, come upon the names of the four cities. Cairo, Mecca, New York, and Tel Aviv. These were the first four cities to report the outbreak of the plague.

She scrolled to the Cairo file and double clicked it. Immediately the screen read: "Access denied."

Thinking it odd, she tried again. Again the screen read: "Access denied."

She went over to Mecca and double clicked it.

"Access denied."

The same was true with New York and Tel Aviv.

"Access denied."

"Access denied."

The fact that she'd been closed out didn't bother her. Except for the genetic information, that was the case with most all of the Cartel's files. And who could blame them? With all of their high-powered meetings and maneuverings, they didn't need her browsing through any ultrasensitive information. Of course that made little difference to Katherine. She seldom if ever found a program she couldn't hack her way into.

No, it didn't bother her that she was blocked out. But it did intrigue her. After all, the agreement was that she could have access to *all* files on genetic research. So what was up? Of course there would be some secrecy in the search for Scorpion's cure. Whoever found it would definitely have the world's undying gratitude, a position particularly helpful to the Cartel in their efforts to court world favor.

But why did each of these cities have its own file? And why were they the only ones to which she was denied access?

Katherine glanced at the time. She still had forty minutes to kill before dinner. So, with a shrug, she started to type. Nothing helped pass the time like a good old-fashioned hacking.

"It will be the ecumenical event of the century." Tanya Chase, the anchor for GBN News, was already on her feet. "Think of it . . . Protestants, Catholics, Jews, Moslems, Hindus, people of every faith coming together before God. And it won't be just at the L.A. Forum. With the satellite feed and local downlinks, we could be reaching every home in the United States and Canada! Not to mention a handful of stations in England, Australia, and New Zealand."

Sarah couldn't help nodding. It was difficult not to get caught up in this petite woman's excitement as she paced back and forth in the clinic's cramped office. She was a lot smaller in person than on TV, but her face was just as tan, her features just as chiseled, and her honey blonde hair (probably not natural) was just as striking. She was dressed to be taken seriously and had a perfect knockout figure (which probably wasn't natural, either). On TV her energy reminded Sarah of someone who'd had a few too many cups of Starbucks, and in person it was no different. Her presence filled the room.

"Let's face it . . ." She finally came to a stop across the table from Brandon. Leaning toward him, she utilized her scooped neck sweater to its fullest advantage. "Something's going on here. The wars, the famine, this new disease. I mean, people are claiming it's the end of the world, and maybe they're right."

"Maybe they are." Brandon kept his eyes leveled at hers, refusing to let them lower. A fact quietly appreciated by Sarah.

"Maybe they are," Tanya repeated. She rose and resumed her pacing. "And if that's the case, then it's time somebody helped us put aside our petty differences. It's time somebody brought us all together with one voice and one accord into the presence of God."

"And you think Jimmy Tyler's the man."

Again she stopped and locked eyes with Brandon. "I know he is."

Sarah watched for Brandon's reaction. Ever since their wedding night, tension had been growing between them. Gerty's e-mail had driven an indefinable wedge between them. They still loved each other, she was sure of that. Probably now more than ever. And the self-control they exhibited did nothing but increase their respect for one another. But every day, Sarah found herself growing more and more resentful. At whom, she wasn't sure. Most likely at God, which did little to help with her feelings of guilt and unworthiness. But she was also resentful toward Brandon. More specifically, she was resentful at his response toward God.

Yes, he was frustrated, she saw that daily. And there were times he could not hide his anger. But, for the most part, he seemed to be taking their command for abstinence as a type of challenge, rising to the occasion and using it to focus more intently upon his work. It was probably just a defense mechanism—she couldn't be sure. The only thing she could be sure of was that as she grew more and more resentful and guilt-ridden, he seemed to grow more and more dedicated ... which made her even more resentful and guilt-ridden ... and on and on the cycle went, like a whirlpool, pulling their relationship down lower and lower.

Sarah turned her attention back to the meeting and addressed Tanya. "Why does Reverend Tyler want Brandon and me to share the platform?"

"Actually, just one of you. Probably Brandon, here, since he's the miracle boy."

Sarah nodded.

"There will be dozens of other ministries represented, so room doesn't permit—"

"No, I understand," Sarah said, barely aware she was tugging her hair over her scar.

"You really think our presence is going to be helpful?" Brandon asked.

"What, are you joking? You guys are getting yourself quite the little following."

"You wouldn't know it by looking at our books." Sarah meant it as a joke, but it came off more weary than clever.

Tanya turned to her. "That's because you don't know how to market yourselves."

Sarah's eyes shot to Brandon. It sounded like someone had overheard their arguments.

He cleared his throat and answered, "Listen, when it comes to finances, I know we're not being all that conventional, but—"

"I know, I know." Tanya held up her hands. "I've heard it all before. You're doing the Lord's work, right?"

"As best as we understand it to—"

"And Jesus never charged for healings, and Jesus never held telethons, and Jesus never took an offering."

Now it was Brandon's turn to look at Sarah. The reporter *was* listening to their arguments.

"But let me tell you something." Tanya was back at the table. "Jesus never had to spend $90,000 renting an arena. He never had to pay for TV equipment or deal with unions. And he sure never had to buy satellite time."

Sarah felt a twinge of justification. It was good to hear someone else use her reasonings for a change.

"And what exactly would Jimmy Tyler get out of the deal?" Brandon asked.

Sarah winced. Didn't he know how good this could be for them? Couldn't he let up just a little?

Fortunately, Tanya was unfazed. "Reverend Tyler will be getting no more than you . . . national exposure and the opportunity to bring hope and comfort to a world torn at the seams, to a world that desperately needs to be brought together in a spirit of unity."

"Careful," he half-teased, "you almost sound like the Cartel."

"In many ways we're not that different. Only what they're striving to do on a political level, we are attempting to do spiritually."

Brandon turned to Sarah. He was obviously interested in her input.

She responded, doing her best not to sound too enthused. "I don't know what it would hurt. And, as Ms. Chase has said, we could certainly use the exposure. I mean, think what that type of publicity could do for the clinic."

Brandon nodded, but he still wasn't convinced.

Tanya leaned back over the table toward him, a little further than the last time. "So what will it be?" she asked.

He kept his eyes on hers, refusing to be distracted. Sarah almost smiled. The woman had no idea who she was up against. How deeply she respected this man. She respected his strength, yes. And, although it could be exasperating at times, she also respected his commitment.

Finally he answered, "I think Sarah and I need more time to discuss it."

"Of course, of course." Tanya pulled back and began gathering her papers. "Take all the time you want. And don't forget to pray about it. Praying is important, too."

Brandon nodded.

Tanya dumped her stuff into a leather satchel and closed it before looking up. "But don't take forever. There are plenty of other ministries that would love to be up on that stage with Jimmy."

Sarah rose to her feet and extended a hand across the table. "I know that, and please tell him how much we appreciate this opportunity."

"I certainly will." Tanya turned back to Brandon, who had also risen to his feet. "And it is just that," she said, reaching out to shake his hand. "An opportunity." She held his gaze, making sure he understood. "A very big opportunity . . . for both of you. And for your ministry. An opportunity that you would do well not to miss."

"Brandon, why are you being so unreasonable?"

"I'm not unreasonable."

"It's a terrific offer and you're just throwing it away. If that's not unreasonable, then maybe I need someone to explain to me—"

"I don't like the man, Sarah. It's as simple as that."

"No one says you have to like him."

"He's a huckster. You've seen him on TV. He's a manipulator. Besides, he's got a lousy toupee."

A week ago the humor would have lightened the mood, broken the tension. But not this evening. This evening, as they prepared dinner in the apartment, before he headed to his mother's for the night, they were having another argument. Something Sarah knew was happening more and more often. And if Tyler's invitation created such a stir, just wait until she brought up the e-mail she'd received from Nepal, the one asking her to help some kid involved with the Cartel.

"The man's a crook, Sarah."

"How can you say that? Look how God has used him."

"God also used Baalam's jackass."

Sarah sighed wearily. "Why are you so closed to this? If we work with him, we'd be reaching a good part of the world. Isn't that what the Scriptures say the two end-time prophets are supposed to do? Reach the world? Well, here's a flash for you, partner. It sure ain't happening for us here in Bethel Lake . . . and it sure ain't happening with our little podunk clinic."

She waited at the refrigerator for a comeback, but there was only silence. She turned and saw him staring down at the table. She'd struck a nerve. He'd obviously been struggling with the same thoughts. But he wasn't about to concede. Oh, no, why should tonight be any different from the others?

"So you're saying we'll accomplish all these great things by endorsing the beliefs of the Jews, Moslems, Hindus . . . or whatever New Age fruitcake has a following big enough for Tyler to pander to?"

"We don't have to endorse anybody."

"Being on the stage with them endorses them."

"We don't have to endorse their beliefs, Brandon. But we can at least endorse them as people. We can at least acknowledge them as fellow seekers of God."

"Please . . ."

"What's that supposed to mean?" He gave no answer and she pursued. "Do you think we're the only ones that God listens to? Are we so arrogant that we think He's only paying attention to us?" Again no answer. "We're talking about a God of love here, Brandon, a God of mercy. Half the world is dying—disease, war, starvation—while the other half is so scared they don't know what to think. There's a whole lot of pain and confusion out there. And no merciful God is going to turn His back on that. We're all on equal ground before Him, and He's not going to let a little tweaked-out theology get in the way."

He looked up at her. "What did you say?"

She did not answer, realizing she might have stepped over the line.

"Sarah, the Bible says no one comes to the Father but through His Son."

"I know what the Bible says."

"Then how can we—"

"And I don't need you to quote it to me."

"But if you believe it, if you believe Jesus Christ and if you really love Him, how——"

She spun on him angrily. "Nobody loves Jesus Christ more than I do, Brandon!" Her throat grew tight. Didn't he know how grateful she was to have her past forgiven? She swallowed. "Nobody . . . not even you." Tears sprang to her eyes. She turned and crossed to the sink, hoping he hadn't noticed. She'd win this argument and she'd win it through logic, not emotion.

When he finally spoke his voice was softer, even a little sad. "I know. I didn't mean that . . ." He hesitated, then tried again. "I didn't . . ." Another failure. This time accompanied by a heavy sigh.

She remained with her back to him. She heard his approach, caught his reflection in the window. A moment later his arms were wrapping around her. The tears came faster, and it was all she could do not to yield to him.

When she trusted her voice, she continued. "Everything's unraveling . . . Instead of becoming clearer, each day is more confusing than the last. There are times I'm not sure what I believe anymore." She took a ragged breath, then continued. "But I know this. That TV show is the first indication that we're on the road to somewhere, that people are actually starting to pay attention to us. And to turn it down now would be one giant step backward."

There was a pause before he answered. "I know what you're saying. And believe me, I have plenty of my own doubts. But . . . it's just . . ." He took a breath, then quietly let it go. He tightened his embrace and rested his head on her shoulder. How deeply she loved this man, how he still made her weak and trembly inside. She knew the discussion wasn't over, but at least for the moment a truce had been declared. She reached down to take his arm, to let him know she was still upset but that it was okay.

And that's when she saw it. "Brandon?"

"Hmm?"

"What's this?"

"What?"

"Here, on the inside of your arm. It looks like . . ." She turned toward him. "Is that a tattoo?"

Brandon looked at it with her. Although the outline was faint, there was no missing a crescent moon and a five-pointed star hovering beside it.

She glanced up at him but he was still staring at it, obviously as surprised as she was. Then she noticed something else. Higher up on his arm. A faint bruise. And another, off to the side.

"Where did you get those?"

She looked back up to him. His eyes were wide with astonishment. He quickly checked the other arm. There was another bruise, a little larger, a little more sickly.

"Brandon?"

He stepped back then quickly peeled off his shirt.

"Bran?"

Now he was examining his chest. There were two more bruises there. And another one, lower on his belly.

"What are they?" she asked.

"Salman . . ." He half-whispered the name.

"Who?"

"Salman Kilyos."

"The guy from Turkey, the one with AIDS?"

He looked up, eyes still wide. "I prayed for him . . . This afternoon I prayed for his healing."

"The Lord finally gave permission?"

"I don't know, not exactly . . . but he was healed."

"Brandon."

He rubbed the back of his neck. "I thought maybe I was just coming down with the flu—you know, kind of achy and stuff, but . . ." He looked back at his arms, examining the bruises. "These were his. I saw them on his arms . . ."

"Brandon, you're scaring me."

After another moment, he looked up at her, his eyes filled with wonder and fear. "I've got . . . Sarah, I've got AIDS."

"What?" She took a half-step back.

He looked down at the bruises, exploring them with his fingers. "I prayed for him, he got healed, and I—"

"Brandon . . ."

"And now I've got his sickness."

He examined the tattoo again, rubbing it. "This was his, too."

Sarah was finding it hard to breathe. "That's not possible."

Brandon continued examining his body. "Everything is fainter, and I'm sure the pain is nothing compared to what he felt, but—"

"Brandon!" The cry stuck in her throat.

He looked back up.

"What is God doing? What does He want from us now?"

Brandon could only stare, then shake his head.

"What does He want? What type of monstrous thing is He demanding from us this—"

"Sarah . . ." His voice warned caution.

"And you would defend him? After this! This is the reward for our obedience? This is how he loves his children?"

"Sarah . . ."

"No!" She began to pace, incredulous.

"There really isn't that much pain, honest." He started toward her, but she would have none of it.

"This is not what God would do. No merciful God would do this!"

He continued toward her, but she backed away. "No."

"Sarah . . ."

"No! This is not a God of love!" She had to get away, to get some space to think.

"But, the pain, it's barely—"

"Stay away from me."

He came to a stop, then reasoned, "Maybe this is some sort of sign. Maybe He's trying to—"

"And still you defend him?" She was shouting, trying to hear herself over the insanity.

He started toward her again. "Sarah."

Her mind reeled. She had to get away, she had to make some sense out of what was—

"Maybe if—"

She turned and headed for the bedroom, then changed direction and went for the closet.

"Sarah . . ."

She threw open the door and grabbed her coat.

"Where are you going?"

She wasn't sure. But she was no longer willing, she was no longer able to listen.

"Sarah." He was reaching out to her again.

"No."

"But—"

"Leave me alone!"

She turned and headed down the hall, stumbling slightly, vision blurry from tears.

"Sarah . . ."

She opened the door and stepped outside. The cool air hit her face but she needed more, she needed to breathe. She started down the steps.

"Sarah . . ."

He was calling, but she barely heard. She had to breathe, she had to get away.

He was on the porch. "Sarah . . ."

Her feet moved as fast as they could down the sidewalk before she broke into a run. She had to get away. She had to breathe. She had to clear her head.

"Sarah . . . !"

CHAPTER 4

And the situation with the Jews?" Lucas asked.

"For the most part they're with us." It was the secretary general again. Same smelly cigar, same overfed ego. "You dangle the rebuilding of the temple in front of them, and they're bound to become cooperative."

"Except for the Hasidim and a few other ultraorthodox sects," another member of the Cartel corrected. Eric looked up from his doodling to see a short round man with a heavy Middle Eastern accent. "It is not giving up Israeli land in exchange for a temple that concerns them. Rather it is that the groundbreaking coincides

83

with the day of your installment as chairman. They are afraid that it puts too much focus upon one man."

The secretary general turned to Lucas. "Unless, of course, you can convince them that you're their long-awaited Messiah."

Quiet chuckles filled the room.

"Maybe we can." Lucas grinned. "Maybe we can." He turned more serious. "What about the Palestinians?"

"They are ecstatic. Finally, a homeland that's more than a token West Bank patchwork."

"And the Arab Coalition?"

The secretary general rolled the cigar in his mouth, then pulled it out. "They assure us that, for the most part, they can hold the extremists in check. But it will be no cakewalk. It's not going to be easy convincing the fringe elements to share their beloved Temple Mount."

"Even though the Dome of the Rock and the temple will be two hundred meters apart?" Lucas asked.

The secretary general nodded. "Even if they're two hundred miles apart. You can create a state for the Palestinians, you can give the Jews their temple, but you still can't control the crazies."

Lucas nodded. "Have we made it clear to the Coalition that we'll soon have another means of control at our disposal?"

"Eric . . ."

"They know that's what we're saying. But, of course, they want to know what that means of control is."

Lucas smiled. "Assure them they'll not be disappointed."

"Eric . . ."

Eric returned to his sketching. *What do you want? I'm busy.*

"I've got something very, very special for you."

If it's another movie, I'm not interested.

"Oh no, my young friend, this is not a movie. This is something entirely different."

Eric pretended to sulk. The last two times it had been very difficult to regain control of his body. Heylel had been too stubborn. Now Eric was going to make him pay. He continued his sketch of the secretary general—complete with cigar, donkey ears, and daggers sticking out of his neck. He waited for Heylel to say more, but there was only silence.

A half minute passed. He pushed up his glasses and focused back on the Cartel. They were yacking about Scorpion again and about finding a cure. He continued to wait. Still no Heylel. Eric was sure he was there; he could feel him. But he remained absolutely silent, and silence was something Eric could never stand much of.

So ... He finally thought.

More silence.

Are you there? Hello?

"Yes, I am here."

So what do you want?

"I think you are ready for the next level."

Eric felt a rush of excitement but tried to hide it. *Next level?*

"There is much more power that awaits you, my friend."

Like what? You keep promising me more power, but where is it?

"I have promised you great things, have I not?"

Yeah, but so far—

"So far you have merely undergone the preparation. And you have done well. You have allowed yourself to be opened and enlarged. Now you are ready to taste and experience powers you never believed possible."

Really? Eric could no longer hide his interest.

"And not just in this dimension. My young friend, you are now ready to travel and experience the powers of all dimensions."

How? When?

"If you wish, we may start at this very moment."

You'll be going with me?

"I'm afraid I must stay behind and talk to these people. But my other friends will be happy to take you. Many of them know the regions far better than I."

Eric briefly focused back on the meeting. The representative of the European Union was talking. "... complete cooperation, as long as we have assurance that the London market will regain its stability and—"

Eric turned inward, back to his conversation. *Where are these ... friends?*

"*We're right here.*" The voice was so close it startled him.

"*Hello, Eric.*" There was another.

"*Hi, there.*" And another. "*Ready to go on our adventure?*"

I'm not sure. How long will we be gone?

"*Time has no meaning where we are going,*" the first voice explained.

"*They need my help now, Eric,*" Heylel said. "*Let my friends take you with them. When you are done you may return.*"

And you'll let me be back in control?

"*If I have completed my task, certainly.*"

Eric immediately saw the fine print. It was the single word *if*. So he replied with a single word of his own. *No.*

"*Eric?*"

Not unless you let me come back when I want to come back.

"*My young friend, be reasonable.*"

I won't leave unless you let me come back when I want to come back.

Eric waited a breathless moment. He was dying to see what they wanted to show him. He'd never been disappointed with any of Heylel's surprises, and he knew this would be no different. But he had to show him who was boss.

"*Let's go, Eric,*" one of the voices pleaded.

"*You won't believe what we'll see,*" another urged.

But Eric continued to wait. The silence lengthened. And then, just when he thought he'd asked for too much and had gone too far, Heylel spoke up. "*All right, my friend. You may return whenever you are ready.*"

You promise?

"Of course I promise. You may return whenever you wish."

Something about Heylel's tone made him the slightest bit uneasy. *Whenever I want?* he asked.

"Whenever you want."

Eric still wasn't entirely convinced, but he did have his word. He took a look around the boardroom. *Well, all right then, just as long as—*

But that was as far as he got. As soon as he had given permission there was such a loud, rushing sound that he could no longer hear himself think. For the briefest moment he felt his vocal chords start to vibrate, his mouth start to move . . .

"Good afternoon, gentlemen, ladies . . ."

And then he was gone, racing into somewhere or something a thousand miles a second. He wanted to scream in fear, in exhilaration, but he moved so fast the cries were swept from his mind before he could think them.

As he pulled their Ford Escort into the Cedar Mall parking lot, Sarah's words kept echoing in his head. *"What kind of God would do this? Is this how he loves his children?"* Brandon turned off the ignition and crawled out of the car. He was stiff and a little achy. The pain wasn't unbearable, just a reminder. But a reminder of what? Of a tyrant God who played hide-and-seek with his will? *"No merciful God would do this!"* He tried ignoring the thoughts, but they kept returning.

He slammed the car door, threw back his hair, and started toward the main entrance. It was 7:45. The bookstore downstairs was Sarah's favorite hangout. It was open until 9:00. He hoped she would be there.

A fog had settled in, absorbing much of the sound of traffic from I–30 while also highlighting the scrape of his shoes against the asphalt. As he walked, his mind continued to spin. What *was* God trying to prove? Yes, he was a God of love and mercy; the Bible made that perfectly clear. And yet, how could a God of love and mercy allow such things to happen? How could he give the two of them such an incredible call on their lives and then go out of his way to keep them in the dark? And what about Salman's sickness? No wonder Sarah was freaked.

But it was more than just Sarah and it was more than just him. What about all the other suffering? Those thousands dying of starvation every day, the Jews and Arabs being wiped out by this malicious virus, the wars raging out of control? It had gotten to the point where he didn't want to turn on the news, afraid of what he'd see.

And yet God, who could see everything, God who was all-loving, who was all-caring, continued to allow these things to happen. Not only allow them, but by the looks of things, endorse them.

The automatic doors hissed open, and Brandon stepped into the mall. He'd barely entered before he heard the first voice ...

"I'm worth something! I'll make you happy! Please ..."

It was a girl, so loud, so close that he turned, thinking she was behind him.

But no one was there.

"I'm somebody, look at me ... please! I've got lots to offer. Please like me. Pay attention to me!"

He glanced about. It was the typical evening crowd—kids, couples, couples with kids, and a few of the elderly. But no one was close enough for him to hear, not like this.

"I'm somebody. Like me. Love me. Please ..."

And then he saw her, standing by the Coffee Beanery, sipping an espresso. She was fourteen at most. Cutoffs too short, midriff blouse showing plenty of firm belly and a pierced navel. But it was the eyes that broke his heart. Under the thick blue makeup was a look of studied indifference. A rehearsed attempt to disguise her neediness and cover her pleas. Pleas that Brandon heard loud and clear.

"Somebody. Look at me. Like me. Love me."

She didn't say a word. She didn't have to.

"Somebody! Anybody!"

"I'll take 'em out. I'll take 'em all out." It was a different voice. Male. Full of humiliation and anger. "Get the old man's shotgun and blow 'em all away. That would show 'em."

Brandon scanned the crowd.

"Let 'em know you don't mess with me."

It came from the kid ahead of him. He couldn't see the face, only the baggy pants and the swagger.

"Anybody, please." It was the girl again. "Please! I'll make you happy. Love me."

"Better yet, I'll blow away their families. Yeah, that would show 'em."

A third voice joined in. "He'll say we can't support it. Not with Julie and college. He'll say we're too old to start another family . . . *I'm* too old. And what about Down's syndrome? Dear God, I'm too old. He'll make me get rid of it, I know he'll make me get rid of it. Dear God, help me! Show me what to do!"

It came from a middle-aged couple off to his left. She was laughing at something he'd said. But underneath, Brandon sensed her anguish. It's not that he was reading minds; these were louder than specific thoughts. They were overriding fears, never-ending anxieties that constantly plagued and haunted.

"Somebody, anybody—"

"Nobody mess with—"

"Maybe I won't tell him, maybe I'll—"

He'd had similar experiences, sensing people's feelings, but only when he looked into their eyes. Never like this.

"Please."

"I'll show 'em."

"Help me!"

And never this loud. He picked up his pace. If Sarah was there, he'd find her and get out as quickly as possible. The sooner the better.

More voices joined in. Some pleading, others crying— the schoolteacher who'd just lost his retirement in the mutual fund that had crashed, the alcoholic housewife, the young mother convinced of her husband's affair—each crying out in private despair.

The voices grew in number and in volume. They were everywhere now. So much pain. So much sorrow. He broke into a trot. How could a God of love allow this much suffering? There was a nine-year-old Jewish girl, eyes red over the death of her father, terrified for the life of her mother. But she wouldn't be terrified for long. The virus would kill her before summer.

A groan rose in his throat ... partially from anguish, partially to drown out their cries. But the cries grew worse, turning into screams of overwhelming need, unbearable sorrow.

Up ahead was the escalator leading down to the bookstore. He quickly headed toward it. But a young man approached from the right—crippled arms, dragging foot. He must have recognized Brandon, because he called out to him, his mouth twisting pathetically. Brandon slowed as he approached. He tried to listen, but couldn't hear. The cry of the other voices was too loud. Not that it mattered. He knew what the boy wanted. And he'd be happy to oblige. Anything to relieve at least one person's suffering. Maybe God wouldn't do anything, but he would. He could at least ease one person's agony.

Brandon reached out and took the boy's shoulders. Immediately he felt the heat. And, immediately, the searing pain. It traveled into his hands and up his arms. Brandon stared in horror as his wrists began to twist and his arms turned upon themselves. He looked back to the boy, but the child paid him no attention; he was looking down at his own hands and arms ... as they straightened.

Brandon tried to speak, to yell, but his mouth was contorting. He felt a drool of saliva spilling from the corner and couldn't stop it. Suddenly his left leg turned in, then crumpled, sending him crashing to the floor. The pain was unbearable. He looked around, eyes wild. People were gathering. With them came even more voices. Desperate voices. Suffering. Screaming. Shrieking.

With the boy's help he struggled to his feet. The kid was talking, but Brandon couldn't hear the words, only stare at the mouth. It was perfectly shaped now, like the rest of his body.

Brandon drew back, horrified, furious at what was happening. No doubt this was more of God's handiwork. Is this what He wanted? For Brandon to take on the suffering of others? Fine. So be it. Let God be the tyrant Sarah had described. Let Him be the monster. But not Brandon. Brandon had a gift. He had the ability to end suffering. And he had something God apparently lacked. He had the love.

A mentally retarded woman appeared in the crowd—mid-thirties, holding her mother's hand. Or was it her caretaker's? It didn't matter. She was simply another victim. Someone else in need of healing.

He reached out toward her. The woman cried in fear, but he managed to grab her hand. She tried to pull away, but his twisted grip was like iron. Again there was the heat. But this time no pain. Only a numbness that raced through his mind like a drug. A drug distorting his logic, dissolving his understanding.

He turned to the crowd. Why were all these strangers staring at him? He didn't hurt them. Why did they want to hurt him?

His left foot gave out again. He lunged forward and fell to the floor. Up ahead was the big, shiny exalator. He liked exalators. They were fun to ride. They made him happy. If he could just reach it, maybe he'd be happy, too.

Suddenly a bad man was reaching for his arm. He couldn't hear him over all the crying and screaming. Why were they screaming? Why were they staring? He didn't do nothing to them. Oh look, there's the exalator. He liked exalators. Why was that man grabbing his arm? He was a stranger. He mustn't talk to strangers. He wrenched his arm free and dragged himself to the bright, shiny stairs of the exalators. He liked exalators.

He struggled back to his feet and reached for the moving black belt. There was that arm again. It grabbed him. He tried to break free, but it held so tight that he had to throw himself backwards to break its grip. But the force caused him to lose his balance, sending him backwards, backwards through the air so he thought he was flying, flying until he hit one of those shiny steps with his shoulder and kept rolling onto his head and flipped over and over again, and then again, screaming in fear and pain, knowing Momma would be mad at him for getting his clothes dirty, but he couldn't stop rolling and screaming and falling down and down and down until he reached the place where he was no longer falling or feeling pain or screaming or hearing those awful voices.

Until he reached the place where there was nothing at all ...

"Eric, sweetheart, wake up." Katherine patted his face gently. "Eric." Then a little harder. "Eric."

He still gave no response.

She was on the polished marble floor with him, his head cradled in her lap. She glared up at members of the Cartel and then at Lucas. "What did you do to him? What happened?"

Lucas kneeled down beside her. Always the voice of reason, he tried to explain, "Katherine, we didn't—"

"What did you do?"

She looked back at her son. By all appearances he was asleep, resting peacefully. "Eric." But he would not wake. "Eric!" She could feel panic trying to take over and used all of her strength to fight it off. "Where is Heylel?" she demanded. "Was Heylel here?"

"Yes," another voice answered.

She looked up to see the fat cigar chewer. "What happened?"

The man shrugged. "He gave us his counsel, and then he left."

"Eric didn't interrupt, he didn't try to take over?"

"That's what's so odd." Lucas continued the explanation. "After Heylel left, Eric simply collapsed, he just went limp." He looked back at her son. Katherine could tell he wanted to reach out and touch the boy, but she also knew he had enough brains not to try.

She turned back to Eric. "Sweetheart . . ."

Nothing.

"Eric . . ."

Now it was Lucas's turn. "Eric . . . Eric, can you hear us? Eric, wake up, son."

Katherine caught some movement under the eyelids. "Eric?"

They shifted several times before they finally fluttered open.

"Eric . . ."

He squinted at the quartz lights over the table, then looked around to get his bearings. When he saw Katherine he relaxed and tried to speak. "Mom." His voice crackled like dry leaves, barely above a whisper.

"I'm right here, baby." She pulled him closer, brushing the hair out of his eyes. "I'm right here."

He slowly closed his lids.

"Eric!"

Then reopened them. As he did, he began to smile.

"What? What is it, sweetheart? Are you okay?"

The smile broadened. "It was beautiful."

"Was it a dream, did you have another dream?"

He shook his head.

"What was it, what did you see?"

"I saw the future."

"The future?"

He nodded. "I was famous, Mom. Everybody loved me."

"Oh, baby." She bent down to kiss his forehead, then stroked his hair again. It was then she caught a glimpse of her hand. It was trembling. Violently. "Everybody loves you, sweetheart. We all love you."

"Katherine." Lucas touched her arm, offering to help. Instinctively, she pulled Eric away. "Leave us alone."

"Kath—"

"No, no more!"

"I know what you must be—"

"You get that doctor here, and you get her here *now!*"

"We're doing all we—"

"You get her here *now*." She glared up at Lucas. "You get her here, or we're on the next plane. You hear me? *Do you hear me?*"

She was shouting now. Her whole body trembled, but there was nothing she could do about it. She continued glaring at Lucas, waiting for a response.

Finally, he began to nod.

Sarah's white sneakers squeaked against the worn linoleum as she raced through Bethel Lake Community Hospital. She was on the third floor, the very floor where she'd stayed when recovering from her accident a year ago. She turned left and nearly collided with a gurney as she continued searching for the room number ... 308, 310, there it was, 312. She burst into the room but was immediately brought to a stop.

There, on the bed, pulled into a twisted fetal position, lay Brandon. His arms were bent and his head cocked sideways. An oxygen line ran to his nose, and a heavy nurse in her late fifties was adjusting some IV lines. But it was the dazed look on his face that took Sarah's breath away. She'd never seen him with such a lifeless expression.

Spotting her, his eyes flickered with recognition. His mouth twitched, slurping back a drool of saliva. It contorted, trying to speak. "Thar ... wa ..."

"Brandon!" She started toward him, but the nurse turned and blocked her path. "No, don't touch him."

"What? That's my husband!"

"Are you Mrs. Martus?"

Sarah's head reeled. "Yes, yes, and that's my husband, Brandon Martus."

"The healer guy, right?"

"Yes, right, right."

"Thar ... wa ..." his voice was wracked with pain as he tried to reach out to her.

Again Sarah started toward him and again she was blocked. "What's going on?" she demanded. "What happened?"

"He was at the mall, doing his ..." The nurse searched for the word. "His thing."

Sarah turned to him. "You were healing people? Brandon, you were there trying to heal people?"

He nodded, wincing in pain at the movement.

She turned back to the nurse. "What happened?"

"I can't be sure, I mean I wasn't there, but—"

"Tell me what happened!"

The nurse took a breath and continued. "The people that he touched, the sick ones that he ... healed." She glanced back to the twisted body.

No more had to be said. The realization hit Sarah hard. "He took on their sickness?"

"Tharwa ... et hoorts."

"I'm not saying that. I mean, it may be what others are saying, but ..." The nurse glanced down at her hands and rubbed them self-consciously.

"What?" Sarah demanded. "Tell me!"

"Well, I've had rheumatoid arthritis for years now. Sometimes it gets to hurting real bad."

"And ..."

"When your husband came in, when we were moving him, he grabbed my hands, and I felt this heat, and ..." She held up her hands and slowly wiggled her fingers. "The pain is gone. Completely."

"Tharwaa ..."

"It's okay, Bran." Sarah moved past the nurse and squatted down beside him. "I'm here, I'm here ..." His face was sweaty, and she knew the pain was excruciating.

"Tharwaa ... make it thtop ..."

"Shhh, it's okay. I'm here, I'm here."

"Doon't weave me." The words pierced her heart. She could tell every syllable was difficult for him. "Doon't weave ..."

"I'm right here, hon, I won't leave you, I'm right here." She took his hand and kissed it lightly. It was only then that she saw his knuckles. Each joint was swollen and inflamed. They were turned and gnarled in what could only be the advanced stages of rheumatoid arthritis.

Sarah looked up at the nurse, but the woman had turned away, wiping her own eyes.

"Tharwa ... et ... hoorts ..."

"I know, honey, I know ..." She could barely get the words out as tears sprang to her eyes. And then, when her throat was too swollen for words, she began to pray.

Dear God ... Dear Lord, what are You doing to us? What are You doing?

CHAPTER 5

How much longer will you be?" Sarah asked as she flipped through the papers inside another one of the clinic's beat-up filing cabinets.

"Just a couple more minutes. The call's supposed to come in at 11:00. I'll have everything fixed up and running by then, no sweat."

Sarah glanced across her tiny office to the dust-coated clock on the shelf. It was crammed into a bookcase with a thousand other books and periodicals in various stages of spilling onto the floor. It read 10:52. "You've got eight minutes," she said.

"No sweat," the kid repeated.

She watched as he finished attaching a TV camera no bigger than a golf ball to the side of her computer monitor. Although videoconferencing had become more and more common, it was one of the many luxuries she and Brandon had decided to do without. She jimmied the filing cabinet until it shut, then leaned against the wall only to hear the brittle paint crackle and fall to the floor behind her. One of the many luxuries.

It had been two days since she'd first noticed the marks on Brandon's arms. Two days of coffee and bad hospital food. Two days with absolutely no change. He still lay in his bed. He was still twisted. And he still writhed in agony, barely coherent ... except for the part where he called out her name. That, unfortunately, she understood perfectly.

Of course his mother had arrived and insisted they take shifts, ordering Sarah to go home and get some rest. And, of course, Sarah had tried to refuse. But Mrs. Martus epitomized the term "Steel Magnolia." Despite her Southern charm and hospitality, there was iron inside the lady. An iron that made sure she got her way, whenever she wanted her way. And before Sarah knew it, she was heading home to get some rest.

But after staring at the ceiling fan in the bedroom for the first half of the night and cleaning the apartment throughout the second, she decided to come to the clinic and get some real work done. That's how she handled stress. Some folks had their wine, their TV shows, their aerobics ... Sarah had her work.

When she arrived, the kid was already there, flirting with Ruth, their receptionist. He was from a local computer store that had been given some very specific instructions. They were to hook up the latest videoconferencing equipment for her without charge.

"And the catch?" Sarah had asked.

"No catch, it's a gift."

"From whom?"

By the look on the kid's face, he must have been waiting all morning to give her the answer. "At eleven o'clock this morning, Lucas Ponte will be giving you a call."

Sarah hadn't been amused. "Right. Tell him I'd love to chat, but I'm having an early lunch with the pope."

"No, I'm not kidding," the boy had said. "They called up the store early this morning and made it real clear what we were to hook up for you."

"They?"

"The guys from the Cartel."

"And you believed they were for real."

The kid had shrugged. "Got me. But the money they wired over was real enough."

That conversation had been thirty minutes ago. After calling his store and being assured that the gift was gratis, that there were "no hidden charges whatsoever either now or anytime in the future," Sarah had finally agreed to the hookup, if only to see who was behind it. Because as practical jokes went, this was about as elaborate as she'd seen.

While the kid puttered with the computer, she returned to her files looking for any material related to what Brandon was suffering. Anything on empathetics (from husbands who actually feel labor pains with their wives to mothers who have to go to the bathroom whenever their children do), to various psychic phenomena, and even to the stigmatics ... those unfortunate souls, particularly Catholic, who so identified with Christ's suffering that for one reason or another their palms actually begin to bleed.

But she could find nothing resembling Brandon's experience, nothing where a healer so empathized with the sick that he took on their illnesses.

There was, however, material on various individuals who referred to themselves as "intercessors"—men and women who felt they were called to intercede and pray for others. People like Rees Howells, who lived in Wales during the first half of the twentieth century. As a man of great faith whose prayers were responsible for several miracles (including what some believed to be major influences on World War II), Howells had stressed over and over again that the first step in interceding was to lose yourself so deeply in the needs of others that you literally start identifying with their suffering.

Perhaps. But to actually take on the suffering? To identify so strongly with the sick that you actually become sick? No. From what Sarah understood of Scripture, that sort of work bordered on heresy. That was Christ's job, to take on the sins of the world, to suffer in our place. It certainly wasn't man's. But if she was right, then why would God—

"Dr. Martus . . . they're on-line."

Startled from her thoughts, Sarah looked over to the monitor. An image of a handsome woman in a navy blue business suit flickered onto the screen. "Dr. Martus?"

"Yes, uh . . ." Sarah moved somewhat clumsily to her chair and sat. "Right here, this is Dr. Martus." She was unsure whether to look at the camera or at the monitor. She tried a little of both.

"My name is Deena Pappopolis." The woman had a slight accent, probably Greek. "I am executive secretary to Lucas Ponte."

"I see, and that would make me Queen Elizabeth."

"Pardon me . . ."

"I appreciate the toys, Ms. Pappopolis, and junior here and I have been having a real in-depth conversation, but what's going on and who are you really?"

"If you will hold the line for just a moment, Mr. Ponte will be able to explain."

"Uh-huh." For a few chuckles someone was really going out of their way. Then again, maybe it was some sort of commercial, or one of those hidden camera things. Whatever the case, she was already weary of it. She had a lot to do and wanted to get to the punch line as soon as possible.

Suddenly the image cut to a man—young fifties, neatly trimmed beard, distinguished looking, and the same trim fig-

ure and riveting black eyes that made the real Lucas Ponte
so immediately recognizable.

"Hello, Dr. Martus."

For the briefest second, Sarah thought he might be real.
She held her tongue a moment and played along . . . just in
case. "Yes?" But even as she answered she remembered hearing of agencies that booked look-alike celebrities for parties
and various affairs. Granted, he was a pretty good likeness, but
on closer examination even she could tell—

"This is Lucas Ponte."

"So I've been told."

She wasn't certain, but she thought she caught a trace of
a smile.

"Actually, I am."

"And I'm the Virgin Mary. Pleased to meet you, Lukey. I
can call you Lukey, can't I?"

The smile grew more obvious. "If you wish. And do I call
you Mary or Mother, or just plain—"

"You can call me impatient," she interrupted, "and plenty
busy. Now who are you, why did you spend money on all this
equipment, and what do you want?"

His charm remained though his tone grew a bit more
sober. "I appreciate your demanding schedule, Dr. Martus, and
please forgive us for the intrusion. But we wanted to make
certain you have been receiving our e-mail."

Surprised, Sarah hesitated, then swallowed. Of course
she'd read the e-mail, had even given it some consideration.
But how did these people know about it? Unless . . . Instinctively her hand shot up to her hair, pulling it over her scar. "I
. . . things have been very busy for us lately."

He continued smiling. "I can appreciate that. Especially
given your recent marriage. Congratulations."

Sarah felt her face flush. She was beginning to accept it
as true—she was actually talking to one of the most influential people in the world. As the fact took hold she felt herself
beginning to unravel under his dark penetrating eyes. What

had he just said? Congratulating her on the wedding? "Yes, uh
. . ." She cleared her throat. "Thank you."

"Your husband is a lucky man."

Sarah's face grew warmer, which made her even more
insecure, which began to irritate her. She didn't appreciate
being made to feel like some self-conscious schoolgirl. She
repositioned herself and swallowed again, only this time there
was nothing left to swallow. "Why, uh, why exactly are you
calling me?"

"Katherine Lyon, the woman who has been e-mailing
you about her son?"

"Yes, now that you mention it, I do recall our staff receiving something." She sounded a little stiff, but definitely more
professional.

"She has asked me to personally contact you, to see if
there is any way to prevail upon you to spend a few weeks of
your valuable time over here. Your training in neuroscience
as well as your expertise in the paranormal may prove quite
valuable in diagnosing her son's problem."

Sarah cleared her throat. "The mother had said something about seizures and spirit guides?"

"Yes, that is correct."

"Surely there's someone closer to you who can—"

"Dr. Martus, I appreciate your modesty, but her son is
very important to all of us at the Cartel. And, consequently, I
believe, to the world."

As she listened, Sarah noticed the kid from the computer
store edging in closer to get a glimpse of the screen. Again she
tugged at her hair. "And you really believe I'm the one to
help?"

"From what I have read of your work in neurobiology and
psychic research, if you cannot help him, I doubt anyone can."

It was another compliment, and it left Sarah even more
unsteady. "Well, I . . . I can't say at the moment. I mean, I'd
have to check my schedule and discuss it with the staff." She
shifted in the chair. "How long of a stay would you anticipate?"

"That would be entirely up to you. However, once you complete your evaluation, you may wish to stay a few days longer and see the Himalayas. Nepal is beautiful this time of year, and it would be an honor for me to show you some of its sights."

Sarah blinked. Was he flirting with her? She tried swallowing again, but with the same lack of success. "Listen." She cleared her throat. "This is all very flattering, but I need some time to think it over."

"Certainly, and please forgive me for this intrusion."

"That's, uh, that's all right."

"But, as I said, the young man is very important to us."

"I understand."

"All accommodations will be first class, and you and your clinic will be handsomely compensated should you decide to come."

"And if I don't?"

"Then I will take it as a personal loss . . . in more ways than one."

He *was* flirting.

He continued. "Do you mind if someone from my office checks with you in a few days, after you have had time to consult your schedule?"

"Uh, yes, I mean no, I mean that would be fine, certainly." She could feel a cool dampness break out across her forehead.

"Good. Well, thank you for your time, Dr. Martus. And again, please accept my apologies for this intrusion."

"That's all right. No problem. I'll let you know my schedule."

"I shall look forward to that. Good day, Doctor."

"Yes, uh, good day."

She saw him reach for his monitor, and suddenly the picture went blank. Sarah stared at the screen for several seconds, feeling her heart pounding in her chest. She took a deep breath, trying to force herself to relax. And then she took another.

On the morning of the third day Brandon was sweating again. Only this time it had nothing to do with a fever. He wasn't sure if he was awake or asleep, but he knew he wasn't in the hospital. He still lay curled in a twisted knot, and he still writhed with the pain. But he was no longer in his hospital bed. Instead, he lay on a moon-shaped platform above a sea of flames, the same crescent moon he had seen tattooed on Salman's arm and now had on his own, the same crescent moon he had dreamed about.

He didn't know how long he lay there before he saw the light—the blazing brilliance that appeared from somewhere behind him. He tried to turn and face it, but the pain in his body was too great.

A moment later he heard the voice. Its power vibrated the air, the flames, the platform—everything shook with the sound—and yet it resonated gently within his own mind.

"Hello, my child."

Again Brandon struggled to turn his head. The pain was severe, but he fought and strained until he succeeded. He had to.

The light was piercing, blinding like the sun, like a thousand suns. He squinted, trying to protect his eyes until, at last, he saw a form in the light—a form carved from the light. It was the form of a man. In one hand he held what looked like seven glowing stars. From his mouth came a razor-sharp, double-edged sword. And behind him were lampstands ... seven as well. It was an astonishing sight. But even more astonishing for Brandon was to see this being quietly kneel down at his side.

That's when he noticed the eyes. They were made of fire—pure, leaping flames of fire. But they were not flames of destruction. They were flames of passion. A burning, consuming passion. A passion that Brandon instinctively knew burned for him. It was so intense and overwhelming that he could not move. All he could do was stare at them and drink in the love. There was no doubt who he was looking at. And there was no doubt of the all-inclusive, all-consuming love.

That's why, before he could stop himself, Brandon spoke. It came as naturally as a little boy talking to his daddy. "Et hoorts."

Sorrow filled the flaming eyes. The voice responded. This time it contained as much pain as it had tenderness.

"I know."

"Why?"

The voice answered gently. *"You say you love. Yet, My child, you know nothing of love. You know nothing of its depth or of its passion."* The voice was tender, yet the words cut deep into Brandon's soul. *"I have given you the briefest taste of My love. These three days you have felt the merest fraction of what I feel, you have ached the smallest trace of what I ache, you have wept the tiniest portion of what I weep."*

Brandon's head reeled. Were such things possible? Could any one person contain such love?

The voice continued, its passion growing. *"I have purchased My bride with My very life. You know nothing of the depth of My love for her; you know nothing of My passion. You who claim to love more than I."*

Suddenly Brandon felt fear, a tremendous terror rising up inside of him as the voice grew in emotion.

"Do you dare speak to Me of love when you know nothing of its meaning? When you cannot comprehend the price I have paid, nor the depths of My devotion?"

Tears sprang to Brandon's eyes. He had to close them. There was no argument to be made. The thoughts running through his mind these past several days, those silent accusations of God, they'd all been heard. They'd all been heard and they'd all been wrong. Brandon knew that was true from the moment he looked into those eyes, from the moment he heard the words. He'd been terribly and ignorantly wrong. A sob of remorse escaped his throat. How could he have been so blind, so presumptuous? Another sob came. And then another. He lowered his head as tears began to fall.

The voice did not respond but waited patiently. Brandon had no idea how long he cried, but finally, when there were no tears left, a hand reached out and touched his cheek. He opened his eyes and recognized it as the hand from his past, the hand from his father's church, the pierced hand that had saved him from the fiery abyss of the serpent's throat.

With excruciating effort, Brandon reached up his own crippled hand to take it. And, as he did, his pain immediately disappeared. But not just the pain in his hand, the pain throughout his entire body ... and his mind. It suddenly ceased.

He looked up, startled. The burning eyes smiled. Reaching out and taking the pierced hand with both of his own, Brandon began to kiss it over and over again as a fresh assault of tears sprang to his eyes and streamed down his cheeks.

"My son ... "

He looked up.

"I have set before you and your bride a great call. I have given you a glorious promise. But you have allowed worldly thinking to turn that promise into worldly glory. You say you are yielded to Me, yet yielded is not the same as broken. The promise I have given must die and face darkness. For only in the darkest places dwell My brightest victories. You and the promise must be ground into the powder of contriteness, then mixed with the oil of My Spirit before My glory is manifested."

Brandon nodded, not because he understood, but because he knew truth was being spoken.

"You are able ... but only if you live in My strength. Only if you hold My hand and look into My eyes. You are able. But if you are not willing, I will understand. My love will be no less, but I will understand and I will find another."

Alarm filled Brandon. Was it possible? Would He really pass him over and choose someone else? After all they'd been through?

The eyes waited patiently until Brandon finally realized they were waiting on him. Impulsively he wanted to shout, "Yes, whatever You want and then some! Anything You choose will be fine with me!" But what of the cost? Look what he and Sarah had been through so far, and they'd barely begun. And if the prophecy in Revelation was to be taken literally, the reward for their obedience would be their murder and their bodies left in the streets to rot. Not exactly the happily-ever-after ending one would hope for. Yes, there would be a resurrection, but ...

What was so wrong with having a normal life? What was so wrong with having a wife he could actually make love to, of having children, raising a family, growing old together? What would be so terribly wrong with just being normal?

Brandon looked back into the eyes. He knew there would be no condemnation if he refused. The flames of passion would burn just as intensely for him regardless of his decision. But, as he stared into those eyes, Brandon realized something else. How could anyone say no to such love, to such all-consuming passion?

Slowly, almost imperceptibly, Brandon began to nod.

The eyes sparkled in delight. And it was that expression that burst Brandon's chest with joy. To think that he, a nobody, could actually make the Creator of the universe smile.

The voice spoke again. *"I will give you a gift few have received. I will give you My heart. My words will become a fire in your mouth that you cannot contain. They will burn until you have completed the warning to My bride."*

"What ..." Brandon's voice was a trembling whisper. "What am I to say?"

"Warn her before it is too late ...
She who preaches to love herself,
when I have commanded her to hate.
She who prays for her will,
but does not seek Mine.
She who claims to be My servant,
yet demands I serve.
She who cries out for answers,
but will not listen.

She who demands healing,
but will not seek Me in sickness.
She who indulges her every whim,
yet allows My least to suffer.
She who is quick to raise the sword,
but slow to drop to her knees.
She who chases her dreams
while forgetting My call.
She who raises her skirts to the world
while ignoring My call to holiness."

"But ... how?" Brandon whispered.

"She no longer has ears to listen, but by seeing, she will understand."

"See what? What are we to do?"

"As My bride's affection has turned from Me, so Sarah will turn from you."

Brandon's protest came before he could stop it. "No!"

The eyes looked upon him with overwhelming compassion. Brandon searched them, hoping for a reprieve, for some other solution.

Again the hand reached out, gently touching his cheek. *"It is the only way. But she will return. Just as My bride will return to Me, so she will return to you. And her act, the returning to your covenant, will be My testimony to the world."*

The lump in Brandon's throat made it nearly impossible to talk. "But ... can't there be ... another way?"

"No."

Brandon looked down, his eyes burning with tears.

The voice continued. *"You and I will share the longing for our bride. And that love, followed by her obedience, is the message the two of you will proclaim to the world."*

Brandon nodded, barely able to breathe for the sorrow.

"Study My letters of love to My bride. Point to their warnings, lest I come and take away her lampstand. Be strong and courageous, My son. Do not tremble or be afraid. For I will be with you. I will be with you always."

Tears spilled down Brandon's cheeks and onto his pillow. The pillow from his hospital bed. The pillow that he was now lying on. He clutched it and continued to weep until it was soaked with his tears.

Sarah was cleaning again. This time she was on her hands and knees in the shower. It was amazing how quickly mineral deposits could build up, especially in the grout, especially in the corners. She'd heard people talk about the city's hard water before; now she understood. For whatever reason, she hadn't seen the accumulation in her first cleaning of the apartment. This time, gratefully, she had. So with spray cleaner in one hand and a brush in the other, she was furiously at work. It was either that or putting down another quart of Swiss Almond Delight which, although kinder to her knees, would be far less considerate of her hips.

She didn't know how long she was down there like that before she heard the front door open. Immediately, she froze. Had she locked it? She wasn't certain.

A moment later, the door shut. Whoever had opened it was now inside the apartment. Sarah held her breath, uncertain what to do. She could call out, demand to know who it was. But that would give away her location. And there, cornered in the shower, on her hands and knees, was not the strongest position in which to ward off an attack. Maybe she should just lay low and stay there in hopes they would take whatever they wanted and get out. It was a difficult decision. Fortunately, she didn't have too long to weigh it. A familiar voice with a terrible Ricky Ricardo accent suddenly echoed down the hall: "Lucy . . . I'm home!"

"Brandon?" She dropped the brush and spray cleaner and jumped to her feet. "Is that you?"

Her husband rounded the corner and her heart leaped. She was so excited that she stumbled over the threshold of the shower.

"Easy!" he warned.

But she didn't care. "Brandon!" Even as she was stumbling and falling, she didn't care. "Brandon!"

He stepped in and managed to catch her just before she slammed into the wall, his arms as strong and healthy as ever. He was laughing now, as he helped her back to her feet, trying to keep his own balance. "Are you okay?" he asked.

She stared at him, not believing her eyes. Then suddenly she threw her arms around him, hugging him, kissing him. "Brandon . . . Brandon, Brandon, Brandon."

He continued to laugh, holding her, until suddenly a dreadful thought filled her mind and she pulled away. "Are you all right, did I hurt you?"

"No." He grinned as he pulled her back into the embrace. "You didn't hurt me at all. I'm fine. I'm absolutely fine."

"And you're positive it was the Lord?" Sarah leaned against their kitchen counter sipping her lukewarm Earl Grey.

Brandon nodded from the table. "Oh, yeah."

"Not some dream, not some hallucination?"

"He was more real than you and I put together."

Sarah paused, carefully thinking it through. Finally she spoke. "Superreality."

"Hmm?"

"That's what Dr. Reichner used to call the supernatural, those dimensions that are higher than our own. Remember? 'Superreality.'"

"He was super something." Brandon looked down at the table, his voice thickening with emotion. "I've never seen such love, I've never felt such intense . . ." But the memory was too much, and he let his words trail off.

Sarah watched silently. It had been nearly three hours since he'd returned to the apartment from the hospital, since he'd strolled in as strong and fit as if nothing had happened. From the looks of things, he'd been made completely well.

But, unfortunately for Sarah, she had other types of wounds, ones far less quick to heal.

Of course she was grateful to have him home. Their first hours of reunion had been pure joy. But now they were down to the cold hard facts . . . and some equally hard questions.

As far as Sarah could tell the vision had been legitimate. There had been no drugs administered except for Percodan to help him relax. Nor had he remained in ICU long enough to develop any of the hallucinations common with longer stays. Granted, what he'd been through would be enough to push anyone over the edge, but nearly everything he described corresponded with other documented visions and accounts, both historically and biblically.

Then of course, there was one other fact: her husband, who had been sick and crippled with pain beyond belief, had been instantaneously healed during the encounter. Psychosomatic? Perhaps. Though Sarah had her doubts. This seemed far less psychological than it did paranormal.

She took another sip of her tea. "Do you remember anything else? Anything else He might have mentioned?"

"Sarah, we've been through this a half-dozen times."

"I know, I know . . ." She couldn't put her finger on it, but she sensed he was keeping something from her. "Nothing more about our relationship?"

He shifted slightly. "He still doesn't want us sleeping together, if that's what you mean."

It wasn't what she'd meant. To be honest, she wasn't sure what she meant. Maybe it was just her own insecurity, her lack of self-esteem—it's pretty hard having self-esteem when God says you're not good enough to sleep with your own husband. But there was something else. She couldn't put her finger on it, but there was something else.

She watched as Brandon reached up and pulled a Bible from the shelf behind him. He opened it and flipped through the pages. How odd, a month ago that book had meant everything to her. And now, almost against her will, she found herself growing uncomfortable with it. Uncomfortable with the way it was invading and overturning every aspect of their lives. *Every* aspect. "What are you looking up?" she asked.

"Remember I told you He said something about 'love letters to His bride'?"

She nodded. "I still don't understand that."

Once again Brandon fell silent, and once again she thought he was hiding something. But what?

He continued. "And those seven stars and those seven lampstands?"

"That's from Revelation," she said. "Toward the beginning. The first couple chapters are the ones that talk about lampstands and stars ..."

"And letters," he said with growing excitement. He riffled through the pages more quickly.

She looked on. Of course she was thrilled to have him back home, and grateful that he seemed completely well. But, then again, she'd never asked for him to be sick. Neither had he, for that matter. So it's not like she should be doing cartwheels in gratitude just because life was almost returning to normal. And what about this business of becoming God's audiovisual aide to the rest of the world? Not exactly the "love, peace, and joy" Brandon had preached to her when she was recovering back in the hospital.

And it's not like they were the first to receive this special attention. After Gerty's e-mail they'd begun studying other Scriptures, discovering how God had used other prophets in the past—men like Isaiah, who was commanded to run around barefoot and naked for three years; or Hosea, the holy man commanded to marry a prostitute; or Jeremiah, who was forbidden to marry at all; or Ezekiel, who wasn't even allowed to cry over the death of his wife.

As far as Sarah could tell, God's track record in dealing with his chosen vessels was anything but pleasant. And if that's how He treated his greatest prophets, she was in no hurry to see what He had in store for them. No, this was not the program she had signed up for. Parting the Red Sea, raising people from the dead, that was more her style. Not this slow, confusing torture. And if that's what He had in mind for them, then maybe it was time to reconsider . . . if, *if* any of it was to be taken literally.

For Sarah that "if" was still the great unanswered question. How much of what was mentioned in Revelation would really happen to them and how much of it was symbolic? How much was literal? How much spiritual? For that matter, the same question could be asked about Brandon's visions, or Gerty's writings, or the hundred and one other signs they'd had. Were they being fools taking everything at face value? Surely if God was Spirit, then He'd talk in spiritual terms, too, wouldn't He? With that in mind, how much of it was up to them to accomplish, and how much of it was up to God? Serious questions. And as the questions churned in her mind, another, more tangible one, surfaced.

"What about Jimmy Tyler's TV show?" she asked.

Brandon looked up.

"Tuesday's the deadline for letting GBN know. During your encounter, did He give you any indication that we shouldn't go through with it?"

Brandon scowled, then slowly shook his head. "No . . ."

"So we can go ahead?"

His frown deepened. "Sarah . . ." She watched as he searched for the words. "Does it feel *right* to you?"

"National exposure, sitting on the platform with one of the most recognizable religious figures of the world? Yes, that feels right to me. That feels real right."

"But this business of, what did He call it, 'pursuing worldly glory.' And remember what Gerty said about the dream and vision having to die first?"

Sarah pulled the chair out and sat across the table from him. "This isn't something we pursued, Brandon. They came to us, remember?"

"I know."

"And to say we're not interested, when we don't have a clear word from the Lord. Isn't it as much a sin to refuse God's blessings as it is to refuse His trials? And couldn't this be just that, one of His blessings, the break we've been waiting for all of this time?"

"I suppose . . ." He was hedging again, obviously struggling with something.

She leaned forward and touched his arm. "What? What is it?"

"It's just . . . well, Tyler wants us to get up there and be a part of this big celebration of unity."

"And . . ."

"And if I'm right about what I heard this morning . . . it doesn't sound like celebration is exactly what God has in mind."

Sarah pushed her hair behind her ear. "No one said you have to get up there and lead cheers. If something needs to be said, we'll have plenty of time to say it later. But later won't come if we don't take these opportunities first."

Brandon continued to think.

She pressed in. "What say we give them a call, give them a tentative yes? And if later God makes it clear we're not to go, then we cancel. That's simple enough, isn't it?"

Brandon gave her a look. One of those that went deep inside of her. The type that, if she let it, would seek out and find her truest, deepest feelings. But not this time. This time she would block it. She'd been doing all she could to ignore the frustration and anger growing inside of her. She didn't need him poking around and discovering what was really going on . . . especially when she wasn't sure herself. Finding an excuse to look away, she rose from the table and crossed to the sink to rinse her mug. "Is that okay, then? I'll call tomorrow and give a tentative yes."

After another long moment he asked, "This is real important to you, isn't it?"

She turned to face him. "Yes, it is. It's very important for *both* of us."

He was still looking at her, but this time she held her ground. She wasn't sure how much he could see, but it didn't matter, at least for now. Now there was the issue of the TV show, whether or not they would take advantage of this obvious, God-given opportunity. Later they would discuss the other issues, like her growing resentment . . . and the invitation to Nepal.

"So?" she asked.

He continued holding her gaze. There was still something else going through his mind, she knew it. But for now, it looked like they'd both be keeping their secrets.

"I'll give them a call then, all right?" She shifted her weight, steeling herself, refusing to look away. "All right?"

Slowly, perhaps a little sadly, Brandon began to nod.

Sarah turned back to the sink and took a silent breath. "Good," she said. "I'll call them in the morning."

CHAPTER 6

Y ou sure I need all this stuff?" Brandon asked.

The makeup person, a petite Sri Lankan in her late twenties who went by the name of Cassandra, laughed as she continued sponging the number seven pancake onto his face. "First timers always say that. Especially you men." She glanced over her shoulder into the lighted mirror facing them. "Just think of this as an opportunity to see what we ladies put ourselves through every day." She grinned over at Sarah who sat in the other barber chair beside them. "Isn't that right?"

Sarah forced a smile. "I'm afraid she's got a point."

Brandon said nothing and sat sullenly as she continued working on his face.

"The bright lights, they wash everybody out. Even those preachers with the ever-tans from Phoenix and Florida, they wear something." She began applying it under his chin. "So, you guys get out this way much?"

Sarah answered, "I spent most of my time on the West Coast. Grew up in Portland, did my undergraduate and graduate work at Stanford, some research at UCLA. But this is Brandon's first time out of the Midwest."

"No kidding?" Cassandra asked. "Get to see many of the sights?"

"We just got in last night."

"Though we found the gridlock on the 405 particularly interesting," Brandon added.

Cassandra smiled. It was obvious small talk came easy to her. "They put you up in the Beverly Hills Hotel? Pretty fancy digs."

Sarah nodded. "I'll say."

"That's one thing about Jimmy, he only goes for the best. You guys get separate suites or a single?"

"I'm sorry?" Sarah asked.

"Depends who did the booking. If it's Sheryl, she makes sure significant others get to *discretely* share a suite. If it's one of the, shall we say, less progressive staff members, then you have to stay in separate rooms."

Sarah cleared her throat. "Actually, we're married."

"Oh, no kidding."

"About a month now."

"Well, congratulations. Didn't see a ring, that's why I asked. 'Course a lot of guys are starting to do that, not wear rings, at least for the cameras. Kinda increases their sex appeal, if you know what I mean." She began brushing Brandon's long dark hair. "And nothing increases the donor base like a little old-fashioned sex appeal, ain't that right, guy?" She gave him a wink in the mirror.

Sarah watched as her husband tried to smile, then glanced down.

"Not that you need it, not with this hair." She reached for a bottle of spray and began spritzing it. "I tell you, I know women who would kill for this. Men, too. It's gorgeous."

Brandon coughed. Sarah couldn't tell if it was from embarrassment or from the hair spray. When he'd finished he gave her the definitive, what-have-you-gotten-me-into look. It was all she could do not to break out laughing. Then, coming to his rescue, she changed the subject. "So, have you known Reverend Tyler long?"

"Twenty years ago this July. He found me on the streets of Colombo, begging for food. He and Bridgett, his wife, took me in. They fed and clothed me, gave me an education, and here I am."

"That's great."

"I owe a lot to Jimmy. And not just me. There was a time nearly every member on staff had a similar story. Always something he did to help somebody—lots of times without folks ever knowing about it."

"Really?"

"I know he comes off a little too slick for some, all show-bizzy and Mr. Entertainment. But underneath that he's a great man. A really great man."

The description of Tyler's genuineness surprised Sarah, and she glanced over at Brandon. But he was busy hearing something else in the woman's voice and studying her actions. After a moment, he finally spoke.

"You said, 'There was a time.'"

Cassandra looked at him. "I'm sorry, what?"

"You said, there was a time when he used to be there for the staff and help them. Has that changed?"

Sarah watched as her husband continued to search the woman, looking for something deeper.

Cassandra shrugged. "We're a lot bigger now." She glanced away, finding something to busy herself with. But

Sarah knew Brandon had found something. The woman continued talking. "In fact, did you know that we now have more stations than any of the secular networks? Isn't that incredible? A Christian network bigger than anything the world has? Praise God."

Brandon nodded as he watched. "And that's a good thing?"

"Of course it's good." Even Sarah could hear the defensive edge coming to Cassandra's voice. "Bigger's always better. At least in ministry. Everyone knows that. The more we grow, the more people we can reach."

Brandon nodded, then answered softly, "And the more of Jimmy everyone loses."

She came to a stop. "What's that supposed to mean?"

Brandon said nothing but held her gaze.

She turned back to her work, a little more briskly. "The man's got pressures you and I can't even begin to imagine. You don't get to be one of the most powerful religious figures in the world without making some concessions along the way."

Brandon slowly nodded. "I understand . . ."

She continued to work, now in silence. Brandon said nothing more. Sarah wasn't sure what all had transpired, but he had found something. Something that had left Cassandra just a little hurt and angry. And something that had left Brandon just a little bit sad.

The silence was interrupted when the door behind them flew open. There, standing in the doorway, was a cameraman with a camera and Tanya Chase with a microphone.

"Hi, guys," she said cheerily. "Glad you could make it."

"Hi," Brandon answered.

"Good to see you," Sarah added.

But Tanya barely heard as she quickly moved into position and motioned for the cameraman to do the same. "We're taping some bumpers to drop in as we go to and from commercial. Little sound bites from our guests explaining why they're so excited to be here. Think you can do that for us, Brandon?"

"Uh . . ." He glanced at Sarah. She knew her husband hated speaking in front of any group, let alone a TV audience, but she gave him an encouraging nod, hoping he'd give it a try. After a moment of reluctance, he agreed.

"Yeah, uh, sure."

"Great. Here we go then."

Cassandra was already removing the plastic sheet from him and turning his chair to face the camera. A bright light glared on above the lens as Tanya shoved the microphone into his face.

"So tell us, Brandon Martus, why are you excited to be here tonight?"

Brandon hesitated, gathering his thoughts.

"Whenever you're ready, Brandon."

He nodded, then finally looked at the camera, wincing slightly at the light. "I . . ." He cleared his throat and started again. "I am grateful to be here so that I can be a part of what Jesus Christ is doing through, uh, *with* Reverend Tyler during—"

"Whoa, hold the phone, tiger." Tanya pulled back the mike and took a step closer. "Can't use the 'J' word on this one."

"I'm sorry?"

"The 'J' word. You know, 'Jesus.' Keep that for the folks back home."

Brandon frowned, not understanding.

Tanya explained. "Lots of secular stations are picking us up. Don't want to antagonize them needlessly. So let's just keep it nice and generic."

"But . . ."

"Just say what you said but don't use the name *Jesus*. Say *God* or *Lord* or something like that instead. That way nobody gets offended."

"Uh . . ." He threw a look at Sarah, who shrugged. It seemed to make sense.

"Just say God instead of Jesus, okay."

"All right . . ."

"Great. Here we go again." She pointed the microphone back at him. "Whenever you're ready."

Again Brandon squinted toward the camera. "I am grateful to be here and to be a part of what God is doing through Reverend Tyler. I think—"

"That's great, Brandon." Tanya gave a thumbs-up. "Just great." She pulled back the mike as the cameraman snapped off the light. "We'll be rolling in about twenty minutes. They'll want you onstage pretty soon. How we doing, Cassandra?"

"Just about there."

"Beautiful. Well, good luck, Brandon." She turned, then suddenly remembered something. "Oh, hang on." She reached into her shoulder bag and pulled out a Bible. "Jimmy wanted all of his guests to have one of these."

"Oh, thanks," Brandon said, "but we've got plenty of Bibles."

"I'm sure you do. But one can never have too many Bibles, can they?" She shoved it into his hands. "Besides, this is the Jimmy Tyler Study Bible." She turned toward the door. "Good seeing you two again and have a great show." Suddenly, she was gone. As quickly as the blonde whirlwind had entered, she had left.

Sarah watched as the door shut. She turned to Brandon with a quizzical look of amusement. But he had already opened the Bible and was scowling down at the title page.

"What's wrong?" she asked.

He didn't hear.

"Bran . . . what's up?"

He glanced at her, then turned the Bible around so she could see the page. "Right here, on the front."

"Yeah."

"It's got Jimmy Tyler's signature."

She still didn't understand. "Meaning . . ."

Brandon's frown deepened as he tried to explain. "Doesn't it seem weird? I mean, the man is autographing God's Holy Word?"

"Aamaa!" The cry was from a young woman, maybe a girl. *"Aamaa!"* With her approaching voice came the slapping of sandals against bare feet and the scraping of stone. Katherine, who was holding a crusted teakettle at the hearth, turned just in time to see a child of twelve barge in. The red dye where she parted her hair signified she was already married. Although this was frowned upon by the government, child brides were still common in Nepal.

"Aamaa!" she cried breathlessly. It was a term of endearment meaning "mother." Since Eric was a god and since Katherine was Eric's mother, she had become "mother to all"—not exactly a term she relished.

"Ke?" Katherine asked.

"The master . . ." The girl tried to speak English but it wouldn't come. It didn't have to.

"Eric?" Katherine demanded. "Something happened to Eric?"

The girl nodded, motioning frantically. *"Chhito!"*

Katherine dropped the kettle on the hearth, tossed aside the rag that served as a pot holder, and raced for the door.

"Chhito!" the girl cried. *"Chhito!"*

Katherine had barely stepped onto the balcony overlooking the courtyard when she saw them—a half-dozen women just outside the gate. She headed for the stairs, flew down them to the courtyard, then dashed across the cobblestones, past the fountain, and through the arched opening.

Outside, on the dirt road, a large pile of grain glowed from the late afternoon sun. But the women, some still holding their winnowing rakes, were no longer working. They had gathered around a body lying on the ground.

Katherine sucked in her breath, fearing the worst—until she saw it was not her son. It was Deepak, his bodyguard. She started toward him, then spotted Eric off to the side. He looked scared and shaken. "Eric?" His face was wet with tears. She headed toward him. "Eric, what happened?"

"I didn't mean to, honest. I didn't—" He ran the few remaining steps to her. She caught him and he buried his face into her arms, beginning to sob. "It was an accident, I didn't mean to . . ."

"Shh, it's okay. What happened?" She threw a look over her shoulder. The body was not moving.

"We were playing . . . just playing. And Deepak . . ." He was unable to continue.

"And what?" Katherine asked. "What happened to Deepak?"

"He made me really, really mad, and . . ." He gulped in a breath of air and continued. "I tried not to be. Honest. I tried really hard to control it this time, but—"

Katherine felt a chill seize her body. "But what? Eric, what happened to Deepak?"

There was another outburst of tears. She continued, more firmly. "What did you do to Deepak? Eric?"

He looked up at her, eyes red and swollen. "I made his heart stop!"

Katherine could only stare.

"I'm sorry." He buried his face into her shoulder. "I'm so sorry."

Instinctively, she patted his back, "Shh, it's okay . . ." Her head was growing so light that as he pushed against her she nearly lost her balance. But she dug in and held on. For both of them she held on.

"God is love. How many times do we have to hear that before we finally get it through these mule-thick skulls of ours? God is love, God is love, God is love. And anyone who doesn't love, is not of God. It don't get any simpler than that, folks!"

Brandon sat watching as Reverend Jimmy Tyler played the crowd, strutting back and forth across the sixty-foot stage. Late fifties, three-piece suit, flashing silver hair—the man literally looked like a Hollywood actor. In many ways he was. He even used the streams of sweat trickling down his face to their fullest advantage—constantly dabbing at them with his handkerchief. And then there were his dramatic pauses, when he poured water from a nearby pitcher and took gulps from a glass. The man was a pro in every sense of the word.

Brandon turned back to the audience, straining to see past the glare of lights. The L.A. Forum held 18,500 people, and by the looks of things, the place was packed out. Packed out and worked up. Between the forty-piece orchestra, the international choir, and Jimmy Tyler's electrifying delivery, they had no choice but to be. There wasn't an indifferent soul in the house.

"I don't care whether you call him God or Allah or Krishna or Buddha, or some Cosmic Force. The point is, God is love. Everybody say that . . ."

The audience joined him: *"God is love."*

Brandon sat in the third tier of seats on the left of the stage. There were about thirty guests on this side. And thirty more on the other. That made sixty guests representing various races, religions, and creeds. Sixty guests whose presence proved their solidarity behind Jimmy Tyler.

"Now, I don't know 'bout you, but I'm sick and tired, I mean I'm fed up to here, 'bout everybody with their own special brand of religion, their own private interpretation of God." He raised his voice into a pinched, mocking tone. "'Well, Reverend, God never does it their way, He only does it my way. Well, Reverend, God doesn't speak through their holy book, He only speaks through mine. Well, Reverend, God only visits my church or my synagogue or my mosque or my temple.' Well, I got news for you, folks, God can go wherever He wants. He can come in any form He wants to touch and heal and bless whoever He wants. And you want to know why? I'll tell you why. God is . . ."

He stuck the microphone out toward the audience. A portion called back, *"Love."*

"Hey." He tapped the mike. "You folks awake out there? I said, God is . . ."

Again they repeated, only this time louder. *"Love!"*

"I can't hear you. God is . . ."

"LOVE!"

"You think we can remember it these next few minutes?" The audience responded positively, but he shook his head, chuckling. "I have my doubts."

The crowd ate it up. So did Brandon's peers sitting on the stage. But not Brandon. Instead, he felt a growing knot of emotion . . . part embarrassment, part confusion, part frustration.

"This is not a time to dwell upon petty doctrinal differences. I don't care what cemetery, er, I mean, *seminary* you folks are from."

The audience chuckled.

"If you ask me, most of them folks are educated way beyond their intelligence, anyways."

More laughter.

"No, this isn't a time to dwell on our differences, this is a time to dwell upon God's love. Because if there's one thing God is, it's . . ."

Everyone shouted, *"LOVE!"*

Brandon continued to watch. It was the mixture of truth and error that he found so confusing. Yes, God was love and yes, He hated religious pride and spiritual elitism. But wasn't it Jesus himself who said the road to heaven was narrow, that He alone was the door, that He was the *only* way to the Father?

Tyler continued. "So what about all of these plagues, this famine, these financial hard times sweeping the globe? What about all these holier-than-thou, self-righteous Bible thumpers who are jumping up and down screaming, 'It's the judgment of God, it's the judgment of God!' Well, I got news for you, folks. That God sure as . . . heaven . . . ain't my God!"

There was a smattering of applause.

"You've all seen the news. Right now eight people in the world are starving to death every second. Eight people! And most of them are innocent babies and children who can't fend for themselves. Innocent babies and children starving to death? Because of God? No, friends, I don't think so. That may be somebody's God, but it sure ain't mine."

The applause increased.

"'I've come that ye might have life and have it abundantly.' That's what my God says."

More applause.

"And what about this Scorpion virus? In seven months they're claiming that if there's no cure, over half of the Jewish and Arab population will be wiped out. Over half! That's genocide, folks, plain and simple. I don't know about you, but that's not my God. It may be somebody's God . . . but He's sure not mine!"

More applause, louder.

"And these wars? Any minute some third power wannabe is going to nuke his neighbor, contaminating the rest of the world until we're all giving birth to three-headed babies. I don't know. That may be somebody's God . . . but He's sure not mine!"

Brandon continued to marvel, amazed at how the man could use truth to preach error. How he could quote Scripture to speak falsehood. Yes, God was a God of love, but he'd read in the Bible again and again that God also used suffering to correct and judge. And it clearly taught that that's what would happen in the end times. So how could Tyler preach that these calamities were just an accident? How was it possible for him to use the Bible to disprove the Bible? Then again, wasn't that exactly what Satan had done with Jesus when he tempted Him in the wilderness? Used God's truth to tell a lie?

But was Tyler even aware he was doing this? Here was a man who had given his entire life to the gospel, just as Brandon and Sarah had. And what of the hundreds of thousands of lives he'd touched? If the two of them could reach only a fraction of those Tyler had reached, their ministry would be more than a success. And it wasn't just the numbers. According to Cassandra, he'd once spent time doing those invisible acts of love, those self-sacrificing acts that others never even knew about. This had been a man who had loved God and had given everything he had to serve Him.

But now . . .

"And what about these out-of-control terrorists with their biological weapons that could wipe out an entire city in seventy-two hours? That may be somebody's God . . ."

By now the audience had picked up his cadence, finishing the line with him. ". . .*but He's sure not mine!*"

It was then Brandon felt something stirring and emerging through all the other emotions. He'd felt it once before, when his father's church was under attack. It was welling up inside of him again. Deep, powerful, unwavering. Anger, but not anger. Something stronger.

"And people today, they're so terrified of these financial crashes that their hearts are literally failing from fear. Did you know that right now the suicide rate in every country is higher than it's ever been in the history of the world? I don't know. That may be somebody's God . . ."

"*. . . but He's sure not mine!*"

Part of the stirring Brandon felt came from the lies, but there was more.

"My God of love promised us peace! Peace among men, peace of mind, peace of the pocketbook! That's what my God of love is about. And God is love, God is love, God is . . ." He held out the microphone.

"*LOVE!*"

"You want a vengeful God? Fine. That may be somebody's God . . ."

"*. . . but He's sure not mine.*"

The sensation raced through Brandon's body like fire until it began to condense somewhere in the center of his chest. So powerful that it surprised, even scared him. Of course God was love, but it was a deeper love, one that involved holiness. If he'd learned anything from his brief encounter at the hospital it was that God's love is not a love giving us whatever we want, whenever we want it ... His is a love that withholds and even disciplines ... a love that doesn't desire to *give* us the best, but that desires to *make* us the best.

Suddenly Brandon understood the sensation consuming him. This anger taking over his heart and mind was not because of the lies. Misrepresentation didn't threaten God. It was because of what the lies were doing to His people. How they were being ripped off and sold a cheapened bill of goods. How they were being duped into believing in a superficial God of superficial love who had no interest in making them whole.

And the more Tyler preached, the stronger Brandon's rage grew until he could barely stand it. His breathing increased. His heart pounded in his ears.

"Dear God," he whispered. "What's happening to me?"

There was no answer. Only the memory of the promise he'd been given in the hospital. *"My words will become a fire in your mouth that you cannot contain."*

And still Jimmy Tyler continued to preach ... and still the fire burned and grew and raged.

CHAPTER 7

$\int$ arah sat at the front of the arena in the roped-off section for VIPs and their families. So far she had to admit that it had been quite a show. The orchestra, the choir, and the soloists had all worked hard to bring the audience into a spirit of love and unity. And they had succeeded. Wonderfully. In fact, Sarah couldn't remember a time she'd felt more inspired to reach out and love her fellow human being.

The pretaped endorsements by top world dignitaries had also helped. Respected men and women, both religious and political, everybody from the Dalai Lama to an emissary from the pope, to the UN secretary general, to the vice president. Tyler's folks didn't miss a beat. They even ended the segment with a prerecorded statement by Lucas Ponte—although Sarah had to admit that she really hadn't paid that much attention to what he'd said. She was too busy reflecting on how this was the same man who'd personally phoned her, and musing upon how his looks held up even when projected upon a forty-foot screen. Then, of course, there was the other matter, the one of his invitation for her to come to Nepal. She had discussed it several times with Brandon, and though he seemed strangely uneasy about their being separated, he wasn't entirely closed to the idea.

Finally Jimmy Tyler himself had taken the stage. Everyone was so primed and ready that the man could have hiccuped and gotten a standing ovation. But he did more than that. A lot more. Even though Sarah didn't appreciate his flashy showmanship, she had to admit it was impossible not to get caught up in his message . . . and in the enthusiasm of those surrounding her.

Still, something wasn't right. She couldn't put her finger on it, but there was something. Maybe it was the way he threw Christianity in with all of the other religions, insisting that it was just one of many roads to spirituality. But there was something else. She knew Brandon hated being in front of people—the poor guy's knees nearly buckled when he tried to make a speech at their wedding reception. She also knew he wasn't crazy about appearing to endorse Jimmy Tyler. Still, there he was, doing both, and for that her respect for him only increased. But, as Tyler spoke, she noticed Brandon's growing restlessness. Since she was in the audience sitting low and close to the front of the stage, and since he sat on the third riser behind two rows of guests, it wasn't always possible to see him. But from the glimpses she caught, she could tell he was definitely uncomfortable. A fidget here, a shift of his weight there. Maybe she was just being overly sensitive. Maybe no one else noticed. But the more his anxiety increased, the more her uneasiness rose. She forced herself to look back at the preacher. He'd opened his Bible and was starting to read.

"For I know the thoughts that I think toward you, saith the Lord, thoughts of peace, and not of evil." He looked up. "Do you folks hear that? God wants us to have peace, not evil. And it's not just in this book. I know you'll find the same thing in the Koran, the Bhagavad Gita, any of them other holy books." He turned to the group of guests on either side. "Am I right, folks?"

Several nodded and agreed.

"You bet I'm right. And you want to know why? Because our God is the *same* God."

Once again Sarah caught a glimpse of Brandon. Now she noticed his face. Was it the lights, or was he getting redder? Even under the makeup he almost seemed to glow . . . and then there was the sweat. His entire forehead was covered in beads of perspiration. *Dear Lord*, she prayed, *help him relax*.

Tyler was back in his Bible. "Then shall ye call upon Me, and ye shall go and pray unto Me, and I will hearken unto you." He looked out to the audience. "You got that people? It's right here in the book of Jeremiah, plain as the nose on your face. If we pray, God has to harken unto us, He *has* to listen. He has no choice in the matter, it's in the contract. He's legally obligated. And you know why? Because He says so! It's right here." He gave the book a rap. "It was true 2500 years ago when he wrote the book of Jeremiah, and it's true today. The Word of God does not change, folks. The grass withereth, the flower fadeth: but the word of our God shall stand forever! Forever! How long will it stand?" He held out the mike.

"Forever!" the audience shouted back.

"Now you're catchin' on." The audience clapped as Tyler wiped down his face and poured another glass of water.

Sarah mechanically joined in the applause as she tried to catch another glimpse of Brandon. A loud *plop* suddenly drew her attention back to Tyler. The man had thrown his Bible down on the stage.

"Ask me what I'm doing." He grinned. "Go ahead, ask me what I'm doing?"

Some of the crowd shouted, *"What are you doing?"*

"What's that?"

More responded. *"What are you doing?"*

He hopped up on the Bible with one foot and grinned. "I'm standing on the Word of God."

The audience laughed.

"Now you little old ladies, don't get your undies in a bunch. I'm trying to make a point here. This holy book is a foundation stone for our society. Fact, some would say for the whole world, am I right?"

More agreement and applause.

"But I've got more than one foot, don't I? Well, don't I?"

The audience shouted back the affirmative.

Continuing to balance, Tyler looked offstage into the wings and shouted, "Boys, can you give me a hand here?" Immediately a half-dozen men ran out onto the stage, each holding a book. "Who's got the Torah?" Tyler asked. A man held out the book. Tyler nodded, "Just set it down there." The man set the book down on the stage near Tyler then stepped back and turned to exit. "What about the Koran?" Tyler asked. Another man raised his book. Tyler nodded, and the man set his book on the other side and exited. "The Bhagavad Gita?" Another man stepped forward and put down his book.

Still on one foot and struggling to keep his balance, Tyler sped up the process. "Go ahead, set them others down, boys— anywhere will do." They obeyed, setting their books on the stage around him, and then turned to leave.

Tyler's balance grew shakier. "We've got more than one foot, so don't we need more than one stone? Isn't that how we stop from falling over?" He grew even more unsteady. "Isn't it?"

Several shouted back. *"Yes!"*

His wobbling grew worse. "Isn't it?"

More shouted, *"Yes!"*

He was beginning to sway, hopping up and down on the one foot. "Isn't it!"

The entire audience yelled, *"YES!"* just as Tyler fell forward, slapping his free foot down on one of the other books. He stood a moment, completely stable, catching his breath. Finally he looked up, grinning. "And that, folks, is called *balance*."

The crowd broke into applause and cheers.

Jimmy laughed, enjoying it as much as the audience. "Do you understand what I'm sayin'?" He began walking on the other books. "We need these other stones, we need these other beliefs. Otherwise we'd topple over, we'd fall flat on our arrogant, spiritually proud faces. Do you hear me? Differences are good! It's the only way to keep our balance."

The crowd clapped in agreement.

As Tyler continued to walk from book to book, something to his left briefly caught his attention. He ignored it and turned back to the audience. "These are our foundation stones, folks. Not just one rock, not just one belief, but several. They all work together in unison to hold up our society, to give us a better stance and help us keep our balance. And that's why we're here tonight, folks. We're coming together as one balanced people!"

Again, something caught his attention, this time a little longer. And, again, he continued. "We're coming together in unity, putting aside our petty religious differences—" Again, he was distracted. There was a commotion up on one of the risers. Sarah craned her neck and to her surprise saw it was Brandon. He had risen to his feet. Others surrounding him were tugging on his sleeve, urging him to sit back down. But he paid little attention. His face was red and he was trembling.

"Reverend Tyler . . ."

At first Tyler tried to ignore him and continue. "Admitting that on our own none of us has all the answers, but when we're united—"

"Reverend Tyler!"

Soon everyone onstage and in the audience was staring at him. Tyler could no longer ignore him. He looked over and grinned. "What's a matter, son?"

Brandon took a step down from his row toward the stage. His voice was thin and shaky. "Reverend Tyler?"

Tyler continued smiling. "Time for a potty break?"

The audience chuckled. Sarah stiffened as Brandon continued down the steps to the stage.

Tyler gave a nearly imperceptible glance to the security guards who stood down in front of the stage near Sarah. They moved in preparation, but Tyler shook his head, indicating that for now he had it under control. They nodded and he turned back to Brandon. "We'll be over in just a few minutes, son, if you think you can hold it."

More chuckles, but the audience's curiosity was definitely growing.

Gripping the arms of her chair, Sarah noticed how wet her palms had become. *What is he doing? What is he doing!*

"You speak from the Bible . . ." Because Brandon had no microphone, his voice sounded hollow as the other mikes onstage picked him up. "You speak from the prophet Jeremiah. But he has other words as well. Other words for you."

"Well, folks"—Tyler threw a smile to the audience— "looks like I'm in for a little Bible study."

More nervous laughter.

Brandon was nearly center stage now, twenty feet from Tyler.

"What's your name, son?"

"My name is not important. It's what the Lord would say to you that matters."

"I see." He gave a wink to the audience. "And what exactly is that?"

Sarah's hand rose to the scar on her face as she watched Brandon take a deep breath. *Dear God,* she prayed, *what is he doing?*

And then he began: "Woe to the shepherds who are destroying and scattering the sheep of my pasture! declares the Lord. Because you have scattered my flock and driven them away and have not bestowed care on them, I will bestow punishment on you for the evil you have done, declares the Lord."

Tyler was unfazed, remaining cool and calm. "Yes, Jeremiah 23, I believe that is." Then turning back to the audience he quipped. "Looks like the boy's been doing his memory verses."

More chuckles.

But Sarah, whose heart was pounding, knew he was wrong. For the past year the two of them had been poring over Scripture, that was true. But they'd barely cracked Jeremiah, let alone put anything to memory. No, this was something else. Something much different.

Brandon continued, his voice still quivering, but growing stronger. "Do not listen to what the prophets are prophesying to you; they fill you with false hopes. They speak visions from their own minds, not from the mouth of the Lord. They keep saying to those who despise me, The Lord says: You will have peace. And to all who follow the stubbornness of their hearts they say, No harm will come to you."

"Well, thank you for sharing, brother." It was obvious the novelty had worn off, and Tyler had had enough. "Now if you wouldn't mind taking your seat, I'll finish making my point, if I can remember it."

But Brandon was far from through. He turned directly to the audience, trying to see through the glare of the lights. "They dress the wound of My people as though it were not serious. Peace, peace, they say, when there is no peace."

Sarah spotted Tyler signaling the security guards to take over. They moved to action. But seeing them, Brandon held out his hand, motioning for them to stop. And, to Sarah's surprise, they did. They continued to stand and they continued to listen, but for some unknown reason, they did not move toward him.

"Therefore this is what the Lord says about the prophets who are prophesying in My name: I did not send them, yet they are saying, No sword or famine will touch this land."

"Guys." Tyler motioned to the security guards. "Can you help our friend find his seat?"

The guards nodded, but did not move.

"Guys!"

Brandon turned from the audience and back to Tyler, his voice more powerful, almost booming. For an amazing moment Sarah thought she saw a flicker coming from his mouth, almost like a flame. Of course it was an illusion from all the bright lights, and it disappeared as quickly as it had appeared. But the rest was no illusion.

Brandon pointed his finger at Tyler and shouted, "Those same prophets will perish by sword and famine!"

The final phrase echoed through the arena until there was only silence.

Sarah's heart thundered in her ears. *Dear God, let it be over. Please, make it be over!*

In the silence, Tyler calmly reached for his glass of water, trying just a little too hard to appear nonchalant. He obviously didn't understand why the security guards were hesitating, but it was important he appear to be in control. "So tell me, uh, I still didn't catch the name." He waited, but Brandon didn't answer. He reached for the pitcher. "Don't you find that all of this shouting and preaching, ever notice how thirsty it makes a fellow? It sure does me. Not that I've had much opportunity these last few minutes."

The audience chuckled as he poured the water.

Brandon approached, keeping his eyes riveted on Tyler, who tried his best to appear amused. They were ten feet apart when Brandon raised his hand and pointed. "The blood of the sheep will be upon the head of the shepherd."

"I see," Tyler said, raising the glass to his lips and starting to drink. But he barely managed to swallow before he gagged, then leaned over to spit it out. He looked down at the glass in stunned surprise. And for good reason. The water inside had become blood red. His eyes widened. He turned to the pitcher. Its contents had also turned to blood. Astonished, Tyler let the glass slip from his hand. It hit the stage with such a crash that he jumped, causing the pitcher to drop from his other hand. It also shattered onto the stage, sending broken shards and splattered blood in all directions.

The audience gasped and began to murmur. Many rose to their feet. The guests on either side of the stage did the same.

Brandon continued his approach.

Looking up from the blood, Tyler took a half step back. Brandon spoke again, "You have lived as a prostitute with many lovers—would you now return to Me? declares the Lord."

That was all the time Tyler needed to recover. Fighting for control, he shot back, "Listen, kid . . . I don't know who you think you are or how you believe these little parlor tricks are going to accomplish anything. But—"

"Repent and return to the Lord!"

Tyler swallowed. "But we've got a lot more important things to cover than to listen to some—"

"Be still!" Again Sarah thought she saw a flicker of flame.

Suddenly, Tyler began coughing, unable to finish his sentence.

And still Brandon continued, breathing hard and speaking intensely. "You son of the devil, you enemy of all righteousness, will you not cease perverting the straight ways of the Lord?"

Tyler tried to respond, but his coughing grew worse.

"The hand of the Lord is upon you, and you shall no longer be able to speak or spread your deceit in My name."

Tyler tried to argue, but the words came out only as coughs and gags.

By now all of the audience had risen to their feet. Some in astonishment, others in anger. Sarah looked around helplessly as they began to shout. "Get him out of here! Get him off the stage!" Others began stomping their feet or booing.

Hearing them for the first time, Brandon turned from Tyler and came down toward the front of the stage to address them. The yelling and catcalls increased. He took a moment and scanned the crowd before breathing deeply and shouting, "Has a nation ever changed its gods? (Yet they are not gods at all.) But My people have changed their Glory for worthless idols. Be appalled at this, O heavens, and shudder with great horror, declares the Lord. My people have committed two sins: They have forsaken Me, the spring of living water, and have dug their own cisterns, broken cisterns that cannot hold water."

Booing filled the auditorium.

Brandon continued looking out at them, his face filling with compassion. Sarah could see the moisture in his eyes.

"Stand at the crossroads and look; ask for the ancient paths, ask where the good way is, and walk in it, and you will find rest for your souls."

The audience was shouting so loudly Sarah could barely hear.

"Like a woman unfaithful to her husband, so you have been unfaithful to Me, declares the Lord."

Items began flying onto the stage. Wadded-up programs, loose change, pencils and pens, anything the audience could find to throw. Some hit their mark, forcing Brandon to wince. But he continued quoting. "Therefore this is what the Sovereign Lord says: My anger and My wrath will be poured out on this place, on man and beast, on the trees of the field and on the fruit of the ground, and it will burn and not be quenched."

Tyler remained bent over and coughing. By now some of the more courageous guests on the stage had started to approach Brandon.

"Return, declares the Lord, and I will frown on you no longer, for I am merciful. I will not be angry forever. Only acknowledge your guilt . . ."

The group onstage continued to close in.

Sarah started to wave, shouting to get his attention, "Brandon, Brandon, look out!" But he didn't hear.

"You have rebelled against the Lord your God, you have scattered your favors to—"

A young man from the right was the first to charge. He hit Brandon from behind and tackled him hard to the ground. As they hit the stage Sarah screamed. She started pushing her way toward them, but the area in front of the stage was already filled with shouting people. She looked back up to the stage. Other guests had arrived and also began struggling with Brandon, trying to subdue him.

"Brandon . . ."

The audience was in a frenzy—shouting, jeering, many applauding his capture.

The group onstage pulled Brandon to his feet. They began to drag him across the stage, toward the wings. He did not go willingly, twisting and squirming, but there were far too many of them.

Sarah was still trying to push her way through the crowd toward the stage. "Excuse me! Please . . . Excuse me!" But it was jammed, choked with shouting, taunting people. She pushed harder. "Excuse me, please—" until an older teen violently shoved her back, shouting an oath. Sarah blinked and stared. She turned, looking around her, not believing her eyes or her ears. How had it happened? How, in just a matter of minutes, had a loving and caring crowd been turned into a shouting mob? The transformation had been so fast, almost supernatural. Such hatred, such fury. And all directed at one person . . .

Katherine glanced up from filling her second suitcase when Lucas entered the room. There was no one else with him. Not his secretary, none of the peripheral folks that usually surrounded him. Not that it mattered. There could have been a hundred, and she'd still have taken him on.

"I don't want to hear it," she snapped. "Nothing you say will change my mind."

He didn't have to speak. His presence in the doorway spoke volumes.

Katherine crossed to the cedar wardrobe, threw open its doors, and gathered a handful of clothes still on their hangers. "You said you could help. You said you could find a cure. Well, you haven't." She headed back to the bed and dumped the clothes into the suitcase.

He remained silent.

She headed back to the wardrobe for another load. "It's not working, Lucas. He's not getting any better. And Heylel's little visits are only making things worse."

At last he spoke—softly, with understanding. "So where are you going?"

"I don't know. Katmandu, for a while. Till we get enough saved to catch a flight home. Anywhere, just as long as it's not here." The last phrase was a little harsh and she knew it. "I know you've tried. You, the Cartel, you've done all you can. But this place, it's nowhere for a kid to grow up. People treating him like a god, you folks hanging onto his every word, acting like he's some cosmic guru. It's not healthy. You can't blame me for wanting my kid to have some semblance of an ordinary life."

"Eric is no ordinary kid."

She threw him a look as she headed for the dresser. It was then she noticed the envelope he was tapping in his hands.

"What's that?"

He glanced down. "Oh, this. It is two one-way tickets to Seattle along with $5,000 cash to help you get started."

Katherine came to a stop. It took a moment to digest the statement. "Why?"

"Pardon me?"

"Why would you do that?"

"Because you are right, this is no place for a child. Or his mother. Especially ones I have grown so fond of."

Katherine eyed him carefully. She'd seen this maneuver before. Sincere concern, mixed with flattery. It was all part of the Ponte charm. She watched as he quietly set the envelope down on the table. Once again she asked, "Why are you doing this?"

"It is the least we can do, considering all we have put you through." He took a deep breath. "And . . ." He seemed to hesitate, unsure whether he should continue.

Katherine knew it was a ploy, but she took the bait anyway. "And?"

"And, given the fact that from the moment Eric leaves these grounds we will be unable to offer him any type of diplomatic immunity."

"What does that mean?"

"The local officials have called twice and have already paid us one visit. They're charging your son with murder."

Katherine's jaw went slack. "That's . . . absurd. Deepak had a heart attack. Eric didn't even touch him. You can't call that murder."

"In the West, you are correct. But I'm afraid these people here are of a much more superstitious nature."

"They're going to arrest him?"

Lucas shook his head. "If Eric stays on the grounds they will not touch him. The government of Nepal would not risk confrontation with the Cartel."

Katherine's mind raced. "But if he leaves the grounds?"

"If he leaves the grounds . . ." Lucas sighed heavily. "Well, as I have said, it is doubtful they will respect our request for diplomatic immunity."

Once again Katherine felt the noose tightening. As it did, her anger grew. "So that ticket, that money is completely useless."

"Not necessarily. A few of the local officials have been known to look the other way . . . when the right money crosses the right hands."

"A bribe?"

He shrugged. "Call it what you will. The problem, of course, lies in knowing which individuals will accept it."

Katherine stared at the envelope. She was being played in perfect Ponte style. "And you just happen to know who those individuals are, don't you?"

He shook his head. "No, of course not. But in time I am sure we could find out."

"How much . . . time?"

"The neurobiologist from the States will be planning to pay us a visit and to run some tests."

"Dr. Martus? When?"

"Shortly, very shortly."

"And . . ."

"By the time she is finished with her evaluation and recommendation for treatment, I am sure we will have found the proper officials."

Katherine could only stare. The trap had been woven so flawlessly that, even now as she stared at him, hating him, Lucas appeared to have nothing but deepest compassion and consideration. The man was a genius.

"But, of course, it is your decision, Katherine. And whatever you decide, we will do our best to be of assistance. We owe a great deal to the two of you. And, as we have proven, the Cartel does not forget its friends." He gave her a brief smile, then glanced at his watch. "Well, if you will excuse me." He turned and headed for the door. But before exiting he turned back for one final comment. "I know you will make the right decision, Katherine. You always have. That is one of your attributes. One of your many attributes." With that he disappeared out the door.

"It was incredible! It was like this fire burning inside of me, and it kept building and building until I thought I was going to explode."

Sarah and Tanya Chase walked on either side of Brandon as they headed down the hallway of the Hawthorne Police

Station. A couple fluorescent tubes overhead were nearly burned out, and they gave the place an eerie blue-green flicker. But Brandon barely noticed. It had been three hours since the event at the Forum, and his adrenaline was still pumping.

"And I knew the words." He turned to Sarah. "It wasn't like the demoniacs we've worked with, where they don't have control of their bodies. I had total control. The words were in my mind before I spoke them. It was just up to me whether I wanted to obey and say them."

"And of course you did." Sarah's voice was flat and noncommittal.

"Well, yes, wouldn't you?"

She gave no answer as they continued down the hall. It was two in the morning and other than a handful of officers, a strung out gang member, and a couple hookers, the hallway was relatively quiet.

Tanya spoke up. "Seems I remember reading something in the Bible about doing things 'decently and in order.'"

Brandon nodded and looked down at the worn yellowed tile passing under his feet. He knew she was right and the thought had crossed his mind more than once. But still . . .

"The only reason Jimmy's not pressing charges is because of how it will look."

Sarah turned to her. "Is that why he's posting bail?"

"Of course. It's the only way he can put a positive spin on any of this."

Sarah quoted the imaginary headline: "Merciful Preacher Forgives Nutcase."

Tanya threw her a look. "Ever consider journalism?"

Sarah gave no answer as they continued walking.

Brandon glanced over at her with his good eye. The other was swollen by a misdirected elbow . . . or fist. Minutes earlier, when he had first been released from the holding cell, Sarah had greeted him with an embrace and tears of concern. But now, as they headed down the hall toward the front desk, he saw only exhaustion and weariness. The evening had been as rough on her as it had been on him. Maybe worse. He reached out, starting to put his arm around her, but she seemed to anticipate the move and shied away.

The action surprised him, and he looked back at her. She gave no response and continued walking, looking straight ahead. He didn't press the issue, but there was no missing the heavy realization as it settled over him. It was true; it had been harder on her, a lot harder.

Once again Tanya broke the silence. "Any idea when Jimmy's going to speak again?"

He turned to her and asked, "He still can't talk?"

"The doctor says it's psychosomatic ... something about having a multimillion-dollar TV broadcast destroyed, not to mention an entire ministry. Earliest estimates say we had an audience share of fifty-nine. That's 133.4 million people, more than watched last year's Superbowl."

Brandon said nothing. His sadness grew heavier.

She continued. "I still don't understand that water to blood thing—how you pulled that off."

Brandon shook his head, as baffled as she was. "Me neither. But in Revelation 11 it says that—"

"Brandon ..." Sarah interrupted.

He looked at her.

"I think we've had enough Bible quoting for one night." At last she turned to him. "Don't you?"

The fatigue and pain he saw made him wince. She'd been through even more than he had originally thought. But there was something else in her. A hurt. A betrayal.

He desperately wanted to comfort her, to somehow take away the pain, but—

"Oh, great," Tanya sighed.

He turned to her. "What?"

She motioned to the double glass doors just outside the lobby. "It's the press."

Brandon turned to see the sizable crowd that had gathered. "What are they here for?"

She gave him a look. "You've got to be kidding."

"What do we do?" Sarah asked in apprehension.

"There's nothing we can do," Tanya said. "The car and driver are parked in front. When we get out there, don't talk to anyone, don't acknowledge their questions, just head straight for the car's rear door. I'll take the lead and break them up, but you've got to stay right behind me. Just keep pushing and don't lose your momentum, or you'll never get through."

"There has to . . ." Sarah slowed to a stop. They were in the lobby now, near the first set of doors. "There has to be another way out of here."

Tanya shook her head. "Better get used to it, girl." She reached for the first door and called over her shoulder. "This won't be the last."

They stepped through the first set of doors and crossed the five feet of space toward the outer ones. That's when the crowd spotted them and came to life. "They're here!" Lights blazed on as cameramen and reporters jockeyed for position. Tanya reached for the outer door and hesitated. Brandon kept Sarah between them, hoping somehow to protect her. After turning and giving them a nod, Tanya pushed open the door, and the assault began.

"Brandon, is it true that—"

"Do you really think you're some sort of—"

"How long has this rivalry between you and Tyler been—"

Everywhere Brandon looked lights glared, cameras jostled, and eager faces and microphones pressed in.

"Come on, guys!" Tanya was shouting. "Let us through! Come on! Come on, now!"

"How soon before you believe the world will come to an—"

"Is it true that you can call down God's judgment any time you—"

"Do you really believe God hates all—"

As they started down the steps Brandon caught a glimpse of the car below.

"Sarah, how long has he had these powers?"

"Is it true, you've only been married—"

And then he felt it, a shattering egg. It caught his left shoulder and splattered onto his face. He looked up. It came from across the street where at least a dozen other people had gathered. But not reporters. These were hecklers. Some hurled insults, others made obscene gestures. Then, of course, there were the eggs. Another one splattered, this time across Sarah's arm. She gave a startled cry as reporters ducked for cover. Others took advantage and pushed in harder. At last Tanya had the back door to the car open.

"Tell us about the next judgment!"

"Sarah, about that scar? Was that something Brandon did? Another one of God's—"

Sarah ducked in, scooting across the seat. Brandon followed.

Tanya slammed their door and opened the front. Reporters swarmed on all sides, shouting, lights blazing. There were more thumps as eggs hit the windows and roof.

"Let's go!" Tanya shouted to the driver. "Let's go, let's go!"

The car lurched forward, fast enough to make it clear they meant business, slow enough not to run over anyone.

A moment later the chaos was behind them. Brandon looked back as a final egg caught the rear trunk and splattered up to the window.

"Well," Tanya called from the front seat, "that wasn't too bad. 'Course the hotel might be a little worse."

Sarah's eyes shot to her. "Hotel?"

"Oh, yeah. Then of course there's the airport."

Brandon looked at Tanya, dumbfounded. "Why?"

"It was the broadcast event of the year, kids. You claimed on national TV that God was judging the world. And your little special effects with Tyler's voice and that blood trick gave them proof of your credentials. Pretty slick move, buddy boy, pretty slick."

Brandon's head was reeling. "I don't . . . understand."

"In ten minutes you succeeded in achieving everything Jimmy Tyler had spent a lifetime trying to do."

"I'm sorry, I still don't—"

"In ten minutes you became the focal point, the representative of God for the entire nation. Not bad for a night's work."

Brandon frowned.

"Of course, He's not exactly the God most of us want to believe in. But when it comes to representing a judgmental tyrant, someone we can blame all of our troubles on, hey, you two win the prize, hands down."

The first-class flight was as luxurious coming home as it had been when they'd headed out. But Brandon barely noticed. All he heard was the dull roar of the 757 and the deafening silence of Sarah sitting beside him. In the last twenty-four hours neither of them had slept. They couldn't. Sarah was pretending to now, but Brandon knew better. It was simply another excuse not to talk.

His actions had erected an impenetrable wall between them. Something he'd have guessed would have been impossible two days earlier. But now . . . not only had he embarrassed and humiliated his wife, branding them both as lunatics, it was likely that he'd also managed to destroy any reputation the clinic had gained. Why had he been so impulsive? What had he hoped to accomplish? And most importantly, why hadn't he given more thought to what it would do to Sarah?

Pride. That's what it was. Plain and simple. Pride that he was somehow holier than Tyler. Pride that he was the only one with the answers. Pride that his interpretation of Scripture was the only one that counted.

But there was an even greater weight pressing down upon Brandon. The words he'd heard in the hospital. About Sarah. About her leaving. They'd never gone away, they'd always remained nagging in the back of his mind. He'd hoped he could stop them—by being the perfect husband, by doing whatever she wanted, by doing whatever God wanted. But nothing had worked. Everything had been in vain. Like riding a runaway train, there seemed nothing he could do to stop the inevitable.

He looked back over to her. Her eyes were open now as she leaned against the window, staring down at the passing farmland. How he wanted to ease the pain, but it was too late.

He looked down at her hand and saw the wedding band sparkle in the sun. He reached out and took her hand into his. She didn't resist. He raised her fingers to his lips, gave them a kiss, then leaned his cheek against them. She still did not respond. He set her hand down onto his own lap and held it. He saw her chest swell as she took a deep breath. And then, without looking at him, she spoke.

"I think, I think I should go." Her voice was dull and life-less as she stared out the window.

The back of Brandon's throat ached. "I understand."

"To Nepal, I mean."

"I know."

"It won't be forever. Just a few weeks." She paused a moment, then continued. "It will give me a chance to work with the Cartel. It will be good for the clinic. It will also help us sort things out."

By now the tightness in his throat was so unbearable he could only nod.

They said nothing more. Brandon closed his eyes. He sat for a long time, thinking his heart would burst. But there was still hope. It's not like she would be gone forever. They were still married, they were still a team. And then, remembering he still held her hand, he gave it two little squeezes . . . their private form of communication.

But instead of responding, Sarah shifted in her seat, gently slipped her hand from his, and continued staring out the window.

CHAPTER 8

Look, save me the brain chemistry lectures," Katherine said, "I've heard them all before. Low serotonin, high noradrenaline, whacked-out neurotransmitters. And the drugs they've pumped him full of ... Prozac, Clozapine, Amperozide, you name it, he's been shot up with it. We even had one quack who wanted to change his diet to chips, cookies, and candy."

Sarah nodded. "High carbohydrates have been known to increase serotonin levels which tends to induce passive behavior."

"And the sugar tends to drive kids through the roof."

Sarah smiled as she strolled with Katherine through the Cartel's long glass and mahogany hallway. To her left was a wall of rich wood with dozens of doors leading to plush offices. To her right was a glass wall and ceiling with the Himalayas looming high above them, their white peaks jutting into a sapphire sky. Below them she could see the ancient three-story compound of stone and stucco where she'd just spent her first night in Nepal.

They walked together in silence for several moments. Sarah liked Katherine and found her candid, no-nonsense approach refreshing, despite the hard shell of defense she'd built around herself and her son. She'd arrived in Katmandu late yesterday afternoon. By the time she'd finished the three-hour, bone-jarring ride up into the mountains, it was too dark to see anything. Thanks to jet lag and all of the excitement, she had not drifted off to sleep until it was nearly dawn. And now, two hours later, Katherine was giving her the grand tour of the Cartel's facility.

"And you believe that stuff?" Katherine asked, finally resuming the conversation. "That we're slaves to whatever chemical happens to be passing through our brains?"

Sarah chose her words carefully. "I believe we are a finely tuned instrument. If just one neurotransmitter alone is off by, say, five percent, it can wreak havoc on the entire nervous system."

"But we're more than just chemistry sets," Katherine argued. "I mean, when Michael Coleman, that fellow who was first infected with the DNA, when he had his problems, he was able to overcome them. It was hard, but he did it."

"How?"

Katherine ran her hand through her short-cropped hair. "You don't think I've asked myself that a million times?"

"And?"

"Michael Coleman was an incredible man."

"That was it?"

Katherine glanced to the floor, frowning.

Sarah knew there was more. "What?"

"Toward the end, when things really got tough, he claimed to have found some sort of faith."

"In?"

"He said it was Christianity. He said his faith in God gave him the power to overcome the evil inside him."

"But you don't buy it."

Katherine's eyes flashed to hers. "My father was a preacher, Dr. Martus. I've seen more than my share of wasted faith and unanswered prayers."

Sarah held her look and then slowly nodded—not because she agreed, but because she understood. It had been two weeks since the Jimmy Tyler broadcast, and things had gotten no better. Well, except for their notoriety. The mail was voluminous, most of it negative. So were the phone calls and visits by reporters. But none of these were as difficult as the attacks on the clinic. Nothing dangerous, just threats, occasional vandalism, and a handful of picketers. Still, that was their life's work, their very service to God. And by the looks of things, God wasn't too awfully interested in accepting that service.

The good-byes had been harder than she'd expected. It was the first time she and Brandon had been apart since they'd fallen in love. And, although he said he agreed that the brief separation would do them and the clinic some good, she knew he didn't believe it for a second.

Unfortunately, she did.

In the forty-eight hours since she'd left O'Hare International Airport she was already feeling a heaviness lifting. Granted, there was still more than enough guilt to go around, but that suffocating frustration, that confusion and resentment which had been building in her for so long, was already loosening its grip. Maybe it was just the exotic location, or the anticipation of working with the Cartel; she wasn't sure. But the sense of freedom both excited her and made her sad.

"So what do *you* think?" Katherine's voice brought her back to the moment.

"I'm sorry?"

"About faith."

Again she was careful with her answer. "I think faith is the catalyst . . . but not the cure."

"Meaning?"

"Meaning I agree with you, that we're more than just chemicals. It's been my experience that there's another level to us, something residing within these . . . 'chemistry sets.'"

"You mean our spirit," Katherine said.

Sarah glanced at her with a smile. "As a Christian I would agree, but the scientist part of me might feel a little better if we were to describe it as 'some form of energy.'"

"Now you sound like a Star Wars movie."

Sarah shook her head. "What I'm talking about is more personal than that. It seems to have a distinct personality. In the labs, to a certain degree, we've been able to catch glimpses of it. No, let me rephrase that. We've been able to catch glimpses of its *effects*. We've been able to see how it can affect the chemistry of our bodies."

Katherine gave her a dubious look.

Sarah continued. "But only if we let it. If not, our bodies can reverse the effect and actually have influence over it instead. It's hard to explain, but when that 'energy' intersects with our chemicals, a hybrid is formed, a unique and very special blend of chemical and spirit, a personality if you will. And that personality can choose to let the 'spirit' override the influence of our chemicals, or it can choose to let the chemicals override the 'spirit.'"

"My dad would have called that personality a soul."

"So would most people of religion. But regardless of the name, it seems to have an ability to make that choice . . . to follow the chemical part of its composition, or to follow the spirit part. And it's that choosing, whether to follow the chemical or the spirit, that I would call 'faith.'"

"So basically you're saying what Coleman said. It was his faith that saved him."

"Yes and no. I'm saying Coleman's faith acted as a catalyst, allowing the spirit to come in and do its work on his chemicals."

Katherine gave a wry smile. "Sounds like you've done a pretty good job of mixing science and faith."

"I don't see any difference between the two. It just takes a little longer for science to get around to proving what we people of faith already accept. I don't believe God performs miracles; I believe God performs 'naturals' that we just haven't understood yet. God performed a 'natural' in Coleman's brain by readjusting the chemicals ... but only as Coleman gave Him permission through faith. God performs 'naturals' when people at our clinic are healed ... somehow He readjusts their bodies. God performed 'naturals' when He raised Jesus Christ from the dead. What makes it a miracle is that He applied His created laws of chemistry and physics in a manner we simply haven't understood yet."

"But what if we don't have the faith to have faith?" Katherine asked. Sarah couldn't be sure, but it almost seemed like Katherine was enjoying the conversation. "Remember that guy in the Bible asking Jesus to help his unbelief?"

Sarah nodded. "I think that brings us back to that Personality, to that Love. Maybe it's that Love that stacks the deck, that gives us the faith to have faith."

Katherine quoted, "'The Author and Perfecter of our faith.' Another one of God's jobs."

"Exactly. But it doesn't negate the fact that faith is a freewill decision on our part, that we still have to be willing to receive that faith."

Katherine sighed heavily. "So you've taken us right back to having to believe in a loving and compassionate God."

"Why's that so hard for you?" Sarah asked.

Katherine hesitated, then answered quietly, "I've been on the receiving end of that 'love' one too many times, Doctor. The death of my father, the murder of my husband, the killing of Coleman." She turned to look out a passing window, starting to lose herself in thought. "Coleman, though ... I have to admit, he almost had me convinced." Then she was back, turning to Sarah. "Until I saw what this God of love let them do to my baby, and what He's continuing to do to our lives."

"And that's your proof that a compassionate Deity doesn't exist?"

"Words are cheap, Dr. Martus. Truth lies in what we do, not what we say. *If* there is a God out there, and *if* He really does love us, He's sure not going out of his way to prove it."

Before Sarah could respond, an office door opened a few yards ahead of them. A woman secretary stepped out into the hallway, followed by Lucas Ponte. For the briefest moment Sarah forgot to breathe. He was even more imposing in person than on the videophone. Over six feet tall, broad shoulders, neatly trimmed beard.

"Lucas," Katherine called.

He looked up at Katherine, then over to Sarah. His grin was instant and made her just the slightest bit unsteady. "Dr. Weintraub. It is so good to see you." He handed his papers back to the secretary and strode quickly over to offer his hand.

Barely noticing the use of her maiden name, Sarah took his hand and they shook. His grip was firm, yet gentle. "Good morning, sir," she said. "It's a pleasure to meet you."

His grin broadened. "I assure you, Doctor, the pleasure is mine." And then, just before he could be accused of flirting, he motioned to Katherine. "It is for all of us, am I right, Katherine?"

Katherine smiled, but there was no mistaking the effort it involved. "Whatever you say, Lucas. You're the boss."

"Really." He chuckled. "So why haven't I ever been informed of this fact before?" Smiling at his joke, he turned back to Sarah. "Did you have a pleasant flight?"

"Yes, thank you." She tugged at the hair over her scar.

"Good, good. And our accommodations?"

"No complaints."

"Excellent."

To some this would have been merely small talk. But Sarah felt the man was genuinely concerned as he asked each question and was equally as interested in each answer. That's the type of sincerity she'd read about, and that's the type of sincerity she now saw in person.

"Well," he said, "I will certainly look forward to speaking with you more in depth, but right now—"

"I'm sure you're very busy."

He sighed. "It's this recent outbreak of earthquakes along the Pacific Rim. You've been reading about them?"

Sarah nodded. "We were in Los Angeles just before they started."

"Now there are geological reports of possible volcanic activity. Hawaii, the Pacific Northwest, Japan ... things may become very serious very quickly."

As he spoke, a young teenager sauntered out of his office and into the hallway. He was thin, almost frail, with sandy blonde hair and glasses. When his eyes connected with Sarah's she caught her breath. For, though they were eight thousand miles apart, Sarah was looking into the very same pair of eyes she'd left back home. Eyes that were already penetrating hers, searching her thoughts, exploring her mind.

Lucas Ponte spotted him and started to make the introduction, but it wasn't necessary. Sarah already knew.

"Dr. Weintraub, this is Eric Lyon."

"Behind me, up on the third story, are the offices to the clinic where Dr. and Mr. Martus had worked for nearly twelve months."

The television picture cut from a close-up of Tanya Chase to a wider angle showing an old four-story brick building in the seedier section of Bethel Lake. Next came a shaky hand-held shot moving down the clinic's hallway.

Tanya's voice continued. "It was behind the doors of these rooms that the couple practiced their 'medicine.' And, although many claimed to have been helped by their efforts, there are the others ..."

The picture cut to a close-up of the mother whose mentally impaired girl Brandon had declined to heal several weeks earlier. "I like Brandon Martus," the woman was saying. "He's a good person. So is Sarah. Debra likes them, too."

The picture switched to the little girl sitting on a tricycle. Her head was tilted and slightly drooped. This was followed by a shot of Mom with her on the floor playing with a preschool toy. As the girl struggled to put the correct block into the correct hole, her retardation became more obvious. The picture returned to the interview as Tanya asked, "How long ago did you visit him?"

"'Bout a month ago."

Back to the two of them on the floor.

"And is she any better?"

"No ..."

"How does that make you feel?"

"I dunno, kinda disappointed, I guess ..." The camera remained on the mother. It was obvious she was struggling with her emotions.

Tanya continued. "Just disappointed?"

The woman shook her head, then glanced away. "I mean, we tried everything else. We was just ..." She swallowed. The camera remained fixed on her and she began again. "We was just hoping that something could be done. I mean with what we heard and everything, we really had our hopes up. We was really, really hoping. But now ..." She sniffed quietly and looked down. The camera remained on her. Finally, she shook her head, making it clear she was unable to go on.

Tanya's voice continued. "Meanwhile, the plague, the drought, and worldwide famine, which Martus claims to be the judgment of God, continue to increase."

After quick shots of suffering patients, shriveled crops, and starving children, the picture cut to a videotape of Brandon standing on the stage of the L.A. Forum, shouting. "My anger and my wrath will be poured out on this place, on man and beast, on the trees of the field and on the fruit of the ground, and it will burn and not be quenched."

Next came a picture of Brandon being dragged off the stage as Tanya's voice continued. "At best, he is accused by many in the religious community of capitalizing upon current world disasters ..."

Now some cardinal spoke. He was an older gentleman, with sensitive eyes and a kindly voice. "Such action is nothing but raw exploitation of the world's suffering. It is an unconscionable act, and quite frankly, I believe the lad owes all of us in the religious community an apology."

Back to Tanya. "At worst, he is accused of actually bringing on the suffering."

Now a local businessman appeared—fortyish, sweaty, and with a loosened tie from the heat. "We all know about his power to heal, and what he did to Reverend Tyler on TV ..." The man shook his head. "You'd have to be crazy not to think he's got some sort of supernatural connection."

Back to Tanya's voice. "Whatever one concludes ..."

Videotape of the egg-throwing protesters appeared, followed by quick shots of graffiti scrawled across the front of the clinic, and finally ending with a handful of hecklers yelling at Brandon as he tried to enter the clinic.

"... Brandon Martus has transformed this once mild Midwest hamlet into a conflicting caldron of controversy."

Back to Tanya standing in front of the building. "And now with the recent reports of seismic activity along the Pacific coast, attention is once again turned to this young man."

Back to Brandon onstage shouting in the background as she continued. "Was this also part of his prediction, part of his 'curse'? Is he somehow responsible? Or is he, as many believe, simply a charlatan, an opportunist out to capitalize upon the world's pain and suffering?"

Back to Tanya. "Earlier we'd reported that we'd discovered that the newlyweds had vowed not to physically consummate their relationship, that they felt sex was too demeaning for ones of such a high calling. And now, in an equally bizarre turn of events, it has been confirmed that after less than eight weeks of marriage the couple has separated. Dr. Sarah Martus was reported as being seen—"

Brandon clicked off the remote. He was practically shaking with anger. Like her boss, Tanya Chase had learned the fine art of using truth to tell lies. Other networks had picked up the story, a couple had even asked for interviews for their news magazines. And, although their coverage was equally as uninformed, no one had gone after them like GBN. Little wonder, after what he'd done to Tyler.

At first Brandon had agreed to the interviews, hoping explanations would somehow clarify things. They didn't. In fact they only caused greater confusion, confirming that he was either a huckster, a fruitcake, or some sadistic wizard capable of manipulating the forces of nature for evil. When the interviews didn't work, he tried remaining silent—an even worse mistake that made him all the more mysterious.

And then, just when it looked like things were starting to settle down, all of this seismic activity kicked up along the Pacific Rim. Mount Baker, Mount Hood, Mauna Loa in Hawaii, and a handful of other semidormant volcanoes in Japan, the Philippines, and Indonesia—all suddenly showing signs of potential eruption. And, once again, fingers began to point at him, questioning and asking if he was somehow responsible.

But by far the hardest thing was having to shut down the clinic. That had happened the end of last week. He'd tried to keep it running, but the threats and rising problems had been too much. The place had become a lightning rod, the galvanizing point of attention for everybody from the media, to the picketers with their placards reading: "HE MAY BE SOMEBODY'S GOD ... BUT HE SURE AIN'T MINE," to the opposite extremists who did Brandon little favor with counterdemonstrations involving signs reading: "TURN OR BURN!"

And where was God in all of this?

Silent, as usual.

Shoving aside an undercooked microwave burrito, Brandon rose from the table, shuffled to the computer, and punched it on. He stayed in Sarah's apartment now, and everything he saw reminded him of her. She'd been gone twelve days, and though she was faithful in answering his e-mail, her responses seemed to be growing shorter and less personal. Maybe it was just his imagination. He hoped and prayed that was the case.

The computer came up and the e-mail came on. Nearly a hundred postings this time. It was amazing how quickly they could find his address and flood his mailbox. Early on he'd learned not to open any whose names he didn't know. One virus and crashed hard drive was enough.

Scanning the list, he could find nothing from Sarah, and his heart sank a fraction lower. There was, however, a name he instantly recognized. He popped it up and began reading so fast that he had to stop and start over:

Dearest Brandon:

I know you are discouraged, but that is a necessary part of the process. The call He has given you is true. You will be doin' great and mighty things for Him. But our understanding of great and mighty is different than His. Ours is vain and will burn. His is life-changing and eternal.

Brandon took a breath and slowly let it out.

Every one of us has a call on our life. I don't care who they are. Like Joseph, God has put a dream in our hearts. But few have the faith to follow that dream through all its steps. You've received the call and that's fine. But that's only the first step. The second came when you messed it up. Like Joseph, you allowed worldly thinking to twist it till it fit into the world's idea of greatness. And if it didn't fit, you gave it a few bends and twists of your own till it did. That's where you've been living this last year as you've tried to accomplish in your flesh what God will do in His Spirit.

But now you've entered the third step, and though it's the most painful, it's also the most necessary. 'Cause it's during this time of discouragement that the Lord untwists the world's twistings, that He removes your handiwork and straightens your dream back into His. Lots of times He lets those closest to us be the most discouraging. For Joseph it was his brothers throwing him into the pit, for Abraham it was his wife laughing at him, for our Lord it was His kinsmen trying to put him away. For you, it is Sarah.

Brandon swallowed hard. The words rang truer than he wanted to believe.

Embrace this third step. I know the wilderness is hot, I know your wanderings seem aimless. But just like He did with the children of Israel, He will feed you, He will give you water, He will provide shade by day and light by night. Hold the Lord's hand, follow Him through the desert, and He will lead you to the land He has promised. But you must do it His way. Because 'Flesh gives birth to flesh, but the Spirit gives birth to spirit.'

Very soon you'll be entering another country. I'm not talking just spiritually, but literally, too. You have seen it lots of times in your dreams, but you haven't sought the Lord about it. When you do, He'll tell you. And when He tells you, obey. For it's the only way your call will bear fruit. Give Sarah my love. Be strong and courageous. Do not tremble or be afraid.

Your servant,
GM

Brandon sat staring at the words.

That's her, isn't it?

Heylel gave no answer, but Eric knew he was in the room. He'd been in the small conference room ever since Sarah had begun setting up the equipment.

That's her, Eric repeated. *She's the one who isn't the one, isn't she?*

There was still no answer. But Eric didn't need one. He'd known it, he'd sensed it, from the moment he'd first seen her in the hallway.

"Now, Eric . . ."

He turned to her. One of the sensors taped to his forehead pulled against his skin, and he winced.

"Here, let me fix that for you."

"It's all right."

"You sure he needs all of this stuff?" Katherine asked as Sarah readjusted one of the dozen sensor wires attached to his face, fingers, skin, earlobes, chest, and calf. "Makes him look like the back of some VCR."

Sarah smiled. "Some of these, like this GSR, measure the amount of electricity his skin conducts. That tells us how relaxed he is."

She reached across him to adjust another wire. Eric noticed that she smelled nice. In fact, everything about her was nice. Nice body, nice hair, nice smile. If it wasn't for that scar running down her face she might have been a real looker.

"This sensor over here is for the EMG—it records his muscle tension—and these around the scalp are for EEG, to register his brain activity."

"Provided he has any," Katherine quipped.

"Ho-ho," Eric replied, "very funny."

"You comfortable now?" Sarah asked.

He nodded.

"Okay, what I'd like you to do is take this in your right hand." She gave him a computer joystick with a trigger, then pointed to the small monitor on the table directly in front of him. "You see that blue line running across the screen?"

"Yeah."

"And the thinner yellow one on top of it?"

He nodded.

"When we begin, I want you to hold that trigger down and concentrate on pushing that yellow line above the blue one."

"You mean like with my mind?"

"Exactly."

"Cool."

As Sarah busied herself with a digital data recorder to record the results, Katherine asked, "And all of this stuff, it's like serious science?"

Sarah nodded. "What we're employing here is something called an RNG, a random number generator. They've been around about thirty years, and they're still the best way for us to measure a person's PK."

"PK?"

"*Psychokinesis*—the ability to move physical objects through mental concentration."

"You're not serious?" Katherine asked. "You don't actually believe people can do that?"

"There are over a dozen labs around the world studying the phenomena, along with other paranormal activity like PSI, remote viewing, automatic handwriting, and the list goes on. In fact, in the past, the United States Department of Defense has spent over twenty million dollars in paranormal research."

"No kidding."

Sarah nodded. "Many scientists are beginning to believe the human brain has a lot more potential than we originally gave it credit."

"And you buy all that?"

Sarah hesitated, then shook her head. "No. I don't believe the human brain is capable of manipulating anything outside the body."

Katherine looked surprised. "But you just said . . ."

"I know."

"Then why are you doing all of this, if you don't believe it?"

"I believe the human mind is capable of connecting with other forces of energy that are able to penetrate our skulls and communicate with our brains by listening to and firing off specific neurons, particularly in the area of the right temporal lobe."

"You're talking about God again?"

"Not always."

"There's something else?"

Sarah finished her work and slowly rose to face her. "The counterfeits."

"Eric?" It was Heylel.

There you are. Eric answered. *Why have you been so quiet?*

Heylel gave no answer.

Eric pressed in. *It's because she's the one, isn't it? Her husband, he was the one we tried to get that research guy— that Dr. Reicher—to stop, wasn't he?*

"Very good."

And she's the one you tried to kill in the car crash.

"Excellent."

But you failed.

There was no answer.

Eric pursued him more forcefully, almost gleefully. *Both times you blew it. And that's why you're not saying anything now, 'cause you're chicken, aren't you? Cause you're afraid of her, you're afraid that she might be able to—*

"SILENCE!"

The voice roared in his mind. It was terrifying, and his entire body gave a shudder.

"Eric," Sarah said. "Eric, are you okay?"

He wasn't sure he could find his voice.

"Eric?"

He glanced up and was grateful to see her reassuring presence smiling down at him.

"Are you okay?" she repeated. "What happened? You look pale. Are you all right?"

"Yeah," he lied. He pushed up his glasses with his little finger. "I'm, uh, fine."

"You sure? You look a little shaken."

"I'm fine. Are we going to do this thing or not?" He hoped his tone would keep her at bay. She studied him another moment before nodding and turning back to the experiment.

He relaxed, but just slightly.

"You'll be hearing some pinging noises," she said. "When you are succeeding in elevating that yellow line, the tones will increase in pitch. When you are not, they will remain the same. Any questions?"

He shook his head and reached for the joystick. "Let's get this show on the road."

Sarah smiled and reached over to flip a single switch. A low drone came through the speaker beside the monitor. "Go ahead. Hold that trigger down and let's see what happens."

"No sweat," Eric said as he pressed the trigger on the joystick. Instantly the low tone turned into a screaming wail. His eyes shot to the monitor. The yellow line had leaped off the blue line and was pegged against the top of the screen.

Sarah reached for the knobs, checking the calibrations.

"What's wrong?" Katherine shouted over the increasing shrillness. "What's happening?"

Sarah shook her head. "I'm not certain!" she yelled.

The shrillness continued increasing in pitch and in volume.

"Turn it off!" Katherine yelled. "Turn that thing off!"

"I'm trying!" Sarah reached for the computer's electrical plug. She gave it a tug, disconnecting it from the power surge box.

But the screaming whine increased.

Sarah stared dumbfounded.

Now Katherine was on her feet. "What's going on? Turn it off! Turn it off!"

"There's no power!" Sarah shouted. "There's no way it can possibly be—"

And then, it stopped. No screaming whine, no glowing monitor with colored lines. Everything was suddenly silent and still. Sarah stared at the monitor another moment, then to the disconnected power cord. Finally she turned to Eric.

He coughed and fidgeted. It was obviously Heylel's doing. As best as he could tell, his mentor was not in a very good mood.

The scissors were dull and he had to cut smaller portions than he wanted, but slowly, methodically, it was coming off. He'd put a paper towel in the sink to cover the drain, and it was already covered with the long strands of his shiny black hair.

Brandon was not sure why he wanted to cut it. It had been part of his identity since high school. He just thought that maybe . . . maybe it was time for a change. But it was more than a change. As he watched the tufts fall into the sink, he knew it was also a type of death. Everything he'd been, everything he was, and yes, everything he wanted to be, had come to an end. There were no tears, no self-pity. Just numbness. Numbness and bone-weary fatigue.

If Gerty wanted him to stop trying, no problem. When you've got nothing left to try with, quitting is easy. Today, maybe tomorrow he'd go down to Bollenger's Printing and Lithograph. See if he could get his old job back. That at least was something he knew how to do. Maybe, in time, Sarah would come back to him. Maybe people would eventually forget all of the craziness. Maybe, someday, *he* could.

He folded up the paper towel, trying to keep as much hair in it as possible, then pitched it into the garbage. Looking back into the mirror, he checked out the sides and top. It wasn't terrible. True, nothing like he'd get at Supercuts, but going to a Supercuts would mean going out in public. And going out in public would mean having to endure the stares, wisecracks, and occasional confrontation.

It had been a week since Gerty's e-mail. And for a week he'd prayed, he'd fasted, he'd done everything he could think of to find out what God wanted.

And for a week there had been nothing.

She'd mentioned something about searching his dreams. But for the most part they had been equally uneventful. No more special guest appearances by Jesus Christ, no more symbolic imagery. Except for the occasional nightmare of the serpent's head along with the addition of that silly crescent moon and star from Salman Kilyos's tattoo, there wasn't that much to speak of. Mostly just memories of Sarah and the constant reminder of how hollow and empty he was without her.

He stared into the mirror. Not thrilled with his new 'do, he went to plan B. He grabbed a can of shaving cream and a disposable Bic from the cabinet. He wasn't exactly sure how to pull it off, but hopefully shaving his head wouldn't be all that different from shaving his face . . . hopefully.

He turned on the hot water. As he waited for it to heat up he thought through the various fragments of last night's dream. It was no different from the others. He and Sarah at the lake, he and Sarah at work, the two of them shopping. Then came a brief appearance of Salman's tattoo. But instead of being inside the church, Brandon was walking across a giant version of the crescent moon and star. To further confuse the issue there were the seven lampstands he'd seen during his vision at the hospital. The same number of lampstands he'd been reading about in Revelation. And leading him through the maze was none other than Salman Kilyos.

Typically absurd and confusing, it was just like everything else. If there was a code to be cracked here, God would have to do the cracking. Because, as in everything else, Brandon had quit trying.

When the water was good and warm, he stuck his head under the faucet to soften his hair for the shave. He didn't hear the knock on the door until he turned off the tap and reached for the towel. Even then he wasn't sure he wanted to answer it. By now every kook in the county had his address.

But the knocking persisted. Toweling off, Brandon stepped into the hall and headed across the worn carpet toward the door.

"Mr. Brandon, Mr. Brandon, are you there?" More knocking. "Mr. Brandon?" The voice was familiar, but he couldn't place it. "Mr. Brandon?"

He arrived and looked through the peephole. To his surprise it was Salman Kilyos, healthier than he'd ever seen him. Before he could stop it, Brandon's mind sorted through the information, searching for the meaning behind the coincidence. For the millionth time he tried fitting together the puzzle, this time including Salman and the dream tattoo. And for the millionth time he hit a wall.

"Mr. Brandon."

"Hang on." He unlocked the original dead bolt, then the two new ones he'd installed, before sliding back the chain and opening the door.

The man stood, smiling in the bright sunlight. "Good morning." When he registered Brandon's lack of hair, his smile wavered slightly. "It looks ... good on you."

Brandon eyed him warily. "Good morning, Salman."

The man's grin broadened. "I have them."

"Them?"

He held out a business envelope. "Our tickets. To Istanbul."

Brandon clutched the door just a little bit tighter. "Istanbul?"

"Of course." The man moved past him and entered the apartment. "After all you have done for me, I figure it is the least I may do for you."

CHAPTER 9

Dear Sarah,

A minute doesn't go by that you don't somehow come to my mind ... wondering what you would say in a situation, what jokes we would make, how we would laugh and talk and argue and pray with each other. I know this time is necessary, but it doesn't make it less painful. Every morning I wake up and feel this huge piece of me missing ... and every day I'm a little more afraid that we are drifting apart and that that piece of me may never return. Stupid, I know, but the fear is always there in the back of my mind. I'm

*glad you're finding the boy so challenging . . . you've always
liked challenges (as long as you can solve them).*

*And what you say about Lucas Ponte is interesting. He's
on the news every night now, as the debate continues about
him taking office and as they prepare to build some sort of
temple in Jerusalem. He sounds like a courageous and caring man—just what our world needs to try to bring the peace
the Cartel is promising. You're right, working with him is a
great opportunity, and it will be interesting to see what purpose his coming into our lives may have.*

Sarah blew the hair out of her eyes and reached for her
mug of tea. She was annoyed at how, even now while reading
a letter from her husband, thoughts of Lucas kept trying to
distract her. Of course she found his flirting to be flattering—
who wouldn't? A man with all of that power and prestige taking an interest in her? It was enough to make anyone give
pause. But that's all she'd done, paused. She'd held off the
invitations to dinner, the requests to privately discuss Eric's
condition over drinks. She was a married woman. And she was
married to an incredible guy. Of course they had their differences; what couples didn't? But they'd work them out. They
had to.

She looked back at the screen.

*I'm glad this trip to Turkey makes sense to you. When
Salman first showed up at my door, telling me that God had
told him to buy the tickets, you can bet I had some doubts.
Of course I remembered how he'd said the crescent moon and
star was the symbol for his beloved homeland, and I knew
what Gerty had said about my going on a trip. But it wasn't
until you pointed out how all seven churches in Revelation
are also in that country that things suddenly made sense.*

*This is where Christ sent the "love letters" that He com-
manded us to study. I wouldn't have made the connection if
it wasn't for your help. Funny, isn't it? Here we are separated*

by thousands of miles, and yet we're still working together as a team. Then again, maybe it's not so funny at all.

I'm on the plane now. We'll be in Istanbul in eight more hours, then we'll catch a flight to Izmir, and drive fifty miles to Ephesus, the first of the seven churches. I tell you though, this sitting and doing nothing for hour after hour can sure make a person crazy. Time is dragging in slow motion.

To make it worse, they're showing a little model of our plane up on the TV screens as it creeps across a map of the world. Talk about painful. It's like watching the hour hand of a clock. Some people can sleep. I can't. Too much excitement.

My hope is that I quickly learn what I must learn to "warn the bride." How that's going to happen is beyond me, but then it won't be the first time He's surprised us, will it? All I know is that the sooner I learn the lessons and the sooner you finish your work there, the sooner we will be back together.

Until then, I love and miss you with all of my heart and all of my body and all of my soul.

Yours forever,
Brandon

Sarah looked at the screen a long time before shutting it off. The room was darker now. She rose and crossed to the overstuffed chair near the window. She was already in her nightshirt—actually it was Brandon's shirt, his blue shirt she loved so much. She eased herself down into the chair and pushed back the curtains. The mountains were on fire with another incredible sunset, making everything glow an iridescent pink.

She wasn't sure why she was crying. Some of it had to do with the letter, some of it had to do with missing Brandon. But there was more.

She pulled her legs up under her chin and held them. High up on the slope above her, some of the Cartel office lights were still burning, including Lucas's. She scolded herself for even looking and quickly redirected her gaze.

She rested her forehead on her knees, face in the shirt, and breathed deeply. Even now she could smell Brandon's smell—a little woodsy, a little trace of aftershave. And, as she breathed in, the memories came . . .

It was true, Brandon was the most incredible man she had ever met. And he always would be. Just as importantly, he loved her. He *cherished* her. She snuggled deeper into the chair. She would sleep there, curled up, her face buried in her husband's shirt, smelling his smell. The tears were gone, at least for now, as she continued to sit, breathing in and remembering his love. But they would return. Off and on throughout the night they would return.

It was late and Katherine was bored. Once again she sat in front of Eric's computer and once again she stared at the antisense files, the ones labeled after the first four cities to be infected with Scorpion—Cairo, Mecca, New York, Tel Aviv. Either the Cartel was getting more sophisticated in protecting their information or she was losing her touch. Maybe a little of both. In any case, her earlier attempts at hacking into these files had been unsuccessful. Now it was as much pride as it was curiosity. She *would* get into those files and she *would* find out why they were restricted.

It was the last resort and one she felt a little uneasy using, but hey, they started it . . .

First she brought up the Cartel's system, complete with the graphic field of their logo, the planet Earth with four different races of hands clasped around it in unity.

Next, she tried to log on as Marshal T. Elliott, the system's administrator. She'd never met the man, but as the S.A. he had the highest security access to the Cartel's computers. He could go anywhere he wanted inside the system. Nothing was forbidden to him. The reason? It was his job to oversee and watchdog the computer system, including, among other things, preventing people like Katherine from breaking into it.

A prompt came up asking for Elliott's password, which, of course, Katherine didn't know. But it didn't matter. This was where it got interesting . . .

Instead of trying to guess the correct password and enter it on the Cartel's graphic logo, Katherine simply typed up a program enabling her to make an exact copy of that graphic logo. Once she captured it, she then designed a shadow TSR, or *terminate stay resident,* program to bring her graphic logo up onto Elliott's computer screen instead of the original. It would work like this:

Elliott would boot up his computer. But instead of the Cartel's graphic logo appearing, asking for his password, Katherine's copy of the logo would appear asking for it. He would then enter his password using the standard nonechoing format which replaced his typed letters with asterisks. Next he would hit *enter.* When he did he would see a momentary flicker on the screen, and then the genuine graphic logo would appear, once again asking for his password.

He would hesitate, wondering if there was a glitch in the system. But the only way to find out would be to reenter his password. He would do so, check out the system to make sure everything was running properly, and when he was satisfied he would continue with whatever work he was doing.

In the meantime, Katherine's copy of the graphic logo, complete with the newly typed password, would be recorded into an encrypted file and tagged with a legitimate file name so it wouldn't stand out. Then, at her leisure, Katherine would simply bring up the file, retrieve Elliott's password, and use it anytime she wanted to go into the system.

It was totally dishonest and deceptively simple. But as any hacker or con artist will tell you, the best deceptions are the simplest.

Katherine's fingers flew across the keyboard as she finished the last of the TSR program and entered it into the system. In a day, maybe two, whenever she had some spare time, she would bring up the graphic field, use Elliott's password, and cruise anywhere she wanted ... particularly into the antisense subfiles listing those four cities.

> To the angel of the church in Ephesus write:
> These are the words of him who holds the seven stars in his right hand and walks among the seven golden lampstands: I know your deeds, your hard work and your perseverance. I know that you cannot tolerate wicked men, that you have tested those who claim to be apostles but are not, and have found them false. You have persevered and have endured hardships for my name, and have not grown weary.

Brandon had read the first part of this letter in Revelation a dozen times on the plane and half that many times in the bus on the way to Ephesus. He'd practically memorized it. And now, as he and Salman walked along the uneven marble road amidst the ruins, it was all he could do to imagine that this was the city, the actual location of the first-century church that Christ had addressed in the letter. This was where Timothy had pastored, where Paul had caused a riot, where many believe Mary spent her last years, and where the disciple John came to die.

So much history here—particularly for someone whose idea of the ancient past went only as far back as the Civil War. It was hard to imagine that he was walking on pavement over two thousand years old, that he could actually see the grooves worn into the street from chariot wheels. And Salman was the perfect tour guide. He was only too happy to be back home in his country and to be showing off its rich history. As the son of an archaeologist, he'd been dragged to most of the major ruins a number of times. And Ephesus, nestled in the fog-covered hills near the Aegean Sea, was no different. He made sure Brandon saw everything . . . the temples, the gates, the palaces, the fountains, the baths, and the brothel. For Brandon one crumbling wall, broken set of steps, and marble column looked like the next, and he had to take Salman's word as to what they saw. However, he was certain about the ancient public latrines—there was something about the long row of clearly defined and still functional marble toilet seats that made their authenticity more than obvious.

"And the vestal virgins"—Salman pointed off to the right—"over here is where they lived. They were highly honored in the city. Their job was never to let the sacred flame go out."

"Sacred flame?"

"Yes. The glory of Rome, that is what it represented, and it burned for centuries. These were glorious times, my friend. The times of the Imperial Cult."

"What do you mean, 'Imperial Cult'?"

"That's when the Roman emperors ruled the world, when they were worshiped as gods."

Brandon said nothing as he looked around the ruins. Despite its fallen state, it wasn't hard to imagine the splendor and majesty of the city.

Salman continued. "And the festivals held for the Imperial Cult, they were the most important times of the city, for any of the cities. People, they would come from everywhere to participate in the processions, the ceremonies, the sacrifices, the feasts—they were wonderful times. The government even passed out money to the poor so they could afford an animal sacrifice. For some it was the only meat they would be able to eat for the entire year."

"All of this to celebrate their ruler-gods?"

"Yes, exactly. The Caesars. And that is why Christians, they were not so well liked."

"Because they didn't worship them."

"Exactly. People, they would worship whoever or whatever they wanted, and that was okay. But if they did not also

worship Caesar, the leader of the entire civilized world"—
Salman ran a finger across his neck with the appropriate
sound effect—"things would not go so well for them."

"And this." Salman motioned to an imposing two-story
structure complete with towering columns, statues, and intricate carvings. "This is the Celsus Library. It was completed
about A.D. 125 and contained twelve thousand scrolls, making
it one of the largest libraries in the world. The walls, they were
twenty feet thick to protect the scrolls from weather and
insects. Magnificent, is it not?"

Brandon had to agree. In fact, the more he took in the
sights of this ancient capital, the more magnificent everything
became. What a world these first-century Christians had lived
in . . . affluent, sophisticated, educated. And what a credit it
was for them *not* to have their heads turned by all of this
wealth and intellectualism—not to mention the flat-out hostility against them for refusing to worship Caesar. No wonder
Christ started his letter to them with such praise.

> I know your deeds, your hard work and your perse-
> verance. I know that you cannot tolerate wicked
> men. . . . You have persevered and have endured
> hardships for my name, and have not grown weary.

These were impressive accomplishments. In many ways
they made this church the ideal role model for today's
churches. Unfortunately, the letter continued . . .

"Mr. Brandon, where are you going?"

"I, uh . . ."

They had traveled about a hundred yards and Salman was
turning to a large structure to his right. "The Grand Theater,
you will want to see this. This is where the riot occurred."

They had discussed the event during the ride to Ephesus.
According to the book of Acts, this was the very amphitheater
where an angry crowd had spent two hours shouting down a
follower of Paul. Brandon had every intention of seeing it, was
looking forward to going inside, but something had sudden-

ly compelled him to head the opposite direction. Something very strong.

"What's this?" he asked, motioning to a long stone road nearly thirty feet wide with broken columns on either side. "Where does this lead?"

"That is the Harbor Street," Salman replied. "It used to lead to the harbor."

"Can we go there first?"

"The sun is nearly down. This is much more important. Did you know that there are over twenty-four thousand seats, and that at one time—"

"That's great, Salman, really impressive—but there's something down here, something I need to see."

"Mr. Brandon, there is nothing at the other end of that road but bushes and blackberry briars."

Brandon nodded. He knew it didn't make sense, but he also knew what he was feeling. It wasn't exactly what he'd felt on the stage in L.A.; it was much more subtle. But it was just as insistent, just as compelling. He knew it didn't make sense, but he also knew he had to obey. "I understand," he called back to Salman. "But . . . there's something down here I need to see."

Salman let out a heavy sigh and started after him. "As you wish, Mr. Brandon, as you wish."

What're all these cloud thingies?

"Clouds?"

Yeah, you know, that misty stuff that's surrounding everybody.

"Ah, you see them as mist. Of course."

What are they?

"They are more of my colleagues. They work with me to protect your people from the harsh and burning light of the enemy."

Eric glanced around the room where he was resting in the recliner . . . well, at least where his body was resting.

Because the conscious part of him, the part that was actually Eric Lyon, floated over his body. It hovered eight feet above the room, looking down at the scene with Heylel. The two of them had made up days ago, and now, once again, Heylel was showing him deeper mysteries. They watched as Sarah conducted another experiment while she talked to his mom in hushed tones. Lucas stood nearby.

How come Mom and Lucas got more of the mist stuff around them than Sarah?

"*Because they have allowed more of us to surround and protect them.*"

But Sarah hasn't?

"*Precisely.*"

Why?

"*Your mother and Lucas are open to our help. Sarah is not. She still believes in Oppressor's ways.*"

Eric felt Heylel shudder at the name. He seldom used it, but when he did it was always accompanied by revulsion and fear. The reason was simple. Heylel had never told him the whole story, but from what Eric gathered, a long, long time ago there was a powerful dictator who kept the universe under his ironfisted control. Heylel was one of this dictator's top generals. But he saw the terrible injustices and led a revolt to liberate the universe from this cruel tyrant. He managed to get a third of creation to stand up with him, but two-thirds did not. The rebellion was crushed, and Heylel and his followers were banished here to earth. But even though they were imprisoned here, because of the kindness of their hearts, they had decided to help the planet's inhabitants by protecting anyone who wanted to be protected from Oppressor's ways.

So, Eric thought, *that's why you're so careful around Sarah? She still follows Oppressor.*

"*Precisely. In her ignorance, she has potential for doing great harm to us . . . and to Lucas.*"

And Lucas is really important, right?

"Yes. The two of you will be a team. And with my help, there is nothing you will not be able to accomplish."

Eric looked back down at Sarah. *But if she's such a threat, why don't you just take her out?*

"Until her time, Oppressor has forbidden us to touch her . . . unless, of course, she gives us permission."

Permission? Like how?

"You have many questions today, my young friend."

If I'm going to help you run stuff, I better learn as much as I can.

He heard Heylel chuckle. *"Yes, as always you are right. And, as always, I am well pleased. There is no one finer in all the world to help me rule."*

And Lucas, don't forget Lucas.

"Yes, and Lucas. You and Lucas. But it will always be you, first."

Eric felt the pleasure swell inside him. This was another reason he liked Heylel, another reason he put up with the outbursts of anger and the struggles for control. It wasn't just because of the power growing inside of him, or the promises of what he would become; it was also because of the respect and admiration Heylel had for him.

So—Eric looked back down at Sarah—*how are you going to stop her?*

"At the moment there is little we can do. Oppressor's light has blinded her to our truth. However, we are attempting to bring her and Lucas together, so he can help."

Together? What, like boyfriend, girlfriend? I thought she was married.

"Of course, but there is always hope."

Like what? How do you do that?

"So many questions."

Tell me.

"We influence her thoughts. We subtly change the patterns of her thinking."

You can do that?

"Only if she gives us permission."

Cool.

"Yes, it is. But we must be very subtle. If our work is too obvious, she will block it. But if she lets us touch her thoughts, if she allows us to gradually rework her thinking, the two of them may very well become lovers."

Too bad you couldn't do that with Mom.

"We have other plans for your mother."

Really? Like what?

"In good time, my friend, in good time. Would you like to see something else?"

Sure, what else do you—

Suddenly his ears roared with rushing wind. But, instead of falling, as he always did during these times, Eric was shooting up . . . at incredible speed. Before he knew it, he was high above the Earth. Below him were the Himalayas. Further north was what had to be China, and to the south lay India as well as the Indian Ocean. But he wasn't just seeing physical land. He was also seeing larger pockets of the same mist and fog that had surrounded the people in the room. Now, however, the pockets blanketed entire regions. In some places it was very thin, in others very thick.

Wow, Eric thought, *this is incredible!*

"It is quite lovely here."

I'll say. And all those misty and foggy places, those are your buddies, too?

"Yes. Instead of concentrating upon just one person, my more powerful friends concentrate on specific regions and—"

Look out! Eric shouted. He lunged to the side as a pencil-thin shaft of light penetrated a clump of mist below them. It sliced through the air just yards from where they'd been floating, and then it was gone.

What was that?

There was no hiding the irritation in Heylel's voice. *"More of Oppressor's works. Take a careful look and tell me what you see."*

Eric squinted, looking out across the continent. *Nothing. Just land, water, clouds, and your mist buddies.*

"*Look closer.*" The voice was more of a command than a request, and Eric knew better than to disobey.

I am, but I don't see any—oh, wait a minute.

"*Do you see them now?*"

You mean those light beams?

"*Yes.*"

They're superthin but, yeah, I see them. They're shooting up all over the place.

"*Yes. And look what they do to our attempts to protect your people.*"

Eric squinted harder, focusing upon one particular patch of mist concentrated over what looked like a city. Several narrow shafts of light were cutting through it, and as he watched, he noticed the mist beginning to dissolve and break up.

"*Do you see what's happening?*" Heylel asked.

It looks like those beams are wiping your guys out.

Heylel said nothing.

Not a lot, though.

"*Enough. By itself, no single ray of light can destroy our protection. But, as you see, the more that penetrate us, the weaker our presence becomes and the harder it is for us to protect you.*"

But what are they? Where do these beams come from?

"*They are people like Sarah, the deluded ones who still follow Oppressor's path. This is their communication with him.*"

That's terrible, Eric thought back.

"*Yes.*"

Isn't there some way to stop them?

"*There are many ways. The best is, as you say, 'to take them out.'*"

But you said he won't let you.

"*No, not on my own. I am only spirit. I need physical tools to manipulate the physical. That is why you and I must work together.*"

Once again Eric felt his importance rising. *Because,* he asked, *with me, you can do anything?*

"*Very good. Together we can do anything.*"

Eric broke into a grin, then recited what he'd heard a dozen times before. *And the more control I give you, the greater we'll become . . .*

Heylel complete the phrase. "*. . . until all is ours.*"

But when? Eric demanded. *You keep promising me that, but when?*

"*Soon, my young friend. You are nearly ready. Your time of glory will be very, very soon.*"

The closer Brandon came to the end of the road the harder his heart pounded. He knew he was about to hear something, to learn something. And he knew it had to do with the other half of the Ephesians letter . . . the warning half. Because, as much as Christ had praise for the church at Ephesus, He also had a stern rebuke.

> Yet I hold this against you: You have forsaken your first love. Remember the height from which you have fallen! Repent and do the things you did at first. If you do not repent, I will come to you and remove your lampstand from its place.

But what did that have to do with the end of this particular road?

As they approached, Brandon noticed they were no longer surrounded by tourists. They were entirely by themselves. And why not? The road went nowhere, and it was nearly closing time. They had walked six hundred yards down the uneven stone pavement until it finally came to an end. The stones stopped abruptly and were replaced by a dirt bank three to four feet high, covered in grass and brush.

There was nothing else.

"See," Salman said, squinting at Brandon who stood between him and the setting sun. "It goes nowhere. There is nothing here."

Brandon turned toward the bank, looking out across the flat land. "But it used to go somewhere."

"Of course. It was the great road to the city; it led to the harbor where the ships docked. All of the world's kings and emperors were greeted upon these very stones."

"But there's no water here."

"Not now. The sea is two miles away."

"I don't understand."

"Ephesus, it used to be one of the mightiest seaports in all of the Roman Empire."

"What happened?"

"The Cayster River. Gradually, over time, it filled the harbor with its dirt and silt. Since no one cleaned it out, the harbor eventually filled up. Now there is only dirt and weeds."

Brandon's head began to swim. There was a truth here. Something profound, if he could just grasp it. He looked down at the bank, then kneeled before it. Without looking at Salman he asked, "And since the city no longer had a harbor?"

"It no longer served a purpose."

Brandon slowly turned to him. "And it was deserted."

Salman shrugged. "Of course. What good was it to anyone then?"

Brandon nodded, but barely heard. He looked back at the bank and reached out to finger the dirt. It was good soil, some of the best . . . just like the Ephesians had performed good works, some of the best . . .

> I know your deeds, your hard work and your perseverance. . . . You have persevered and have endured hardships . . . and have not grown weary.

And yet it was that excellent soil that had slowly replaced the most important thing to the city—its harbor . . . just as— now he had it—just as the excellent works of the church had slowly replaced its love.

Yet I hold this against you: You have forsaken your first love.

Unnoticed, silently, the good quality soil had replaced the city's harbor ... Unnoticed, silently, the good quality works had replaced the church's love.

Now Brandon understood. That's why he'd been led to the end of this road—to see this truth.

But there was more. The truth didn't end with this city or this church. Wasn't this also what the makeup woman had said about Jimmy Tyler ... at first he was full of love, but gradually his works consumed him? That somehow they'd "lost" Jimmy Tyler? "You don't become one of the biggest ministries in the world without sacrificing something," wasn't that what she had said?

The thoughts swirled in his mind. How much of it was his own thinking, he didn't know. How much of it was inspiration, he wasn't sure. But understanding raced into his head, almost faster than he could absorb it ...

Wasn't that the main reason he'd hated church, the reason his friends never darkened its doors, because of the lack of love? Wasn't that what everyone needed more than anything—sincere, genuine love? Sure, there was the teaching, the preaching, the programs—and they were all necessary and they were all good. But, somehow, amidst all of the programs and good ... love had been forgotten.

But not just their love for others ... more tragically, he sensed it was the Ephesians' love for God. Their "first love"— that zeal, that joy for being saved, that excitement he'd seen on Sarah's face the first time she understood how loved and forgiven she was. For him, for those who had grown up in the church, it had become old hat, cliché—as lifeless as some other religion's ceremony or prayer beads. Like the silt, good religion had replaced heartfelt love. Godly works had replaced fervent passion.

But what could be done?

"Mr. Brandon, Mr. Brandon, are you all right?" The concern in Salman's voice made it clear he saw the moisture welling up in his eyes.

Brandon nodded and reached into his backpack. He fumbled for his pocket New Testament and Psalms and pulled it out, quickly flipping through the pages to Revelation.

Remember the height from which you have fallen!
Repent and do the things you did at first.

What had he done at first? What had Sarah done?

They'd thanked God, they'd worshiped and adored him. Not from rote, but from their hearts. They didn't recite dusty hymns from dusty hymnals, they didn't recite overhead projection verses. They *truly* worshiped, using their minds *and their hearts*. That's what had started to fade . . . the love from their hearts.

He turned back to the Bible and read.

If you do not repent, I will come to you and remove
your lampstand from its place. . . . He who has an ear,
let him hear what the Spirit says to the churches. To
him who overcomes, I will give the right to eat from
the tree of life, which is in the paradise of God.

But how could the others be warned? How could today's church be reminded of the subtle deception that was slowly creeping in and—

Brandon had the answer before the question had completely formed. Slowly, he rose to his feet and looked back down the road toward the amphitheater. In the distance the multiple rows of stone seats reflected gold in the setting sun. He fought off an involuntary shiver.

But he knew . . .

He would be the one to tell them. Once again, he would be required to stand in front of a crowd. And, just as in L.A., and just as in that amphitheater two thousand years ago, the answer would be booed and shouted down. The thought made him cold inside. But just as surely as he felt the cold gripping his gut, he knew it would be done.

Not here, not now. There were still lessons to be learned. But in time it must be done . . .

CHAPTER 10

Get out of the street! Hurry!"

Sarah glanced over her shoulder and saw a trickle of people rounding the corner and racing down the street toward her. A trickle which quickly grew into a torrent, and then a mob. And still they poured in. Hundreds, maybe a thousand, all shouting and waving their fists at a frame of burning bamboo held high above their heads.

"In here!" Katherine shouted as she pulled Sarah across the wet cobblestones and into the open doorway of a shop. "We've got to get out of the street *now!*"

They reached the doorway just as the first of the crowd began to pass.

"What's going on?" Sarah shouted. "What are they doing?"

"Watch!"

Sarah pulled further into the safety of the doorway as the throng came by. The trip to Katmandu had been Katherine's idea. "To get you into the city and see some sights," she'd said. And they had seen sights . . . everything from the tea shops to street flower vendors, to the temples complete with spinning prayer wheels, to painted holy men . . . to human bodies being cremated right there on the banks of the Vishnumati River. It took nearly an hour to get the stench out of her nostrils, and she knew she'd never be able to entirely remove the image. Even more unsettling for her was that this same river, where they poured the remaining ash, was where other people ceremonially bathed and cleansed themselves from their sins.

Then there were the children. Everywhere she looked, especially in the temple areas, there were dirty, ragged children. Some begged by playing what looked like cheap, miniature violins, holding them in their laps and lifelessly running a bow back and forth across untuned strings. Others were more direct, dogging them and tugging at their clothes for any money they might have.

"Where do they all come from?" Sarah had asked.

"Lots are orphans."

"They have no home? People don't adopt them?"

"This is a Hindu state, remember."

"What does that mean?"

"It means everyone believes in reincarnation."

"But what's that got to do with these poor—"

"If a child's parents are killed, people figure it's judgment for the evil the child committed in his past life. It's his punishment."

"You're not serious."

"Of course I am. People don't want to interfere with the judgment of the universe, so they leave the kid alone."

"They won't help him?"

"Worse than that. Usually the child is thrown out of the village in hopes that he'll starve to death and die quickly."

"I can't believe that. It's so . . . inhumane."

"That's because you're looking at it through Western eyes. People here feel it's the exact opposite. By helping the child die, they're doing him a favor. They're helping him pay for his past sins, so he can be reincarnated to a better life."

"That's terrible!"

"That's reincarnation." And then Katherine had added, "Guess it doesn't matter what religion people believe in . . . the Supreme Being still winds up embarrassingly short in the love department."

"You really hate Him, don't you?"

Katherine had shaken her head. "I don't hate Him. I just don't believe Him. Truth isn't in words but in action, remember? And I sure don't see any action of a loving God here."

That conversation had been over an hour ago. Sarah had wanted to come to God's defense, but over the weeks, as she had learned all that Katherine had been through, from widowhood, to alcoholism, to fighting for the survival of her only child, she knew there was little the woman would hear. As a preacher's kid who'd seen the worst of life and then some, Katherine seemed to have every reason to doubt God's love. And Sarah, with her own personal doubts and frustrations, knew this was not the time to try and stand up for Him. Yes, she still believed there was some sort of call on her life, but every day that believing grew just a little bit fainter, and every day that call became just a bit more dim.

Now the two of them stood in the doorway watching the crowd and the burning frame of bamboo approach. But it was more than just the burning bamboo that the people held above their heads. Lashed to it by his hands and feet was a nearly naked man, his body painted with various symbols and images representing evil. It was he and not the burning bamboo that the crowd was shouting and screaming at.

"Do you know what's happening?" Sarah yelled over the noise.

Katherine nodded. "The man tied up there represents Ghanta Karna, one of the world's most dreaded demons."

"Demons?" Sarah shouted.

"That's right."

By now the man and burning frame were directly in front of them. He writhed and screamed, shouting oaths back at the crowd, which only agitated them more.

"They're not going to burn him to death?" Sarah cried.

Katherine laughed. "No, no. It's all a show, part of the ceremony. By the time they get to the river, he usually frees himself and makes his escape."

"Usually?"

Katherine shrugged and smiled.

Sarah turned back to the crowd. The burning bamboo had passed, and the mob was already beginning to thin.

"So you see, my friend," Katherine said, no longer shouting, "Western religions don't own the market in their belief in demons or, how did you put it the other day, in 'counterfeits.'"

Sarah nodded, watching the last of the crowd head down the street. "I see your point." Then with a grin she added, "But I think our way of handling them is a little easier."

"A good old-fashioned exorcism?"

Sarah looked at her. She was unable to tell if she was mocking her or not. "I've seen it work, Katherine. A half-dozen times at the clinic, I've seen people completely delivered of demonic influence in the name of Jesus Christ."

Katherine glanced away, pretending to watch the remaining stragglers, but it was obvious her mind was someplace else. "Do you think . . ." She cleared her throat. "Do you think that might be what Eric is suffering from?"

Sarah said nothing. The suspicion had been growing in her mind throughout the tests. Eric's psychic abilities, his hosting another "consciousness," his violent behavior—these were all classic patterns of demonic activity. Then there was the increasing difficulty in regaining control from Heylel.

Katherine turned to her, waiting for an answer.

As always, Sarah carefully chose her words. "There's a strong possibility, but his problem could still be physical or psychological. I know others have run tests, but there's still a possibility he may be suffering from schizophrenia or from multiple personality disorder."

"They're not the same as possession?"

"Not always. Possession can display those symptoms, but they can also be created by a chemical imbalance or a psychological disorder. It's not always easy to know the differ—"

"The stuff I've seen my son do, what he's been through—it doesn't sound like any psychological disorder to me. And Heylel . . . there's no way that creep is a part of my son. There's absolutely no way they're connected."

Sarah slowly nodded. "You may be right. But it's important that we finish checking out the natural causes first."

"Aren't you done with that yet?"

"Just about."

"Well, I suggest you hurry and get a move on, Doctor."

Sarah looked at her.

"The sooner you finish up your tests and get down to a major face-to-face with this Heylel thing, the better off we'll all be."

Surprised, Sarah asked, "So you think it's demonic?"

"Come on." Katherine stepped into the street. "Let's head down to the river and see if the poor guy makes it."

To the angel of the church in Smyrna write:
These are the words of him who is the First and the Last, who died and came to life again. I know your afflictions and your poverty—yet you are rich! I know the slander of those who say they are Jews

and are not, but are a synagogue of Satan. Do not be afraid of what you are about to suffer. I tell you, the devil will put some of you in prison to test you, and you will suffer persecution for ten days. Be faithful, even to the point of death, and I will give you the crown of life.

He who has an ear, let him hear what the Spirit says to the churches. He who overcomes will not be hurt at all by the second death.

Brandon stared hard at the page. It was the second letter Christ had sent to the churches in Revelation. But instead of commanding the people to repent and return to their first love, as he had at Ephesus, this letter promised persecution and urged the church to be faithful "even to the point of death."

Persecution? Death? For the church? For His beloved bride? All of his life Brandon had been taught that God protected His own, that Jesus, the loving Shepherd, would not allow anything to happen to His flock. But this . . .

You will suffer persecution . . . even to the point of death.

It didn't make sense. It wasn't the gospel he'd been taught.

"Mr. Brandon, Mr. Brandon, why the scowl?"

He glanced over to see Salman climbing the steep stone steps of the fortress wall. In his hand he held a sheet of newspaper rolled into a cone. "The children," he called, "they have given us more sunflower seeds."

Brandon smiled. There was no doubt about it, the two of them had become the local children's special project. This was their third day living inside the ruins of Kadifekale, an ancient acropolis of broken walls, crumbling arches, and an underground cavern suitable for sleeping. For three days they had sat atop this nine-hundred-foot hill overlooking the city of Ismir, which in ancient times had been called Smyrna. And for three days the Kurdish children who lived around the ruins had been bringing them sunflower seeds, goat milk, and flat bread baked on the inside roof of stone ovens. These Kurds were the outcasts of Turkish society, yet they were the first to offer hospitality. By day the impoverished children came to them with food. And for the nights, though it was so warm they really didn't need it, an old woman who sold handwoven goods to tourists insisted upon giving them two brightly colored blankets.

Salman remained by Brandon's side the entire time. He didn't have to. He could have easily found a cheap hotel down in the city. But he stayed. Regardless of the discomfort, regardless of the inconvenience, he stayed to explain, to translate, and to tell his stories. Salman Kilyos was a born storyteller, and he loved to practice his gift whenever he could. Their friendship had grown, and a day didn't go by that Brandon didn't thank God for the man's commitment. Their bond was strong . . . and unlikely. But no more unlikely than the journey they were making.

"Hold out your hand."

Brandon obeyed and Salman poured out a large pile of the unshelled seeds.

"Thanks, Salman."

"No problem. But you still do not answer my question. Why the frown?"

"Take a look at this." Brandon handed the Bible to him and pointed to the two small paragraphs in Revelation chapter two. Salman took it and began to read. Although he claimed to be a Christian, Brandon had his doubts. Somehow he suspected it was all part of the Salman Kilyos con. A sincere con, but a con nonetheless. After all, ninety-eight percent of Turkish citizens claimed to be Moslem. For Salman to be part of the two percent and to be a Christian to boot seemed more than a stretch. Then there was his hatred of Ponte and the Cartel. During their frequent conversations with local

Muslims, Salman would be the first to side with the most radical fringes, agreeing that Ponte was up to no good, and insisting that he was an "infidel of infidels." An interesting description considering Salman was supposed to be Christian. Still, each time Brandon tried to talk to him about the Lord, Salman insisted that he already knew.

As Salman read, Brandon looked back out over the city from their vantage point high atop the wall. A wall that, according to Salman, had been built by Alexander the Great around 300 B.C. It was a million-dollar view of the city and harbor beyond. A million-dollar view that he and the Kurdish children had for free.

"Of course ... this is nothing."

Brandon turned to Salman as he handed him back the Bible. "What's nothing?"

Salman shrugged. "Christians, they have been martyred and killed in my country for hundreds of years. Remember what I was telling you about the Imperial Cult?"

"The religion forcing everyone to worship Caesar?"

"It lasted two hundred fifty years."

"That long?"

Salman nodded, pouring a half-dozen sunflower seeds into his mouth. "And the very first martyr to give his life in Asia, he was killed right here on this hill."

"Seriously?"

"Yes, of course, right here. His name, it was Polycarp. Surely you have heard of him?"

Brandon shook his head.

"His death, it is most famous." Brandon didn't answer and Salman continued, a little incredulous. "Your father he was a preacher, and you do not know this story?"

Suddenly, Brandon felt a little stupid. Truth be told, other than the Bible, he knew next to nothing about Christian history. But as Salman repositioned himself, and poured a few more seeds into his mouth, he had a feeling that some of that was about to change ...

"The year, it was A.D. 156. And the Imperial Cult, they are after Polycarp in a bad way. He is eighty-six years old and as bishop of this church, he was ordained by none other than Saint John himself."

Brandon nodded. Once again he was impressed at the country's rich history.

Salman spit out a couple shells and continued. "His congregation, they insist Polycarp flee the city for his life. Reluctantly, he obeys their wishes, but his location, it is soon found out. And instead of trying to get away, he stays. In fact, he offers the arresting officers food and drink.

"Later, as they drive him back to the city in their carriage, they beg him to change his mind and vow allegiance to the emperor. But he refuses. When they arrive, they take him to the amphitheater to meet the governor just on the side of this hill."

"This hill, here?" Brandon repeated.

"Yes, yes, of course. Anyways, the governor, he orders Polycarp to deny Christ. 'Have respect for your old age,' he says. 'Swear allegiance to Caesar and denounce Christ, then I will release you.'"

Salman paused to drop a few more seeds into his mouth and to no doubt create more suspense.

Brandon fell for it. "Well, what happened? What did Polycarp do?"

"This story, I do not believe you do not know it."

"Will you tell me what happened?"

"I thought everybody—"

"Tell me."

Salman couldn't hide his amusement. He spit out some shells, then continued. "Polycarp, he says, 'For eighty-six years I have been Christ's servant, and he has never done me wrong. How can I blaspheme my king, who has saved me?'

"And the governor, he says, 'I have wild animals I will throw you to.'

"And Polycarp says, 'Bring them on.'

"Now the governor, he sees Polycarp is not afraid so he says, 'If you are not afraid of my animals, then I will burn you by fire.'

"Meanwhile, the Jews inside, they are really getting hot under the collar, so they race to the gates screaming to the crowd outside, 'Polycarp is a Christian, Polycarp is a Christian, Polycarp is a Christian!' And the crowd, they yell back, 'Burn him! Burn him! Burn him!'"

Salman paused to drop a couple more seeds into his mouth.

"And?" Brandon asked.

"The governor, he agrees. But Polycarp, he says he doesn't need to be lashed to a stake. He says all they have to do is tie his hands, and he will remain in the fire. So they do. They tie his hands, put wood all around him, and light the fire. And Polycarp, he doesn't cry, he doesn't scream, all he does is shout to God, 'I thank You that You have thought me worthy to share the cup of Christ among Your witnesses!'"

"So he was burned to death?" Brandon asked.

"No . . . not yet. The wind keeps blowing the flames away from him. He feels the heat, but the flames will not kill him. The pain, it must be unbearable, yet eyewitnesses say he had a look of joy on his face until the end."

Brandon ventured, "And the end came—"

"—when a soldier finally runs him through with a sword." Salman said nothing more.

There was no sound, only the hot wind blowing up the hill and through the coastal pines overhead. The story had unnerved Brandon. This was not the "happily ever after" gospel he'd been taught in Sunday school. Why hadn't Polycarp gotten away? Why didn't the governor suddenly have a change of heart or be converted? And why the long, lingering death?

Something was wrong. This was not the good-times, trust-God-to-fulfill-our-American-dream message that Brandon had heard from his father's pulpit all of his life. This was a faith where people gave up their lives. It wasn't a faith where they recited the magic words and cruised to heaven. Yes, there was salvation, yes, it was free . . . but it wasn't cheap. It cost Christ his life, and it cost these people theirs.

Of course there was joy, Polycarp had it even as the fire surrounded him . . . but the fire still surrounded him.

And he was still killed.

Was the church ready to hear of such a thing? If, God forbid, persecution ever returned, was the bride prepared to give up everything for Him?

Was *he?*

Was Sarah? In all of his excitement to share the gospel with her, had he forgotten to mention the fine print . . . that to live Christ's life, she may have to die?

Brandon looked back down at the Bible.

> Be faithful, even to the point of death, and I will give you the crown of life. He who has an ear, let him hear what the Spirit says to the churches. He who overcomes will not be hurt at all by the second death.

For Brandon, the first two messages had been revolutionary . . .

If the church in Ephesus wanted to maintain their lampstand they had to return to their first love. If the church of Smyrna wanted the crown of life they would have to be faithful even to the point of death.

But there was more. As radical as these first two messages were for Brandon, he could only guess what the next five would contain . . .

"So you believe that this Heylel, that he's some sort of . . . spirit?"

Sarah toyed with her soda straw as she sat at a wrought iron table next to the Cartel's lap pool. "I'm not certain," she said, "but it's a possibility we have to consider." She looked up, searching Lucas's eyes for any sign of ridicule. There was none. There never was. Just the deep thoughtfulness and consideration she had grown to expect.

And there was something else . . . the connection. She'd felt it the first time they'd spoken in the hallway. And, over the past three and a half weeks, it did nothing but grow each time they met. Which they did, frequently, but only if it applied to business. That was Sarah's unspoken code of ethics, the perimeter of defense she'd built around herself. With what she felt stirring inside of her, she needed a defense. But it didn't stop her from wondering what would have happened if they had met just a year earlier.

He cleared his throat. "And as a scientist, by using the word *spirit* you mean . . . ?"

It was a good question, his questions always were. She took a breath and began to explain. "As you know, there is growing scientific evidence to support what you and I would call the supernatural. You've no doubt seen the results of some of the tests I've run on Eric."

"Yes, I have, and they have been most impressive."

"But it doesn't stop there. Many physicists and mathematicians agree there is evidence that our universe does not end with three dimensions."

He looked on, waiting for more.

"There are several mathematical models that point to at least eleven dimensions, probably more."

"And the reason we do not see these dimensions?"

"Lower dimensions can never see higher dimensions."

"How convenient." It was a good-natured tease and she appreciated the camaraderie. But she also rose to the occasion. She took the straw she'd been holding and laid it on the table.

"If this straw was a two-dimensional creature living on this table, it would understand length"—she indicated the length of the table—"and it would understand width." She motioned to the width. "But it would have no idea of depth, of up and down, since up and down doesn't exist in its world. In fact it would see none of this." She motioned to the rest of the room.

"Nor would it see us," Lucas added.

"Exactly." She took the straw's wrapper and laid it on one side of the straw. "No matter how many walls it built around itself"—she took a napkin and laid it on the other side—"we could still see it."

"Since it doesn't know there is any '*above*' to build a roof over itself."

"Precisely." She lowered her face closer to the straw. "And no matter how close we got, it would never know we were here."

"Unless?" Lucas asked.

"Unless we moved something that it could see in its own dimension." She blew the paper out of the way.

Lucas stared at the paper, slowly formulating his thought. "And you believe that Eric is starting to see into these other dimensions?"

"Yes. I believe that somehow your DNA experiment has made his nervous system more susceptible to their influence."

"*Their* influence."

"The spirits . . . the inhabitants of this other dimension."

"But is that so wrong?"

"Not if they're the good guys."

"Good guys . . . you mean like angels?"

Sarah nodded. "Unfortunately there are other inhabitants of that world . . ."

Lucas listened intently.

"Judaism, Christianity, other religions—many acknowledge their existence and have names for them. Our culture calls them . . . *demons*."

Lucas frowned. "And you believe that this is what Heylel may be?"

"I'm not sure, but I think in a few days we'll need to find out."

"But he's been so helpful, so generous."

"I understand."

"So much of what we have been able to accomplish has been through his counsel."

Sarah waited as Lucas explored the idea. It was a lot to digest at one time, but if any man was capable of doing so in an intelligent and unbiased manner, he was the one. As she watched, she again found herself wondering what would have happened if she'd have connected earlier with a man of such strength and maturity, a man who knew exactly who he was and where he was going ... instead of someone so young who, although incredibly kind and compassionate, was still ... so young.

She pushed the thought out of her mind as she had a hundred other times. But, as always, it came back. Initially, she had tried to replace it with memories of Brandon. She'd even tried to pray them away. It helped some, but when it came to praying to a God that, at times, she barely understood, or daydreaming about one of the most dynamic men in the world, well, there was little contest.

"What do you propose we do?"

She glanced up, momentarily forgetting where they were. "I, uh, we've already completed the psychological aspects of his testing. In just a few days we will be through with the physiological as well."

"And then?"

"Then I'd like to move toward the spiritual. I'd like to speak with Heylel directly. I'd like to convince him to reveal more of his identity."

"Many of us have tried."

"I appreciate that, and I may be equally as unsuccessful. But my experience in these areas might give me a slight advantage."

Lucas nodded quietly.

Sarah took a deep breath and let it out. The meeting had been more taxing than she had anticipated. Then again, she was always nervous with Lucas. She glanced back up and caught him smiling at her.

"What?" she asked self-consciously.

"I appreciate your candidness, Doctor. Many would be reluctant to openly voice such opinions, especially ones of such unconventional nature."

Sarah caught herself tugging at her hair and stopped. "And that's all they are," she emphasized. "Opinions."

"For now."

"Yes, for now."

He remained smiling.

Realizing the meeting had come to an end, Sarah reached down and gathered her papers. "Well, then, that's the direction we'll pursue." She started to rise. "I'll let you get back to work now and—"

"Please." He motioned for her to sit. "I have one other area to discuss with you. If you have the time."

"If *I* have the time? Well, yes, certainly." She sat back down.

"As you know, the Cartel is in the final stages of bringing together the world powers. In a matter of days, and for the first time in history, we may have finally secured world peace."

"A remarkable accomplishment. And as their chairman, you should be quite proud."

Lucas shrugged off the compliment. "A figurehead, that's all I am." Before she could disagree, he continued. "Your work has proven very interesting these past several weeks."

"Thank you."

"And this business of bringing science and the supernatural together is quite intriguing. I'm wondering if it wouldn't be prudent for us to investigate a similar union here at the Cartel. As we enter this new paradigm of history, many things will change. Perhaps it would be well to create our own department bringing these two disciplines together. And what person would be better to head it up than yourself?"

Sarah chuckled. "Is the chairman offering me a job?"

He looked at her, his intense eyes making her feel a little uneasy at the joke. A little uneasy and a lot weak. He spoke quietly. "I know your clinic has closed."

"How did you know that?"

"It is my job to know everything ... especially concerning the people I care about." He hesitated, appearing uncertain if he should go on. "And I care about you, Sarah. By now, you must know I care about you very much."

Sarah's heart stopped. Everything froze as she tried to grasp what she'd just heard. She opened her mouth, but no words would come. She tried moving her lips. Nothing happened. Then, as always, Lucas, the gracious and understanding one, came to the rescue.

"I am sorry. I have embarrassed you."

"No, that's—"

"I was out of line. Thinking only of myself. Please forgive me." For the first time she could remember, he seemed flustered, unsure. "I don't know what I was thinking. It is just ..." He leaned forward, staring at his palms. "In my position, there are so few people that I trust, that I can confide in." He paused, then continued. "And sometimes, ever since Julia died, sometimes this loneliness—" He glanced up and saw her discomfort. "Ah, but I have done it again. Please, please, I apologize. What you must think of me. And you, a married woman with such deep convictions. Please, accept my apologies. I don't know what I was thinking. When it comes to world powers, I have a good understanding. But these matters of the heart, I guess they'll always be foreign to me."

Sarah looked on, stunned and moved. The more he struggled, the more endearing he became. Here was a major world power, suave, sophisticated, countries bowing at his feet, yet he had suddenly turned to jelly when speaking from his heart. A heart that had apparently placed much of its affections upon her.

He shook his head, unable to look at her. "I am sorry."

"No." She cleared the hoarseness from her throat. "That's okay. Really."

He continued shaking his head.

"Lucas?" He looked up. There were those eyes again. For a moment she forgot to breathe. "Don't worry about it. I'm not offended. Actually, it's quite a compliment." She reached down and regathered her things, preparing to leave. "Most women would consider it an honor." Somehow she was able to rise to her feet and actually stand. "But you're right, I am a married woman and I am committed to my husband."

"Certainly." Lucas also rose to his feet. "I understand completely. Believe me."

She smiled. "I do believe you."

He nodded, but kept his eyes riveted on hers.

"Well." Again she cleared her throat as she checked her papers. "If I have your permission then, when we finish Eric's neurological tests, we'll change gears to see if there's anything spiritual."

"Yes, certainly, whatever you think is best."

"Good." She shifted the papers to her other hand and suddenly reached out to shake his. It was an odd gesture, a little clumsy, but it was the best she could think of considering the circumstances. "Well then, good afternoon, Lucas."

He took her hand and they shook. "Good afternoon."

She moved past him. She heard the click of her pumps against the marble tile, and knew she was making progress toward the glass doors, but she wasn't sure how. He was still staring, she sensed it. She arrived, pushed open the doors, and stepped into the main building. Somehow she was able to continue forward.

Brandon had been ravenous. And the lunch of cheese, flat bread, cucumbers sprinkled with lemon juice, and a large bowl of yogurt with a glob of unprocessed honey plopped in the middle was a welcomed feast. Once again the food came compliments of Salman's swift tongue. This time he'd convinced the restaurant owner that it would bring him great fortune to feed the "holy man and his disciple." That had been half an hour ago. After that, word quickly spread through the city of Bergama. Now it seemed every time Brandon glanced up from their sidewalk table he caught more faces staring at him. Concerned faces. He'd smiled politely, then did his best to ignore them. And still the crowd continued to grow.

A thousand feet above them on a mountaintop overlooking the city stood another acropolis. It had once been called Pergamum and was the address of the third letter. Of all the locations so far, this one made him the most nervous. He wasn't entirely sure why, though he suspected much of it had to do with Jesus Christ calling it "the throne of Satan."

"Some more drink?" Salman held out a bottle of sweet cherry juice, a favorite of Turks. Brandon shook his head and watched as the young man set it down and refilled his glass from another bottle. Its blue and white label read "Raki." It was also a favorite, but with a bit more kick—a forty-five-proof kick, to be exact.

"I'm still not sure how you pulled this off," Brandon said, marveling at the food before him.

"Take a look around you, my friend. We are in the Bakir Valley—the most fertile in all of Turkey. Nowhere in the world do they grow finer tobacco or cotton."

"But what's that got to do with—"

"Their livelihood, it depends upon farming. And the drought, it is wiping them out."

Brandon looked back up at the faces. "But what's that got to do with me?"

"Mr. Brandon, you're the man who called down this drought."

"What?"

"Please, I saw it on TV—'My anger and fury will be poured out on the trees of the field and the fruit of the ground and it will burn and not be quenched.'"

"But that didn't necessarily mean—"

"So if you can call down a drought from heaven, then you can call it back up and make it rain again." He leaned forward with a smile. "As long as they don't make you too angry."

"Is that what you're telling them?"

Salman shrugged and broke into a grin.

Now the anxiety on their faces made sense. So did the growing crowd. "Salman, I didn't—"

"Well, looky who we have here."

He glanced up and saw Tanya Chase approaching. Looming beside her, his hands stuffed into his pockets and looking miserable in the heat, was her sullen and balding cameraman, the one from L.A.

"We figured you'd show up," Tanya said as she peeled off a 500,000 lira bill, amounting to about two U.S. dollars, and handed it to the boy who had brought her. "It was just a matter of time." She pulled up a chair and joined them. The cameraman followed suit. "You remember Jerry, don't you?"

Brandon and the cameraman exchanged nods.

"Waiter, waiter." She motioned to Salman's glass. "I'll have whatever he's having. Oh, and one of those cheese and honey desert things." She turned to Salman. "What are they called?"

Struck by her beauty and her boldness, Salman was only too happy to be of assistance. "*Hershmalem*. It is called *Hershmalem*."

"Yeah," Tanya called, "one of those *Hersh*-whatevers."

"Make that two," Jerry muttered.

The waiter nodded and disappeared into the crowd. Brandon watched as Tanya reached for an olive on his plate. "How did you find me?" he asked.

"We knew you'd gone to Turkey. Figured it wasn't exactly a family vacation, with your wife leaving you and all."

Brandon ignored the barb.

"Hometown rumor has it you fancy yourself one of the two witnesses in Revelation. So ..." She reached for another olive. "Doing our best to think like a delusionist, we figured you'd head for Patmos, the island where the book was written. When you were a no-show there, Jerry here guessed you'd be hitting the seven churches." She glanced at her cameraman. "Nice work."

He shrugged and said nothing.

She glanced around the sidewalk. "You seem to be drawing quite a crowd."

Brandon did his best to keep his voice steady. "What do you want from me?"

"I'm just a reporter after a story."

"Haven't you done enough damage already?"

"*Me?* Haven't *I* done enough damage? Look around you, Brandon. Look at all these people suffering. And not just them. What about the thousands that have been killed in the Pacific Northwest? What do you have to say to—"

"Wait a minute. What thousands?"

"Don't tell me you haven't heard? The volcanoes. Baker and Hood, they've both gone off. Washington and Oregon look like war zones. Twelve thousand dead and counting. And Mount Bandai is getting ready to blow in Japan."

"And you think . . . I'm responsible?"

"You tell me. That's why I'm here. And while you're at it, maybe you can explain again why you believe this God of yours, who's supposed to be an all-merciful, loving Father, has reduced Himself to the level of throwing cosmic temper tantrums."

Brandon blinked in surprise. But before he could respond, a little girl's scream suddenly cut through the din of the sidewalk and traffic. Another followed. People turned, looking across the cobblestone road toward the plaza on the other side.

There was another cry, only this one was from a woman.

Other guests at surrounding tables rose, stretching their necks for a look. The screaming continued.

"What is it?" Brandon asked as he stood, trying to see. "What's going on?"

Then he spotted her across the street. A young mother was being held by two other women as she shouted and pointed. Twenty, maybe thirty feet beyond, pressed against the base of an Ataturk statue, was her two-year-old daughter. She was screaming in terror at the fifty-pound mongrel crouched in front of her, snarling. And the more she screamed, the more incensed the dog became.

"He's rabid!" Salman said.

"What?"

"Look at the foam. The dog, he has rabies."

Now Brandon saw it, the white foam frothing and falling from the animal's lips. For the briefest second he wanted to move to action, to try and help. But he felt a check in his spirit. Something told him to be still and to simply watch.

Those closest to the plaza began backing away. Some crowded into the safety of doorways. An older gentleman was doing his best to ease the hysterical mother away.

But the dog saw none of it. His attention was focused only upon the little girl and her awful noise.

A handful of men, four to five, began shouting. They stepped out from the crowd, waving their arms, their hats, doing anything they could to draw the animal's attention. But the girl's cries were too loud, too immediate. The men moved closer, pleading with her to be calm, to be quiet, but she would have none of it. She started toward one of them. The dog immediately crouched, ready to spring. The man shouted for her to stop and she froze, still crying.

Another yelled and started running toward the animal. He came within ten feet before the dog saw him and spun around. The distraction worked, but only for a moment. Because as the man veered off for safety, the little girl's cries drew the dog's attention back to her.

Another one tried. Approaching slower. Shouting louder. Waving his arms until he caught the animal's attention. The dog turned and the man ran. But again the little girl's cries focused the animal's attention back on her. It crouched lower, snarling at the insufferable noise.

Others, near the safety of doorways or behind open windows, shouted and hollered, but they were too far away. The animal was focused only upon the girl, when suddenly—

"Sevim!"

Heads jerked around to see another man running toward the plaza. He was a farmer, dressed in dark clothes, racing directly for the animal.

"Sevim!" It was obviously her name. He shouted other things in Turkish that Brandon did not understand.

"What's he saying?"

"He is the father," Salman explained.

"Sevim!"

The crowd murmured as the man raced across the dead grass and dirt of the plaza. By the look of things he had no intention of stopping.

"What's he going to do?" Tanya yelled. "Is he crazy?"

Salman's response was the same. "He is the father."

The man closed the remaining distance. The dog spun toward him snarling, white froth dripping from its fangs. But, before it could attack, the man leaped at the beast with a ferocious cry.

The dog was strong, fifty pounds of crazed muscle— lunging and biting, clawing and tearing. But the father fought relentlessly, crying out in pain and rage, as he tried to grab the animal's head.

The crowd watched in horror and fascination.

And still the battle continued. Snapping teeth, tearing flesh. The man's face and arms were covered in blood. Some of the others worked in closer, hoping to snatch away the little girl. But it was still too dangerous.

The snarling changed to gasps and grunts as the father wrapped his bleeding arms around the animal's chest and began to squeeze. If he couldn't break its neck, then he would crush it to death.

The dog yelped and writhed, twisting its head, lunging for the father's face, but the man continued to squeeze. With superhuman strength he began breaking ribs, crying in rage until he let the animal slip a foot between his arms, then grabbed its head and lathering muzzle and jerked it hard to the right.

The dog went limp and dropped to the ground.

The little girl shouted and started toward him, but she was immediately swept up by the surrounding men.

Chest heaving, dripping in sweat and blood, the father looked down at his arms, at his torn and bloody clothing, and finally at the dog that lay at his feet. He was as dazed and as astonished as anyone.

Others approached, motioning him to follow, careful not to get too close, lest they, too, become infected by the saliva.

"Did you see it?" Tanya turned in amazement to Brandon and Salman. "Did you see what he did? How he risked his life?"

Salman nodded. "He is the father."

"Such love, such anger. I've never seen anything like it. No one else would get in there. But he did. And did you see what he did to that animal?"

"It was about to destroy his child."

"Yes, but such passion . . . and rage."

"He is the father."

As Brandon watched the scene, his understanding grew. God's anger, His wrath had nothing to do with the throwing of what Tanya had called temper tantrums. Instead, it had everything to do with His love, with His overwhelming passion for His children. Instead of petty rage, it had everything to do with awesome love . . . and with destroying the very thing that was destroying those He loved. Because, as Salman had so clearly put it:

"He is the Father."

CHAPTER 11

Dearest Sarah,

I'm constantly amazed at how great God's love is. It seems every time I turn around I see it appearing in deeper ways. Of course I'm clueless about how to use all this information to "warn the bride." Then again it's better I don't know or I'd probably freak. I guess not knowing is just another part of that love.

What you said about Eric's EEG doesn't sound good. If strong delta waves are what demoniacs and psychics experience during their trances . . . and if that's what Eric's brain is doing *when Heylel is around, then I think it's pretty clear we're talking possession. As a Christian it shouldn't be a problem for you to send him running . . . if that's what Eric wants. But if he doesn't, that's a whole 'nother ball game. Let me know what happens.*

Is the heat as unbearable where you are as it is here? And the pollution from those volcanoes—the sky here is getting so thick with haze that it's almost impossible to see the mountains just across the valley.

I miss you, Sarah. Not a moment goes by that I don't think of you. Sometimes it's in the way I hear a person laugh, or see them tilt their head, or when I watch other couples together. It's like you're everywhere. Everything speaks of you and reminds me how much I want for us to be together. Of course I wish you would write more, but I understand when you say you're so busy. But not forever. Soon we'll be back in each other's arms, and we'll never let each other go again. I look forward to that moment with all of my heart and with all of my soul.

Yours forever,
Brandon

Sarah closed the lid to her laptop computer. Of course he was right about Eric. The kid was displaying typical signs of demon possession. Well, not quite so typical. Because this Heylel, or whoever he was, was not displaying typical signs of being a demon. The profound insights he was sharing with the Cartel, the intense visions he was giving the child . . . these were not normal for what she'd confronted in the past. Still, everything else pointed in that direction . . . and she knew what course must now be taken.

Then there were Brandon's comments about the drought and the volcanoes. Who knew what effect the millions of tons of contaminants in the atmosphere would have? At one point a third of the world had reported "darkness at noon." And it was anyone's guess how those pollutants would affect the rest of the ecosystem. People were already complaining about water so bitter that it was unfit to drink. And it would only get worse.

But neither of these issues weighed as heavily upon Sarah as the other. She sighed wearily as she snapped off the computer and walked barefoot across the worn pine floor to her dresser. She slid open the top drawer and looked at Brandon's neatly folded shirt. She reached down and unfolded it. As always, the women of the compound had done an excellent job washing the clothes. Every morning they left for the river with baskets full of dirty laundry. And every afternoon they returned with wonderfully clean and fresh-smelling clothes.

She pressed the shirt to her face and drew in a deep breath. There was only the smell of soap and fresh water now. No trace of Brandon remained. She felt the burning in her eyes. The tears happened almost nightly now. She peeled off her clothes, letting them drop to the floor, and slipped into his shirt. She crossed toward the bed, holding one of the sleeves to her face. There was nothing at all.

She curled up under the blankets. It was late, but sleep would not come. The knot in her stomach and the heaviness in her chest made that impossible. The last thing in the world she wanted to do was hurt him. He was such a good kid, so committed, so loyal. But that was the problem, he was a kid.

And Lucas Ponte was a man.

She rolled onto her side, pulling the spare pillow into her and clutching it tightly.

To the angel of the church in Pergamum write:
These are the words of him who has the sharp, double-edged sword. I know where you live—where Satan has his throne. Yet you remain true to my name. You did not renounce your faith in me, even in the days of Antipas, my faithful witness, who was put to death in your city—where Satan lives.

Nevertheless, I have a few things against you: You have people there who hold to the teaching of Balaam, who taught Balak to entice the Israelites to sin by eating food sacrificed to idols and by committing sexual immorality. Likewise you also have those who hold to the teaching of the Nicolaitans. Repent therefore! Otherwise, I will soon come to you and will fight against them with the sword of my mouth.

He who has an ear, let him hear what the Spirit says to the churches. To him who overcomes, I will give some of the hidden manna. I will also give him a white stone with a new name written on it, known only to him who receives it.

Brandon woke within the ruins of a large round room. There was no sound, just crickets and a soft wind blowing across the dry grass of the Bakir Valley. The moon was nearly full, but because of the smoke high in the atmosphere, it produced a red hue that gave an eerie glow to the crumbling walls above him. He rose up on one elbow and spotted Salman sleeping a few yards away. At first he didn't understand why the man slept curled on the dirt with no blanket to soften the hard ground . . . until he looked down and saw that he was sleeping on two.

Earlier, Brandon had complained about the rocky ground, and Salman had offered him his blanket. Of course Brandon had refused. But after he had fallen asleep, it appeared that Salman had stolen over and somehow slipped it under him. Brandon smiled. The greatness of the man's heart continually surprised him.

It had been Salman's idea for the two of them to sleep here at the Sanctuary of Asclepion, just a couple miles below the main acropolis. "It was one of the main healing centers of the world," he had said. "Named after the 'healing god.'" He'd given Brandon a wink. "Something you can relate to, I am sure."

It was also upon Salman's insistence that Brandon had agreed to sleep inside the remains of this treatment center, or dream house. "It is where the patients used to sleep," he'd said. "It is where they waited for Asclepion to give them dreams for the priests to analyze."

Although Brandon wasn't superstitious, he wasn't crazy about sleeping in the remains of some building once used for occult practices. But, between arguing with Tanya—who kept wanting to chronicle his pilgrimage "for the folks back home"—and visiting the mind-boggling sights up on the acropolis earlier that afternoon, Brandon had little energy to argue.

Yet now he was wide awake.

When sleep showed no promise of returning, he rose and stepped out of the ruins. High above he could see the acropolis hovering in the distance, its white marble pillars glowing crimson in the moonlight.

"Where Satan has his throne," that's what Christ had said of the area. But what did that mean? And where was this throne? Brandon had been up on that hill all afternoon but hadn't found an answer. Nor did he receive any further insights into the letter. Maybe that's why he was unable to sleep. And maybe that's why he had this sudden compulsion to return. Without the noise of tourists, the incessant chattering of Salman, or the scrutiny of Tanya and her cameraman, maybe now he could learn something.

It would take less than an hour to climb back up to the top. The night, although bathed in the moon's unearthly red glow, was peaceful, and the solitude would be a good time for waiting upon the Lord. Although, even as he started forward, Brandon nervously wondered what time would ever be good for visiting Satan's throne.

"Dr. Martus . . . Dr. Martus, over here!"

Sarah looked up from her papers to see one of Lucas's aides motioning to her. The pressroom bustled with noise and confusion as members of the Cartel and other significant figures took their position onstage. Last-minute adjustments were being made to lights, makeup, and the pleats on the navy blue backdrop curtain. The reason? Less than an hour ago the Cartel's scientific team in Brussels had found the cure to Scorpion.

Now they were about to make it public.

"Dr. Martus . . ." The aide continued motioning for her to join them.

Sarah glanced to the other distinguished members taking the stage, then turned back to him and shook her head. He'd obviously made a mistake; she had no business being in their company.

She returned to the report that had been thrust into her hands, a copy of the preliminary findings. Although viral diseases were definitely out of her field, from what she understood, the results looked very promising. No wonder everyone was so excited.

"Dr. Martus . . ." It was Ponte's voice. Her head jerked up, and she saw him standing on the back riser, motioning for her to join them.

She pointed to herself. "Me?"

"Come, come," he called, "you're part of this, too."

She hesitated, not understanding.

"Carlos, Deena," he called to his aides, "please help Dr. Martus up here."

A moment later Sarah was being guided through the crowd and up onto the platform.

"Over here." It was Lucas again. "Please, bring her here, beside me."

The crowd parted, not without a few raised eyebrows. Sarah felt her ears growing warm as she moved up the risers, until she was standing beside the grinning Lucas.

"What do you think?" he asked, referring to the report in her hands.

"From what I can tell it looks great."

His grin broadened. "Good, good . . ."

"All right, everybody, if I may have your attention, please?" It was the press secretary, a short man with a nasal voice. He was clapping his hands and calling from below. "May I have your attention. If everyone would look this way, please?"

Sarah and the group turned toward him. He was surrounded by a small battalion of video and still photographers. Lights blazed as cameras whirred and clicked. Instinctively, Sarah's hand rose to tug on her hair, but just as quickly Lucas reached out, took it, and gently brought it down to her side. She shot him a quick look of gratitude, but he did not respond. Instead, he continued posing and smiling for the cameras. He was, however, doing something else. Hidden by the others in front of them, he continued to hold Sarah's hand.

And she did not withdraw it.

The climb was steep, but Brandon made good time. In fact, he was surprised at how quickly he'd arrived. Unfortunately, that wasn't his only surprise. He'd not quite crested to the top of the hill when he heard rustling in the grass behind him. But it was more than rustling. It sounded like rushing water. Lots of it. He threw a look over his shoulder and saw that the entire hillside below him was now alive with snakes. Millions of them . . . slithering through the grass, crawling over rocks, and swarming across the broken ruins. He knew they weren't real. They couldn't be. At least not real in the physical sense. It was a vision, like so many he used to have—back when heaven had first called him, back when hell had used every power at its disposal to stop him. But, vision or not, it was just as frightening. And, on another level, just as real.

They came from the Asclepion healing center he'd just left. He suspected they represented the snakes the people there had worshiped as part of their healing. He didn't know if they were poisonous. He wasn't sticking around to find out. Although tired and winded from his climb, he picked up his pace.

As he stumbled up to the top of the hill, the first ruins to come into view was the Altar of Zeus. Only now it was no longer ruins. Instead of five rows of broken steps leading to rocks and grass, it was now a magnificent altar with dozens of polished marble stairs along with intricately carved reliefs, columns, and statues. And there, standing at the top, directly behind the altar, was a dazzling bright form of a man at least ten feet tall.

He radiated such power that, at first, Brandon thought it might be another vision of Christ. Or at least an angel. He glanced over his shoulder. The snakes continued their approach up the hill. Maybe the creature would stop them, maybe it would protect him. But as Brandon turned back to him, he noticed the eyes. They burned like Christ's, but instead of burning with love, the flames flickered and leaped with hate.

Brandon continued to run, veering to the right to give the thing a wide berth. That's when it roared, shaking the very ground under his feet. He stole a quick look over his shoulder and to his horror saw that the creature had started down the altar steps. And there was only one place it was going . . . after him!

Already exhausted from the climb, he forced himself to keep running. He staggered up a slight knoll and entered the large flat area that Salman had described earlier that afternoon as the Sanctuary of Athena, the goddess of wisdom and war. But instead of the broken pillars overrun with grass and shrubs that he'd previously seen, there was now a giant two-story marble building and gate. And exiting that gate, heading straight toward him, was another figure of light, almost as tall, but female. In her arms she carried several books. Her mouth did not move, but he could sense her calling out to him. There were no words, but he felt an incredible attraction to her. A powerful impulse to sit down and discuss what was happening, to search the books she was holding for some clue, to put their heads together and try to reason out what was going on.

But this was not the time for sitting and reasoning. The snakes were gaining on him; so was the creature from Zeus's altar. He darted around her to the left ... and a moment later she, too, had joined in the pursuit.

Up ahead was where the library had once been. Salman had said it had contained two hundred thousand scrolls. When it was standing it was the second largest library in the world. Well, it was standing now. And as far as Brandon could see, there were no glowing giants or slithering snakes anywhere around it. That was good enough for him. Near exhaustion and gasping for breath, he staggered toward it hoping to find someplace inside to hide and rest.

He arrived and entered the first room of the massive building. That's when he heard the voices. At first only two. They came from the shelves. No, they came from the scrolls on the shelves. He didn't understand the language, but they were murmuring, as if alive. Others joined in. He sensed they were giving opinions, advice. Soon there was a dozen—each trying to be heard above the other.

With legs turning to rubber, he stumbled through the dimly lit room. The voices grew in number, hundreds of them now, coming to life as he passed the shelves, shouting at him, yelling at him, desperate to be heard.

He entered a second room. More voices. Growing to a roar. Deafening. He covered his ears. He had to get out. He couldn't think. He forced his legs to keep moving, but they no longer had feeling. His lungs burned for air. Off to the side, he spotted the red glow of moonlight. It was coming through a distant doorway. He headed for it, staggering, stumbling, fighting to keep his balance until, finally, he burst outside into the night air.

He could go no further. He had to stop and lean over, to fill his lungs, to regain his strength. The voices faded only slightly, but even that was a relief. So many attacks on so many fronts. *Why, God?* he prayed. *What's going on?* Glancing up he saw he was standing on the top row of a huge amphitheater. Just beyond, off to the right, was the temple of Bacchus, the wine god. *Tell me, what are You trying to say?*

Suddenly he felt his spirit quicken, his understanding expand . . .

This is exactly what the people of Pergamum had faced every day of their lives. The occult practices of Asclepion, the hostile Greek and Roman religions, the spiritual warfare, the intellectual reasonings, the overwhelming information—all constantly attacking their minds and their spirits. And when the assault was too much—Brandon looked down to the theater and over to the temple of Bacchus—they had plenty of diversions to distract and numb the pain.

> I know where you live—where Satan has his throne. Yet you remain true to my name. You did not renounce your faith in me . . .

What faith these Christians must have had. To withstand so many attacks on so many levels. And yet—his mind focused more sharply—wasn't that exactly what the church of today faced? Today, in this age of information with all of its truths and science and spirituality? So much information attacking from every side. And so many opportunities to throw up our hands, to give up, to quit the fight and zone out with the world's diversions. Although separated by nearly two millenniums, the cultures suddenly appeared identical.

Amidst such assault how could either culture distinguish the difference between truth and error? Amidst such cacophony, how could anyone hear, let alone discern, that still, small voice of God?

And yet, didn't our culture have at least one advantage? Brandon turned his head toward the Temple of Trajan that loomed above and to his right. As the center of the Imperial Cult, it was the crowning masterpiece of the acropolis and towered over the entire valley, making it clear where the ultimate power and authority lay. At least Christians today didn't have to worry about the totalitarian government that Salman had described. At least they didn't have to worry about worshiping a one-world dictator.

The thought had barely registered before he heard the snakes. They'd rounded the library and were rushing toward him in a giant wave. From the other side came Athena with her pleas for reason, and behind her, Zeus with his thundering demands.

There was no place to go. It was either down into the theater or up to the Temple of Trajan. He'd known since Ephesus that his future involved a large arena, but he also knew that it wasn't now. He turned to his right and scrambled up the rocky remains toward the temple.

And that's when the rules changed . . .

He'd barely reached the temple with its moonlit, blood-red pillars, when an unearthly cry spun him around. To his astonishment, he saw the snakes engulfing Zeus. But it was more than that. Zeus was also engulfing the snakes and Athena . . . as she was engulfing them. All of the creatures were coming together, joining forces, turning into one large entity—a darkness that resembled none of them separately, but all of them corporately.

Brandon watched, paralyzed with fear.

I know where you live—where Satan has his throne.

Suddenly, he understood. Satan's throne wasn't just the altar of Zeus, or Athena, or the medicine of Asclepion, or the library with its thousands of "truths." It was all of these combined. And now they had all come together, combining forces here at the center of Imperial Cult worship. As he watched, the black shadow collapsed upon itself, condensing into a denser, more tangible form . . . one he recognized immediately. It was the giant serpent head from his dreams.

It started toward him.

Brandon stepped back. "Stay away!" he cried hoarsely. "Stay back!"

It said nothing, but continued its approach. Brandon could see its tongue flickering in and out and back and forth. His thoughts raced. There had been no way to battle this thing in his dreams nor when it had appeared in his father's church. If he couldn't stop the thing then, how could he stop it now?

He struggled to remember Christ's words, his letter to the Christians here. Surely God had not left them defenseless. If this was Satan's throne, God must have given them something to fight with. But what? What could defeat all the noise, the deceptions, the falsehood? What had the letter said?

I will fight against them with the sword of my mouth.

But what did that mean?

The serpent's head closed in. It slowly opened its jaw, revealing the swirling, fiery abyss inside. An abyss that had nearly consumed him before. The wind increased. It began pulling at him, tugging at his clothes, his body, exactly as it had in the church. Desperately, he looked for an escape, but it was already cornering him against the back wall of the temple.

His mind churned, running the phrase: *Sword of my mouth, sword of my mouth, sword of my mouth*. He recalled the small, double-edged sword he'd seen inside Christ's mouth at the hospital. The one that had replaced His tongue. It was a scary image, almost obscene, but now . . .

The sword, the sword . . . Wait. A verse was coming to mind. One of those he hated memorizing back in Sunday school. *"The Word is sharper than any double-edged sword . . . able to divide, to divide—"* He couldn't remember the rest, but that was enough.

The mouth was a dozen feet away now. Its jaw unhinged, opening even wider. Now there was nothing but fire. Fire and wind screaming in Brandon's ears, trying to pull him in.

Other memories of other confrontations raced through his mind. What had other people done? What had Jesus—

He remembered the battle between Jesus and Satan. In the wilderness. It had been one of his dad's favorite stories. How the most evil force of the universe fought the Creator of the universe. Not with guns or bombs—they hadn't even tried to nuke each other. Instead, these two powerful forces of the universe battled with the most powerful weapon of the universe: They quoted God's Word. Wielding it back and forth, like swords, like—

That was it! That was the sword of Christ's mouth, His Word!

Even in L.A., wasn't that how he'd silenced Jimmy Tyler? Not with *his* words, but with *God's*. And maybe that's what was bringing God's judgments down on the world now. Not what Brandon had said up there on that stage, but what God had said through him. That's where the power was. That's the weapon that had been given them!

Brandon reached into his back pocket for the New Testament. He'd barely touched it before he heard the scream.

"Nooooo!"

He looked up. The head had stopped its approach. He finished pulling out the Bible and with trembling hands opened it—somewhere, anywhere, it didn't matter. But, even as he did, he noticed the wind beginning to subside.

Again he looked up. The serpent head was already beginning to lose its form, turning back into a nebulous shadow. Brandon watched, transfixed, as the shadow started to dissipate, allowing the red moonlight to penetrate it. A moment later it had turned into a fine mist, then wafted and blew until nothing more of it remained. Nothing but two words, or at least Brandon's impression of those words.

Soon . . . The voice echoed inside his head. *Very soon* . . .

And then it was gone. There was no sound, except Brandon's heavy breathing. No shadows, except those cast by the crumbled ruins. And no more majestic temples. Everything was exactly as he had seen it that afternoon with Salman.

A thousand feet below, down in the city, the first Moslem call to prayer began. Dawn was about to break. Other mosques around the city joined in until the entire valley echoed in competing calls to worship.

So many voices.

Brandon would head back down to join Salman soon enough. But for now he needed to rest. To rest and to contemplate what he'd seen. It was true. The struggles of Pergamum were no different than those of today's church. So much information, so many versions of *truth*. Both cultures had their roaring distractions. But both had an identical weapon available, not only to battle those errors, but to uncover the truth.

Because, just as surely as love was required for Ephesus, and faithfulness to death for Smyrna, so truth was required for the survival of Pergamum.

Katherine stared at the computer screen, unable to believe what she saw.

Earlier she'd pulled the system administrator's password, *Mongoose Warrior*, from her encrypted file. Then, using his name and password, she'd logged onto the system and was given free access to all files. Everything went exactly as planned. No problem . . .

Until she started reading the classified information on Scorpion. She'd already checked the Cairo and Mecca files. Now she was scrolling through the New York one. Like the others, it contained a brief log of time and events. And, although the locations and times were different, the sequence was nearly identical—particularly in regard to the "dehydration of product," "transportation of product to specified site," and "dispersal of product over site."

It was this last phrase that sent a shudder through her. With trembling fingers, Katherine brought up the fourth and final file. "Tel Aviv."

Again there were minor alterations, but the basic sequence of events was the same . . . dehydration, transportation, and finally, the dispersal of product over site.

She closed her eyes and took a deep breath. Was it possible? Here were the first four cities that Scorpion had struck. And here, before her, was a record of the Cartel producing and releasing something over those very same cities.

No. The thought was too outrageous. It had to be a coincidence. A bizarre coincidence. Her thoughts raced, exploring a thousand other options. There had to be something else, some other tie-in that could either prove or disprove the possibility. Something more that could—

Wait a minute. Dates and times. Yes, of course. The incubation period of Scorpion was between twenty-eight and thirty-one days. If she could find the date that its outbreak was first reported in each of the four cities, and compare that to the date of the product's dispersal, that would be more than enough proof.

For the briefest moment Katherine hesitated, afraid of what she would find. Then the anger kicked in. Anger over the wasted months and years. And anger over all the deceptions that she'd suspected but could never prove. Fueled by this anger and with growing resolution, she jotted down the release dates and exited the system.

A moment later, she logged onto the Internet and began her search of dates and locations.

Sarah leaned over Lucas Ponte's bathroom counter and stared into the mirror. Her face was flush from the wine and her eyes watery. "Get a hold of yourself," she whispered crossly. "Stop it. Stop it right now." She grabbed a tissue and dabbed at her eyes, careful not to smear the mascara.

The dinner had been Lucas's idea . . . part celebration, part sitting down with Katherine and Eric to lay out her beliefs about Heylel and to explain what must be done. That was the only reason she'd agreed to come to Lucas's living quarters, because Katherine and Eric would be there. But, for whatever the reason, mother and son had not shown. And, after waiting nearly an hour (and consuming two, or was it three glasses, of Chianti), they agreed to start eating dinner without them.

The dinner was excellent. Greek salad, sautéed mushrooms, veal scallopini, and more vino, lots and lots of vino. They talked about everything. And they laughed. Lucas did not bring up his feelings about her again, at least not in words, though she could see it in the hundred and one ways he was attentive to her. In fact, as best she could tell, those feelings had grown.

So had hers.

An hour didn't go by that she didn't catch herself thinking about him, about them. His sensitivity, his maturity, his power . . . who he was, and what she could have been with him.

"Stop it," she repeated. "You're a married woman. You have a husband."

She took a deep breath to clear her head, then adjusted the spaghetti straps to her dress and tugged at its hem. Why she had worn such a skimpy thing was beyond her. She turned from the mirror and with determined resolve strode across the white marble floor toward the door.

When she reentered the room she saw that Lucas was no longer sitting at the table. He had dimmed the lights and had stepped over to look out the large picture window with its moonlit view. His silhouette was impressive. That tall frame, those broad shoulders, a physique that he obviously took great care—

Stop it!

Sensing her presence, he turned. "There you are," he said. "Are you all right? I was beginning to worry."

His concern was touching. "Yes." She cleared the raspiness from her throat. "I'm fine." As she passed the table she had to briefly reach out to steady herself. There was no doubt about it; it was definitely time to be going.

Lucas turned to look back out the window. "Beautiful, isn't it?" She arrived at his side, so close they were practically touching. The mountains glowed brilliantly. The shadowed terraces spilled to the valley floor where lights from the tiny village twinkled. He continued, softer. "How could anything be more perfect?"

She quietly agreed.

"That's one of the many reasons they selected this location. Certainly not because of its easy access." He chuckled, and she felt his arm brush hers. Suddenly she was very aware of their closeness. "Though, I must say, sometimes this isolation, this loneliness ..." He took a deep breath. She felt his arm swell against hers, then deflate as he quietly sighed.

How hard it must be on him. So powerful, yet so lonely. Here was one of the mightiest men in the world, beside her, alone with her, yet having no one with whom to share his intimate thoughts. What she could do for him, how she could help—

No! You're a married woman. There's Brandon! Your vows!

She continued to stand beside him, absorbing the scenery, feeling the warmth of his presence, wondering if he felt hers. Her head was growing light as feelings of well-being and euphoria washed over her.

Your vows! That piece of paper!

But that's all it was, a piece of paper. There was no moral contract, nothing physical had taken place. Their marriage had never been consummated. In some cultures that meant it wasn't even legal. Could she really be considered unfaithful? Unfaithful to what? A written document, a piece of paper? What about faithfulness to her own heart?

"Sarah ..."

She looked up at him, wondering if he knew her thoughts, seeing and feeling the room move slightly.

What about Brandon? What about God?

She waited for him to say more, but he did not. Instead, he looked down and shook his head, unable to continue. But she knew. She always knew. She could see the glint of moisture in his eyes. She touched his arm, offering support, assuring him she understood, that she felt it, too. The impossibility of their situation.

And then he looked at her. Those soulful, penetrating eyes that reached in and held her heart, that dissolved her very insides. The room started to move again, and she tightened her grip on his arm for support.

What about Brandon? What about—

He slipped his arm around her waist, helping her to stand. He understood everything. They were close, their bodies touching. Closer than they'd ever been. She could feel his breathing, the pounding of his heart.

She was no longer certain if she was standing or being held. It didn't matter. The room was moving again, and they were so close, and so much alike, and so perfect for one another.

His mouth moved toward hers.

What about—

She tried to think of Brandon, of God, of some reason to resist. But they no longer mattered. There was only Lucas, their embrace, his pounding heart, the spinning room . . .

She closed her eyes, felt his warm breath on her face. She tilted back her head until, finally, their lips found one another's.

CHAPTER 12

To the angel of the church in Thyatira write:

These are the words of the Son of God, whose eyes are like blazing fire and whose feet are like burnished bronze. I know your deeds, your love and faith, your service and persever-ance, and that you are now doing more than you did at first.

Nevertheless, I have this against you: You tolerate that woman Jezebel, who calls herself a prophetess. By her teaching she misleads my servants into

sexual immorality and the eating of food sacrificed
to idols. I have given her time to repent of her
immorality, but she is unwilling. So I will cast her
on a bed of suffering, and I will make those who
commit adultery with her suffer intensely, unless
they repent of her ways. I will strike her children
dead. Then all the churches will know that I am he
who searches hearts and minds, and I will repay
each of you according to your deeds. Now I say to
the rest of you in Thyatira, to you who do not hold
to her teaching and have not learned Satan's so-
called deep secrets (I will not impose any other burden on you): Only hold on to what you have until I
come.

To him who overcomes and does my will to the
end, I will give authority over the nations—

"He will rule them with an iron scepter;
    he will dash them to pieces like pottery"—

just as I have received authority from my Father. I will
also give him the morning star. He who has an ear, let
him hear what the Spirit says to the churches.

The sun had set an hour ago, but the darkness offered little relief from the heat. Brandon had spent all afternoon
inside the coffee shop reading his Bible. A television set
droned quietly in the background as a large electric fan swept
back and forth across the sweating men who sat around
Formica tables drinking tea, discussing politics, or playing a
tile game called Okay. They were a hundred yards down the
street from the ruins of Thyatira, now called Akhisar. There
was little to see. Just more dried grass and scrub pines in ruins
that were no bigger than a city block . . . a city block located
directly in the center of the existing town.

Salman was up in the hotel room resting. Despite Brandon's protests, Tanya Chase had insisted upon paying for their

room. "Don't be ridiculous," she'd scolded him when he'd tried to refuse. "It's good for all of us. They'll kick you out the second you try to sleep in those ruins, and Jerry and I have no intention of traipsing all around the countryside tracking you down wherever you decide to camp out."

It seemed a fair trade-off: a real bed to rest his travel-weary bones, for life under some minor media scrutiny that would be inevitable anyway. But there was another reason he had agreed. Although Tanya insisted she was only going after a story, pushing him to make his "great declaration to the world" so she could wrap it up and put it to bed, Brandon saw something else. A softening. Maybe not on the outside, but something was happening to her heart. As she and Jerry continued to hang around, watching him day in and day out, occasionally discussing the Scriptures, something was happening to her. Slowly, but surely, something was happening. He turned back to the New Testament and smiled quietly. There seemed to be no end to God's miracles.

As he continued reading and waiting on the Lord, an unusual truth had started to emerge. But this one wasn't about the church of Thyatira . . . it wasn't even about the church of today. It was about Brandon Martus. A truth exposed and revealed by "He who searches the hearts and minds." A truth about the Jezebels in his own soul. The sins he was tolerating and allowing to dwell within his own heart.

All of his life he'd been taught that holiness was a good thing to pursue, a worthwhile . . . pastime. But it was nothing as important as life and death. After all, if we sinned, there was always Christ's sacrifice on the cross to pay for it. And if we wanted to indulge a little longer or deeper in those sins it may not be for the best, but it was okay. Christ's grace was endless; there was no ceiling to the debt we could run up on His credit card of forgiveness.

But now . . . as Brandon studied the Scriptures, he was beginning to see a much different God, with a much higher purpose. He turned back and reread 1 Peter:

But just as he who called you is holy, so be holy in all you do; for it is written: "Be holy, because I am holy."

Brandon was beginning to understand that holiness wasn't a suggestion. It wasn't even a goal. It was a command. A command just as important as not killing, not stealing, not committing adultery.

He flipped over to Galatians 5:19–21. He'd read it several days earlier—a virtual shopping list of immoralities.

The acts of the sinful nature are obvious: sexual immorality, impurity and debauchery; idolatry and witchcraft; hatred, discord, jealousy, fits of rage, selfish ambition, dissensions, factions and envy; drunkenness, orgies, and the like.

Of course he wasn't guilty of all of these, at least not on the outside. But, like the church of Thyatira, how many of these immoralities did he secretly tolerate on the inside? And if that wasn't bad enough, there was the final verse. The kicker:

I warn you, as I did before, that those who live like this will not inherit the kingdom of God.

"Will not inherit the kingdom of God." Did God honestly expect him to live a life that pure and holy? Yes, he knew holiness was something God *preferred*, and he always figured if he succeeded, great, but if not, no sweat. After all, he no longer lived under the law, but grace.

Yet these verses seemed to take the matter far more seriously. He felt compelled to flip over to the book of Romans.

Don't you know that when you offer yourselves to someone to obey him as slaves, you are slaves to the one whom you obey—whether you are slaves to sin, which leads to death, or to obedience, which leads to righteousness? But thanks be to God that, though you used to be slaves to sin, you wholeheartedly obeyed the form of teaching to which you were entrusted. You have been set free from sin and have become slaves to righteousness.

Was it possible? All of his life Brandon had been taught that he had been set free from the *penalty* of sin. But now he was seeing something deeper. According to these verses and others like them he was not only free from sin's punishment ... he was free from its *power*.

He turned to 1 John.

No one who is born of God will continue to sin, because God's seed remains in him; he cannot go on sinning, because he has been born of God. This is how we know who the children of God are and who the children of the devil are: Anyone who does not do what is right is not a child of God.

It had always been there, in the Scriptures and some-where in the back of his head, but it had never taken hold. He had never known the importance, no, the *requirement* God made regarding holiness. Did others? Did the church? Had she preached it here in Thyatira? Did she preach it today? Or, in her zeal to save people, had she forgotten the second half of the gospel—the fact that God not only freed us from the *penalty* of sin ... but that he freed us from the *power* of sin. A power we could choose to embrace—or ignore. But one that if ignored would bring a devastating penalty.

I warn you, as I did before, that those who live like this will not inherit the kingdom of God.

The concept was astonishing.

"Brandon?"

He looked up. It was Tanya.

"I think you need to see this." She tried to avoid his eyes, but it was too late. He already knew something was wrong.

"What's the matter?"

The men in the coffee shop had started to murmur. This was a place for them to gather; no women were allowed.

"What is it?" Brandon repeated.

Tanya turned and left the shop without a word. Brandon quickly gathered his papers, stuffed the New Testament into his back pocket, and followed. His heart was already beginning to pound as he stepped outside and into the night.

"You scum . . ." Katherine searched for a more degrading term, but she was shaking so badly she could barely speak. "You despicable monster."

"Good evening, Katherine." Lucas turned to squint at the clock across his living room. "Or should I say good morning." Even as he stood in his disheveled state of mussed hair and swollen eyes he looked gorgeous. "To what do I owe this honor—and how, might I ask, did you get past the electronic security?"

"I know a little about computers, remember."

"Ah, of course." He finished tying the belt to his robe while heading past the leather sofa to the bar at the end of the room. "May I get you something to drink?"

It was then she noticed Sarah's open satchel and scattered briefs on the coffee table . . . and her shoes beside the sofa. "Dr. Martus is here?"

Lucas glanced up. "Hmm? Oh, yes. I am afraid your friend had a bit too much to drink at dinner, and she is now sleeping it off."

Katherine threw an involuntary glance to the bedroom with its door half ajar. "She had dinner here? With you?"

He was searching through the bottles in the cabinet. "Does that surprise you?"

"I just thought she was smarter than that."

"Yes, well, when you and Eric failed to show, our evening became a bit more—how shall I say—intimate."

"When Eric and I failed to show?"

"Yes, we waited, had a few drinks, but you never—"

"We were never invited."

"Ah, an unfortunate oversight by my staff. I shall have to speak to Deena. Here we go." He pulled out a bottle from the back. "Scotch is still your preferred drink, is it not?"

It was now or never. Katherine played her card. "I know about Scorpion, Lucas."

He glanced up. "I'm sorry?"

"I know the Cartel . . . I know that you created the virus."

He paused just a fraction of a second, then reached for two glasses. "Created . . . the virus?"

She remained silent. She'd thrown him off balance, and now he was stalling to recover.

He opened the bottle and began to pour. "I have been accused of many things, Katherine, but I must admit this one really surprises—"

"I saw the files, Lucas." She stepped further into the room. "Cairo, Mecca, New York, Tel Aviv—the first four cities to break out with the plague. I don't know how you created it, but I know you transported and air-dropped the Scorpion virus over each of those four cities. I know that you purposely started the epidemic."

He hesitated. By now her heart was pounding like a jackhammer. She watched his every move, waiting to see what he would do, what he would say. After an eternity, he turned and crossed toward her, drinks in hand.

"You're right, of course." He arrived and held out a glass. She only stared at him, her rage building. When it was obvious she wouldn't take it, he carefully set the glass on the coffee table, beside Sarah's papers, and eased himself into the leather sofa. "Please." He motioned for her to sit opposite him.

She remained standing.

He became very quiet, staring down at his glass a long moment. Katherine shifted and waited. Finally, he spoke, but he did not look up. "It was a very difficult step to take." His voice was soft and thick with emotion. "And, although the

Cartel fully endorsed the action, I am the one who must take the ultimate responsibility."

Katherine watched, refusing to be taken in. Still, she had to ask, "Why?"

He looked up. "The Arabs, the Jews, you know they will never get along. We all know this. The rest of the world, we may agree to live in peace, but not these two cousins. And that is what they are . . . cousins. Did you know that both come from the line of Abraham? The Jews from Isaac, Sarah's son— the Arabs from Ishmael, her handmaiden's child?"

She said nothing.

He continued. "That is why it wasn't hard to design a virus to attack only their gene pool."

She repeated the question. "Why?"

"It seemed so unfair, for the entire world's peace to be held hostage by nothing more than a . . . family squabble."

"So you decided to wipe them both out."

"No, no. Is that what you think?" He looked up at her, his eyes full of hurt, even betrayal. But it didn't work. Not this time. Katherine would not be drawn in. "No, that's not it at all," he said. "You must understand, the only way to bring these two parties together, to force them to cooperate, was to somehow provide them with—how shall I put it—an incentive."

Katherine frowned, not understanding.

He continued. "The Jews, the Arabs, they are dying off by the thousands."

"Try millions."

Lucas shrugged. "Yes, you are right. And here we are, an organization dedicated to world peace that is suddenly holding the only cure."

Katherine's jaw went slack. "You're . . . blackmailing them? If they don't cooperate, you're going to withhold the vaccine?"

"Blackmail is a very ugly word. As I said, our purpose is only to provide an incentive."

"They'll never go for it. The people will never—"

"The people will never know. But their leaders already do. And by all appearances they are already coming around."

"That's not possible."

"We are talking life and death here."

"You're talking genocide."

"That would be their decision, not mine."

Katherine reached out to the sofa to steady herself as Lucas continued.

"In less than a week, every major country will have given the Cartel the authority we need to enforce world peace. That's when I will officially be taking office and when we'll have the groundbreaking for the new temple. Think of it. For the first time in five thousand years, the Jew and Arab will exist side by side in peace. Not that there won't be tensions. But, as I have said, we do hold the incentive."

Katherine's voice was dry and raspy. "That's ... monstrous."

"It is the only way."

"The only way? Innocent Jews and Arabs are being destroyed all around the world, and you say it's the only way?"

Lucas leaned back and sighed wearily. "It is an unfortunate by-product, yes."

"By-product?" She was practically shouting. *"By-product?"*

He said nothing.

Unable to contain her anger, Katherine was ready to explode. She had to do something. Anything. She spun around and started toward the door.

"Where are you going?"

"I don't know, but we're going. We have to get out of here."

"Katherine, if you're thinking about disclosing this information to the general public, I assure you, it will not be—"

She spun back at him. "I'm not disclosing anything. I'm getting out of here. You're sick, Lucas. Deranged! All of you! And we're not going to be a part of your sickness any longer!"

"So you're taking Eric and leaving?"

"That's right."

"Despite the authorities."

"We'll take our chances."

"And if Eric chooses to stay?"

"I'm his mother; he'll leave if I tell him to leave."

"I'm afraid that may be wishful thinking."

She looked at him, incredulous. "What?"

"Eric is more connected to us than you would like to believe. He is more connected to me. I've made sure of it."

When her voice finally came it was husky and full of venom. "You scheming, manipulative—"

"Katherine, please, let us forego name-calling, shall we?"

She turned on her heels and stormed back to the door. There was nothing left to be said. Now there was only action. She'd get them out of there. She had to. And if Eric put up a fuss ... well, she was still his mother, wasn't she? She could still make him obey, couldn't she?

"Katherine ..."

But even as she flew out the door, slamming it behind her, doubts began to rise. Lucas had sounded so confident, and he was always so thorough. What other tricks did he have?

Brandon raced outside, past the children kicking the deflated soccer ball, barely noticing the old men sitting at the tables, puffing on their giant hookahs.

Something inside of him was beginning to *know*. Once again his spirit was quickening. Once again the world surrounding him grew less and less real as the understanding became more and more vivid. The truths of the letter to Thyatira hadn't been completely revealed, not yet. There was something else.

He pulled up alongside Tanya. Her heels clicked against the tile sidewalk, drawing the attention of every male whose vision was not completely impaired. "Is it Salman?" he asked.

She looked straight ahead. "I told Jerry not to tape it, as a courtesy to you. But sometimes his ambition gets out of hand." She said nothing more, her face flashing from light to shadow as they walked under the bare bulbs strung from the fronts of shops to the mulberry trees lining the street.

The hotel was a dive at best. A handful of apartments in one of the five-story buildings that surrounded the square. They'd barely arrived outside the structure when Brandon heard the music and looked up. Three stories above, on his balcony, a young couple was locked in a passionate embrace. And by the noise coming from inside he suspected they weren't his only company.

He entered the lobby with Tanya and started up the concrete steps. Brandon didn't need the Spirit of God to fill in the details. Salman was on the road, Salman finally had a place to stay, Salman was unwinding and letting off a little steam with some newfound friends. No big deal. But other impressions rushed in. Salman drunk, Salman carousing, Salman having sex. The thoughts were unsettling, and he knew he'd have to speak to him. Still, it certainly wasn't his style to judge or condemn—

"Nevertheless, I have this against you: You tolerate that woman Jezebel, who calls herself a prophetess. By her teaching she misleads my servants into sexual immorality ..."

The words surprised him. Surely God wasn't talking about Salman. The guy was a baby Christian, nominal at best. Brandon's job wasn't to judge. He was to be loving and kind. Salman would eventually come into deeper maturity and—

"I have given her time to repent of her immorality, but she is unwilling."

He grabbed the iron railing as they moved up the stairs. *Lord, that's too harsh.*

There was no response.

He's a good friend. It's not my job to judge.

"You tolerate ..."

He's a good man. Look at all he's done.

"He is unwilling."

Only for now. He will be later. We just have to give him more—

"I have given him time to repent, but he is unwilling."
It's just ... sex. It's part of today's culture. Everybody is—
"You tolerate ..."
That's so ... judgmental. It's so ...
"You tolerate ..."
Brandon was growing more desperate. *Please ... I wouldn't even be here if it wasn't for him. Look at all he's done for me, all he's given up.*
"You tolerate ..."
But You say we're supposed to love, we're supposed to be merciful and forgiving.
"I have given him time to repent, but he is unwilling."
They were on the second story now. He gripped the railing tighter, fighting back the anguish. *I can't. I can't do that.*
"I have this against you."
Please ... what about Your love? But even as the words came, Brandon knew their answer. He'd already seen God's love back in the hospital, back in the square with the rabid dog. The love that surpassed human sentimentality, a love that destroyed anything that threatened His beloved. In desperation, Brandon turned back to the other argument, the one minimizing Salman's sin. *It's just ... sex.*
"And eating the fruit of the tree was merely eating the fruit of the tree."
The insight was so powerful that it nearly slowed him to a stop. It was true. Rebellion was rebellion. It made no difference what shape, what form. It made no difference how large or small, how injurious or benign. Rebellion was rebellion.

They arrived at the third-story landing and crossed to the apartment. The music throbbed as Tanya stepped aside to let him open the door. He leaned against the handle, steeling himself. This was hard. Next to saying good-bye to Sarah and losing the clinic, this was the toughest.

Taking one last breath, he turned the knob, pushed open the door, and stepped into the party. There weren't a lot of people. About a dozen. Some talked, others danced to the

clanging rhythms and mournful wails of contemporary Turkish music.

He called out to the nearest couple. "Where's Salman?"

"*Ne?*" the young man shouted.

"Salman, where is Salman?"

His partner, a bottle blonde, motioned toward the bedroom.

Brandon looked over to the closed door. Heaviness grew
in his chest as if a huge stone had been placed on it. He started
through the crowd and had barely crossed halfway when the
door opened and Salman appeared, tucking in his shirt. The
girl with him was sixteen, seventeen at most. She reminded
Brandon of the girl at the mall. The one so hungry for love
and attention.

Salman looked up and for a moment appeared startled to
see him. "Mr. Brandon!" He recovered and sauntered toward
him. Disguising his uneasiness with a grin, he arrived and
slapped Brandon on the back. "Welcome!"

Brandon swallowed hard, took another breath, and then
quietly gave the order. "Leave."

"I am sorry. What?"

Although he tried to sound angry, the ache in his heart
gave him away. "Leave."

"But the party, it has just begun." He glanced about.
"Banu, Banu!" He motioned for one of the nearby girls—easily as young as his. She wobbled toward Brandon in high
heels, obviously drunk, the interest in her dark eyes embold-
ened by the alcohol.

Salman laughed. "You're in luck, I think she likes you."

Brandon repeated himself. "I want you to leave, and I
want you to leave now."

Banu wrapped her arms around one of his. He barely
noticed as he remained focused on Salman. "What you are
doing is wrong." The words came harder. He had to breathe
between each sentence. "It is wrong and you know it."

Salman chuckled. "Wrong? It is a little indulgence. A little reward after our hard labors."

"It's wrong." From the corner of his eye he noticed Jerry across the room, hoisting the camera on his shoulder, beginning to tape.

"Maybe it is a little wrong," Salman admitted with a twinkle, "but a little wrong is sometimes good. Banu, show Mr. Brandon how good a little wrong can be."

Before he could stop her, the girl had reached her arms around his neck and pulled herself up to him, kissing him fully on the lips. He tried to push her away, but she clung with tenacity. He tried again, harder, until he finally broke her grip. But the force sent her staggering backwards. She hit a table filled with glasses. It collapsed and crashed with her to the floor. Booze splashed, glass shattered, and people gasped. Suddenly, Salman and Brandon were center stage.

Trying to ignore the stares, Brandon repeated himself as evenly as he could. "What you are doing is wrong."

"Wrong? Celebrating with a few friends, it is wrong?"

Brandon spoke more softly. "You know what I mean."

"No, I do not. You tell me which is wrong." He raised his voice so everyone in the room could hear. "Is it wrong for someone to buy an airline ticket for a friend in trouble? Is it wrong to be his companion and guide in a country he would be lost in? Is it wrong to live outdoors with him, to starve with him, to suffer with him? Is that wrong? Or is it wrong for that friend to suddenly throw him onto the streets as thanks for his hard work and dedication?"

Salman's logic was irrefutable. Brandon had no argument, only what he knew to be true. "You must go, Salman. If you repent, if you sincerely ask God's forgiveness, then maybe—"

"Repent? Repent of what?" There was no missing the contempt filling his voice. "Of being a man? Of having manly desires?" He reached for the girl he'd slept with, pulling her mouth toward his, kissing her passionately, long and hard. The crowd voiced approval.

"There," he said, finally releasing her and catching his breath. "That's what I think of your repentance. Or would you prefer me to treat her as you do your own wife . . . never fulfilling your duties to her as a man!"

Brandon wasn't angry. He knew it was the alcohol talking. He also knew it was Salman feeling the betrayal of their friendship. And who could blame him? Certainly not Brandon. Instead, Brandon slowly nodded and looked at him with deep sincerity. "I am sorry, my friend."

The word triggered something in Salman. Suddenly his voice grew husky with emotion. "Friend? This is not how you treat a friend." His jaw stiffened, making it clear he was trying to maintain his anger. "This is how you treat an enemy. And you"—he pointed an accusing finger—"you do not even know the difference."

He turned to one of the group. "Orhan! The newspaper, bring it here." A young man in his twenties produced a newspaper. Salman grabbed it and threw it down on the table. "That!" He slammed his hand down on the front-page photo. The one of Lucas Ponte standing with a handful of dignitaries. "That is your enemy! He is all of our enemy!"

Brandon glanced at it, then back at Salman. He'd heard the speech about the evils of Ponte and the Cartel a dozen times—if not from Salman, then from his militant friends. This was an obvious attempt to change the subject. But Brandon would not be sidetracked. "I'm sorry, Salman." There was a large lump in his throat. "We can no longer work together."

"Look!" Salman roared. "Look at the picture!"

Brandon glanced back down. Salman's finger was not on Lucas Ponte; instead, it was pointing to a woman. A woman standing beside him, looking on with deep gratitude. But it was far more than gratitude . . . she was looking at him with heartfelt admiration.

Suddenly Brandon could no longer breathe. He gripped the table, having to lean against it just to stand. Salman continued to talk to him, to berate him, but he no longer heard. People from the party moved in for a better look, but he barely noticed.

All he could do was stare at the photograph of his wife gazing at Lucas Ponte with adoration . . . and burning love.

CHAPTER 13

Sarah dragged herself up the courtyard stairs. Her head throbbed, her mouth felt like cotton, and she still didn't completely trust the ground under her feet. She'd barely made it to the second flight when her stomach heaved and she bent over vomiting. But it was more than just wine that had made her sick. Sarah Martus was sick with guilt.

Lucas had been kind and understanding as always. Once she woke, he had done everything to convince her to stay. He'd even offered to sleep on the sofa. But she had to get away, she had to sort things out. It was Katherine's shouts and slamming of the door that had awakened her. She didn't hear all the words, couldn't understand the argument, but she knew Katherine was awake and that she was at least one person who would listen.

She pulled herself back to her feet, wiped her mouth, and somehow started across the landing. Fortunately, Katherine's door was open and her light on. Pausing to gather herself, Sarah pushed her hair behind her ears, straightened her clothes, and approached.

Inside, Katherine flew around the room, packing furiously. She glanced up, was briefly startled at Sarah's presence, then continued. "What do you want?"

"I . . ." Sarah squinted at the glaring light. "Where are you going?"

"We're leaving. Eric and me, we're out of here."

"But . . . the treatments . . ."

"They're over. You did what you could."

"What about the deliverance session? I haven't gotten together with Eric to—"

Katherine stopped. "To what? To cast out his demon?" She motioned cynically to Sarah's appearance. "You, the mighty woman of God?"

Sarah's face grew hot as she adjusted her dress.

Katherine continued. "You can't even control your own libido, and you think you can get some demon to obey you?"

"I . . ." Sarah stammered, "We didn't . . ."

Katherine turned back to her packing, her voice dripping with disdain. "Please . . ."

The conversation was racing faster than Sarah could keep up. Suddenly she heard herself blurt out, "I love my husband!"

Katherine looked back to her. "You really believe that, don't you?"

Sarah nodded, already feeling tears in her eyes.

Katherine shook her head, then resumed packing. "That just makes you more pitiful than I thought."

"Katherine . . ." It was more plea than argument.

But Katherine continued packing, not looking up. "As I've said before, Doctor, truth is in what we do, not what we say. You say you love your husband, yet you sleep with Lucas Ponte. You tell me which is the truth."

Her stomach was churning again. Brine filled her mouth as she leaned against the frame of the door, swallowing it back.

"Not that I blame you. What woman in her right mind would pass up the opportunity—especially a woman with so much . . . ambition."

Ambition . . . there was that word again. The one that had haunted her all of her life. The reason behind her abortion, her sordid past. The reason she'd become a Christian and tried to start over with a clean slate. Yet, here it was again, raising its head, just as Gerty had warned, just as Brandon had sensed. Nothing she did could free her of it. Katherine was right. How much of her attraction to Lucas was love and how much of it was simply his power? Surely, it was more than coincidence that she happened to have fallen for one of the most influential men in the world.

But Katherine wasn't finished. "You two are cut from the same cloth; you always have been." She reached for the door, making it clear she wanted her privacy. Sarah took a step back. "But be careful, my friend. Lucas Ponte is not as he appears. But then again, I guess, neither are you."

She shut the door, leaving the indictment ringing in Sarah's ears.

To the angel of the church in Sardis write:
    These are the words of him who holds the seven spirits of God and the seven stars. I know your deeds; you have a reputation of being alive, but you are dead. Wake up! Strengthen what remains and is about to die, for I have not found your deeds complete in the

sight of my God. Remember, therefore, what you
have received and heard; obey it, and repent. But if
you do not wake up, I will come like a thief, and you
will not know at what time I will come to you.

Yet you have a few people in Sardis who have not
soiled their clothes. They will walk with me, dressed
in white, for they are worthy. He who overcomes
will, like them, be dressed in white. I will never blot
out his name from the book of life, but will
acknowledge his name before my Father and his
angels. He who has an ear, let him hear what the
Spirit says to the churches.

Just outside the small village of Sart, the Hall of the
Imperial Cult towered fifty, nearly sixty feet above Brandon's
head. Of everything he'd seen in Turkey, this reconstructed
portion of building with its multiple columns, balconies, and
towering brick walls was the most foreboding and intimidating. Part of it was its architecture, part of it was its history.
Built during the peak of the Roman Empire, it symbolized the
power of the ancient one-world government, and just as
importantly, the worship of its leader.

But there was something else that frightened him. He
couldn't put his finger on it, but he knew it involved Sarah,
it involved himself, and somehow it involved the future. But
what did this ancient past have to do with their future?

"I just spoke with Salman."

He turned to see Tanya approach through the grassy field
that had once been the Sardis gymnasium.

"How is he?"

"He's in the village. Wants to team up with you again. If
you'll have him."

Brandon felt a surge of joy. "Of course I'll have him. I'd
love for him to join us."

"So would he. Except . . ."

"Except?"

"His girlfriend from the party is with him. He says she's part of the deal."

Brandon's heart sank just as quickly as it had leaped. He glanced away, then answered softly, "I'm sorry to hear that."

"That's your answer, then?"

"My answer is the same as it was back in Thyatira."

"I told him it would be."

The two grew quiet. Only the wind and the rustling of dry grass broke the silence.

Changing the subject, Tanya finally asked, "Have you been up to the Citadel yet?" She motioned toward the craggy hill across the road and above them.

He shook his head.

"Not much up there, though the history's kind of interesting."

"How's that?"

"About twenty-five hundred years ago the Pactolus River was *the* source of gold in the world. That made the ruler, here, a fellow by the name of Croesus, the richest man on earth. And that's where he stored his riches, right up there in the Citadel."

Brandon looked at the hilltop. As Tanya spoke, he listened carefully. So far every church letter from Revelation had also been related to that city's history or geography. He suspected this would be no different.

"The place was absolutely impregnable," she explained, "except for one small opening in the wall. So Croesus stationed two watchmen there to guard it. Everything was fine, until Cyrus, King of Persia, decided he wanted the ruler's gold. But there was no way to get in and get it. So he brought his army into this valley, and he waited and waited and waited."

"Until?" Brandon asked.

"Until one night both watchmen fell asleep. That's when Cyrus made his move. He broke through the wall, stormed the Citadel, and defeated Croesus, taking all of the man's gold and riches."

"All because the watchmen fell asleep?"

"Exactly."

But if you do not wake up, I will come like a thief, and you will not know at what time I will come to you.

Immediately Brandon recognized the symbolism. Five hundred years after Croesus, a church at this same location had existed which seemed to have had a rich history of good works. There was no false teaching, no lack of love, and no immorality. Christ had nothing against them . . . except that they had fallen asleep. They had rested on their past accomplishments. Like the two watchmen they had slept when they should have been on duty. And eventually . . . Brandon looked around the ruins . . . *the thief had come to steal*. And now there was nothing.

Again he wondered how similar that was to today's church. He wondered how often good people pointed to past accomplishments as an excuse not to act, as a reason to retire from the battle. But the battle always continues. And, like Cyrus, the enemy is always waiting . . . waiting for us to quit, waiting for us to retire, waiting for us to fall asleep . . . so he can storm the gates.

Wake up! Strengthen what remains and is about to die, for I have not found your deeds complete in the sight of my God. Remember, therefore, what you have received and heard; obey it, and repent.

The more Brandon thought on this truth, the more he understood. Christian service is not historical fact, it's contemporary action. It is not past glory, it is current doing. Retirement would have to wait until heaven. Because right now the battle continued to rage for the hearts and minds and souls of people God loved more than His own life.

"Brandon . . . Brandon?"

He looked up, returning from his thoughts.

"There's another bit of information you need to know . . . considering Sarah and the Cartel and all."

He couldn't hide the anxiety in his voice. "What's that?"

"The last of the holdout countries has agreed to endorse the Cartel. Seventy-two hours from now, in Jerusalem, the Cartel will be given full authority over matters of world peace. That's when Lucas Ponte will officially be installed as their chairman."

Brandon looked back up to the Hall of the Imperial Cult. Once again, he felt the stirring of the Spirit, the movement of pieces falling into place. He gave an involuntary shudder. Something had been happening. Something under his very nose. And now it was stirring from its slumber.

"Wake up!"

"Brandon, are you all right?"

"It's happening." His voice was barely above a whisper.

"What?"

"The Imperial Cult."

"What are you talking about?"

He swallowed hard and continued. "One world government, one world leader . . . Ponte and the Cartel, they're coming into power. They're bringing everything to an end, exactly as it began."

"Whoa, wait a minute, now you're sounding like Salman."

He turned to her. "Salman was right."

"What? You're not serious?"

He was as surprised as she was. "It's been staring me in the face all this time, and I just hadn't seen it. About the Cartel, about Ponte . . . Salman was right." Brandon slowly shook his head, amazed at his own thickheadedness.

Tanya continued searching his face. "You really believe that?"

He turned back to her. "I *know* that."

An eerie silence crept over them.

Tanya cleared her throat. "So what are you talking about here? Some sort of Antichrist thing?" She tried to show her scorn, but it came out more as a nervous chuckle.

Brandon answered quietly, "Whoever he is, he will rise up to become the next ruler of the Imperial Cult—he will become the next world . . . god."

"Come on," Tanya scoffed.

Brandon said nothing.

She continued. "Who are we kidding? The people would never allow something like that. They'd never stand for it."

He agreed. "Not if they knew."

More silence, more thinking.

Finally Tanya spoke again. "If you really think it's true, then the people have to be warned. Somebody has to tell them."

Brandon nodded. He knew she was trying to capitalize on the situation, but that didn't stop the pieces from moving about in his mind, from him seeking some way to try and make them fit. She saved him the trouble. "Brandon . . ."

He glanced at her.

"It's you."

The words caught his breath.

"It's you, isn't it?"

He shook his head. "No."

"But—"

"There's nothing I can do."

"But you agree, the people have to be warned. And if you're supposed to be some sort of end-time prophet guy, shouldn't that be your—"

"No . . . I'm not the one." He turned away.

"But if it's true, if you *really* believe it's happening, then somebody has to warn them, somebody has to wake them up."

The phrase spun him back to her, but she had no idea what she'd said. Without a word he turned and began walking away.

"Brandon?"

"No . . ."

She scrambled to his side, doing her best to keep up with his long strides in the grass. "If you seriously believe that, then you need to say it. You need to go public and say it."

He remained silent. He'd "gone public" once before, in Los Angeles. And one disaster like that per lifetime was enough.

But Tanya didn't let up. "Isn't that your job?" He knew full well she was more interested in a story than the truth, but that didn't make her any less right. "Who's going to tell them if you don't?" Nor did it prevent her from going for the jugular. "And what about Sarah, who's going to warn Sarah?"

The question nearly stopped him, but he pushed ahead. "I'm not ready."

"The installation is in three days. When *will* you be ready?"

He gave no answer.

"We could fly to Jerusalem. I could pull a few strings, maybe arrange a public face-to-face. Shoot, we might even be able to stage a debate if—"

"No!"

And still she dogged him. "Okay, then we could make that tape I've been asking for, broadcast it over GBN, and—"

"No!"

"Why not?"

"I'm not the one . . . I can't do stuff like that."

"Brandon?"

"It's not me."

Growing out of breath, she slowed to a stop. "Brandon?"

"Leave me alone!"

"Brandon!"

But he kept walking, practically running, doing anything he could to get away from her. But the truth remained. And it would remain, gnawing away at him the rest of the day . . . and on into the night.

CHAPTER 14

Sometimes death rushes in like a flood, sometimes it trickles in unnoticed. For Brandon both cases were true. The first death, the flood, had hit him with the TV broadcast back in L.A. The trickle death had slowly seeped in as he traveled the villages of Turkey until, suddenly, he was over his head and drowning at Sart. Yes, he had received insight. Yes, he had learned truths to warn the bride. But, at last, he understood who he would have to oppose in order to proclaim those truths. That's when he realized how absolutely unqualified he was.

And that's when he had given up.

It's not that he was rebelling against God. It was just a cold hard fact. There was no way he could step up and take on the world's most powerful organization. Would the Lord be disappointed? He didn't know. But he did know it was not his fault that God had picked the wrong person for the job.

His tears, his protests, and yes, his shouting at the Lord, had continued throughout yesterday afternoon and on through the night. Pacing, yelling, crying, raging . . . until he was entirely spent. Now there was only fatigue . . . and a sad, melancholy peace. There was something peaceful about being dead.

He was sitting on one of a half-dozen stone sarcophagi strewn about the tiny ruins of Philadelphia. Except for an occasional puttering moped on the street behind him and the distant shouts of children playing, the morning was still. The mulberry trees offered shade from the relentless sun as well as a haven for a family of doves cooing in its branches.

Funny, a month ago he'd dreamed about taking on the world for God. Now he realized he was unqualified to do anything except give up. But that was okay. He'd tried, he'd put up the good fight. He simply didn't have what it took. In time, maybe Sarah would return to him, though he wondered what he could possibly offer in comparison to the great Lucas Ponte. In time, someone else would warn the church about her need to prepare for Christ's return. In time, someone else would stand up against this new Imperial Cult.

But it wouldn't be him. That much was certain. For him, it was over. It was painful, yes. It left him numb, of course.

But it was over.

The sun continued to rise and the day grew hotter. More out of habit as well as some curiosity, Brandon eventually pulled out his pocket New Testament and flipped it open to the sixth letter, the one addressed to the church that had inhabited these ruins.

And, after a long pause, he began to read:

To the angel of the church in Philadelphia write:
> These are the words of him who is holy and true,
who holds the key of David. What he opens no one

can shut, and what he shuts no one can open. I know your deeds. See, I have placed before you an open door that no one can shut. I know that you have little strength, yet you have kept my word and have not denied my name. I will make those who are of the synagogue of Satan, who claim to be Jews though they are not, but are liars—I will make them come and fall down at your feet and acknowledge that I have loved you. Since you have kept my command to endure patiently, I will also keep you from the hour of trial that is going to come upon the whole world to test those who live on the earth.

I am coming soon. Hold on to what you have, so that no one will take your crown. Him who overcomes I will make a pillar in the temple of my God. Never again will he leave it. I will write on him the name of my God and the name of the city of my God, the new Jerusalem, which is coming down out of heaven from my God; and I will also write on him my new name. He who as an ear, let him hear what the Spirit says to the churches.

The words were comforting. There were no rebukes, no commands, nothing that needed to be repented of. Just encouragement and the promise that if he held on to what he had, God would reward him. No problem there—when you've got nothing left, hanging on isn't hard.

There was, however, one phrase that stuck in his mind. He tried to dismiss it, but it kept returning. *"I have placed before you an open door that no one can shut."* Of course the promise could have merely been for the church here, or for today's church in general. But, somehow, he suspected there was more. Then again, what purpose did an open door serve for a dead man with dead dreams and dead hopes?

The answer came back just as clearly, just as sadly . . .

None.

"Brandon . . ."

He glanced up to see Tanya wind her way through the ruins toward him. They'd dropped him off earlier that morning and had left to check into a hotel. He was grateful for the ride from Sart to Philadelphia, but could have done without her continual persistence for him to go to Jerusalem and confront the Cartel ... or to at least make a video that she could broadcast. On the other hand, Tanya could persist all she wanted. Another nice thing about being dead is, persistence doesn't matter.

"I've got something for you." She approached, waving a piece of paper. "I printed it up from the Internet. I don't recognize the name, but she sent it to you in care of my e-mail."

"She?"

"Yeah." Tanya handed him the paper. "Somebody by the name of Morris—Gerty Morris."

The name startled him, and she saw it. "You know her?"

He nodded, then looked down at the paper she had given him. How could she have known? How, over a year ago, did Gerty know who to send this through to get it to him? Both a chill and a sense of anticipation started to rise in him. It was happening again. He could feel it. The fear. The excitement. Already he was starting to breathe harder. His spirit was quickening. Once again, God was making his presence known. There was no mistaking it. More importantly, He was about to make His will known.

My dearest Brandon:

This is gonna be my last letter to you. My prayer is that you've made your journey safely and that now you're preparing to be doing battle.

Brandon almost laughed. Prepared to do battle? If there was one time in his life he was unready to fight anybody for anything, it was now. He continued reading:

'Cause it's only when you're the weakest and the most defeated, that you're the most pliable in His hands. It's only when your vision is dead, that God's vision comes alive.

Brandon gripped the letter more tightly.

I have told you of the four steps to fulfilling your dream. First you received it, then you twisted it into your version of greatness, and now, at long last, it's dead. But it is only dead as Abraham's dream of Isaac was dead on the altar, as Joseph's dream of ruling his brothers was dead in prison, as our Lord's dream to save the world was dead on the cross, as Moses' dream of freeing his people was dead when he fled to the wilderness.

The words began to blur from the moisture welling up in his eyes. Were such things possible? Had this been planned all along?

Unlike Moses, your time in the wilderness was short. But your death is just as thorough. God commanded Moses to throw down his staff so He could transform it. But, just as importantly, he ordered Moses to pick it back up. You are God's now. Brandon Martus is dead. His dream is dead. His call is dead. No one can be harming or hurting you 'cause no one can harm or hurt a dead man. No one can be killing you 'cause no one can kill a dead man. All that you are is Christ's . . . and all that is Christ's is yours.

Now it is time for the fourth and final step. Now you must be picking up your staff. You have received the call. You have distorted it. You have watched it die. Now, you must let Him resurrect it.

He has set an open door before you, Brandon Martus, that no one can close. All you got to do is walk through it. The seed has fallen to the ground and died. Now it is time for it to sprout and bear fruit. Your work is complete. Now, pick up your staff and watch as God completes His.

Good-bye, my brother. I look forward to meeting you again.

GM

A full minute passed before Brandon looked up. He did not bother hiding the tears streaming down his face.

"Hey." Tanya reached out and touched his knee. "Are you okay?"

He nodded and quietly whispered, "Yeah."

"You sure?"

"Yeah." He forced a grin. "For a dead man, I couldn't be better."

Sarah raced across the courtyard. Even from this distance she could hear the screaming. She ran up the outside steps and sprinted toward the men's quarters, not slowing until Eric's room came into view. Outside, a handful of disciples had gathered. Others remained below in the courtyard. Both groups stood in silent concern as, inside, the mother and son were embroiled in a terrible fight.

That's why Katherine had called her. Eric was out of control. He had to be stopped. Given his history of violence, Sarah had grabbed her medical kit, including some Versed, a powerful sedative, and come as fast as she could. The guard stationed outside the door recognized her and stepped aside. Sarah nodded, took a moment to catch her breath, then pushed open the door.

The room was a war zone. Torn posters, broken chairs, even the computer screen was smashed. She spotted Katherine first and then Eric. He was holding two men against a wall by their necks. Their feet dangled just off of the ground.

"Eric!" Katherine was screaming. "Eric, let them go! Eric!" She turned to Sarah, her face wet with perspiration. "I told him we were leaving! I told him, but he refused. He said we're going to Jerusalem!"

Sarah looked at the two men pinned against the wall. Their eyes bulged; their faces glowed a bright red. And Eric, far too scrawny to be exerting this type of strength, was a study of deep concentration.

"You're killing them!" Katherine screamed. "Eric, let go! Eric!"

Sarah took a couple steps closer.

"I brought them in to help us pack," Katherine cried. "That's when he went crazy. Eric!" she shouted. "Eric!" She turned back to Sarah. "It's like he doesn't hear me, like he's not even there!"

Sarah nodded. She'd reached the same conclusion. Eric's rage, his superhuman strength, the look in his eyes. There was no question in her mind that it was time to make her move. She'd seen Brandon do this a half-dozen times at the clinic. Sometimes she'd helped. But this time she was all on her own. She took another breath, then shouted, "Heylel!"

Eric showed no signs of hearing. For the briefest moment Sarah thought she was mistaken. She cleared her throat and tried again, this time with greater authority. "Whoever you are . . . I order you to stop this!" Still no response. "In the name of Jesus Christ, I order you to stop it, now!"

In an incredible display of strength, Eric slowly brought the men down until their feet touched the floor. But he did not let go of their throats. And he still did not acknowledge Sarah's presence.

"Release them completely!" Sarah shouted. "I order you to release them, now!"

The hands withdrew from the throats, and the men slipped to the ground, coughing and gasping for air.

Then, ever so slowly, Eric turned to face her. She braced herself, expecting the worst. She was not disappointed. His eyes locked onto hers with such hatred that she gave an involuntary gasp. His lips curled back into a maniacal grin.

Katherine started toward him. "Eric—"

"No." Sarah held out her hand to stop her. "Don't. That's not Eric." She turned back to the boy. "Are you?"

The grin broadened.

"You're the one they call Heylel, aren't you?"

At last the mouth moved. "Very good." It was still Eric's voice but much deeper and more guttural. "But tell me, Dr. Martus, who exactly are you?"

Sarah swallowed, unsure of the question.

Katherine took a step closer. "What have you done with Eric? Where's my boy?"

The head swiveled in her direction. "At the moment he is preoccupied with more private instruction."

Katherine bristled and took another step toward him. "What are you doing to my son?"

Sarah touched her arm. "Easy . . ."

But Katherine didn't notice. Her voice trembled as she spoke. "What do you want from him?"

"Why, the same as you do, Katherine. I simply want his happiness."

The answer appeared to set her back. "How?" She pointed toward the men rubbing their throats, struggling to their feet. "By using him to destroy people? By turning him into some kind of monster?"

"Oh, but Katherine, he has already become that."

The statement made her shudder. The voice continued. "But you mustn't blame me, my dear. Turning your son into a monster was not my doing. That was the hand of your scientists. I am merely completing spiritually what they had begun physically."

Katherine's trembling grew worse. The voice continued. "It is the perfect marriage, don't you think? Man's desire to become God . . . joining forces with mine?"

Katherine bit her lip.

He continued. "And the two shall become one."

"No . . ." She gasped. "That's . . . my son."

And still the voice continued, relishing the torture. "Not anymore, Katherine Lyon. He is mine."

"No . . ."

"Oh, yes. Your little boy barely exists. He's given me nearly everything. After all, he understands the importance of our goal and—"

"Goal?" Sarah had seen enough. She quickly stepped between the two. "What is your goal? What are you going to do with him?"

The eyes shot to hers. "Why, rule the world, of course."

The candidness surprised her. But he wasn't finished.

"Just as the Christ was the incarnation of your Oppressor, so Eric has become the incarnation of me."

Sarah went cold. "Who . . . who are you?"

"I am the voice of reason, the Illuminated One. I am he who is committed to enlightening your planet and setting it free."

"Free? Of what?"

"Of he who claims love, yet demands holiness. Of he who offers freedom, while demanding servitude."

"You're . . . talking about God?"

"I am speaking of Oppressor. He who cast me from heaven, who imprisoned my host upon your planet."

Sarah caught her breath. She'd encountered several demons but never one who made such boasts. When she finally found her voice, she repeated her question. "Who . . . are you?"

"Oh, but Sarah, you know me." The casual use of her name made her stiffen. "You've always known me." Eric took a half step closer—his eyes focused so entirely upon her, their hatred so cold that she felt an icy embrace wrap around her chest, making it nearly impossible to breathe. "I was there when you put Suzie Burton into the hospital."

"*What?*"

"You remember . . . that little bicycle incident?"

The comment stunned her. "It . . . it was an accident."

"Yes, that is what you told your parents. That is what you told everybody. But you and I know better, don't we?"

Sarah's face reddened as thoughts of her most embarrassing childhood moment filled her mind. "I was eight years old."

"You were not eight when you cheated your way through calculus to get that scholarship for Stanford."

Shame poured in on top of her embarrassment. "How did—"

"I was there with you and your best friend's boyfriend, in the backseat of his parent's Nova. Remember?"

More memories rushed in ... along with other emotions—remorse, humiliation. The accusations came faster.

"When you 'borrowed' that money from your mother's purse, when you stole from your employer's till. When you were so drunk at that frat party you didn't even know who or how many young men—"

"Stop it!"

But Heylel didn't stop. The blows came harder and more rapid. "I was there when Harrison was conceived—"

"Harris—?"

"Your baby boy. That's what you were going to name him, remember?"

Sarah was reeling. "I—"

"I was there when you sacrificed him for grad school. I was in the abortion clinic when they reached inside of you—"

"Please ..." She gasped. "Stop ..."

"When they grabbed your baby's skull with the forceps—"

"Stop it!"

"When you let them crush—"

"Stop it!" She covered her ears. "I will not listen!"

But the voice was also screaming inside her head. "I was there when you let them kill your baby boy, Sarah! When you sacrificed your only child for your selfish *ambition!*"

There was that word again, like a blow to her chest. And still he spoke, driving each phrase home with a vengeance. "Ambition! That's all you are, Sarah Weintraub. That's all you'll ever be!"

She tried to answer, but she could barely breathe.

"I was there when your ambition nearly killed Brandon, your own husband!"

Mustering all of her strength, Sarah cried, "That's history! I'm a Christian now! I'm forgiven!"

"Are you?"

"Yes . . ." She gasped. The words tumbled out by rote, using the last of her energy. "Christ died on the cross for my sins. I'm forgiven, I'm a new creature in Christ."

"Is that why you drove your husband to humiliate himself on national television? Is that why you destroyed the clinic? Is that why you destroyed your own marriage? Because you are a new creature?"

Sarah had no defense. And still the blows came, so relentless she grew weak at the knees. "Is that why you're here, because you've changed? Is that why you're Lucas Ponte's concubine?"

"Please . . ." She could barely hear herself speak. She could barely think. There was only the voice and its awful truth.

"Is that why you're an adulteress? Tell me, Dr. Martus, is there anybody you won't sleep with to further your goals? Is there anyone you will not prostitute yourself to?"

She shook her head. "I am not—"

"Of course you are. You always have been—you always will be. The whore of Babylon."

Her body convulsed in a stifled sob.

"You have not changed. You never will change. That is why Oppressor selected you. The whore of Babylon. That is what you are. The harlot full of ambition . . . adultery and ambition, that is all you ever will be. Admit it! Who better to symbolize the prostitute! ADMIT IT!"

Another sob escaped.

"Who better to be the whore! ADMIT IT!" The entire room vibrated with his roar. "ADMIT IT! THAT IS ALL YOU ARE. THAT IS ALL YOU WILL EVER BE!

"ADMIT IT!

"ADMIT IT!"

Almost imperceptibly, Sarah began to nod. She could no longer deny the truth. A truth she'd been running from for months, for her entire life. There was no change. She'd tried, but it had done no good. There'd never be change. Not for her.

"Sarah Weintraub . . ." the voice sneered, spitting out the words. "Liar, cheater, thief, adulterer . . . killer of her marriage, killer of her children, killer of all she touches . . . You're pathetic. Disgusting. You're worse than Eric ever could be. At least Eric is honest enough to admit what he wants. But you . . . the whore of Babylon. THE WHORE OF BABYLON!"

Sarah continued to sob, uncontrollably now. She felt Katherine at her side, heard her speaking words of comfort. But it didn't matter. Words no longer mattered. Truth was truth. There was no hope. Not for her. Not even God could help her. Not now, not ever . . .

The remains of Laodicea were so isolated and so desolate that the mere act of walking through them made Brandon's heart heavy. There were no glimmering marble ruins here, no towering columns or arches. There were only broken-down walls and scattered piles of brick and rubble. There were no trees, not even brush—just one barren hill after another covered in dry, dead grass. For one of the richest cities in the Roman empire, it was now one of the most forsaken. For one of the wealthiest of the seven churches, its physical remains were the least.

The sun had just dropped behind the hills as Brandon stretched out his blanket beside the ruins of what a faded metal sign claimed to have been the actual church building. Earlier he had given in. He had finally agreed that tomorrow he would make the videotape for Tanya. Granted, a tape wasn't exactly the same as standing up to the Cartel in a dramatic confrontation, but it was better than nothing.

That was scheduled for the morning. But tonight, he had just wanted to be alone, to spend time out in these deserted hills, meditating on the last of the seven letters. He had no idea what the future held. Perhaps he'd take Tanya up on her offer to go to Jerusalem. He didn't know.

But that was okay, dead men don't need to know anything. They don't have to do anything. They don't have to be anything.

As the wisdom continued to take root, the peace continued to grow. If there was a battle, it would not be his. If there was a confrontation, it would only be as the Lord directed. He was merely along for the ride.

He reached for his pocket Bible. Although he planned to turn to Revelation, Psalm 37 caught his attention. He glanced down at the first few verses and began to read.

> *Do not fret because of evil men*
> * or be envious of those who do wrong;*
> *for like the grass they will soon wither,*
> * like green plants they will soon die away.*

Brandon paused to look out over the hills of dead brown grass. Hills that had once been so full of commerce and life were now withered and dead.

> *Trust in the Lord and do good;*
> * dwell in the land and enjoy safe pasture.*
> *Delight yourself in the Lord*
> * and he will give you the desires of your heart.*
> *Commit your way to the Lord;*
> * trust in him and he will do this:*
> *He will make your righteousness shine like the dawn,*
> * the justice of your cause like the noonday sun.*
> *Be still before the Lord and wait patiently for him;*
> * do not fret when men succeed in their ways,*
> * when they carry out their wicked schemes.*
> *Refrain from anger and turn from wrath;*
> * do not fret—it leads only to evil.*
> *For evil men will be cut off,*
> * but those who hope in the Lord will inherit the land.*
> *A little while, and the wicked will be no more;*
> * though you look for them, they will not be found.*
> *But the meek will inherit the land*
> * and enjoy great peace.*

"Peace, *great* peace." That was his inheritance. It was not up to him to fret or worry about evil. God would take care of it in His time. He had promised to use Brandon and that was fine, but only as He chose, not as Brandon schemed or planned or worried.

Dead men don't worry.

He rested against one of the ancient stone blocks of the church. Behind him, in the distance, he heard a pack of wild dogs. They sounded like they were near the remains of the Laodicean stadium. He had visited that area a little earlier and had sensed, just as he had in Ephesus and in Pergamum, that such a place would be part of his future, maybe part of his physical death. But that was okay.

Dead men don't die.

Ahead of him stretched one rolling hill after another. He could hear the distant tinkling of sheep bells as a shepherd guided his flock to safety for the night. The symbolism was not lost on him: the barking dogs versus the gentle shepherd protecting his flock from approaching night. And night was approaching . . . faster than he'd imagined. In the dimming light he quickly turned to Revelation, to the final letter to the final church:

> To the angel of the church in Laodicea write:
> These are the words of the Amen, the faithful and true witness, the ruler of God's creation. I know your deeds, that you are neither cold nor hot. I wish you were either one or the other! So, because you are lukewarm—neither hot nor cold—I am about to spit you out of my mouth. You say, "I am rich; I have acquired wealth and do not need a thing." But you do not realize that you are wretched, pitiful, poor, blind and naked. I counsel you to buy from me gold refined in the fire, so you can become rich; and white clothes to wear, so you can cover your shameful nakedness; and salve to put on your eyes, so you can see.
> Those whom I love I rebuke and discipline. So be earnest, and repent. Here I am! I stand at the

door and knock. If anyone hears my voice and opens the door, I will come in and eat with him, and he with me.

To him who overcomes, I will give the right to sit with me on my throne, just as I overcame and sat down with my Father on his throne. He who has an ear, let him hear what the Spirit says to the churches.

It was darker now. And Brandon's heart was heavier. He looked out over the bleak, forsaken hills. It was obvious the church had not paid attention to the warning. According to the guidebooks, there had been a major textile center here— so successful that apparently they had no need for Christ's garments. A medical center so famous for its eye balm that they didn't need Christ to help them see. A church so wealthy that they didn't realize they were "wretched, pitiful, poor, blind and naked." And, because they felt no need to repent, Christ had apparently spit them out of His mouth. As Brandon scanned the stark desolation before him, he wondered how different today's church, in all of its affluence, was. He also wondered how different, if any, its fate would be.

As he thought of today's church his mind drifted to Sarah. Their fates were so intertwined, he saw that now. As always, Gerty had been right. Sarah's actions symbolized a portion of the church—her ambition, her wanderings, her ... He swallowed back the thought, but knew it was true ... her adultery. Yet, even this knowledge hadn't stopped his love and longing for her. Nor did he suspect it stopped the Lord's love for His bride. If anything, her unfaithfulness only increased His desire to hold and console her.

With a quiet sigh, Brandon closed the book and stuffed it into his back pocket. He lay down and watched the stars begin to appear. But sleep would not come. Eventually he threw off the blanket and rose to his feet. He started to pace. He started to pray. Before long, he was wandering the deserted hills, praying and pacing.

He prayed as the last light of evening faded ... and he would still be praying at the first light of dawn.

Sarah sat alone in the dark.

It was her last evening in Nepal. She'd agreed to accompany Lucas and his entourage to Jerusalem. What other choice did she have? Heylel had been right. She couldn't return to Brandon. She was not worthy of him. And this business of being an end-time prophet? Who was she kidding? She wasn't qualified to serve God, she wasn't even qualified to be a Christian. What had Katherine said about actions speaking louder than words? She could claim to be whatever she wanted. But the truth was in what she did. And what she did proved her to be nothing but an ambitious, manipulating ... adulterer.

"The whore of Babylon"? Not a bad description. But instead of selling her favors for money, she'd held out for a higher currency: power.

She'd not slept with Lucas again; in fact she'd barely seen him. But she knew it was just a matter of time. Word had already spread that the two of them were "an item." Not that it mattered. Not now. Now that she'd finally seen the truth.

Sarah looked around the room. All her bags were packed except for the notebook computer which she'd left charging on the table for tomorrow's trip. But its tiny light was already glowing green indicating its battery was charged. She rose and crossed to it. For the briefest moment she thought of turning it on, of seeing if there was any e-mail from Brandon. But she fought off the temptation. It didn't matter. Not anymore.

She unplugged the power cord and packed it away.

"Okay. Stop tape, please."

For what must have been the hundredth time, the red light went off from Jerry's camera, and for the hundredth time he lowered it from his shoulder.

"I'm sorry, guys," Brandon apologized.

"No, that's okay," Tanya said, though there was no missing the weariness in her voice. "Just take a couple minutes to gather your thoughts and we'll start again. Do you want some water or anything?"

Brandon shook his head.

"Okay, let's just relax a couple minutes then."

Brandon sat on a nearby pile of stones and rolled his head, trying to stretch the stiffening muscles in his neck. They'd been at it all morning, and as far as he could tell they were no closer to getting it right than when they had started. But it was understandable. How do you condense a month's worth of learning into a single speech . . . especially when the person giving the speech doesn't know the first thing about speaking?

Brandon had so much to say, messages from each of the seven letters, and it all wanted to come out at once. From Ephesus, the warning for Christians to return to their first love. From Smyrna, to prepare them for possible persecution. From Pergamum, that they could cut through the distracting voices with the sword of Christ's mouth. From Thyatira, the insistence upon holiness. From Sartis, to wake up and quit resting on past accomplishments. From Philadelphia, the opportunities opening up to proclaim the gospel. And finally, from Laodecia, that wealth and strength will be the church's downfall if she doesn't humble herself and receive Christ's real riches.

And, if that wasn't enough, there was his knowledge of the Cartel—how the organization of peace would eventually turn into another Imperial Cult whose ruler would set himself up to be worshiped as God.

How could someone like Brandon say all of this? Sure, he'd jotted down notes and had practiced, but everything he said still came out jumbled and confused.

"Don't worry," Tanya had assured him earlier, "we can save it in the editing."

Maybe she was telling the truth, maybe she wasn't. Still, it would be nice to get it right at least once.

"Brandon?" He looked up as she knelt next to him. "Can I make a suggestion?"

"Sure, anything."

"I've got bits and pieces of what you're trying to say—"

"I know and I'm sorry. I've got an outline, but—"

"Why don't we try another approach?"

"Another approach? Like what?"

"Do you remember back in L.A. how easy the words came for you, how you said they were like fire?"

He nodded. "They burned so hot I couldn't hold them back."

"So let's do that. Instead of trying to remember everything, just relax and let the fire come."

"I'm sorry, I don't know what—"

"I mean get out of the way. Stop trying to do it on your own."

Brandon frowned.

"You've been talking about being this dead man, right?"

"Right."

"So be dead. Stop trying. I'll tell Jerry to stand by while you pray or do whatever you do. And if you feel this fire stuff starting to come, just let us know and we'll turn on the camera."

"And if it doesn't come?"

"Well, no offense, my friend, but we couldn't be any worse off than we are now." She flashed him a grin, which he couldn't help but return. She patted his shoulder, then rose to go speak with Jerry.

Waves of heat shimmered off the tarmac at Tribhuvan International Airport. The temperature outside was insufferable, but it dropped a good twenty degrees as soon as Sarah stepped into the Cartel's Gulfstream Five corporate jet. Toward the front of the cabin was a plush sofa, a handful of overstuffed swivel chairs, a wet bar, and a large mahogany table. Beyond that was an office meeting area, and past that what looked like quarters for sleeping.

"Sarah." Lucas glanced up from his paperwork and motioned for her to sit in one of the chairs beside him. As usual he was all charm and attention. Gesturing around the plane, he asked, "What do you think? It's on loan to us for a trial run."

She continued looking around the cabin, taking in the rich wood paneling, the communication center behind them with its phones, faxes, and computers, and the royal blue curtains tied back from the windows with gold rope. "It's . . ." She couldn't quite find the words. "Nice. Very nice."

"You don't think it's too much?"

She joined him and took a seat. The upholstery was leather, probably calfskin. "A person could get used to it."

"Good." He grinned. "How was your ride to the airport?"

"A little bumpy. But I'm sure we managed to miss a few potholes along the way."

He chuckled while reaching out and patting her hand. "Well, that shall all be changing. Very shortly we will leave behind the potholes and all the other joys of life in the wilderness."

"You're not going to return?"

He shook his head and sighed. "I don't think so. The work before me is too great. I am afraid the days of semi-seclusion have finally come to an end."

Unable to miss the sadness in his voice, Sarah was about to comment when something outside the window caught her eye. A police jeep had pulled up just past the jet's white wing. Two officers had emerged and were now intercepting Katherine and Eric on their walk from the car to the plane.

Eric had won the argument with his mother about remaining with Lucas and the Cartel . . . at least for now. Not that Katherine had much say in the matter. Just the same, she took great pains to stay glued to her son's side every available second. Sarah had barely spoken to her since the encounter in his room. Except for the not-so-subtle warning about getting too close to Lucas, Katherine had returned to her usual distant and aloof self.

Outside, the argument grew more animated. It appeared the police were trying to escort Eric away.

Sarah turned to Lucas. "Do you see this?"

He had returned to his work. "Hmm?"

"The police, it looks like they're trying to arrest Eric."

He glanced over at the window. "You're not serious?"

"Take a look." They watched as the altercation grew more physical, until the officers were actually pulling Eric toward their jeep. "Shouldn't you do something?"

"Mr. Chairman?" An aide knelt at Lucas's side. "The American secretary of state is on the phone."

"Now?"

"Yes, sir."

He rose from his seat and turned to Sarah. "I am afraid I must handle this."

"What about Eric?"

"I think . . ." He gave a slight smile. "I think Eric can take care of himself."

"But—" Sarah motioned toward the window, confused.

"Trust me, he will be fine." And after another smile, Lucas was gone.

Sarah turned back to the window. Now the larger of the two officers was stumbling backwards. He was grabbing his collar, ripping at it, trying to loosen it. Others looked on, not understanding. He motioned wildly, clawing his neck. He stumbled against the jeep, then dropped to his knees, tearing at his throat. His partner raced to his side, shouting, trying to understand what was happening. Other members of the party moved in to try and help.

But not Eric. He had simply turned and started toward the plane again. For the briefest second he glanced up, and his eyes locked onto Sarah's. They were filled with smirking amusement. She looked away and over to Katherine. The woman was ashen white, watching with a hand over her mouth. Sarah turned back to the officer. He was sprawled out on the concrete, his body heaving, gasping for air.

She spun around to Lucas, who was in the communication center, chatting away. He nodded to her with a reassuring smile and continued to speak. She turned back to the window. The officer on the ground had stopped moving. As far as Sarah could tell, he was no longer breathing.

A chill crept through her body. "Eric can take care of himself," he'd said. "Trust me . . . he will be fine."

It had started. Not because Brandon had forced it, or even sought it. It began simply as he thanked the Lord. He started thanking him for the small immediate things—the stark beauty of the rolling hills in front of him, their various shades of brown and gold and beige. The rocks at his feet— their shapes, their colors, their texture. He glanced over at Tanya and Jerry. What wondrous creations they were, each with their unique looks and gifts and personalities—Tanya with her honey blonde hair and perpetual drive, Jerry with his sweating bald top and sullen weariness. What marvelous diversity.

These first few thoughts of thanks were purposely willed by Brandon. But once the pump had been primed, the praise came easier. Soon it was taking on a life of its own. The worship began to blossom, growing until he was caught up in it wholeheartedly. But not just worship over what God had created . . . worship over who God was. His goodness. His faithfulness. His majesty. With the worship came a reverent sense of awe . . . and with that awe came the love.

As he basked in his love for the Lord, he began to feel the Lord's love for him. It became a cycle. A cycle of adoration and love, one for the other, spiraling, drawing them closer and closer into each other, until Brandon was totally and completely immersed. And with the immersion came the spilling over. Unable to contain the love, it overflowed, pouring out from him toward all of creation. Once again Brandon was experiencing the Creator's heart. And with that heart came the fire. It was the same fire he'd seen in the Lord's eyes. The same all-consuming passion.

Tears filled his eyes. But they were not his tears. The love, the gut-wrenching ache was God's—his longing to embrace his children.

And still the fire grew, radiating through his body until it centered in his chest. So much needless pain, so much self-inflicted suffering . . . when all they had to do was listen. The rules were not for him, they were for his children, for their well-being. Why wouldn't they see? Why wouldn't they obey?

Tears spilled onto his cheeks. He couldn't stop them. So much love. So much pain. He felt Tanya touch his knee. "Tell us," she said softly, "tell us what you're feeling."

He tried to speak, but the ache was unbearable.

"Tell us . . ."

He looked up. There was Jerry with his camera lens four feet away. But it was no longer just a lens. It was God's children, millions of suffering children who needed their Father, who needed to be held. It was his bride, longing for her bridegroom, aching for his embrace, hungry for the only one who could satisfy her.

A Scripture leaped into his mind, another memory verse. But it was more than a verse. It was alive—filled with the very presence of God, filled with his fire. At last Brandon opened his mouth, and at last he began to speak.

"When I shut up the heavens so that there is no rain, or command locusts to devour the land or send a plague among my people . . ."

He took a ragged breath and continued: "If my people, who are called by my name, will humble themselves . . ."

Other words rushed in. They were not Scripture, but he knew they could be trusted, he knew they came from the fire.

"My children! My bride! I have chosen you from before the beginning of the world. You carry my name, yet you do not live my life. Though I have given you power, you have not used it to pursue my holiness. Hear my plea. Heed my warning. Quit seeking your desires, quit seeking your kingdom. Humble yourselves and receive mine. Receive all that I am."

More words poured in and Brandon obeyed, speaking them as they came to his consciousness.

"I am eternal. All else you pursue will burn. You fast in vain. You pray and plead and beg, but your efforts are futile. Look into my eyes and know what is eternal. Only when you behold my glory will your desires conform to mine. Only when you know me can you pray in my name.

"Repent! Turn! I have given you the power to overcome. All you need to do is choose: your wickedness or my holiness, your death or my life. For without repentance there is no forgiveness. And without forgiveness we have no fellowship."

For the briefest second, Brandon caught a glimpse of life without God, and it nearly devastated him. A heaving sob escaped, and it was all he could do to hold back others.

"Humble yourselves!" he shouted. "Seek my face! Turn! Then will I hear from heaven and will forgive your sin and will heal your land. My bride . . . my precious bride." The words choked in Brandon's throat as he realized he was also speaking to Sarah, *his* Sarah. "How my heart yearns for you. How I love and adore you . . . more than I did my very life. How I long for this time of suffering to end, and for the cup of my wrath to be emptied. But you will not have it.

"You try to stop evil by changing others. Yet you do not cease from your own evil. Repent. Repent and turn your heart toward me. Repent and see if there is anything I would withhold from you. My arms are opened wide."

He continued to shout, pleading to the camera, pleading to Sarah, to whomever would listen. He could no longer tell if they were his words or the Lord's. He suspected they were one and the same.

"Turn from your adultery. Let my love break your grip on iniquity. Let my love strip you of your sin. Turn and run into my arms that I may hold you as I once did. Come to me that we may again share the intimacies of husband and wife. That we may again be one."

The final words came heavy and uneven. "For when we are one . . . when you are lost in my arms and when our hearts are intertwined, all of creation watches in awe. When we are one, delighting in each other's pleasure, there is nothing, absolutely nothing you can withhold from me, and nothing I will withhold from you."

Brandon was hit by another set of wracking sobs. And then another. But there were no more words. Just the tears. He lowered his head. He had felt God's presence; he had been consumed by his love and had spoken his words.

Now there was only silence.

PART THREE

For Sarah Martus the ride from Ben Gurion International Airport to Jerusalem was an eye-opener. In some ways she'd forgotten the world-wide fame of Lucas Ponte, let alone the international importance of the upcoming event. But now, everywhere she looked, there were reminders. There were the crowds standing outside the airport with banners to greet them. There was the fifty-two-kilometer drive to the city with every other streetlight along the highway supporting a different country's flag. And as the motorcade wound its way through the limestone cliffs, there were the honking cars and waving drivers. They had no idea which of the three limos Lucas was in (one of the many Israeli security precautions), so they waved at all of them.

When Sarah had pointed out the fervent devotion, Lucas had shaken his head and smiled. "It's not for me; it's only what I stand for."

"You mean the upcoming peace?" she asked.

"Yes." He sighed with weary satisfaction. "Finally our planet can have some rest."

Sarah nodded. Amidst her own life's turmoil, it was easy to forget the significance of the last few days . . . and the upcoming ones. Still, there was the matter of Eric and her knowledge of who or what he was hosting. And, since there was no place for Lucas to hide or duck the issue inside the limo, she decided to bring it up again.

As always, he listened with great attention. When she had finally finished voicing her concerns he spoke. "And yet, as far as you can tell, Heylel offers no physical danger to the boy."

"That's true. But the psychological trauma for anyone, particularly in these early stages of adolescence, can be devastating. Surely, Katherine has told you what she's seen."

Lucas shook his head. "A few brief remarks, but nothing of substance. Katherine can be quite elusive when she wants to be."

Sarah frowned. "But you knew about the death of his bodyguard? His outbursts of violence?"

"Oh, that. Yes, yes of course. That I knew. That's why we initially invited you to join us."

"And now this incident at the airport."

He shook his head. "Terrible, terrible." He leaned over to his secretary who was brooding over an itinerary in the seat facing them. "Deena, when we get to the hotel be sure to send our condolences to the family."

"Certainly." She jotted down the note.

"Also flowers."

Deena nodded and continued to write.

Sarah watched. What had Katherine said? "He's not as he appears." She was beginning to understand. She saw it on the airport tarmac, and she saw it now. Lucas Ponte, the ultimate statesman—not only had he a gift for saying the right thing at the right time, but he was a pro at keeping his hands clean and avoiding any unpleasant confrontation.

This time, however, she would not give up. "My point is—"

"Oh." He turned back to Deena. "And something for his partner, perhaps a gift reminding him that the Cartel would greatly appreciate his discretion in this matter."

"I understand."

"Lucas?"

He turned back to her. "Yes, Sarah." The sincerity in his eyes was so earnest that she almost believed him. Almost.

"If Heylel is so dangerous," she asked, "to both Eric and to others, why do you keep going to him for counsel?"

"Because he has always proved accurate."

"That's it?"

"Should there be more?"

"He's a killer."

"Lucas?" Deena interrupted. "Excuse me, Sarah." Without waiting for permission, she continued. "You have a meeting scheduled with the vice-chair at 1:15, but if you meet with Premier Orowitz at 2:00 I'm afraid we could create some diplomatic upsmanship. Perhaps it would be better to . . ."

She continued speaking, but Sarah barely heard. It had happened again. The interruption. The sidestep. As they spoke, she turned and looked back out the tinted window. They were in the city now, heading down Jaffa Road. She craned her neck, hoping to catch a glimpse of the Old City, but the buildings blocked her view.

When Deena finally finished, Sarah turned back to him. She would not be put off again. "Lucas?"

He was studying his papers. There was the slightest trace of impatience in his voice. "Yes, Sarah."

"If Heylel is a killer, if he's so dangerous, it seems incongruous that you would work with him toward world peace."

Lucas looked over to her, then broke into a smile. "You know so little of politics."

"I know Heylel is incredibly evil."

"We provide Heylel a service. In return he rewards us with his counsel."

"And that service . . . is Eric?"

"Eric has voiced little opposition, and for his participation Heylel has promised him great things."

"You mean to let him rule the world." Lucas hesitated, and she took advantage of the opportunity. "He's just a boy, Lucas. You're letting a boy prostitute himself for some sort of demonic power. Don't you see it? The Cartel, all of you, you're all prostituting yourselves for whatever information this Heylel has to offer."

"Sarah . . ."

"What about your ethics? What about your ideals, what about—"

"Ideals?"

"Yes, what about—"

"Ideals?"

Sarah came to a stop.

There was the smile again. This time he gently shook his head. "Sarah, Sarah, Sarah. The world is a very hostile place. Ideals are interesting in theory, good for classroom discussion. But I am afraid they don't fare so well in world politics. Take a look out there."

Sarah turned to the window. They were approaching the King David Hotel, and people were lining the street to catch a glimpse of them. Some waved, others clapped.

"These people, they are not interested in ideals. They are interested in survival. They want to live. They want their children to live. And in the end they will do whatever is necessary to make it so. In the real world everyone must pay a price. Everyone must prostitute themselves some way. It's how we survive." He patted her hand. "Prostitution does not have to be an evil thing, Sarah. Surely you understand that by now. You, better than most."

She wasn't sure she'd heard correctly. "Pardon me?"

The car, which had pulled into the driveway of the hotel, came to a stop. "Ah, here we are."

Sarah glanced outside. People were gathered along the driveway. They crowded onto the sidewalk and spilled over to the front yard of the large YMCA building across the street.

The car door opened and a young man in a dark blazer appeared. "Welcome to Jerusalem, Mr. Chairman."

Lucas smiled and turned on the charm. "Thank you ... Mr. . . . ." He paused, waiting for a name.

"Zimmerman, sir. William Zimmerman. I'm head of security."

"Thank you, William." Lucas stepped out of the car, and the crowd broke into cheers. He waved as bodyguards appeared from nowhere and quickly escorted him toward the entrance of the large six-story stone structure.

Inside the car, Deena had gathered her things and stepped outside to follow. But as Sarah scooted across the seat to join her, she turned back and motioned for her to stay put. "You don't get out here."

"I'm sorry?"

"For appearances. It is best you wait until the limo pulls to the service entrance on the side."

"Service entrance?"

She nodded. "We don't want the conservative factions to get the wrong impression, do we?"

Sarah sat stunned.

Deena smiled. "Don't worry, we've secured a suite for you beside Lucas's. I've been told it has a discrete connecting door." Before Sarah could react, Deena smiled and shut the car door. The limo gave a slight jolt and pulled away.

"But you can fight it, I know you can."

"Mom . . ."

"Just like Coleman, remember? You still have free will."

"Mom . . ." Eric watched his mother rise to her feet. She began pacing around the large fifth-story suite that overlooked the Old City.

"Maybe if we were to pray," she offered. "Maybe if we were to ask God—"

"Mom!" The sharpness of his voice turned her back to him. "I don't want him to leave."

She crossed back to him. "Sweetheart . . . it may be exciting now, he may be making all sorts of promises. But eventually, eventually you'll have to pay the price."

"I don't care."

"You don't . . . care?"

He nodded and pushed up his glasses with his little finger. She took a deep breath and eased herself beside him on the sofa. He could tell she wanted to brush the hair out of his eyes the way she used to. He was grateful she didn't try.

"Don't you see?" she asked. "You've become a different person. The sweet, loving Eric I used to know is—"

"That Eric was a wimp!"

"No." The kindness in her voice made him uneasy. "That Eric was sensitive and kind. And he always used his gifts for good. Remember?"

He felt his old weaknesses trying to creep in, and he glanced away.

"Remember how he used to help people? Remember how you healed my face? How you helped that little blind girl at the compound?"

"Tell her." He wasn't sure if it was his thoughts or Heylel's. *"Tell her the truth."*

He rose and moved away from her toward the window. The Old City and its wall rested on the hill just a few blocks away. It had a green hue from the bulletproof glass in front of him. "You don't know what you're talking about."

"I know what I see." Her voice remained gentle.

"We *are* using my gifts for good!"

"Killing that policeman at the airport yesterday?"

"He was in our way."

"And Deepak? He was a good friend, Eric. One of your favorites."

He felt himself faltering. "He . . . he made me mad."

"Eric, sweetheart . . ." She was up again, crossing toward him. "You have to make this thing stop."

"No!"

"Do you want me to take over?" That was definitely Heylel speaking, though the two were becoming so close, it wasn't always easy to tell. And that was the idea—to become so much at one with each other that when he thought, it was Heylel thinking, that when Heylel spoke, it was him speaking.

His mother continued, softer. "I know you love Lucas, but—"

He turned on her. "Love has nothing to do with it! He's been valuable to us in the past, and he'll be even more valuable in the future. Just you wait."

His mother hesitated, then continued. "I know you like the idea of the Cartel listening to you, that it makes you feel important—"

"I am important!"

"—but these people are not good, Eric. They're evil."

"They're going to help us rule the world!"

His mother hesitated. "Maybe. But that doesn't make them good. They've done things, sweetheart. Awful things. And they'll continue to do them. They'll continue to do them until—"

"If you're talking about Scorpion, I already know."

That stopped her. But only for a moment. "You . . . know about it?" Her voice was a little unsteady.

Eric had the upper hand now. It was important to keep it. "Of course."

"You knew that all those people—that the Jews and Arabs—were being murdered?"

"Knew about it?" He let out a short laugh. This would get her. "We told them how they could do it!"

"Eric ..."

"Sure. Me and Heylel, we drew them the diagrams, we showed their genetic guys how to make it."

She could only stare.

"And that won't be the end of it," he said. "Others are going to try to stop us, and we're going to kill them, too. We'll kill them all. We'll kill anybody who gets in the way. Anybody."

He wanted to keep going, but his mother was already fighting back tears. It was enough for the time being. After all, she was still his mother. At least for now.

If Brandon had been impressed by Turkey's history and culture, he was overwhelmed by Jerusalem's. With a past history thirty times longer than the United States, the Old City was home to four hundred holy sites, thirty denominations, three Sabbath days, seven alphabets, and fifteen languages. It was a jarring cacophony of life-threatening politics, swarming humanity, fierce prejudice, devout holiness, deep-rooted hatred, and beckoning merchants ... all crammed within a half square mile of narrow streets and stone buildings. But there was something else here—beyond the history and humanity.

There was the desire to touch holiness.

Brandon felt it no stronger than in the Church of the Holy Sepulcher, the large structure built over what many believe to be the hill where Jesus was crucified as well as the tomb from which he rose. Tanya had dropped Brandon off here while she went to persuade a news producer friend into editing and beaming his taped message back to the States. That had been nearly two hours ago, and Brandon was no more tired of the place now than when he had arrived.

For the first hour he'd been lost, wandering the grottos and carved-out niches staked out by somber-looking clergy of various sects. He choked on the incense and smoking candles, was jostled by the waves of pushing pilgrims, and was amused at the chants and songs of competing clergy all pretending to be oblivious to each other. It wasn't until he'd completely circled the inside of the church and started up the steep nineteen stone steps to Calvary that Brandon started to feel a connection. Even then, it wasn't immediate.

At first, like so many others, he was put off by the gaudy lampstands, the hanging candleholders (attached to nearly every square foot of ceiling), the pretentious amount of gold and silver (including the loincloth of the life-size crucifix looming above and behind the altar), the inlaid pearl, the religious icons, and the intricate mosaics covering the entire ceiling of vaulted arches. In fact, for Brandon, the whole place gave new meaning to the word *kitsch*. If Christ really had been crucified here, why did they have to turn it into such an overindulged spectacle of bad taste?

But as he sat on a worn marble bench against the sidewall, he began to see something deeper. He began to sense the awe and the love here. He saw it in the hundreds of faces parading past the crucifix stuck into the rock. He saw it in the line of those patiently waiting to stoop under the altar and reach into a small hole to touch part of that rock. He saw it in the nuns kneeling, the Greek Orthodox priest meditating, the Armenians moving their lips in whispered unison, the Protestants standing to the side softly singing, a lone Coptic priest silently weeping. He saw it as each attempted, in their own way, to touch the infinite, to express their inexpressible appreciation for what had been accomplished on that hill so many centuries before.

And the longer Brandon sat, the more he understood. He tilted back his head to look up at the mosaic ceiling above him—dozens of stars and angels in a midnight blue sky. Each stone was laid with such care and precision that it actually looked like an intricate painting. The work must have been excruciatingly difficult. Wasn't this all the same? Wasn't this the same as the old black woman who was now being helped down to her knees so she could touch the rock? Wasn't this simply another attempt at trying to embrace God, some way of expressing the inexpressible? And although the pictures, candles, and gaudiness were not his style, just as many of the theologies parading before him were not, Brandon felt their reverence, awe, and love.

And, as he felt their love, he sensed a deeper Love returning.

Feeling God's love and sensing his presence were happening more and more for Brandon. Now that he'd given up his own life, he was more open to experiencing God's ... no matter what form it came in. He found it interesting that he was no longer concerned about affirming his own views of Christ. In fact, the more he lost himself in Christ's love, the more he realized his views didn't matter. All that mattered was Jesus Christ. Not Brandon's theology, not Brandon's ministry. God would advance these as he saw fit. All that mattered was Jesus Christ and him crucified. Everything else was vain ... as vain as the debate over which brand of worship here was better ... or which type of art was the most tasteful.

As he felt God's love, he felt the fire—the burning desire to draw each of these children into his arms. To encourage them to bask and soak and drink in as much love as they could. Because there was no end to it. The love for each was infinite. And there was no spot on earth where that love was more apparent than here.

Here, where the God of the universe unleashed his wrath upon his Son. Here, where at any moment, the Son could have cried, "Enough, let them suffer their own punishment!" Here, where, sin by sin, anguished torture upon anguished torture, the Son received full punishment for each of our failures ... where, for six excruciating hours, all of creation watched in stunned silence as the human race, who had once sold itself into slavery, was being repurchased.

Such love. Such infinite, unfathomable, indiscernible love. That was the love that saturated Brandon and fed the fire. And that was why here, on this tiny hill, in this noisy, eclectic sanctuary, Brandon closed his eyes and began to pray for the bride. For God's bride . . . and his own.

Sarah sat naked on the edge of the white Jacuzzi, staring at the water as it filled the tub. She was drunk. She'd been drunk for hours. A fully stocked bar was one of the perks in the VIP suites. She had taken a fancy to the Coke and Puerto Rican rum. She'd hoped it would silence the voice, the one she'd been hearing to some degree or another ever since the encounter in Eric's room at Nepal. The one she'd first heard on her wedding day . . . *the whore of Babylon!* But it did not. Instead, the more she drank the louder it grew . . . and the more relentless it became. *Adultery and ambition, that is all you are!*

In Nepal she'd been able to drown it out with the preparations for Jerusalem, with the excitement of the installation, and with the love and respect she had felt from Lucas. But now . . . *Prostitution . . . surely, you understand better than most.* That was yesterday afternoon, the last time she'd seen him in person. He'd been in meetings ever since.

For whatever reason, security thought it was best she not leave the hotel, at least until after the installation. So with Lucas gone and Katherine making a point to stay cloistered in her room with Eric, Sarah was left pretty much on her own.

Except for the voice. *You have never changed, you never will.*

She'd tried the TV, but all she seemed to see was Chairman Ponte speaking with some president, Chairman Ponte talking with this group, Chairman Ponte offering assurance to that group. Anticipation for tomorrow's installation was high, and rightfully so. With the Cartel pulling strings behind the scenes and pressing for last-minute favors, it looked like it would be the international event of the decade. And her boyfriend was right in the center. But for now he was the last thing in the world she wanted to see. Not since the little incident out on the terrace.

She'd been sunning herself at the hotel's pool, one of the few distractions she'd found since she'd arrived. She'd already lost track of the number of glasses of Chardonnay she'd put down when she spotted Lucas dining up on the terrace. He was chatting with a handful of Hollywood celebs. Big names. So big that she thought strolling up to the table and meeting them would be interesting—especially since their talk didn't appear to be too official—especially since one of the actresses seemed to be becoming a bit too affectionate.

Sarah pulled herself from the lawn chair, waited for the ground to stop moving, then placed one foot in front of the other and headed toward the terrace. She'd barely made it halfway when Lucas spotted her. She smiled. But, without even acknowledging her, he glanced to one of the security men and discreetly nodded in her direction. Taking his cue, security quietly crossed the lawn and cut her off.

"May I help you, Doctor?"

"I'm going up to say hi."

"I don't think that's such a good idea. Chairman Ponte is preoccupied at the moment."

"No, he's not. He's right there." She tried to pass him, but the man blocked her.

"I'm sorry, ma'am, he's asked not to be disturbed."

"What?" The ground had started to move again. "Do you know who I am?"

"Yes, I know exactly who you are."

"Then you'll let me by."

Again she tried to move around him, and again he blocked her. "I am sorry, Doctor."

She raised her voice louder. "I want to see Lucas. Let me by."

"Doctor, maybe you should go back to your room."

"Lucas!" she waved her hand. "Lucas!"

Other tables glanced in her direction, but not Lucas. He became more engrossed in his discussion.

"Lucas!"

"That's enough, Doctor." The security man motioned to one of the dining guests, who immediately rose to his feet and joined them. "Show Dr. Martus to her room, will you please?" The "guest" nodded and took her arm.

"But that's . . ." Sarah tried to twist free. "Lucas and I, we're, we're . . ."

"I know what you are," the security man answered. "Good day, Doctor."

The guest began leading her around the terrace and up toward the hotel. She tried to break free, but his grip was like iron. "Lucas! Lucas!" Other tables turned and stared. By now she'd drawn nearly everyone's attention. Everyone but Lucas's. He continued talking and laughing in perfect oblivion.

That had been forty minutes ago.

Sarah turned to the bathroom counter behind her and poured the last of the rum into her glass. When she set the bottle down, she missed the counter and it crashed onto the marble floor, sending shards of splintered glass in all directions. She looked down, startled at her own clumsiness, then felt the tears coming to her eyes.

Can't you do anything right?

She closed her eyes, but the voice continued. *You can lie. You can cheat. You can kill.*

"I know exactly who you are, Doctor." That's what the security guard had said. And maybe he did. But did she?

Adulterer.

I know exactly what you are, Doctor . . .

Behold, the Whore of Babylon!

And she was learning more and more who the great Lucas Ponte was as well . . .

Be careful, he's not all that he appears.

She'd seen it before, but had done her best to deny it. Lucas Ponte . . . master of charm, perfecter of politics. Wasn't it interesting how once they'd slept together he had never again mentioned his offer for her to join the team? Wasn't it interesting that he was always insulated from the dirty work of power? Wasn't it interesting how he always pretended to listen, but how he always got his way ... even when it came to Eric ... even when it involved the young man's destruction?

No, Lucas Ponte was not as he appeared.

But, then again, neither are you.

Liar ... Baby killer ... Adulterer ... Whore ...

She looked back to the water in the tub. Is that really what she'd become? The great Sarah Weintraub, doctor, cutting-edge neurobiologist, end-time prophet ... now reduced to nothing but an elaborate call girl?

"Brandon!" The name surprised her. It came deep from her gut before she could stop it. "Bran ... don ..." But even Brandon couldn't help now. No one could. Naked and all alone, Sarah lowered her head and tried to cry tears of self-pity. But they would not come. There was no pity. Not anymore. It was hard to pity someone you hated so deeply.

CHAPTER 16

I tell you, kiddo, it's the biggest broadcast I've ever been a part of. We've got downlinks in nearly every country. In theory we could be reaching every household with a television in the entire world."

"If those households are interested in tuning in," Tanya corrected.

"Oh, they'll be interested. With the promos and all the past coverage on Ponte, they'll think it's the media event of the century."

Tanya looked at Ryan Holton skeptically.

"See for yourself." He motioned to the row of monitors along the top of the wall of the Channel

Two newsroom. They monitored the competing channels beamed in from other countries. Except for one screen showing the latest volcano disaster in the Philippines, and another playing a fabric softener commercial, all others were broadcasting various aspects of Lucas Ponte's visit to Jerusalem or commenting upon the upcoming installation.

Tanya whistled softly. "The Cartel's doing all this?"

Ryan nodded. "They're twisting some pretty heavy arms. Every major network in the world is being 'encouraged' to support this 'pivotal moment of world history.'"

"That's how it's being promoted? A little rich, isn't it?"

He shrugged. "The people are eating it up."

Tanya looked out across the newsroom. A dozen reporters, all under thirty and most chain-smoking, were typing at computer terminals or working the phones. Israel had basically two major networks. Channel One, run by the government, and Channel Two, which was owned and operated independently. The latter's facilities filled the entire ninth floor of the impressive Egged Building on Jaffa Road. On the outside the building looked modern and impressive. On the inside it was purely functional. Worn carpeting, low ceiling, fluorescent lights, and grimy white walls. But Channel Two was the best. And that's why Ryan Holton had chosen to use their services. Because he was the best.

Tanya had fallen in love with Ryan's good looks and sharp intelligence right out of college. And, despite their breakup two years later, she knew a part of her would always love him. But he wanted a family and she wanted a career. Then there was her faith. Not that it prevented them from living together for nearly ten months. Still, she claimed to be a devout Christian. And Ryan—well, Ryan's only devotion was to being a great TV producer/director and a faithful friend. He had succeeded in both.

Tanya stared up at the various screens showing Ponte meeting this dignitary, Ponte visiting this site, Ponte chatting with this common person. According to Ryan, the images were being broadcast all around the world. "These guys are good," she conceded. "Very, very good."

Ryan nodded. "They've got the power, kiddo, and they know how to use it. You should see what they're letting me do for the broadcast. I've got twelve cameras with live feeds from around the world. Endorsements from Moscow, the Vatican, Washington, that sort of thing. Another half dozen for immediate man-on-the-street responses, and fourteen stationed around the Temple Mount where I'll call the show."

"They let you bring remote trucks onto the Mount?"

"No, the trailers are parked just outside the Wall. We had to string cable over it *and* the cemetery beside it. But they're letting me bring in a couple Jumbotron screens so the crowd at the back of the Mount can see what's happening up onstage."

"Sounds like you've got your plate full."

He flashed her a smile. "Just the way I like it."

Another pause settled over the conversation. Nearly eighteen months had passed since they'd last touched base. She hadn't even known about his divorce, though she suspected it coming. And as far as his looks went? The more worn and weathered he became, the more handsome it made him.

He tapped the tapes she'd handed him. "You say this kid is the one who ruined your show in L.A.?"

"Yeah. Any chance of scoring some time in one of these edit suites?" She motioned to the cramped rooms behind them. "Turn Jerry loose on an Avid so we can put together something for broadcast?"

Ryan broke into a mischievous grin. "Payback time, huh?" Before she could respond, he asked, "Did you know your boss is in town?"

"Jimmy Tyler?"

"Yeah, he's staying over at the Hyatt. During the ceremony he'll be one of the dignitaries on the platform. Not that he'll be doing much talking." Ryan glanced back to the tapes in his hand. "So what you're looking for with these is a little eye for an eye, am I right?"

Tanya shook her head. "Not really. Actually, I believe there's something legit about him."

"You're not serious?"

She nodded. "He's young, and he's made his share of mistakes, but what I saw in Turkey and what I have on tape proves he's not some religious con artist. And he's definitely not a fruitcake. I think he just might be the genuine article."

"A prophet crying in the wilderness?" Ryan teased.

Tanya shrugged, doing her best to maintain her skepticism. After all, that was a reporter's stock-in-trade. "The kid's got a lot to say . . . I just think somebody should give him the opportunity to say it."

Ryan held her look a moment, then glanced down at the tapes. "We've booked time on all their Avids until after the installation."

"Prerecorded segments during the broadcast?"

He nodded, then referred back to the tapes. "What do you have, about three hours here?"

She nodded. "I'm looking for an eight-, maybe ten-minute piece when it's completed."

"Do you mind working at night?"

"Hey, we'll take what we can get."

"Send Jerry up. Have him start digitizing them. Once they're loaded I can give up one of the machines."

Tanya broke into a smile. "Thanks, Ryan."

"No problem, kiddo."

"What do I owe you?"

"This one's on the Cartel."

"You're serious?"

"Sure." He grinned, then added good-naturedly, "'Course it might cost you some drinks with me when you're done. Maybe stop by the hotel . . . we've got plenty of catching up to do."

Tanya knew what he meant, and she was not offended. After all, they were both single again, and he *was* looking pretty good. But she'd already planned her answer. "I don't think so, Ryan."

There was a flicker of surprise in his eyes, and she explained, "Don't get me wrong, there's nothing in the world I'd rather do than spend the night catching up on old times."

"But?"

"You know my faith, my religion."

He looked perplexed. "It never stopped you before."

"You're right." She inhaled, then let it out. "But, this kid. I don't know. After listening to him . . ." She dropped off, trying to find the right words.

"He really got to you, huh?"

She looked up at him, then slowly nodded. "Yeah . . . he really got to me."

As Brandon remained in the church praying, a deeper urgency began to rise up within him. At first he thought it was coming from the old Brandon Martus, the dead one, the one trying to make him worry and draw him away from the presence of God. This sort of thing happened frequently, but he was getting used to its tricks. In fact, he'd learned a few of his own. He'd discovered the best way to keep the old man dead was by focusing upon Christ. He discovered if he filled his mind so full of worshiping and dwelling upon him, he could literally force the old thoughts to flee. Sometimes this would take ten seconds, sometimes ten minutes, but if he persisted, it always worked. He could enter the presence of God and remain until the Father's thoughts became his thoughts.

Except for now.

Now, the more he dwelled upon Christ, the more his thoughts filled with Sarah. He bore down harder, closing his eyes, concentrating upon Jesus' grace, his tenderness, his glory. And yet the thoughts of Sarah continued to grow and expand. An idea began to take shape. Was it possible that the reason he couldn't remove the thoughts of Sarah was because they were the thoughts of the Father?

Eyes still closed, he sensed a difference in the light striking his face. Somebody had approached and was standing in front of him. He heard faint, labored breathing, but kept his eyes shut and continued to pray. Then he heard the brush of clothing and felt something touch his arm. He opened his eyes and saw a frail old woman leaning toward him. She was hunched over and wore a loose dark brown dress and a cream-colored Palestinian head scarf. Her face was leathered and grooved from decades of sun, and her once-blue eyes were watery gray from cataracts.

She patted his arm again, this time motioning for him to rise and follow her.

He smiled, but indicated that he was praying.

She took his arm. He looked down at her hand. It was mostly bone and blue veins. She pulled, motioning that he must come with her. Her grip was weak but persistent, and when he looked back into her eyes, he sensed how important it was for her that he obey. Finally, reluctantly, he rose from the marble bench.

She did not release her grip, but continued to pull. She hobbled toward the steep steps and started down them, relying on him for balance, until they reached the main floor of the church. Once there, she turned and started toward the exit.

"Whoa, wait a minute." Brandon brought them to a stop. "I have friends. They are coming to pick me up."

She paid no attention and continued to pull, motioning for him to follow.

He spoke again, louder and slower. "I must stay." He indicated the church. "Here. I must stay here."

She shook her head and continued to pull. It was obvious the woman would not let up until she got her way. Brandon scanned the crowded church, making sure Tanya had not already arrived. When he didn't see her, he looked back at the woman's anxious eyes. Finally he agreed to follow.

They stepped through the wooden door and into the blazing bright courtyard. He winced at the sunlight reflecting off the limestone pavement and buildings. She led him to the right, up the steps, and out onto St. Helena, a narrow street. Fifty yards later they turned left onto Christian Quarter Road. Like all the other streets and roads in the Old City, it was a crowded walkway jammed with small shops hawking everything from onions to leather coats, Turkish delight, batteries, dried dates, blue jeans, pistachios, and a thousand and one tourist trinkets—from cheap olive wood chessboards to holographic pictures that changed from Jesus to Mary and back to Jesus again as you walked past.

And still the woman pulled, tirelessly, treading up the worn stones until they turned right again, past more shops, and eventually arrived at a square just inside Jaffa Gate. A square big enough for a few cars.

"Taxi?" A driver called out. "Taxi?"

Brandon shook his head.

They continued through the square toward the towering wall of giant stone blocks. The woman was puffing now, struggling to breathe. Brandon tried to slow her down, indicating that she should sit on one of the benches and catch her breath. But she would not stop. They stepped through Jaffa Gate and out into the new city.

And still the voices accused.

Failure! Destroyer! Whore!

As Sarah's hopelessness grew, her need to be near the one person who had ever given her hope increased. She struggled to rise from the edge of the tub. Her first unsteady step ended with a sharp burn. She looked down to see a jagged piece of the broken glass cutting into her right heel. She watched the dark blood spread out onto the white marble. But it didn't matter. She continued walking, stepping on other pieces of glass, hearing them pop and snap under her bare feet, feeling the sharp pain as they tore into her toes, her arches, her heels. But it didn't matter. In fact, it almost felt good, proof that the universe was still a sane place that demanded justice.

She staggered into the bedroom, leaving bloody footprints on the beige carpet. Some of the glass remained stuck in her feet, but it didn't matter. She arrived at the dresser and pulled open the bottom drawer. She dug through the cloths until she found it. Brandon's shirt. She pulled it out, sending the other clothes tumbling to the floor. She slipped it on. Of course the smell was gone, but there were still the memories.

She hugged herself, holding it close, shutting her eyes and imagining it to be Brandon's embrace. She wasn't sure how long she stood, lost in his goodness, his kindness, his love. It had been the happiest time in her life, in both of their lives. Until she had ruined it . . .

Adultery and ambition, that is all you are!

"No!" she whispered harshly.

Liar!

"No!"

Cheater!

"Stop it!"

Thief! Murderer!

She wrapped her arms tighter, holding Brandon's shirt closer. But the comfort had already faded. There was nothing he could do. Nothing anyone could do. For the briefest second she thought of praying. But she'd failed at that, too.

You have never changed, you never will.

It wasn't God's fault. It was nobody's fault . . . but hers. Like everything else, she was the one to blame.

Killer! Adulterer!

She lowered her head, but the tears still did not come. Now there was only the self-hatred, the accusing voice, and the unbearable pain. These were things no one could stop.

Or could they?

She turned. With unsteady steps, she shuffled back toward the bathroom. A plan was beginning to form.

Baby killer!

There was a way to silence the voice. There was a way to stop the pain.

By now the water was pouring over the top of the tub, mixing with the blood on the marble and darkening the carpet where it soaked. Another mess of her making.

She sloshed across the floor, her feet finding another piece of broken glass before she arrived and turned off the water. Now everything was quiet. Strangely still, except for the echoing drip of the faucet. And the voice.

Stooping down, she rummaged through the pieces of glass until she found just the right one—blunt at one end, razor sharp at the other. There was a way to stop the pain and the voice. And, as a doctor, she knew the least painful and most effective way to do it. Holding onto the tub for balance, she rose back up and then stepped into the water. For the briefest moment she started to remove Brandon's shirt, then thought better of it. It was all she had left. And she needed him now more than ever.

She lowered herself into the water, sending more of it spilling over the side and onto the floor. But it didn't matter. No one would know. The Cartel would see to that. It would be too much of an embarrassment. But, then again, she was always an embarrassment.

She looked at the water. It was turning pink from her bleeding feet. She looked down at her wrists. This much she could do right. After all, she was a doctor. Taking the piece of glass in her right hand, she lowered her left arm into the warm water. There was barely any pain as she expertly opened the vein. She switched the glass shard to the other hand and slit open the other vein. Darkness spread into the water.

Sarah set the glass on the side of the tub. As she scooted down into the water, more sloshed onto the floor. But that was okay, everything would be okay. All she had to do was wait. She pulled Brandon's shirt tighter around her body and drew his collar up around her face. This is how she would go to sleep. This is how she would die. Dreaming of Brandon, of all that they had, of all that they could have been.

"Mom," Eric whined from inside the limo. "Lucas is already there. Come on."

"Right, honey, just a second." Katherine stood in the open car door. Lucas had sent word for Eric to join him as he reviewed the preparations at the Temple Mount before tomorrow's installation. They were just leaving when a slight commotion in front of the hotel caught her attention. A young man and an old Palestinian woman were being blocked from entering by two plainclothes security. Normally such a scene wouldn't concern her, but there was something vaguely familiar about the man, and she felt drawn to check it out.

"Mom!"

"I'll be right back." She turned from the limo and walked briskly toward the entrance. "Excuse me," she called. "Excuse me, is there a problem?"

The young man looked at her. He was in his mid-twenties. And, although the face was unshaven and his hair closely cropped, she recognized the steel gray eyes instantly. They were the same eyes from the photos Sarah had shown her. "You're Dr. Martus's husband?"

He was surprised at the recognition and nodded. "Yes, I'm Brandon Martus. And you're—"

"You know these people, Ms. Lyon?" the older of the two security guards asked.

"Yes, I . . ." Katherine glanced back to Brandon. "This is Brandon Martus, Dr. Martus's husband." There was no missing the glance between the two guards. They'd all been briefed on Sarah's relationship to Lucas.

She turned back to Brandon. "You're here to see Sarah."

"Is she here?" He sounded surprised.

"Of course."

"Mom!"

Katherine glanced back to the limo. Eric was growing agitated. If she didn't hurry, he could have another outburst. She turned to the older guard and asked, "You'll see to it Mr. Martus gets to her room?"

The guard fidgeted. "Ms. Lyon, I'm not sure if he's cleared security for—"

"He's the woman's husband."

"Yes, I can appreciate that, but—"

"Mom!"

"Certainly a man's entitled to see his own wife."

"I agree, but—"

She heard a car door slam and turned to see the limo begin pulling away. "Eric!" She started after him. "Eric, wait a minute! Eric!" The car picked up speed. "Eric!" She ran a half-dozen steps before slowing to a stop. The limo pulled out of the driveway and onto King David Road, where it took a right and disappeared down the street. Frustrated and angry, Katherine turned and stormed back to the group.

"He'll be okay," the guard said as she arrived. "We've got two of our best people with him."

She gave him a look, then called out to the doorman, "Order me a taxi."

The older guard shook his head. "Can't do that."

"What?"

"Not until we get you some security."

"Then get me some!"

"It will take at least thirty minutes."

"Then do it," she snapped. Spotting Brandon and the old lady still waiting, she asked, "So are you going to get them up to see Dr. Martus or not?"

The older guard hesitated, not wanting to upset Katherine any more than she already was.

"Well?" she demanded.

More hesitation.

"Ponte's not even here! What's the risk in taking this man up to see his own wife?" she demanded.

Finally, reluctantly, the guard turned to his partner and motioned toward the entrance. The partner nodded and escorted them to the door, but not before the older guard called, "He can go, but not the old woman."

"What?" Katherine turned to him.

"Not the old lady."

"She's obviously a friend."

"Not the old lady," the man repeated.

Katherine realized it was a power play, the only way for the guard to save face. But before she could continue, the old woman produced a business card on paper-thin stock. She handed it to Brandon, pointing to the card, then to herself.

"What's this?" Brandon asked.

Again, she pointed.

"It's her home," the guard answered in mild irritation.

Brandon frowned. "I don't understand."

"It's an invitation. If you don't have a place to stay she's offering her home." The guard motioned her toward the street and ordered something in Arabic. She nodded, but before she turned to leave, Brandon reached out and took her hand.

He spoke loud and slow. "Thank you."

She patted his arm, gave a semitoothless smile, and pointed toward the heavens. Brandon understood and nodded.

Once again the guard ordered her to leave. This time she obeyed, turning and starting to shuffle down the driveway toward the road. Katherine watched as the younger guard ushered Brandon through the large revolving door and into the hotel. She hesitated a moment, glanced at her watch, then turned to the first guard.

"Thirty minutes?"

He nodded.

She sighed in frustration. "Call me," she said, then turned and followed the other two inside. The lobby was two stories of yellow marble, dark wood, brass, and freshly cut flowers. The floor was made of long, alternating slabs of green and yellow marble. Along the walls were portraits so dark and indiscernible that Katherine figured they must have cost a fortune. Not that she cared. All she cared about was getting back to her son.

She caught Brandon's elevator just before the door closed and rode up with him and the security guard. It was there in the privacy of the small elevator that the guard motioned to Brandon with upturned palms. "May I?"

It took a moment until Brandon suddenly understood. Without a word he raised his arms and the guard quickly, but expertly, ran his hands over his back, chest, and sides, then down each of his legs.

"Thank you."

Brandon nodded as Katherine continued to watch. He was a good-looking kid, intriguing. Then there were those eyes. Sarah was right when she'd said there was nothing they didn't see. And when they caught her evaluating him, even she felt the slightest bit uneasy, as if he was somehow able to see into her.

She cleared her throat. "I take it Sarah isn't expecting you."

"No, I uh . . . no." He was nervous, and for good reason. She wondered if he had any idea what he was walking into.

"My name is Katherine. Katherine Lyon."

"Eric's mom?" The eyes were kind, but still probing.

"Yes."

"How is he?"

"He's okay. He's fine."

She tried to hold his look, but couldn't. He obviously knew she was lying. It was time to change the subject. "Sarah's . . . she's been going through some tough times."

His answer was quiet and full of understanding. "I know."

She looked at him, wondering how much he did know. The elevator came to a stop and the doors opened onto the hallway of the sixth floor. This was the location of the Royal Suite, the suite in which nearly every visiting head of state had stayed in the past fifty years. Deciding to tag along, Katherine stepped out of the elevator and followed the guard as he escorted them down the hallway of plush blue carpet and dramatically lit limestone arches. In the center of the hallway to the right was a white tiled door with a guard posted on either side. Each was armed with an Uzi. They passed the two guards, who gave stoic nods, and then approached a door another twenty feet further down the hall.

When they arrived their escort knocked loudly. There was no answer. He tried again. The result was the same. He turned to Brandon and gave a shrug.

But Katherine would not be put off. "I guess he'll have to wait inside until she returns."

The guard gave her an uneasy look.

"You do know the security code, don't you?" Katherine asked.

He nodded.

Katherine sighed heavily, trying her best to intimidate him—no easy job since he was Israeli. "Then will you please open the door so this man can go in and wait for his wife?"

The guard hesitated.

"You see how dirty he is."

More hesitation.

"Look, I take full responsibility. Just let him in there and get cleaned up before she arrives." Unable to clearly read him, she set her jaw more firmly. "Either that . . . or we go down, drag up your boss, and waste even more time that you fellows obviously don't have."

She held his gaze, unblinking. Finally, more in irritation than compliance, he reached for the keypad and pressed four buttons. The door clicked and he pushed it open. Brandon entered, followed by Katherine. The guard said, "We'll call you when a car is available," then turned and headed back down the hall.

Almost amused, Katherine shut the door and turned to Brandon. "Well, that went rather—"

But he'd noticed something off to his right. She followed his gaze to the carpet leading to the bedroom. It looked like footprints. "What on—"

"Sarah?" He sprinted into the room. "Sarah!" He turned right, following the stains into the bathroom.

Katherine was right behind him. The best she could tell, the footprints looked like blood. Then she saw the soaked carpet near the bathroom entrance and the rose-colored water on the bathroom floor. She heard splashing as Brandon reached into the tub and then she saw him rise up, holding Sarah's limp body in his arms. The young woman's face was the color of snow. She wore a blue work shirt stained crimson, the same color as the water streaming down her pale white legs and arms. And then she saw the wrists.

Brandon carried the dripping body past her. "Sarah . . ." he cried softly. "Oh, Sarah." He brought her to the bed and laid her down. "Sarah . . . Sarah, can you hear me? Sarah!"

Finally Katherine could move. She crossed to the bed stand and picked up the phone.

He looked up. "What are you doing?"

"I'm calling the front desk for a doctor."

"No."

The response surprised her. "What?"

"Not yet."

"She needs help."

"Not yet."

Katherine hesitated, not understanding—then she started to dial.

Brandon's hand shot to her arm and gently held it. "Please . . ."

"If we don't call now, she'll—" That's when she felt the heat from his hand. She looked down. It was wet with water and blood. But the palm felt like fire. She looked back up at him.

"Please," he asked, "just give me a few seconds . . ."

She knew she should refuse. But there were those eyes. They were full of absolute knowing, of intense passion. Against her better judgment, she slowly lowered the phone.

Brandon turned back to Sarah. He'd already pulled one of her arms from the wet shirt. Now he removed the other, bringing the sliced, bleeding veins into full view. Katherine winced at the sight, but Brandon barely seemed to notice. Instead, he began applying pressure to the wounds. But on closer look Katherine saw he wasn't applying pressure. He was merely holding them.

She looked back up at him. His eyes were closed and his lips silently moved. She looked down at the arms. Was it her imagination, or had the flow of blood stopped? She tilted her head for a better look. As best she could tell the wounds under his hands were no longer bleeding. It was amazing. But that wasn't all. Because as she watched, Katherine saw something even more astonishing.

At first she thought it was an illusion, the play of light and shadow on Sarah's arms. But it wasn't. Instead, the collapsed veins, the very ones Brandon was holding, actually began to swell. Not a lot, just enough as if they were filling back with blood. The swelling continued to move up her arm, until it began branching out into other vessels. And, as Katherine watched, she could actually see color returning to the arms, then the shoulders and chest.

"That's incredible," she whispered. "What are you doing?"

Brandon didn't answer. His eyes remained closed and he continued praying.

She looked back down. The color was moving into Sarah's abdomen now, then her thighs, and up into her face. She could actually see the arteries in the woman's neck plumping up. The process continued, lasting well over a minute, until Brandon was finally done. At last he opened his eyes. And when he removed his hands, wiping the sweat from his forehead, Katherine saw another amazing fact. The cuts in both of Sarah's arms were gone. Completely.

"Let's get her under the blankets," Brandon said.

Katherine nodded. She pulled back the sheet and blankets while Brandon slipped her under the covers. But Sarah's head had barely touched the pillow before her eyes began to flutter . . . then slowly open.

Katherine touched his arm. "Look . . ."

He already saw.

It took several seconds for Sarah's eyes to focus. When they did, she recognized Brandon smiling down at her and closed them again, obviously thinking it was a dream. But this was no dream. When she reopened them, he was still there, still smiling.

Her lips quivered, trying to smile back.

Katherine glanced up at Brandon. He was practically beaming.

Sarah tried to speak.

"Shhh," he whispered. He brushed the matted hair from her forehead. "Just rest."

"I thought . . ." Her voice was a breathy crackle. "I thought I'd never see you again."

He grinned. "You were wrong."

Tears filled her eyes. "Bran . . ."

"Shhh . . . I'm right here."

They streamed down her cheeks and onto the pillow. "Don't leave me . . ."

"Shhh . . ."

"Please . . ."

He bent down and kissed her forehead. Then he rested his face on the pillow beside her. He was crying, too. "I won't leave you," he whispered, his own voice breaking. "I won't ever leave you."

Sarah gave a faint smile. Then she closed her eyes and slept.

CHAPTER 17

In some ways Sarah felt like they had never been apart—as if her loathsome behavior were from some other life, from some other Sarah. It was almost like she was once again the clean Sarah, the Christian Sarah, the Sarah her husband had cherished and adored. For Sarah his presence was like a cool wind blowing through a hot, stench-filled room. A breeze that filled her sails, lifting her, reminding her how she could soar with his love as her only support. But those feelings soon gave way to heavier reality. A reality that tasted like tarnished metal in her mouth, that felt like an overcoat soaked in her own sweat, reeking with her own filth and odor, so heavy with failure that she could barely move, much less fly.

And she knew Brandon knew. Those eyes knew everything. That's why she avoided them, why she found excuses to look around the room, out the window, anywhere but at him. She knew he knew. And, regardless of what happened, things would never again be the same between them.

She'd barely slept an hour. When she awoke, other than being ravenously hungry, there seemed to be no other side effect. Even the hangover was missing. Brandon figured it came with the fresh blood supply, though he joked that it shouldn't be a recommended cure for too much partying. Sarah returned the humor by mentioning the scar still remaining on her face. "What's the matter?" she'd teased. "You couldn't make it a package deal?"

At Katherine's insistence a doctor had come up and given her a quick look over. As far as he could tell everything was fine. And, once she'd been assured that Sarah was okay, Katherine headed for the Temple Mount to find her son.

Now, Sarah sat on the edge of the bed finishing off a lunch, courtesy of room service, as Brandon filled her in on his travels through Turkey. He described what he'd seen and learned, and explained how an unquenchable fire to warn and prepare the church had returned and continued to burn in his soul.

"It's like the fire I felt in L.A., but different." He paused, then shook his head. "No, no . . . I'm what's different."

"How so?"

"I've given up."

Sarah frowned.

"I'm not running my life anymore, Sarah. I've given up and died. No more agendas, no more trying to make God's will happen, no more anything."

"And this is good?"

"Yes. Because when I'm dead, that only leaves Christ. Remember that verse Gerty gave us. Unless a kernel of wheat falls to the ground and dies, it remains a single seed. But if it dies, it produces many seeds? Well, that's what's happened. I've died. I've traded my life in for his. And, if you ask me"— he flashed a grin—"I think I got the better end of the deal."

Sarah returned the smile, a little less sure. "How does that tie in with the fire?"

"Now I'm letting it burn however it wants." He rose to his feet. "I've stepped out of the way, Sarah. I'm letting God do it. It doesn't matter how stupid or ignorant it feels, I'm letting God call the shots. To be honest, I've never been so free, I've never felt such peace . . . and power."

"It sounds a little frightening."

"Of course it's frightening, but if you're dead, what difference does it make? And I've noticed something else."

"What's that?"

"When I get out of the way and let that fire do its thing . . . there's a lot less chance of me getting burned." He gave her another grin and she responded in kind. But it lasted only a moment, before the guilt rose up again and began pulling her down.

It was true, during their time apart Brandon had gone through some obvious changes. He'd left a boy and returned a man. But it was more than that. He was freer. He was more at peace than she'd ever seen him.

And what changes had she undergone?

Whore of Babylon!

The voice was still there. Even Brandon's presence could not remove it. *Oh God!* she cried out in silent prayer. *Can you forgive me? Can you ever forgive me? Can Brandon?*

He reached out and took her hands. "Hey," he whispered. "I missed you."

She glanced away, fighting back the tears. He knew. And yet he still loved her, he still treated her with adoring respect. Was it possible . . . was it possible that God . . . did he feel the same way toward her? Even now?

"You up for more food?" Brandon asked, reaching for the phone.

"Yeah . . ." she answered hoarsely.

"What'll it be this time?"

After placing the order, Brandon urged her to tell him what she'd been through since they'd been apart. It was hard, but through the tears, the anger, and the self-hatred, she told him . . . everything.

She could see by the workout he was giving his jaw that it wasn't easy for him. She could also see the hurt in his eyes. But she saw no anger, nor any condemnation. When she finished she was exhausted, feeling much like a limp and very dirty dishrag.

Nearly a minute passed before Brandon finally spoke. "So . . . where do you want to go from here?"

"Where do *I* want to go? Where do *you* want to go? You're the one I've wronged. You and God. I'm the one that's ruined everything."

"You've ruined nothing." Brandon's voice was soft but firm. "There's nothing you've ruined that God can't restore. If you let him."

"Brandon, it's not that simple."

"Sure it is."

"What about *your* emotions, your feelings of betrayal? You have the right to be furious with me."

"If I had any rights, I might be."

"Brandon . . ."

"But dead men don't have rights." He knelt down at her side. "Sarah, you're God's gift to me. Whatever he gives of you to me, I rejoice in; whatever he withholds, I accept. When you're dead everything is a gift."

"But what about your feelings? Your emotions?"

He paused a moment, thinking it through. "They're like children," he said. "When they're good, I enjoy them. When they misbehave, I don't let them rule my home. Like every other part of me, they are subject to Christ."

"Brandon . . ." She closed her eyes in frustration.

"What?"

"Feelings are important . . . you just can't repress them."

Brandon smiled warmly. "I'm not repressing anything." He reached out to her face and gently brushed back her hair. "Christ is in charge, Sarah. Not my feelings. Christ has already paid the price for your sin. He's already forgiven you ... how can I do anything less?"

And then it happened. Almost before she knew it. A deep, heaving sob. And then another. And another. Suddenly the floodgates were opened. It was as if all the bile that had been building up over the weeks, over the months, was suddenly coming up—doubts, ambitions, adultery, attempted suicide—all of it—and with an intensity that completely overwhelmed her. "I'm sorry!" she gasped between sobs. "I'm so sorry."

She felt him sit beside her, his arms gently wrapping around her. He pulled her closer. "I know," he whispered softly into her ear, his own voice filled with emotion. "I know ... and I forgive you."

At that exact moment she knew the Lord had forgiven her as well. For as her husband continued to hold her, she could feel the arms of Christ gently wrapping around her, tenderly embracing the depths of her soul. The experience was so intense, so powerful, that she could not speak. She didn't have to. All she could do was cry—each silent sob bringing another failure to the surface, another failure that the Lord instantly removed and discarded. It was as if she was taking a long, refreshing shower, but from the inside ... as if the water was loosening and washing away the filth of every failure, cleansing and forever rinsing away the foul stench that had been clinging to her for so many months.

How long they held one another like that she did not know. But when they were finally finished, she was exhausted. As she pulled back, wiping her cheeks, she saw her husband's own red eyes and wet face. "Sorry about that." She sniffed as she reached out to wipe his cheeks with her hands. He grinned and did the same for her. Now it truly was as if they had never been apart.

Eventually, the conversation resumed. Soon they began talking about Eric. Sarah recapped all that she had discovered, speaking of the tests she'd run, what they'd revealed, and about the long delta brain waves that were recorded whenever Heylel was present.

Brandon slowly nodded. "So we're talking about basic demon activity?"

Sarah shook her head. "Not so basic. Don't forget, the genetic structure of his blood has been altered. According to the lab reports, his DNA is like no other in the world. There's no telling what combination of hormones and neurotransmitters his blood is triggering his brain to release."

"Meaning?"

"Meaning, it could just be creating some sort of unknown connection between the physiological and the spiritual."

Brandon whistled softly. "Poor kid, he got it from both ends, didn't he?"

Sarah nodded. "The worst science has to offer and the worst of the spiritual world."

"We're agreed then," Brandon asked, "that Heylel is demonic?"

Sarah paused. "I think ... Brandon, he might be more than that. I think the evil is more powerful than just a demon's."

"More powerful than a demon? The only evil more powerful than a demon is ..." Brandon slowed to a stop. "Are you saying what I think you're saying?"

She nodded and watched as he fought off a shiver. The same shiver she'd experienced the first time she'd worked through the possibilities. But something else was running through Brandon's head as well. She could see the wheels turning. Once again he rose to his feet.

"What is it?" she asked.

He started to pace, trying to piece it together. "You're saying we have a person like no other in the world."

"Correct."

"A human who has been biologically manipulated and now may be hosting Satan himself."

"That's only speculation."

He nodded. "But he is a multiple murderer, and he does offer supernatural counsel to the Cartel."

"Yes."

"The very organization that's ushering in this one-world peace thing, that's setting Lucas Ponte up as its figurehead."

"I don't see the connection. What's that got to do with—"

"I'm not sure, but somehow it's connected to the Imperial Cult."

"Imperial what?"

"The one-world government that was killing off Christians for not worshiping their Caesars. That's what they thought the Antichrist was back then, back when Revelation was first written, back when they believed 666 was the code for Nero's name."

"What are you saying?"

"I'm not certain. But here we are, the two witnesses in Revelation—"

"At least one of us."

He ignored her and continued. "We're in Jerusalem where we're supposed to have some kind of showdown with the forces of hell . . . and there's supposed to be an Antichrist and a false prophet and—"

"That's only if you're taking everything literally."

Brandon turned to her.

She continued. "We've always agreed that some of Revelation was to be interpreted historically, like your Antichrist Caesar stuff, and that some of it was to be interpreted spiritually, and that only some of it was to be taken—"

"—literally. Yes, the three views of Revelation, that's how it's always been interpreted."

"So . . . what are you saying now? I mean which is it, historical, spiritual, or literal?"

"Yes."

"What?"

"It's all three!"

"At the same time?"

"Yes." Brandon grew more excited. "Don't you see, you're the one who's always talked about a multidimensional God. One that's everywhere at the same time."

"Omnipresence is one of his characteristics; the Scriptures make that clear."

"So if he's omnipresent, if he's multidimensional, why can't his writings be, too? Why can't he be talking about a historical event as well as a spiritual event as well as a literal future event . . . all at the same time?"

Sarah's head began to spin.

Brandon crossed the room back to her. "That's what I learned in Turkey. Even though those seven letters were written to seven specific churches in history, they also have deep spiritual and symbolic significance, while at the same time applying to issues facing today's church."

"Yes, but—"

"That's what Scripture always does with prophecy, even the ones about Christ! That's why nobody figured them out until after he came. Yes, they pointed to events in Old Testament history; yes, they pointed to spiritual events; and yes, they pointed to very real and tangible future happenings . . . all at the same time! Don't you see? A multidimensional God writing on multidimensional levels!"

Sarah forced herself to speak calmly. "So you still believe there's a literal quality to all of these events in Revelation?"

"There's something. We'd be fools if we thought we could figure it out before it happens. I mean, that's what they did with Christ's first coming. Nobody got it right. Three hundred prophecies and not a single Bible scholar got it right. Nobody can figure out prophecy until after it happens. But there's too much here just to be coincidence. Eric . . . the Imperial Cult . . . Ponte . . ."

An eerie silence stole over the room. Was it possible? Were they smack-dab in the middle of Revelation without even knowing it?

The knock on the door caused them both to jump. "Room service."

Brandon crossed over to the door and opened it. A young bellhop rattled in with a cart. "Sorry I'm late. Everyone's watching the shooting on TV."

"Shooting?" Sarah asked.

"Didn't you hear?"

"Hear what?"

"Some majnoon just shot Chairman Ponte. Over at Temple Mount. Gunned him down in cold blood."

"What's the kid doing!"

"Somebody stop him!"

"Eric!" Katherine cried. She struggled to move, but she was pinned to the pavement by a security guard. "Eric?" He had tackled her to the ground when the shooting had started. Now she was fighting to catch a glimpse of her son through the running feet and fallen bodies. "Eric!"

"Somebody grab the kid!"

They'd been a hundred yards north of the Dome of the Rock when the shot rang out. A single bullet fired by a sniper across the courtyard. Katherine had been standing so close to Lucas that she'd actually seen blood and bone explode from his chest. Now he lay eight feet away—the front of his body soaked in blood, his eyes fixed open in a death stare.

But she could not find her son. "Eric!"

They'd just left the stage, fifty yards from the newly opened East Gate, and were strolling toward the site of the temple groundbreaking. That's when the shot had been fired.

"Let me go!" It was Eric. She recognized his voice immediately. "Let me go, I can help!"

There was a scuffle. She caught a glimpse of Eric's trousers and shoes.

"Eric!"

"I can help him. Let me—"

"Let him go." It was a member of the Cartel. The secretary general.

"But, sir—" a guard protested.

"Let the kid go." The command was firm and unwavering. "Now!" And then a little more reflective. "Let's see what he can do."

"Okay, everybody," another guard spoke up. "Step back now, let's clear the area."

Instantly, the weight came off Katherine. Another guard was helping her to her feet. Now at last she could see the whole picture. There was Lucas lying on the ground in a widening pool of blood, and standing directly above him was her son . . . *safe*. The relief was immeasurable.

"Eric!" she called. "Eric!"

But he didn't hear. Instead, he stared down at the lifeless body.

"Everyone stand back." Security continued moving the crowd. "Give us some room here . . ." She felt hands around her arms, pulling her back with the rest of the crowd.

"But I'm the boy's mother. I'm—Eric!"

It did no good. She was pulled back fifteen feet until she became part of the perimeter surrounding Eric, the secretary, and the body. She watched breathlessly as Eric slowly lowered to his knees. She knew how much he loved the man, and she'd give anything to be by his side to comfort him. But when she looked at her son's face, she saw no tears. She saw no emotion at all.

Eric gently took Lucas's right arm, which had fallen across his abdomen, and stretched it out onto the stone pavement. He did the same with the other arm. The crowd grew still. In the distance an approaching EMS vehicle could be heard. Eric reached down and straightened one leg and then the other. Then he rolled the head forward until it faced up. Finally he reached down to the staring eyes and closed them.

A gentle breeze stirred through the courtyard. News cameras adjusted for better positions. Everything became absolutely silent.

Still on his knees, Eric lifted one leg over the body until he was straddling it. A faint murmur rippled through the crowd. Then, ever so carefully, he stretched out and lowered himself directly on top of the body—chest to chest, arms to arms, legs to legs.

The murmuring increased. Security started to move in, but the secretary repeated his order. "Leave him."

"But, sir—"

"Watch."

Eric took a deep breath and lowered his head. He put his mouth directly over the man's mouth, face to face, lips to lips . . . and then he blew. It was a type of mouth-to-mouth resuscitation, but one like nobody had ever seen. Eric exhaled completely, then turned his face to let the air escape from the corpse's lungs. He took another breath and repeated the process. The crowd began to fidget, a couple voiced concern, but Eric paid no attention.

Katherine watched. She wanted to cry out his name, but she knew he would not respond. He took a third breath and blew it into the mouth of the body. The crowd grew more restless.

Then, ever so faintly, the fingers of Lucas's left hand began to twitch—once, twice. A moment later, those of his right hand started to move.

Katherine looked on in astonishment.

Suddenly the right foot jerked. Then Lucas's entire body convulsed. Then, at last, he began to cough.

The crowd whispered and buzzed in amazement.

A moment later Eric crawled off of the body, and a moment after that, Chairman Lucas Ponte opened his eyes.

Sarah stared at the medical chart, not believing what she saw. Blood pressure, ECG, respiration rate, everything about Lucas was normal. He wasn't even running a temperature.

She turned to the physician who'd let her take a look at the chart. "What about the chest wound?"

"What chest wound?" he asked.

"It's all over the news. Eyewitness reports. A bullet tearing through the chest. Lots of blood."

"The reports are wrong."

"I'm sorry, what?"

"There is no chest wound. There is no wound of any kind."

She searched his face.

He shifted uncomfortably and repeated himself, "There is no wound. Now, if you'll excuse me."

She nodded, then motioned to the chart in her hand. "May I look at this another moment?"

"As you wish." He turned and exited past one of the two sets of security guards stationed at either end of the long ICU bay. The room was designed for nine separate beds and ICU stations, which was still only a fraction of those available in the new emergency wing at Mount Scopus Hospital. But today it was cordoned off with only two occupants ... Chairman Lucas Ponte a few beds over, and directly at her side, young Eric Lyon.

Both were sleeping. And why not? Raising someone from the dead is probably just as exhausting as being raised from the dead. The thought gave Sarah little comfort as she turned back to Lucas's chart. Against Brandon's advice she'd insisted upon rushing to the hospital. He'd accompanied her as far as the waiting room. But having no security clearance, he was now sitting out there with Katherine sipping lukewarm Nescafe.

Sarah flipped through Lucas's chart until she reached his EEG, the measurement of the brain's electrical activity. This was her specialty. If there was any abnormality she could probably spot it. But she was not prepared for what greeted her. According to the chart, Lucas Ponte was registering the exact same delta waves that Eric displayed whenever Heylel had entered him. In fact, their patterns appeared absolutely identical. A fist-sized knot formed in her stomach.

"Quite a coincidence, isn't it, Doctor?"

She looked up to see Ponte, across the room, wide awake. "Lucas ..." She took a step toward him, then caught herself. She wasn't entirely sure why. "You gave us quite a scare."

"I gave myself quite a scare, Dr. Martus."

It was the way he spoke. Something about how he used her name. She did her best to cover the uneasiness. "You're not feeling any pain? No side effects?"

"Not a thing. Well, except my vision seems to have been slightly affected. Still, at my age, spectacles become a reality sooner or later. They want us here for overnight observation, but I guarantee you we'll be out of here by nightfall."

"It's . . . amazing."

"Yes, it is. So you see, Doctor, your husband is not the only one who can perform miracles."

The knot tightened. She unconsciously reached for the newly healed skin on her wrists. "You know . . . what happened?"

Lucas smiled. "Yes, Doctor, I know everything about you."

There was that phrase again, that tone. She glanced down at his chart.

"It really is quite remarkable, isn't it?" he said. "For two entirely different people to have identical brain waves?"

"You've seen this?"

"No, as I have said, my vision seems to be suffering slightly. I asked them to test it. What do they have it down as?"

She looked back at the chart. It read 20–400. "They have you down as—"

"20–400, yes."

She looked up, startled. "How did you . . ." She slowed to a stop. He was grinning, but not at her. He was looking just beyond her. She quickly turned and was startled to see Eric now sitting up in the bed beside her. He was busy reading the chart in her hands.

"Eric," she said, "how are you feeling?"

"Just fine, Dr. Martus."

She felt a slight chill. Something wasn't right, something about the voice. She continued. "That was quite a feat you pulled on the Temple Mount."

"Yes." Eric smiled and pushed up his glasses with his little finger. "But it wasn't me, Doctor. You of all people should know that by now."

The chill grew deeper. She forced herself to continue. "I was just telling Lucas how remarkable all of this is. I mean, to go through that kind of trauma with virtually no side effects."

"Except for my vision and those brain waves," Lucas corrected.

She turned back to him. "I still don't understand. If you can't read the chart how did—"

"A hundred and sixty over a hundred!" Lucas interrupted. "That's ridiculous, I've never had blood pressure that high!"

Sarah glanced down at the chart. Sure enough, that's what they'd written down, 160/100. She looked back up. "How did you know, if—" She came to a stop.

The grin increased. She slowly turned back to Eric. Once again, he'd been reading the chart in her hands. She spun back to Lucas, whose grin broadened, almost menacingly.

"That's . . . that's not possible," she stuttered. She turned back to Eric, who wore the identical grin.

"What's that, Doctor?" Lucas asked.

Her breathing came harder. She started backing away.

"What's that, Doctor?" Eric asked. It was a different voice but the same.

She turned back to the boy. He was gloating in delight. So was Lucas. It was a game. It had to be. The two of them were playing some sort of game.

"What's that, Doctor?" Now it was Lucas.

She bumped into a bed table on wheels, nearly knocking its contents to the floor, then she turned and started for the door.

"What's that, Doctor?" She didn't know who it was that time. She didn't care. All she knew was she had to get out of there. She had to breathe. She broke past the guards, through the doorway, and out into the hall.

"Brandon . . . Brandon Martus!"

Brandon turned from his conversation with Katherine and looked across the milling crowd of press and security that filled the waiting room. Tanya Chase's honey blonde hair emerged through the faces. She was pushing the wheelchair of an old man.

"Look who I found!" she called.

At first Brandon didn't recognize him.

"It's Reverend Tyler," she exclaimed as they pulled up to his side. "You remember Jimmy Tyler."

Brandon stared at the man. He'd put on a good fifteen years . . . and had lost twice that many pounds. He was hunched over and drawn, and when he looked up at Brandon his eyes were full of pain and helplessness.

Brandon dropped down to his side. "How are you, sir?"

The old man gave a hacking cough, then motioned to the back of his hands and the back of his arms, indicating their sensitivity to touch.

"It's Scorpion," Tanya explained. "He's come down with the virus."

Brandon nodded. He knew the symptoms. First came the nausea and fevers, then the sensitivity to touch. Next the lining of his blood vessels would start to leak, followed by his organs bleeding, filling his stomach and intestines. Eventually blood would begin seeping out of his nose, mouth, eyes— every orifice in his body. Slower than Ebola, it was just as deadly, and because of its more leisurely pace, it was even more torturous.

Tanya continued. "I told him what you've been up to, about the video we made. And he's agreed to broadcast it, in its entirety, on his network."

"That's great," Brandon said.

"In fact," Tanya said, "Jerry's over at the station right now, editing the piece."

Brandon looked from her back to Tyler. "Thank you," he said gently.

The old man shut his eyes and nodded, accepting Brandon's gratitude. It was clear he wanted to bury the hatchet. But as Brandon started to rise, he grunted and motioned for him to remain a moment. Brandon stooped back down. With more grunting and pantomime, Tyler pointed to Brandon, then to himself, and then up to heaven. It was clear he wanted Brandon to pray for him. He motioned to the back of his hands and his arms. He wanted him to pray for his healing.

Brandon nodded, only too happy to oblige. He reached toward the old man, who greedily took his hands into his. That's when Brandon felt the check. Something wasn't right. He wanted to pray over Tyler, but somehow he shouldn't. He looked at the old man. It made no sense. Tyler's eyes were full of pain and sorrow—and there was no mistaking his contriteness. So why couldn't Brandon pray?

"No, not yet." The command resonated in his head.

Why? Brandon asked.

"His repentance is not real."

I don't understand.

He waited for further clarification. But none came. The command had been given. Brandon looked back into the old man's eyes. They were brimming with tears of thankfulness. But slowly, sadly, Brandon had to withdraw his hands. "I'm sorry," he whispered. "I'm ... sorry."

The withered hands reached out to his, trying to pull them back, his eyes filling with growing fear and confusion. The expression broke Brandon's heart. He could clearly see the man was repentant. But he had his orders and regardless of how unreasonable they seemed, he would not disobey. "I'm sorry," he whispered softly.

Suddenly the man's countenance shifted. His eyes flashed with anger. He coughed, clearing his throat, and before Brandon could rise, Jimmy Tyler spit a mouthful of phlegm into his face. Brandon winced but did not move. Instead, he looked at Tyler. The man seethed with rage.

Now Brandon understood. There was no repentance here. No contriteness. There was only the desire to stop the pain, to end the Lord's discipline. And wanting to stop God's discipline is a far cry from wanting to repent.

But even now, Brandon was filled with compassion. A Bible verse came to mind. He didn't know where it was in Scripture, but he knew it was from the Lord. And, despite its apparent harshness, he knew it must be said. Because, past the harshness was God's love, his infinite yearning to touch and save his child.

As gently as possible, Brandon spoke, "Not everyone who says to me, 'Lord, Lord,' will enter the kingdom of heaven, but only he who does the will of my Father who is in heaven."

Tyler stared at him, his anger hardening to hate.

But there was more and Brandon continued. "Many will say to me on that day, 'Lord, Lord, did we not prophesy in your name, and in your name drive out demons and perform many miracles?' Then I will tell them plainly, 'I never knew you. Away from me, you evildoers!'"

Brandon searched the man's face, looking for any trace of humility. There was none. Then, quietly, tenderly, he added his own postscript. "I'm sorry," he whispered, "I'm so very sorry." Slowly he rose to his feet, wiping off the spittle with his sleeve.

"Are you okay?" Katherine asked.

He nodded. "Yeah . . ." He turned back to Tyler, but the man had already grabbed the wheels of his chair and started rolling himself through the crowd.

Brandon, Tanya, and Katherine watched silently as he disappeared into the mob.

"I don't understand," Tanya said. "It would have been the perfect solution. Jimmy would have gotten his healing, you would have gotten your broadcast, and God would have reached the world with his message. Everybody would have won."

Brandon shook his head. "Everybody, but Jimmy . . ."

"What?"

"God is as concerned about the one lost sheep as he is the ninety-nine."

"Brandon . . . Katherine?"

He turned to see Sarah working her way through the crowd. Even then he noticed how drawn she looked.

"What's the matter?" he asked as she arrived. "Are you all right?"

"Yes." She nodded, a little out of breath.

"Are they still sleeping?" Katherine asked.

Sarah shook her head.

Brandon repeated, "What's wrong?"

She turned to Katherine. "Eric, your son's eyesight . . . do you know what it is?"

"His eyesight?"

"Yes, the prescription for his glasses. What's his eyesight?"

"Not great, but—"

"What is it?"

"Uh, 20–400, I think. Why?"

If Sarah was pale before, she turned absolutely white now.

"What's wrong?" Brandon repeated. "Sarah, what is it?"

She glanced around.

"Sarah?"

"We've got to talk," she answered quietly. "In private."

"Back at the hotel?" Katherine asked.

Sarah shook her head. "No." She glanced at the security and the press milling about. "We've got to talk someplace where we won't be recognized and where we won't be heard."

CHAPTER 18

It had been Brandon's idea to meet at the home of the old Palestinian woman. Actually, he hadn't even thought about her until he'd stuffed his hands into his pockets and pulled out the card she'd given him with her address. But as soon as he saw it, he knew that was the place.

She lived in the Palestinian village of Silwan, just south of the Mount of Olives. The flat-roofed buildings made of ancient stone and rubble stood two, sometimes three, stories high. They were packed tightly beside each other and clung to the steep hillside. Directly to the west lay the Hinnom Valley, once called Gehenna. According to

Tanya this was where, in the Old Testament, the Israelites had sacrificed their babies to Baal and later, where Judas had hung himself. For Sarah, it seemed everywhere she looked there was history. In fact the taxi ride from the hospital to Silwan had taken them through the Kidron Valley, the very valley Jesus had crossed during his triumphal entrance into the city on Palm Sunday and prior to his arrest five nights later.

"That's the Garden of Gethsemane," Tanya said as they passed a church and small olive grove to their left.

The group turned to look and Brandon half-whispered in awe, "That's where it all began . . ."

"What do you mean?" Sarah asked.

"That's where the war was fought . . . where the fate of the entire world hung in the balance."

"What about Calvary?"

Brandon shook his head. "The decision to go there, to die to his own will, that war was waged right here."

"Dying to self," Sarah said as she looked back out the window, recalling their earlier conversation. "Even Jesus Christ had to do it."

Brandon nodded. "That's the only battle that counts."

Sarah glanced at her husband. There was so much wisdom there now. So much maturity.

The taxi pulled up to the address, and everyone was certain the driver had made a mistake. It was nothing but a garage carved out of a hillside with an impoverished two-story house beside it. But the driver insisted this was the place, and reluctantly the four of them piled out. The sun had already dropped behind the hill as they approached the entrance, a large corrugated door with the address spray painted across the top left corner. Off to one side a patch of wild roses withered from the heat. On the other, a grape arbor was propped up by a barrel used for burning trash.

Katherine banged on the steel door. The reverberating echo set off one or two neighborhood dogs. Sarah looked around. An old bedspring set atop cinder blocks served as a fence separating them from the neighbors. After a louder set of knocks and more barking dogs, the door finally slid open. The hunched woman with the nearly toothless grin greeted them. She'd already met Brandon and Katherine, but not Tanya or Sarah. After carefully shaking each of their hands, she ushered them inside.

It wasn't much. A tattered throw rug lay across cracked concrete. Two lamps (one without a shade) lit the bright yellow walls. A worn wooden table and three chairs sat in one corner, while the bench seat of an old car served as a sofa against the far wall. But the poverty had little effect upon the woman's hospitality. They'd barely taken their seats before she disappeared into what must have been the kitchen/bedroom and returned with a large serving tray. On it were four small glasses of coffee with the consistency of grainy syrup, along with four glasses of water to help wash it down.

"Okay." Tanya turned to Sarah. "You definitely have our attention. Now, what's going on?"

Sarah finished her sip of coffee, set the glass down, and began. "I don't think Lucas Ponte . . . I don't think he's with us any longer."

"What's that supposed to mean?" Katherine demanded.

"It means that what made up Lucas, his personality, his soul, whatever you want to call it . . . I believe it's no longer controlling his body."

"But he's alive," Katherine said, "you just saw him. You said you talked to him."

"I talked to somebody, but I don't believe it was him." She took a breath and continued. "I believe it's the same personality, the same entity that inhabits and controls Eric."

"You mean . . . Heylel?" Katherine asked.

"Lucas Ponte's brain waves are identical to your son's when Heylel inhabits him."

"Long deltas?" Brandon said.

"Exactly."

"Who is Heylel?" Tanya asked.

"That's the million-dollar question," Katherine muttered.

"But he inhabits your son?"

Katherine held her look a moment, then glanced away. Silence stole over the group until Tanya turned back to Sarah. "So you're saying the Lucas Ponte we know is dead."

Sarah nodded. "I believe so."

"And inhabited by this Heylel?"

"That's only one of his names. I believe he has others."

"Such as?"

"This is only speculative, there's no way to prove it, but I believe . . ." It was harder for Sarah to say than she thought. She backed up and tried again. "I believe what was once Lucas Ponte is now being—"

Katherine finished her sentence. "—controlled by Satan."

The group turned to her in surprise.

"I was with you in Eric's room," she said to Sarah. "I heard his claims. To be honest, I've suspected something like that for a while."

More silence. Finally Brandon spoke, staring at the floor. "The Antichrist." Uneasy glances were traded across the room. He looked up. "He is the Antichrist that was prophesied to rise up and rule the world." Turning to Katherine, he continued. "He and the false prophet."

"Which would be my son," Katherine flatly concluded. Without waiting for his response she turned to the group. "That's what Heylel has been promising him from the beginning, to rule the world."

"And . . ." Tanya was thinking out loud. "Tomorrow's installation is . . ."

Brandon answered. "Tomorrow's installation is the beginning of their reign."

Another pause. "Is there any way we can stop it?" Tanya asked. "If this is true, shouldn't somebody try to stop it?"

"Enter Revelation's two witnesses," Katherine said as she turned to Sarah and Brandon.

Sarah said nothing, waiting for Brandon to respond. He began shaking his head. "No . . ."

Tanya scowled. "But if that's who you're supposed to be, isn't that what you're supposed to do? If you really are the two witnesses, then you have to stand up to him and—"

"No," Brandon interrupted. "My job"—he threw a glance to Sarah—"*our* job has been the same as it's always been. We're to proclaim truth—through the Word of God and through our lives. Nothing more."

"But we're talking the Antichrist here," Tanya argued. "The great deceiver and destroyer. If you don't get in there and physically stop him, who will?"

Sarah ventured, "I think what Brandon's saying is that our weapons are not physical . . . they never have been."

Brandon nodded as Katherine quoted, "He who lives by the sword, dies by the sword."

"So what's left?" Tanya demanded.

"What always has been," Brandon replied. "To warn the world, to prepare the saints of God."

"Prepare?" Tanya asked. "For what?"

Brandon answered, "For the return of Jesus Christ." The group exchanged looks. He continued. "Christ is on the brink of returning. But his bride isn't ready. She needs to repent, to prepare herself."

"And," Sarah interjected, "she needs to be warned that Lucas is the counterfeit messiah and not to be followed."

Brandon nodded. "That's our job—to proclaim the truth. Nothing more."

"But how?" Tanya repeated, then suddenly she had an answer. "The videotape! Of course. You can tell them through the tape we made of your message from Turkey!"

Katherine shook her head. "You need more than some tape. I've seen these guys operate; they can spin and distort truth any way they want."

Sarah nodded. "I'm afraid she's right."

Katherine continued. "What you need is to present something live and in person, something they can't come back and twist all up."

Brandon agreed. "And it has to be done before the installation. Before anyone bows their knee."

"Or," Sarah said thoughtfully, "during it."

"You mean get him up there on the stage, like in L.A.?" Tanya asked. "Get Brandon to prophesy and call down some sort of curse on Ponte?"

Sarah threw another glance at Brandon. The idea literally made him stiffen with fear. Still, it had some merit.

Katherine shook her head. "There's no way Heylel will let you get close to the stage, much less get on it."

"Maybe . . ." Sarah turned back to the group. "But I've seen how he operates. And if there's any residue of Lucas left, I have a pretty good handle on him, as well."

"Meaning?" Tanya asked.

"Meaning, I might be able to convince him."

"That's absurd," Katherine scoffed. "He's worked years for this moment. He's got far too much pride and ambition wrapped up in this to share it with anybody."

Sarah began to nod. "And that's the key."

"What is?"

"His pride and ambition."

"What are you talking about?"

"If this Heylel really is who he claims to be, who we think he is, what's his one weakness, what's his Achilles' heel?"

The group stared at her blankly.

"His ambition," Brandon ventured. His voice sounded weaker. Obviously the thought of going back onstage had taken its toll.

"Exactly," Sarah agreed. "Everything we read about Satan in Scripture . . . his temptation of Adam and Eve, his promises to Christ, his being kicked out of heaven . . . everything points to him trying to usurp God's authority, to a pride and ambition that wants to rule." She turned back to Katherine. "Look at his promises to your son."

Katherine agreed. "Pride and ambition . . . that pretty well covers it."

Sarah nodded. "Unfortunately, I've had a little experience in that area myself." She continued. "If there was some way we could play off of that pride . . ."

"You actually think he'd give Brandon permission to speak?" Tanya asked.

"Only if he thinks he can make a fool out of him," Katherine answered.

"And out of God," Sarah added.

Brandon coughed nervously. "Given my past record in front of crowds, I'd say that's a strong possibility."

"But it doesn't matter." Sarah turned back to him. "All you have to do is deliver the truth. It doesn't matter how stupid he makes you look or how foolish you feel. It doesn't matter if he cuts you down or verbally destroys you."

Brandon held her look, still obviously nervous, but at least understanding. "Because dead people don't die," he said.

"Precisely. All that matters is that you speak the truth. That's all God ever commanded us."

Brandon swallowed. "And . . . the rest is up to him."

"Yes!" Sarah was excited. "Don't you see? Our strength is that we don't have to be victorious, we don't have to win!"

"And Satan's weakness is . . ."

"That he has to!"

A moment passed as the group slowly digested the paradox. Sarah caught Brandon's eye and gave him a small smile of encouragement. He tried to return it, but the fear was obviously too great.

"And what about my tape?" Tanya asked. "Any chance of convincing Lucas or Heylel or whoever to let us play the tape during the broadcast, too?"

"Don't be ridiculous," Katherine scoffed.

Tanya countered, "It's no more ridiculous than winning a war by losing it."

"You want me to ask Ponte if he'll also play the tape?" Sarah asked.

"Doesn't hurt to ask."

"And if he says no?"

Tanya grinned. "Ponte's not the only game in town. I've got a few other strings I can pull."

Another moment passed before Katherine asked, "What about Eric?"

Sarah scowled, thinking it through. "I'm not sure of the logistics . . . but I doubt even Satan can inhabit two places at once."

"Only God is omnipresent," Tanya offered.

"I may be splitting hairs, and maybe it's only a matter of microseconds, but I believe Heylel probably moves back and forth between your son and Lucas."

"Then who's inhabiting Lucas when Heylel is in Eric?"

"Maybe some weaker power, maybe nobody. But you bring up an interesting point . . . if we can keep them separated, there may be less consolidation of power."

Katherine nodded. "Lucas thrived off of him in life; now he's doing it in death."

Sarah agreed.

"I should keep Eric away from tomorrow's ceremony, then?"

"Can you do that?"

"I'm still his mother, aren't I?"

"I don't know, guys . . ." Brandon's voice was thin, the way it always sounded when he was nervous. "To expect Sarah to talk Ponte into letting some hick like me up onstage." He turned to Tanya. "I mean, you saw me in L.A. And in Turkey I could barely put two sentences together for that tape. And now you want me to get up in front of the whole world?"

"Not you, Brandon," Sarah answered softly.

He turned to her.

"You're dead, remember?"

He tried to hold her look, but his eyes faltered. He turned to the rest of the group. "And Tanya, you're going to try and drop in some tape during an international broadcast?" He rose to his feet and began to pace. "Listen to you people. I mean, who are we kidding? There's no way we can pull this off."

Sarah knew he was speaking out of fear. Getting back onstage in front of all those people was his worst nightmare. She glanced around the room. Everyone sat silently, weighing his words, maybe even coming to his same conclusion. It might even be the right one. It certainly made more sense. But still ...

Finally, Tanya looked up at him and asked, "So you don't think we should even try it?"

All eyes turned to Brandon. He had crossed to a small barred window, keeping his back to them. Sarah knew the pressure he felt was enormous, the thought of going back onstage, terrifying. A half minute passed before he finally answered, his back still toward them. "I don't know if it's possible or not." He paused, then continued. "But I know what I've always known." He slowly turned to face the group. "The bride has to be prepared ... and she has to be warned of Ponte's seduction."

"And all of these 'impossible odds'?" Sarah asked.

His voice was softer now as he answered. "You said it yourself. If we fail, all we do is wind up looking foolish. Our job is to proclaim the truth ... the rest is up to the Lord."

"The whole thing is ludicrous," Katherine muttered.

Brandon turned to her. "Probably ... but what other course do we have?"

She started to respond, then glanced away. It was obvious she had nothing further to say.

Once again silence stole over the group. Finally, Brandon repeated himself quietly, but with more determination. "Our job is to proclaim the truth. The rest is up to the Lord."

For Sarah, one of Jerusalem's many surprises was the close proximity of everything. According to Tanya even the walk from Silwan to the King David Hotel was less than thirty minutes. That's why she'd decided to take it. It would give her a chance to clear her head, to sort through the day's events ... and to prepare for the upcoming talk with Lucas or Heylel or whoever he was. If his prediction was correct he was probably already out of the hospital and back at the hotel, where she should speak to him as soon as possible.

Katherine had asked if she could accompany her. Of course Sarah had agreed. From what she'd seen of Eric's iron will and explosive temper, she figured Katherine's task would be as difficult as hers, and she'd probably need just as much time to think things through. Tanya had taken a taxi downtown to Channel Two to check on the progress of the editing. And Brandon, at everyone's insistence, had agreed to stay behind at the old woman's home. Everyone had their assignments, and his was to prepare for the unlikely possibility of speaking tomorrow.

The moon was full, and because of the growing impurities in the atmosphere, it cast a dull red glow over their shoulders as the two of them made their way along the single-lane road that passed through the Hinnom Valley. To their right towered the south wall of the Old City, and to their left was a steep ridge with occasional cliffs.

"So this is where the Israelites sacrificed their kids," Katherine mused. "What did Tanya call it, 'The Valley of Sorrows'?"

Sarah looked around them. The narrow ravine was silent and tranquil, the air still warm and smelling of dust and sage. There was no trace of the suffering that had filled this valley so many thousands of years ago.

"I wonder what that must have felt like," Katherine said, "sacrificing your own kid." Sarah turned to her as the woman continued thinking. "Giving up your child's life in the belief that you're securing the safety of millions."

Sarah wasn't sure what she was saying, but she didn't like the sound of it. "Katherine . . ."

Katherine turned away, looking up at the cliffs. "He's a monster, Sarah. My son is a killer. He's killed before and he'll kill again and he'll keep on killing. Only it won't be by ones or twos. Soon it will be by the thousands, maybe millions."

"You don't know that for certain."

"Of course I do. And so do you. But if somebody could stop him—"

"Katherine . . ."

"Were the mothers' actions here really so despicable . . . sacrificing one life in the belief that they could save millions?"

"Katherine, what are you saying?"

At last she turned to face her, and for the first time Sarah could remember, there were tears in the woman's eyes. "He's my baby . . . He's all I've got."

Sarah took her arm. "I know. I know . . . But there's got to be some other way."

"What?"

"I don't know. But sacrificing your only son . . ."

Katherine said nothing.

Sarah continued. "Eric still has a free will. Somewhere deep inside of him he must still be able to make decisions. If you could just reach him, talk to him. If you could get him to see that Heylel is wrong and that God's ways are better. If you could convince him that God's love is greater than all the—"

"Don't you dare talk to me about God's love!" The outburst surprised her. "Not after what I've been through."

"But—"

"No God of love would allow this type of torture. And if he did I certainly wouldn't want anything to do with him."

"Katherine . . ."

"I'm serious. No more!"

Sarah nodded and answered softly, "I'm sorry."

They walked in silence for several minutes before conversation finally resumed. They talked about how Katherine might convince Eric to go with her tomorrow. Perhaps a tranquilizing drug to sedate him would be helpful. Sarah had some Versed back at the hotel with her medical supplies. She could give her a small vial and show her how to use the syringe if she was interested.

Katherine had agreed.

Eventually the conversation turned back to Heylel— what Sarah should say, how she would have to again stand before his accusations, how she would have to use all of her strength and intelligence to persuade him to let her husband speak. Then again, maybe she wouldn't have to use her strength and intelligence at all. Maybe she would simply follow her husband's example and die. Die and let God do it. But how? They were fancy words, but how could she actually put them into practice?

Sarah shook her head. She couldn't. Not yet. But she could pray. And, as silence again stole over the conversation, that's what she did.

The elevator doors opened and Tanya stepped into the rundown foyer just outside Channel Two. She nodded to the guard who had been dozing at a small metal desk. She pushed open the double glass doors and entered the newsroom. Compared to this morning's crowd, there were only two kids working the computers and puffing cigarettes, which almost made the air breathable. No one acknowledged her presence as she headed back to the edit suite where she and Jerry had begun their work.

But Jerry wasn't there.

The overhead fluorescents were on, but the monitors and computer editing system had been shut down. Tanya scowled. Maybe he was on break. But that wouldn't explain why he'd turned everything off.

Beside the keyboard, she spotted a stack of three tapes. She crossed to them and read the backs. One was labeled "Brandon Martus, Turkey montage." It was marked with a red "edited master" sticker. The other two were the original tapes they'd made of Brandon's speech back in Laodecia.

Tanya was puzzled and angry. She had left clear instructions that Brandon's speech was the first thing to be cut together. And later, only if he had the time, was he to put together something on his travels through Turkey. But, by the looks of things, Jerry had done just the opposite. He'd wasted valuable hours editing Brandon's travels and hadn't even touched his speech.

Something was wrong. This type of incompetence wasn't like Jerry.

Tanya stepped out into the hallway and poked her head into the next edit suite. A stringy-haired brunette was hunched over the keyboard, mumbling and smoking.

"Excuse me?" Tanya asked. "Excuse me?"

"What?" the girl demanded without looking up.

"The gentleman that was in here with me this afternoon. You don't happen to know where he went, do you?"

There was no response.

"Excuse me."

The girl swore at the picture playing on her monitor. She hit a few keys, and tried again.

"Excuse me."

"Here," the girl called over her shoulder, "take a look at this." On the monitor a shaky handheld shot zoomed into a crowd on Temple Mount, then it cut to a closeup of Eric placing his mouth over Ponte's, lip to lip, and slowly exhaling. Tanya watched with morbid fascination until the picture abruptly ended and the girl turned to her. "So what do you think?"

"It's fine . . ."

"Not too weird."

"You're using it for tomorrow's broadcast?"

"Maybe. The director wants tons of prerecorded drop-ins. Probably won't use half of 'em, but he wants them just in case."

Tanya nodded. "That's his style. So tell me, did you happen to know where the guy in the next suite went?"

"How should I know?"

"I just, uh—"

Without a word the girl turned back to the keyboard and resumed working. It was clear the conversation was over. Frustrated, Tanya stepped back to her room and mulled over the situation. The good news was the last take of Brandon's speech in Laodecia was great. It would only take an hour or so to tighten it up. The bad news was it had been a long time since Tanya had operated the Avid editing system on her own.

Still, valuable time was ticking away. So, with a heavy sigh, she eased herself into the sticky vinyl chair, booted up the system, and went to work.

"So tell me, Dr. Martus, how was your meeting?"

Sarah stiffened. "What meeting is that?"

"Come now," Ponte chided. "As I have told you, there is little I do not know. Your husband, he has gone through many impressive changes, am I correct? Making someone of your filth and immorality even less worthy to remain in his company."

"I'm not here to talk about my past behavior."

"Past, future, it is all the same with you, Doctor. You will never change."

Sarah recognized the ploy. It was the same one Heylel had used in Eric's room in Nepal, and more recently when she had tried to kill herself. But she would not fall for it. Regardless of her past, regardless of her future, she was forgiven. Maybe she didn't fully understand it as Brandon did, but she knew it in her head. Just as her husband had forgiven her, so had her God.

She remained standing at the end of the conference table in the north section of the Royal Suite. Lucas Ponte, or what was left of him, sat at the other. He looked as he always had, except for the pair of glasses he now wore. A stack of papers lay on the table before him. It was 10:00 P.M. and they were alone.

Sarah cleared her throat. "If you know about our meeting, then you know what we would like from you."

"I only know when and where you had the meeting. My associates were forbidden from entering."

The fact gave Sarah some comfort. It was good to know there were still limits put on his powers. Bracing herself, she went straight to the heart of the matter. "We know who you are and what you plan to—"

"You know nothing of me!"

The shouting surprised her, but she held her ground. "I know what I've read."

"You know only what Oppressor has written. You know only his version of truth. You know nothing of the glory that was mine—of my vast power and majesty. I was his greatest accomplishment, his shining act of creation. I led the stars in their songs, I was the bright and exalted one, directing all of heaven's host in his worship."

"Until you got greedy."

The eyes locked onto hers in icy rage—the hate so intense that she physically felt air pulled from her lungs. "They *wanted* me to rule! A third chose me as king! A third! And now"—a seething chuckle escaped from his throat—"his beloved children are about to do the same."

The emotion was so dark and cold that instinctively, Sarah started to pray. *Dear Lord*—

"Stop it!" He ordered. "Stop it!" The voice echoed through the suite. He took a moment to regain control. "I cannot hurt you. Even now there are forces surrounding you that prevent my approach. But not forever, Sarah Martus. Rest assured, your time is nearly at hand." Leaning back with the faintest trace of a smile, he began to quote. "When they have finished their testimony, the beast that comes up from the Abyss will attack them, and overpower and kill them. Their bodies will lie in the street of the great city ... where also their Lord was crucified."

Sarah steadied herself. She was all too familiar with the prophecy, but that didn't stop him from continuing. "For three and a half days men from every people, tribe, language and nation will gaze on their bodies and refuse them burial. The inhabitants of the earth will gloat over them and will celebrate by sending each other gifts because these two prophets had tormented those who live on the earth."

Ponte paused, then shrugged. "An unfortunate ending given your loyal and unswerving commitment. Then again, that's how Oppressor always operates, making impossible demands upon those he claims to 'love,' while offering little in return. But if you were to serve me"—he tilted his head—"well, now, that would be a different story. For I know how to reward my servants."

Suddenly Sarah's mind swam with immeasurable pleasures. Feelings, emotions, impressions—gorgeous men desperate to please her every whim, access to the highest powers,
unlimited glory, worldwide adoration—pleasures so overwhelming that Sarah had to lean against the table to stand.

And then, just as quickly as they came, they were gone—
leaving her gasping in the sudden silence.

"You see." Lucas chuckled quietly. "I do know how to
reward."

"I thought . . ." She took a gulp of air and finally managed
to look up. "I thought you couldn't touch me."

"I can't, not without your permission."

"Then what was—"

"Just a few of the doors you've left open to me."

Sarah looked back down at the table, her mind and body
still reeling from the assault.

"Those are *my* promises, Dr. Martus. Those are *my*
truths."

She knew she couldn't withstand another attack, not like
that. She had to play her card and get out of there. "But . . .
your truths," she said, "they're only half-truths. What of the
pain they bring, the suffering that follows?" She looked up at
him. "What of the whole, the eternal truth?"

Lucas laughed. It wasn't malicious, just amused. "Eternal truth? Nobody is interested in eternal truth." He pushed
up his glasses with his little finger, just as Eric always had.
"The only truth they are concerned with is mine."

"Is it?"

"Open your eyes, Doctor. Take a look at the world.
Nobody cares for the eternal. My truth is all that counts. My
pleasures are all they pursue. They have made their decision,
Doctor. Through their own free will they have chosen me to
rule. By their own volition they have rejected Oppressor and
have selected me."

"You're wrong."

Lucas looked at her, waiting for more.

Sarah made her play. "They have chosen you out of ignorance. They have chosen your truth because they know no better."

"They have always had Oppressor's Word."

"Distorted by you."

"No, my pleasures have distorted many of its teachers. Their teachings have, in turn, distorted the Word."

Sarah could feel the ground slipping away. His logic was too strong. *Dear Jesus,* she silently prayed, *help me, please help*—Instantly, she understood that Heylel was again trying to distract her. She shook her head. "No, that doesn't matter," she said. "What matters is that tomorrow the world will be making their choice out of distorted facts and ignorance. And making a choice out of ignorance is not making a choice at all."

"My dear Doctor, even with all the facts, they would choose me. Even if every man, woman, and child knew every detail, they would still choose my truths over Oppressor."

"Possibly."

"Definitely."

"But you'll never know, will you? Not for sure. You'll always wonder if they chose you because you really are the greatest, or simply because they didn't know better."

Another smile crossed Lucas's face. "You are very clever, Doctor."

She said nothing.

"And your solution to my dilemma is . . ."

"Let the people make an intelligent choice. Give them all the facts. Then, if they want to follow you, so much the better."

His smile broadened. "But you've forgotten one important fact, Doctor. They *will* follow me, regardless. Oppressor's prophecies must be fulfilled."

"Then you'll have nothing to lose. They'll follow you regardless, even when they know the facts. And you can rule with the satisfaction that they truly have rejected God and that they really have chosen you to be their ruler."

There was a moment's pause. "You make an intriguing argument, Doctor." He pushed up his glasses. "So tell me, how would they hear these facts?"

"Let my husband speak from your stage tomorrow."

Lucas burst out laughing. "You would have Brandon Martus debate me?"

"No, not a debate. Just let him speak from his heart for a few minutes."

"The boy is terrified to stand in front of the smallest group. He will make an utter fool out of himself. He will completely discredit your cause."

"Then you'll have nothing to lose, will you?"

"Except, as you have said, if he embarrasses himself and your position, the people will still be unable to make an intelligent decision."

Sarah's mind raced. Had she just defeated her own argument? Suddenly another thought came, another opening. "That's why we'd also like to play a video. In case Brandon gets tongue-tied."

"The video he and Tanya Chase made in Turkey."

Again Sarah was unnerved at how much he knew. "Yes."

Silence settled over the room. She waited patiently.

Finally Lucas spoke. "You have presented your case well, Doctor. Allow me to think upon it. The prophecies must be fulfilled. The people will choose me and reject Oppressor, this we know. But to have them make this choice with the full knowledge of who they are rejecting and who they are choosing ... this would be an even greater triumph."

Sarah nodded. "Exactly."

He turned his gaze fully upon her. "I know what you are planning, Doctor. Do not think your cleverness has deceived me. But your proposal has every possibility of making tomorrow's victory all the sweeter. Through your own wiliness you may have actually made my victory greater. You will have my answer in the morning. Good night, Doctor." He looked back down to his papers and resumed his work. The meeting was over.

Sarah turned and saw herself to the door. She felt a sense of triumph, but even now, wrapping around it, there was a deeper sense of dread. She'd sensed the Lord sharpening her mind so she could effectively state her case. But had she out-thought herself? Had she inadvertently played into Heylel's hand, giving him, as he had said, an even greater victory? Only time would tell. And, glancing at her watch, she realized that time was fast approaching.

CHAPTER 19

Brandon sat in the deep silence of the Garden of Gethsemane. He watched the dappled patterns of moonlight that had filtered through the olive trees as they inched their way across the ground. The stillness was absolute. He wasn't sure why the Franciscan caretaker had left the gate unlocked, but he knew this is where he wanted to be. This is where his Savior had been.

Earlier he had prayed and paced and cried and prayed some more. *Are we doing the right thing . . . what am I to say . . . are we stepping out where we shouldn't . . . is this really your will?* Around and around the questions went. But there had been no answer.

Only silence.

And with the silence came the doubts. What was he thinking? He'd already proven his inability to stand in front of people. He ruined one man's ministry, destroyed his own. He'd subjected Sarah and himself to unbelievable ridicule and scorn. And now he was expected to do it all over again? This time in front of billions of people? What *was* he thinking?

And with the doubts came the fear. Memories of glaring television lights, unblinking cameras, a hostile audience yelling and booing him, hating him. And it would be worse tomorrow. Much worse. This was no national broadcast he was appearing on, this was *international;* it was going to be shown around the world. And this was no televangelist he was going against. This had every appearance of a standoff with Satan himself!

What was he thinking!

Please, Jesus ... I'm not ready for this ... there has to be some other way ... tell me some other way ... whatever you want, just tell me ...

The silence continued.

He wasn't sure what he had expected. A word would be nice, another guest appearance by the Lord would be even better. He'd even settle for one of those supernatural impressions he sometimes felt in his spirit.

But there was nothing.

He didn't know how long he had sat there waiting, listening to the silence—maybe an hour, maybe two. But eventually he heard the faint squeak of the iron gate. He'd finally been discovered. He was about to be thrown out. Not exactly the answer he'd hoped for. The sound of feet crunching gravel approached. He pulled into the shadows with the futile hope that he wouldn't be noticed. But, of course, he was.

"Brandon ... is that you?"

"Sarah?" He rose to see her coming up the path, then quickly moved to her for an embrace. "What are you doing out here? How did you find me?"

"I went to the house. The old lady said you were coming here. And the caretaker, he said he was expecting me."

Brandon looked at her in surprise. "The caretaker . . . he knows?"

Sarah shrugged. "He pointed out where you were sitting. Said he was concerned about all your pacing wearing out his grass."

Astonished, Brandon looked over his shoulder toward the garden gate. There was nothing there but shadows. That's all he'd ever seen. Pushing aside the thought, he turned back to Sarah. "You shouldn't be out here, not alone."

"I talked to Lucas."

"What did he say?"

"I think he'll go for it."

"That's . . . good."

"You don't sound too excited."

"No, I think that's great. It's . . . great."

"And . . ."

He looked at her. She was staring up at him, searching his face. He'd never been good at hiding things from her. This was no different. Finally, he confessed, "I'm scared, Sarah."

"I know."

"I mean, it's one thing to dream up all these clever plans, but to actually go through with them . . ."

She nodded.

"In just a few hours I'm supposed to go up onstage, in front of the whole world, and have some sort of showdown with the Antichrist? Who are we kidding? I still don't have the faintest clue about what I'm going to say or do. At best I'm just going to wind up looking like the world's biggest jerk."

She took his hands and answered quietly, "What does it matter? As long as you're dead in Christ, what does it matter what you look like?"

He looked at her, appreciating what she was trying to do, but it didn't work. He broke from her and turned to resume his pacing. "Those are just words. They sound real good in theory, but this isn't theory. This is reality. And tomorrow's reality is that I'm going up there battling the most evil force in the world, and I'm not the slightest bit qualified."

"You're right, you're not. You never have been."

He looked back at her.

"But isn't that your strength, Brandon? Hasn't the key to everything you've done so far been your weakness? Think about it. Hasn't your success been knowing you're unqualified, knowing that the only way you can possibly succeed is by relying on God?"

"This is different."

"How?"

"It . . . just is."

"Why . . . because it's bigger?"

He tried to answer, but could not.

She stepped closer. "You keep talking about dying—about letting the old man die and letting Jesus rule. That's all well and good. I mean, that's really important, but I think you've missed something even more important."

He waited.

"You've missed faith, Brandon. Without faith you've got nothing, without faith you are nothing. Yes, be dead, yes, let Christ rule . . . but then have the faith that he *will* rule."

"You don't think I want that? You don't think I've been trying to believe?"

Her answer was soft. "Then maybe . . . you should stop trying."

"What's that supposed to mean?"

"It means dead people don't try."

She was beginning to make sense, in an odd sort of way. And she was starting to break through. "What am I supposed to do about all of these fears, about all these emotions?"

She approached him, looking up into his face. "Let me tell you what a good friend once told me about emotions. He said they're like children. We can enjoy them when they're good, but we don't have to let them rule our house."

Brandon gave her a look.

She reached out her hands and rested them on his waist. "It's not a matter of emotion, my love. It's a matter of choice. Just as you chose to die in Christ ... you have to choose whether or not to believe."

"You make it sound so simple."

"It is simple ... it's not easy, but it is simple."

He closed his eyes for a moment and then sighed. "For a scientist, you're a pretty good theologian."

She smiled. "I have a pretty good teacher." She snuggled into him and he wrapped his arms around her. She was right, of course. But how had she done it? How, in just a few seconds, had she managed to calm the storm? The woman was amazing. He'd almost forgotten how amazing.

She said nothing more but simply rested her head on his shoulder and waited. It felt good holding her like that. Natural. Like she always belonged. Pressed against him, he could feel her warmth, and with that warmth came the assurance. He could do anything with her there. Anything at all. He took a deep breath of the night air and slowly let it out. She snuggled in closer.

"It's getting late," he said.

"Yes."

"We should be heading back."

"I know." Then, looking up at him, she held his gaze for a long moment. He felt a strong impulse to kiss her. He reached down and brushed the hair from her face.

"What about you?" he whispered.

"What about me?" she said, tilting back her head, lifting her face closer.

"We keep talking about my death in Christ ... what about yours?"

She gave no answer but closed her eyes and raised her mouth to his. He lowered his head and their lips found one another.

When they parted he looked back down at her. "Well?"

"I'm working on it," she said as she pulled his mouth back to hers. "I'm working on it." They kissed again longer, slower.

When they had finished, Brandon looked down at her. She smiled, and it made him warm all over. Without a word they turned. Still holding one another, they headed back down the path toward the gate. And there, walking in the moonlight, through the garden, for the first time that Brandon could remember, he felt like they were truly one.

Tanya had spent much of her professional life around remote television setups, and she wasn't the least bit surprised to see that everything for tomorrow's shoot was state of the art. After all, Ryan Holton was in charge. The equipment and trucks were parked along a narrow road that ran parallel to and a mere twenty feet from the Eastern Wall. It was a typical arrangement: a boxy-looking generator truck to supply the electricity, a semitruck whose long trailer served as the production center, and the miles and miles of black cable. What was not typical was the scaffolding that carefully suspended the cable, preventing it from touching the thousands of graves packed tightly along the outside of the wall.

It had always amazed Tanya that such a location had been chosen for a cemetery ... until she learned the method behind the madness. Tradition claimed that Jesus Christ, upon his return, would enter through the large Golden Gate in the center of the wall. This explained why in the seventh century the Moslems had sealed it up with stone. Then, as an added precaution, they had buried their dead directly in front of it. After all, the Law said a priest could not walk over the grave of a human, and since Jesus was a priest, and since there was nothing but wall-to-wall graves in front of the gate, it was obvious in their minds that they had efficiently blocked the second coming of Jesus Christ.

The blue and white production trailer was lit by two self-contained quartz lights on either end. Besides various storage bays underneath, the trailer had three separate doors leading to three separate rooms. The front room was where the director, technical director, and production assistant sat. Before them would be rows and rows of monitors along with a switcher to change cameras and an effects board. This is where Ryan would call the angles and direct the show. Behind him and just slightly higher was the sound engineering room. Here the sound technicians would sit, checking levels and watching the broadcast over the director's shoulder through a pane of glass. And finally, at the back, was the VTR, or videotape replay, room. This was where the show would be recorded and where the prerecorded tapes would be dropped in and played on Ryan's cue.

It was this last room that Tanya needed to enter and discretely place her two edited tapes. She'd not heard from Sarah and had no idea what if any progress she'd made with Ponte. She'd put a call in to Ryan, but he was not available. She'd left a fairly detailed message on his service but knew that it would be unlikely she could see him before the show. So, as far as she could tell, prepositioning the tapes for the VTR operator was her next best option.

A single guard with an M-16 was posted outside the trailer. He didn't look Israeli but appeared to be part of the international coalition . . . which meant he might be easier to con. Gripping the plastic shopping bag that held the tapes, Tanya took a brief breath and stepped out of the shadows toward the trailer. She walked with what she figured to be the right sense of purpose and professional boredom.

The guard heard her and turned.

"Good evening," she said, nodding.

"I.D. please." He sounded American, from the south. He tapped his chest indicating where her crew I.D. should be hanging from her neck.

"It's right . . ." She looked down, then feigned surprise at its absence. "That's funny, it should be . . ." She pulled aside her jacket to look. "Oh great . . ." She glanced back up, pretending to be flustered. "I left it back in his van."

"Van?"

"Yeah, Ryan Holton's."

"The director?"

"Yeah, it got in our way when we were . . . I mean to say, he took it off when, we, uh . . ." She ran her hands through her hair, pretending to be even more embarrassed. She caught a flicker of amusement crossing his face. Good, it was working. "Look," she said, "if anybody found out about us, I'd probably lose my job. But he's kind of nervous, you know preshow jitters and everything, and, well hey, a girl's got to do what she can to get ahead . . . if you know what I mean." She dropped off, pretending to fidget some more. "Look, if you'll just let me deliver these two tapes for him, I'll be on my way."

He shook his head in amusement.

"What?"

"You showbiz people, you're all alike, ain't you."

She looked up through her bangs and smiled. "Yeah, I guess we are."

"Let me see in the bag."

She crossed to him and opened it. For the briefest moment she thought of leaning forward and distracting him a bit further—after all, she was wearing her favorite V-neck pullover—but something inside said no. Something about Brandon and what he'd been saying.

After checking the tapes, he motioned her toward the trailer. "Go ahead."

She gave him another smile. "Thanks." She crossed to the aluminum steps leading to the VTR room, climbed up them, and entered. It was small, almost claustrophobic. Two chairs faced a narrow desk which faced various rows of monitors. On the side wall hung cables and patch cords. The rear wall consisted of a dozen tape machines with two metal racks holding videotapes. These were the tapes to be dropped in during tomorrow's broadcast.

For some unknown reason, a wave of uneasiness crept over her. She wasn't sure why. Maybe it was because in just a few hours this tiny space would be responsible for influencing the entire future of the world. A sobering thought. But it wasn't her first. She would always remember the confrontation she'd had with a congressman in Washington when she'd first started out. He'd openly ridiculed her choice of profession, and when they were alone in the elevator she got in his face with one of the best sound bites of her life. "Listen, congressman," she'd said, jabbing a finger at him, "you folks may legislate what the people want, but we *tell* them what they want."

It was true back then, and it was just as true today . . . and tomorrow.

Pushing aside her uneasiness, Tanya unfolded the plastic bag and reached for the first tape. It was the one she'd just finished editing over at Channel Two, the speech Brandon had delivered with such conviction at Laodecia. As she pulled it out of the bag, she noticed her hand shaking.

"What's the matter with you, girl," she scolded herself. "It's just a segment." But she knew it was more than that. She knew that if played, this single tape could change the entire outcome of the broadcast.

She turned toward the metal tape rack and riffled through the tapes, looking for the ideal place to put it. They would be positioned in the rough order Ryan would call them. She hesitated, then decided to put the speech in the fifth or sixth position, well after the logos and intros, but not too far into the show.

That's when she heard the voices. Men talking, outside.

She froze, listening carefully, but she couldn't make out the words. She knew it wasn't the crew. They wouldn't be called for three or four more hours.

Her heart began to pound.

Quickly, she pulled the other tape from the bag, the montage of Brandon's travels through Turkey. She hadn't had time to view it, but she trusted Jerry. Despite their differences, despite his annoying habits and ever-present ambition, he was good.

Suddenly the trailer vibrated as heavy feet moved up the steps. Tanya reached for the rack, trying to drop the tape in somewhere, anywhere ... when the door quickly opened.

"Hold it right there, please."

She stopped, hand in midair.

"Turn around slowly, if you do not mind."

Tanya obeyed. As she turned toward the door she squinted, trying to make out details of the silhouette standing there.

"Ms. Chase? Tanya Chase?"

She continued to squint. "Who's asking?"

"What is that you have in your hand?"

"Oh, this?" She referred to the tape. "I was just putting this back where I—"

"May I see it, please?"

"Sure." She handed him the tape. That's when she saw the dull glint of light reflect off what looked like a silencer. Her mind raced as she did her best to sound calm. "What's all this about?"

The figure turned and handed the tape outside, to someone just out of sight. "Is this the one you edited?"

Another voice read the label. "'Brandon Martus, Turkey montage,' that's the one."

Tanya immediately recognized him. "Jerry ... is that you?"

"Good." The first figure nodded and retrieved the tape.

"Jerry!"

"You gave us a scare, Ms. Chase," the silhouette said. "Mr. Jerry has worked very hard on that for us. We were afraid you might have misappropriated it."

"Worked ... for you?" She tried to see past him. "Jerry, what is this about?"

"Please, go ahead and put this back where you had it."

Tanya took the tape. "What do you mean, 'worked for you'?"

"Please ..." The gun motioned toward the rack.

Tanya turned and dropped the tape into the second shelf, wherever there was room. Knowing the best defense was an offense, or at least a belligerent attitude, she tried to turn the tables. "Now, tell me, exactly who are you and what is Jerry Perkins doing—"

There was the faintest flash from the muzzle of the silencer, a muted *zip-thud*, and a roaring explosion inside her chest. The force was so powerful that it threw her back into the wall. She tried to gasp, but for some reason she could not breathe. Her chest raged with fire and she clutched a handful of patch cords before she slid to the floor. There was another flash. But this one brought no pain as it slammed her body hard into the floor. If she could have breathed, she would have cried out. The room was already growing bright white. She was losing consciousness.

"What did you do?" It was Jerry's voice, screaming in protest, but sounding very, very far away. "What did you . . . No, don't. What are you doing? No, please. We had a deal! Please, for the love of—"

She heard two more *zip-thuds* . . . and then there was nothing. By now the whiteness was everywhere and her eyes were unbelievably heavy. She had to close them, just for a moment. No, she was a reporter, she had to see what was happening. She could no longer hear Jerry, she could no longer hear anything. And her eyes, they were so heavy. She would close them, just for the briefest moment. Slowly . . . she lowered her lids . . . just for a second . . . only for a second.

Rose-colored moonlight spilled through the window and onto Eric's face as his mother watched him sleep. He was always so peaceful when he slept. There was no sign of the explosive anger or the violence. There was no sign of Heylel. Just the sweet, tenderhearted child she had once known.

She remembered one day when he was six and she had dropped him off at day care—how, after she'd kissed him good-bye, she had watched him from the car. She remembered how his little body stood at the foot of the stairs, lunch box in hand, staring up at the huge house before him. How badly she wanted to jump back out and race to him, scooping him into her arms, explaining that she had made a mistake, that he was too young, that she'd never let him go. And she remembered how he had turned, giving her a brave little smile, more for her sake than his, and started up the porch steps, never looking back again.

The thought brought tears to her eyes. It always did. Over the years she'd gradually given up hope that she could ever find peace and happiness. Those days had come and gone. But not for Eric. His whole future lay ahead of him. That's why she'd invested so much into him, providing every opportunity she could afford for him. She thought if she could draw the line and stop the suffering with herself, letting him enjoy peace and goodness, then her life would have had some purpose.

That had always been her hope. And looking down at the sweet, innocent face before her, that hope was almost revived. Almost.

In the next room sat the vial of Versed and the syringe Sarah had given her before leaving—plus another full vial Katherine had stolen after Sarah had left. Two cc's would be all that was needed to sedate Eric to the point of cooperation. It would still allow him to walk, if she helped support him. Any more than that could be dangerous. By Katherine's estimate, she now had twenty cc's.

There were many important decisions she'd have to make in the next few hours. But right now she was too exhausted. Not that she'd be able to go to sleep. But, at least for now, she could curl up in the armchair across the room and watch her child in the moonlight. Here, she would muse and smile over memories of what he had been . . . and here, she would silently weep over what he would never be.

The walk from the Garden of Gethsemane to the old woman's house was only twenty minutes, and no matter how slowly they took it, it was coming to an end far too soon.

There were so many issues Sarah wanted to discuss and catch up on, but they'd all have to wait. All but one.

"Brandon . . . I want to go up on that stage with you tomorrow."

He slowed to a stop. They were less than fifty yards from the door. "Are you crazy?"

"I think it's important."

"Why?"

"I've always let you stand up and take the heat. I've always hid in the background and let you be the one to get the beating."

"I don't have a problem with that."

"I do. We're a team, Brandon. That's what the Lord has always told us—in the Scriptures, in the prophecies. We've gone our different directions, but we're together now, just like he said. We're a team."

Brandon nodded.

"If you go up there, I want to go up there."

"But . . . what are you going to do, what are you going to say?"

"I don't know. Do you?"

"That's not the point." He shook his head and resumed walking. "No, I don't think it's a good idea."

"Brandon . . ." She caught up to him. "If you and I are supposed to represent Christ and his bride, isn't there a time when the bride has to stand up with her husband and share in his suffering? Isn't that one of the things you learned in Turkey, that the bride should expect persecution?"

"Yes, but—"

"So what type of symbol am I if I sit back and let you take all the heat?"

He picked up his pace, obviously agitated. "I don't think it's a good idea," he repeated.

She stayed glued to his side. "Why not?"

"It's . . . it's not right."

"Of course it is."

"It's too dangerous."

"Brandon . . ."

He said nothing.

"Brandon, talk to me. Brandon."

He didn't slow until they reached the front of the old woman's home.

Finally he turned to her. "Look, you know the prophecies. If they're to be taken literally, you know there's a chance that tomorrow could be our last day alive."

"Exactly. *Our* last day."

"It's not right."

"You keep saying that. What's not right?"

"Jesus Christ laid down his life for his bride."

"Yes . . . and he requires the bride to do the same for him. That's what you've been learning, Brandon. That's what those letters say." He tried to look away, but she wouldn't let him. As she searched his face she saw the fear and concern. "It's all right," she whispered. "I want to do this."

"But . . . I'm afraid. I mean it's one thing for me . . . but for you . . ."

"It's okay."

"Sarah . . ."

She put her fingers over his lips, silencing him. "You've given up your life," she whispered, "now let me give up mine."

He looked into her eyes a long moment. But this time she felt no uneasiness. This time she had nothing to hide. At last, he began to nod, almost imperceptibly.

She rose up and kissed him on the cheek. "Thank you," she whispered.

They turned back to the house. He reached for the steel garage door and pulled it open. Both were surprised at what greeted them. The lights were off and the old lady was nowhere to be found.

"Hello?" Brandon called. "Hello."

Everything was dark except for faint flickering coming from the next room.

"Hello . . ."

They exchanged looks, then moved in to investigate. They passed the table and chairs, the car seat sofa, until the other room came into view. But the woman wasn't there, either. Instead, a queen-sized mattress with clean pillows and a pulled-back sheet lay in the center of the floor. Beside the head of the mattress sat an ornate wooden tray with two recently filled champagne glasses and an opened bottle of sparkling grape juice. From the ceiling hung several white crepe paper streamers. They came together in the center above the bed, where two cardboard wedding bells hung. Everything was bathed in the soft romantic glow of a dozen flickering candles.

Brandon and Sarah stood speechless.

When Sarah found her voice it was barely above a whisper. "How did . . . how did she know?"

Brandon shook his head and nervously cleared his throat. "Do you think maybe the Lord's trying to tell us something?"

Sarah said nothing.

"Well." Brandon cleared his throat again. "It's not exactly Chicago's Hyatt Regency . . ."

By now Sarah was so overwhelmed she could barely speak. "No," she whispered as she wrapped both arms around Brandon. "It's a thousand times better."

CHAPTER 20

Brandon held Sarah in his arms throughout the night. He found everything about her intoxicating ... the slow breathing of her sleeping body against his, the softness of her breath upon his chest, her warmth, her smoothness, the smell of her hair. Everything filled him with both peace and exhilaration. And, as the hours passed, he tried his best not to fall asleep so that he might savor the time for as long as possible.

But her presence was more than physical or even emotional. Yes, he was whole now, complete. But there was something else here. Something deeper, something ... spiritual—a truth he could almost grasp, but not quite. If Sarah's presence could bring him such joy and if Sarah represented the bride of Christ ... was it possible that he, as a part of that bride, could bring equal joy to his Lord? Was it possible that as a mere human he could bring such pleasure to the Creator of the universe ... simply through his presence and fellowship? Could this be part of the "profound mystery" Paul spoke of in Ephesians?

Brandon tried to explore the idea, but it was deeper than he could think—at least for now, at least for tonight. Instead, he was content to simply lie beside his sleeping wife, enjoying her presence. Eventually he rose up on one elbow and looked down upon her lovely face, quietly thanking God for his goodness. But soon his eyes grew tired and he had to lay his head back down on the pillow. Still, even as he drifted off to sleep, he was rejoicing over his bride and silently worshiping his Lord.

"Brandon ... Bran ..."

He woke to see Sarah smiling down at him. It was morning and she was already dressed. Even more surprising, she had cut her hair. So short, that it no longer hid the scar.

She bent over and kissed him lightly. "Good morning."

"Hi." He grinned, then reached out and pulled her to him.

They kissed again, and when they parted she whispered, "It's getting late."

"You cut your hair."

"Yes."

"It's like the picture," he said. "The one Gerty sketched of us confronting the serpent head. Remember?"

"Yes, I know."

Suddenly he understood. Sarah had finally accepted all of Gerty's words. And all of Revelation's.

"Today's the day, isn't it?" he asked.

"I think so."

He sat up. "Are you frightened?"

"No." She shook her head and sat beside him. "Not when I'm with you. When I'm with you, I can face anything."

Her long jagged scar was in plain view now, its shiny pinkness accentuated by the harsh morning sun. As he looked at it, he felt his hands beginning to grow warm. The palms first and then radiating out into his fingers. He glanced down and saw their growing redness.

So did Sarah.

He looked back up into her face. Then, slowly, tenderly, he raised his hand toward the scar. But before his fingers touched her cheek, she took them and gently moved them away. "No, Brandon."

He looked at her, puzzled.

"This is who I am. Today of all days, I want to be exactly as he's made me."

A smile spread across his face. He didn't fully understand, but he realized this was her way of accepting all that God had called her to be. Like the cutting of her hair, this was a confirmation, a marker proving she had totally and unequivocally given Jesus Christ complete control of her life.

He leaned over and kissed her again. She sighed in quiet contentment, then whispered, "We better get going."

He nodded and rose to dress.

Moments later she called from the other room. "Brandon. Come look at this."

He slipped on his shoes and entered the room. On the table sat two sesame bread rings, several slices of goat cheese, some grapes, and two oranges.

"This wasn't here last night, was it?" she asked.

Brandon slowly shook his head. "I guess there's no end to her surprises."

"I guess not."

Although there wasn't a lot of food, it was enough and it was refreshing. After they'd finished eating, Sarah suggested they spend some time in prayer. Kneeling had never been their habit, but they both felt it was appropriate for today. Lowering to their knees, they held one another's hands and began to pour out their hearts to the Lord. They thanked him for his goodness and his faithfulness. They blessed him for his protection these many months and for accomplishing his will regardless of their doubts and failures. Finally, they asked for the courage and faith to finish the task he'd set before them.

"And, above everything," Brandon concluded, "we ask for your perfect will to be done. Regardless of our success or our failure, we ask that you accomplish your purposes fully and completely . . ."

"Yes," Sarah agreed. "Your will and only yours."

"Because it is in your name that we pray . . . and that we live or die . . ."

They both said amen together but remained kneeling in silence for several more moments. When they finally looked up, Brandon saw Sarah's eyes were brimming with moisture. So were his. But they were not tears of sadness or fear. They were tears of appreciation.

As they rose and prepared to leave, they outlined the plan one more time. The installation and groundbreaking were scheduled to begin at 11:00. Lucas and his entourage would have already left the hotel. Sarah would speak with him at the Temple Mount, confirm his decision, and get word to Brandon, who should be standing nearby.

"Do you know what you're going to say yet?" she asked.

He shook his head. "It's like I have two different topics. One is a judgment against evil, and the other is a warning and encouragement for the bride. I'm not sure which he wants."

"It will come," Sarah assured him. "Whatever is to be said, it will be said."

"I wish I had your confidence."

"We just prayed for his will to be done, didn't we?"

"Yeah."

She broke into a grin. "Then even you can't mess that up. Whatever is to be said, will be said."

He chuckled softly and they started for the door. "What about Tanya?" he asked. "If Lucas says yes to showing the tape, how will you get word to her?"

"She said she had other avenues. I don't think we have to worry about Tanya Chase."

Something about the phrase rang truer than Sarah had intended, but Brandon couldn't tell what. All he knew was that she was safe now—very, very safe.

"What about Katherine?" he asked.

Sarah turned to him. "As you're praying about what you're going to say, send up a prayer or two for her—she needs it."

Brandon caught something terribly troubled in her eyes, but she said no more. He made a point to pursue it later, as they headed toward the city. They stepped outside. The haze of ash was much thicker and the heat was already unbearable. He reached for the steel door and slid it shut.

"Do you think we should lock it?" Sarah asked.

"Probably wouldn't hurt." He reached for the padlock and snapped it into place. Finally, they turned and started up the steep road leading toward the Old City.

"She was so sweet," Sarah mused. "I wish we could have left her a gift or note or something to show our appreciation."

Brandon nodded in agreement, though he suspected she already knew. She seemed to have known nearly everything. They'd barely taken a half-dozen steps before they spotted a middle-aged Palestinian at the next house, locking his own door.

"Excuse me," Brandon called. "Excuse me. Do you speak English?"

The man turned. "Of course."

"I was wondering. The old woman that lives there?" He pointed toward the garage.

"What?"

"The old lady that lives there . . . in that garage? If you happen to see her, would you mind—"

"There is no old lady living there."

Brandon pointed, "No, I mean in that garage, right there."

"That's what I said, nobody lives there."

"Well, actually," Sarah explained, "there is. We had—"

"The owners, they have been away for nearly a month."

Brandon frowned. "But the woman who lives in the garage—"

"I told you, no woman lives there."

"Well . . . maybe she's like homeless or—"

"I watch their property. I feed their canary. There are only two keys, one for the garage, one for the house. I have them both. Nobody lives there." He finished locking his door, then turned and headed past them up the road.

Brandon and Sarah looked at each other, then back to the garage. Neither could say a word.

"Momm . . . whas woong? Mommm . . ."

Katherine put her hand to Eric's forehead. "Oh, sweetheart, you're burning up."

He frowned, obviously trying to clear his mind. "Whas . . . gooing on . . ."

"You're delirious, dear. We've got to get you back to the hospital. Here, let me help you get dressed."

It pained Katherine to lie to her son, but she could think of no other way. This would at least ensure his cooperation. And if Heylel should drop in and experience Eric's drugged state, he might buy it as well. She had her doubts, but it was worth a try.

He'd winced slightly and stirred from his sleep when she'd injected the Versed a few minutes earlier, and now it was performing exactly as Sarah had promised. She'd already called a taxi, leaving clear instructions for the driver to meet them down in the lower service entrance. She wanted to avoid the lobby and the security personnel she knew would be present.

After dressing Eric and grabbing her handbag with the other vial of the drug, Katherine led him out the door and down the hall toward the elevator. Unlike Ponte's Royal Suite, upstairs, there were no guards on this floor. The two of them arrived at the elevator and waited as Eric drifted in and out of coherency . . . sometimes appearing nearly wide awake, other times dozing off into dreamy sleep.

The elevator arrived. Katherine walked them both inside and pressed the button to the basement. With any luck they'd be able to go straight to the service entrance without stopping on any floors.

Unfortunately, Katherine's luck had never been good. They stopped at the fourth floor to let on an old Jewish couple and at the second to let on a child. Neither party asked questions, and she didn't offer any explanations. It took forever, but they finally arrived at the lobby. The doors opened and it was just as she had feared—the place was crawling with security.

The child exited first, followed by the couple. As they left, Katherine did her best to block Eric from any curious onlookers. When the doors were clear she reached out and pressed the *close* button. Once again time seemed to crawl until the doors started to shut.

"Ms. Lyon . . . Ms. Lyon." A hand suddenly appeared between the doors, slamming one side and causing them to reopen. It was the security guard from yesterday. The one who had led her and Brandon up to Sarah's room. "Is everything all right?" he asked.

She nodded. "For the most part."

He'd already spotted Eric. "Is he okay?"

Eric opened an eye, gave a smile, then drifted back to sleep. As he did he shifted his weight against Katherine, nearly throwing her off balance.

"Whoa." The guard moved to the other side to assist.

"I'm not sure what's wrong," Katherine said. "It's probably a complication from yesterday. I told them they should have spent the night at the hospital for observation, but with today's installation and everything . . ."

"Here, let's get him out and—"

"No, that's okay. I have a taxi downstairs. He's waiting to take us back to the hospital."

"Without security?"

"No, I called you guys. There's probably somebody waiting there now."

"Just the same." He pushed the *close* button. "I better go down with you and make sure."

"No, really, you don't have—"

But the doors were already closing. Fortunately, Eric remained sleeping as the elevator crept to the basement. Doing her best to make small talk, Katherine asked, "Is everybody else over at the Mount?"

"Just about. Couple more groups to transport, including yourselves. I'll let them know the situation and see what arrangements we can make for you."

"Thank you."

At last the doors opened.

"Here..." The guard began to help Eric out of the elevator.

"That's okay, I can handle it from here."

"Don't be ridiculous."

They stepped out of the elevator and headed down a dimly lit hall with Eric between them. The boy did little to help.

"That's funny," the guard said. "I don't see anyone here. You sure you called us?"

"Absolutely." Katherine breathed harder as Eric grew heavier. "He's probably just outside."

But when they stepped through the doors and into the bright sunlight there was no one there. Just an idling taxi with its Palestinian driver standing outside, grabbing a quick smoke. When he spotted them he quickly crossed to the passenger door and opened it.

"You seen anybody else here?" the guard asked as they arrived. "Any security people?"

The driver ground out his cigarette and shook his head.

The guard surveyed the area. "This is not right."

"Maybe he's up on the street," Katherine offered. She pulled Eric toward the door. "Here, help me get him inside."

The guard obliged, easing Eric into the car. But when he rose again, he still saw no sign of help. "Listen," he said, raising his sleeve toward his mouth. "Just stay put a moment and we'll find out what's going on."

"We don't have time to wait," Katherine insisted. "He's getting sicker by the minute."

The guard motioned for her to hang on and then turned to speak into the mike hidden in the cuff of his blazer sleeve. As he did, Katherine quickly crossed to the other side of the car and climbed in. "Mount Scopus Hospital, hurry."

The driver, who was still standing outside, motioned to the guard.

"Hurry!"

He did not move.

"Now. Let's go. *Let's go!*"

He hesitated.

"Now!"

Finally, reluctantly, he crossed back to the driver side, trying unsuccessfully to catch the guard's eye. But the man still had his back to them. At last the driver climbed behind the wheel and shut his door.

"The hospital," Katherine ordered. "It's an emergency!"

"But"—the driver motioned toward the guard—"the man . . ."

"Hurry! Hurry!"

Muttering something in Arabic, he put the car into gear.

"Now, let's go!"

They started forward.

Hearing the movement, the guard finally turned. "Hey, wait a minute. Wait a minute!"

"Go!" Katherine shouted. "Go!"

"But—"

"I'm paying the fare, not him. Let's go!"

More than a little frustrated, the driver accelerated. He looked nervously through the rearview mirror as the guard started after them.

"Keep going!" Katherine cried. "Keep going!"

The driver cursed in Arabic but continued driving. They headed up and around the building. Katherine stole a look over her shoulder. The guard was squinting to read their cab I.D. number and shouting back into his sleeve.

The cab pulled up to King David Road and the driver started to turn right. This would take them past the hotel's entrance and ensure certain capture.

"No!" Katherine shouted. "Turn left! Turn left!"

"But the hospital, it is—"

"Left!"

Throwing up his hands in frustration, the driver uttered another oath and turned left, causing more than one driver in the opposing lane to slam on his brakes, giving opportunity for the driver to curse even more.

Katherine looked over her shoulder.

"Where to now, lady?"

She gave no answer, continuing to look out the back window as they headed down the hill until the hotel disappeared from sight. When she turned back she recognized they were heading toward the same area she and Sarah had walked the night before.

"Lady . . . you still want hospital?"

"No, uh . . ." She looked around. "No, drop us off here."

"What?"

"Here, right here!"

"But we have not—"

"I'll pay you full fare, just drop us off here. Now! Stop the car and drop us off!"

As she hoped, her anger got her way. He swerved toward the right curb near the bottom of the hill. The cab barely stopped before she jumped out, grabbed Eric, and threw a handful of bills at the driver. Then, with minimal help from Eric, they crossed the busy street against the light and headed east, toward the Valley of Hinnom.

The Temple Mount was packed. The area of paved limestone north and east of the Dome of the Rock, the expansive park of cypress and olive trees north of that, even the rooftops that surrounded this twenty-five-plus acres of the most hotly contested real estate in the world were crammed with people trying to see the ceremonies on the stage which was located less than a hundred yards from the Golden Gate. And if they couldn't see the stage, there were always the two Jumbotron video screens rising high into the air on either side.

Brandon stood and watched the opening ceremonies upon the stairs called the Scales of Souls. These were a series of steps directly under the stone arches where Muslims believed men's souls would be weighed on Judgment Day. To his immediate right, on the stone pavement, was an area many believed to have been the site of the original temple, and just past that was the famous gold-roofed Dome of the Rock, one of the most holy sites in all of Islam. Inside was the rock upon which Jews, Christians, and Muslims believed Abraham had offered Isaac up to the Lord. The Mount was a somber, reverent place, and it seemed that everywhere Brandon looked some major religious event had occurred.

He had a strong sense that those events weren't entirely over.

He directed his attention back to the stage where an orchestra was playing various national anthems as country after country marched forward presenting their flags. Lucas Ponte sat onstage surrounded by nearly a hundred dignitaries. He watched the ceremony with the perfect mixture of strength and humility, nodding graciously to each flag bearer who placed their flags into one of the hundreds of holders surrounding the stage.

Brandon turned to look out over the crowd, searching the sea of faces for Sarah. She should have been there by now, but he saw no sign of her.

A cheer rose up and he turned back to the stage. The last of the flags had been presented and the music had changed to something noble and stirring as a video clip on the life of Lucas Ponte appeared up on the Jumbotrons. It covered everything from his humble beginnings as a grandson of Italian immigrants in Chicago, to photos of his valedictorian speech, to his emerging social consciousness at Notre Dame, to his stint in the Peace Corps, to his political career which started locally, then rose to Illinois governor, culminating in his illustrious career as president of the United States. It included the tragedy of losing his wife to cancer and yet his determination to fill out his second term for the good of the country, followed by his decision to continue serving the world through his work with the Cartel. It spoke of the organization's struggles to usher in world peace and their recent cure for the Scorpion virus. The piece was stirring and worked the crowd into such excited anticipation that the entire Mount roared in appreciation as Lucas Ponte was finally introduced and approached the lectern.

Brandon turned back to the crowd. They shouted, they cheered, they clapped, many wiped tears from their eyes. He'd never seen anything like it. And still the roar continued. A full minute passed, and then another as, up on the screen, Ponte smiled in both appreciation and humility, while wiping away a tear or two of his own. It was quite a performance.

"Brandon . . . Brandon . . ."

He turned to see Sarah working her way through the crowd toward him. When she arrived he shouted over the noise, "Are you okay?"

She nodded.

"Did you talk to him?"

She leaned forward. "What?"

"Did you talk to him? What did he say?"

"He said yes."

Brandon's heart sank and soared.

"It won't be for long," she shouted. "Just enough to call you up onstage—to use you as an example of his 'accessibility' and 'open-mindedness.'"

"He hasn't missed a trick, has he?"

"He doesn't think so."

The cheers started to subside. They turned back toward the stage. Several more seconds passed before the applause quieted down enough for Ponte to begin.

"Friends . . ."

But that was all it took before the crowd started up again. Brandon turned back to scan the cheering, shouting, tear-stained faces. And he was expected to go up against this? Was he crazy? They'd rip him apart!

That's when he felt Sarah take his hand. He looked at her. She smiled, doing her best to appear encouraging.

When the crowd finally settled, Ponte resumed. "Standing before you this day, upon this sacred and holy site, I can only say that I am overwhelmed. Humbled and overwhelmed."

More applause. When it ceased he continued. "Jerusalem . . . the city of peace. Yet, for how many centuries, no, for how many millennia has that name been scorned and mocked. Jerusalem . . . she who has been destroyed and rebuilt eighteen times. Jerusalem . . . she who has changed religions eleven times. Jerusalem . . . she who has never been a city of peace . . . but the symbol of seething hatred and unspeakable violence."

A hush fell over the Mount. A quarter million people grew very, very still. Ponte said nothing, holding the pause for as long as possible before he continued. "But all that is about to change. Starting today, Jerusalem will finally become all that she was destined to be. Starting today, Jerusalem will be a city of hope, of understanding, and most importantly, a city of peace!"

The crowd clapped and cheered.

"But not just a city of peace. Starting from this moment forward she will become the symbol of humankind's ability to overcome our barbaric past, the symbol of our entrance into a new age, the center of a new world order whose one and only theme is . . . peace!"

More cheers.

"Peace!"

Still more.

"Peace!"

Once again the roar was deafening. Brandon looked down and shook his head, marveling. But when he glanced back up, something above the stage caught his attention. A cloud of mist had begun to form. And as the crowd cheered and Ponte resumed, it continued to grow.

"And why are we entering that peace? It is not because of anything I have accomplished." He motioned to the dignitaries behind him. "It is not because of anything my friends, your leaders, have accomplished. No." He pushed up his glasses and continued. "It is simply because our time has arrived. Just as seasons come and go, so do the seasons of human history."

The cloud began to condense, slowing taking the shape Brandon had seen far too often.

"And now we are entering into a brand-new season. The season of humankind. A season where we will no longer focus upon our differences in race, in nationality, and perhaps even more importantly, our differences in religion—for, as this city can attest, it is differences in religion which have proven the most dangerous of all."

"Brandon . . ."

He threw Sarah a glance. She was staring straight ahead. "You see it, too?" he asked.

"I see something."

"This is the day, perhaps the first since the glory of Rome, that we will be able to throw off the yoke of religious division, that we will no longer allow it to manipulate and control our destiny . . ."

A tightness began to grip Brandon's gut. He suddenly felt very, very cold—not only about what he was hearing, but about what he was seeing. For there, hovering over the stage, with Lucas Ponte directly below it, was the head of the serpent.

At the mouth of the Hinnom Valley lay a grassy park. Despite the ceremony on the Mount two miles away, a Palestinian family sat under one of the many pine trees enjoying a picnic lunch. They seemed the quintessential family—a husband, wife, two beautiful children. They ate and teased, shouted and laughed, obviously enjoying each other's company. Katherine couldn't help but stare as she and Eric made their way across the narrow ravine to the dirt road leading up the other side. That's all she had ever wanted, a family like that.

And she'd nearly had it, too . . . until her husband's murder, until her father's death, until her bout with alcohol. And then, just when everything looked hopeless, Michael Coleman came upon the scene. Like her father and Sarah and a dozen others, Michael had also spoken of faith and of God's love. And then, just when she was starting to believe that there might really be some goodness in life, that there might really be a God of love, Michael was also taken. End of topic. End of discussion. End of hope.

Now there was only Eric.

The drug had barely started to wear off. She thought of giving him another injection, but Sarah's earlier words about free will and that he could still denounce Heylel rang in her ears. As far as she could tell, that was his last remaining chance. And, since it's hard to make a freewill decision doped up out of your mind, she decided to let more of it wear off.

They continued climbing the ridge.

"Whar we goin'?" His speech was still slurred, but he was definitely more coherent. "Whar you takin' us?"

"Just a little farther, sweetheart. See those nice cliffs over there?" She pointed to where the Hinnom and Kidron Valleys met. "I thought maybe we could sit there and talk."

"Talk?"

"Yeah, you know, like we used to. Just the two of us."

"Wha abou Lucas . . . an Heylel. Whar's Heylel?"

"They're busy, sweetheart. Right now it's just you and me. Just you and me . . ."

"But those of you who know me, who know what I have been striving to accomplish these many years, know of my insistence upon tolerance and mutual respect."

The crowd applauded in agreement.

Brandon looked on, his mouth bone dry, as he watched the serpent's head condense over the stage.

Sarah turned to him. "That's what killed your father—what attacked you?"

He nodded.

"Just because we do not agree with any one person does not give us the right to deprive that person of their voice. Just because their views are extreme, or even hurtful, does not give us the right to silence them. That is not the mutual respect and love for which I have worked so long and hard. Despite our disagreements, they are still our brothers and sisters, they are still part of our unique oneness. Because we are all one, my friends. We are one people ... we are one community ... we are one planet!"

The applause grew more enthusiastic.

Brandon threw another look at Sarah. Her eyes were riveted to the serpent's head. She appeared even more frightened than he was. He reached out and put an arm around her. She barely noticed.

"That is why I have personally invited a dissenting voice to come and briefly share our platform. You may disagree with what he has to say, perhaps even find it repulsive. Some would insist that his narrow religious thinking is a throwback to the very hatred and intolerance we are eliminating here today. Others may see him as a symbol of what has crippled and shackled our human spirit for so many centuries. So why do I invite him? Because he still deserves the right to be heard, because he is still my brother, he is still part of our human family."

By now the image of the head was so clear Brandon could see the tongue flicking in and out ... just as it had in his visions, just as it had in his father's church ... moments before it had opened its mouth and consumed him.

"Many of you from the West may remember the televised event featuring our good friend, Reverend Jimmy Tyler." Ponte turned to those onstage behind him and acknowledged the man in the wheelchair. With great effort, Jimmy Tyler raised his hand in a wave. "That was when this young man I am about to introduce first came to the world's attention. But for those of you unfamiliar with him, a news crew has assembled a brief video that should serve as an adequate introduction before he comes forward."

"All right, Tanya," Sarah whispered.

Brandon nodded.

"In it you will hear statements that may strike you as outrageous, even offensive. You will see things that may defy science and the laws of physics. Do I believe such things are possible? What I believe is of no consequence. All I ask is for you to listen to his claims, look at the world around us, and draw your own conclusions. Ask yourself if his views are not the embodiment of the chains that have enslaved our planet since the beginning of time. Ask yourself if the writhing our planet is currently undergoing is nothing but a final effort to, once and for all, throw off those shackles."

Brandon lowered his head. He was being set up. Even now, even with world opinion on Heylel's side, even with the prophecies clearly stating the people would follow him, he was still stacking the deck.

"And let me apologize in advance for any bias you may note in this videotaped introduction. Although the news team tried to be objective, it was obvious they found the material deeply disturbing, and like the rest of us, they are only human ..."

Ponte stepped back, motioned to the screens, and Brandon and Sarah joined the rest of the world in watching.

The narrator's voice was unfamiliar to him, but the images were crystal clear.

"Born of religious parents, Brandon Martus was raised in a strict fundamentalist Christian household ..."

A series of photos flashed upon the screen. Seeing his parents displayed before the world filled Brandon with both anger and sorrow. Was there nothing this man would not stoop to?

"But it wasn't until the death of his sister in an auto accident for which he was responsible that Martus began to experience the deeper aspects of guilt and condemnation for which his faith is known."

The screen showed photos of him with his little sister— images that brought instant tears to his eyes. He had to look down. A moment later he felt Sarah moving closer to him for support.

But it was only the beginning. Soon the video was discussing his "so-called psychic powers," replaying portions of the older report Tanya had broadcast that included interviews of angry and disappointed patients. Next came the photos of Sarah and mention of their "sexual repressions" and "failed marriage."

He glanced at Sarah. She was taking it no better than he.

After that came clips from Jimmy Tyler's TV rally. Images of Brandon shouting, Brandon screaming, Brandon approaching Tyler and yelling, "The blood of the sheep will be upon the head of the shepherd!" This was followed by the pitcher of blood, the shattering glass, Tyler choking and coughing helplessly as Brandon, appearing out of control, shrieked, "The hand of the Lord is upon you, and you shall no longer be able to speak or spread your deceit in my name!" All of this was intercut with shots of the Los Angeles audience booing and throwing things onstage . . . as the live audience on the Mount also grew more and more agitated over what they saw.

New images began. A video of a party with plenty of drinking, dancing, carousing. At first Brandon didn't recognize it, until he caught a glimpse of Salman. This was the party he had thrown at Thyatira. There were other shots, angles of half-naked men and women which may or may not have been part of the party, but which definitely gave it every appearance of an orgy.

Now they were back in L.A. with Brandon onstage shouting: "Surely as a wife treacherously departs from her husband so have you dealt treacherously with me!"

Now, back to the party—shots of young Banu snuggling into Brandon's arms with the narrator explaining, "But such hypocrisy cannot be hidden for long . . ." A closeup of the intoxicated girl. " . . . especially when it comes to underaged children, no more than fourteen or fifteen years old."

The anger and disapproval of the Temple Mount grew louder.

More angles of Brandon screaming onstage, "You have played the harlot with many lovers!"

Back to Brandon at the orgy where he was seen abusing the child by throwing her across the room into the table, sending glass and booze crashing all around her.

By now the Mount's anger had turned to audible boos and hissing. And still the video continued . . .

"But I don't wan' things diff'ren'!"

"Eric, sweetheart—"

"Heylel promised . . . and nothin's gonna stop us! Nothin'!"

For the briefest moment Eric's anger had pushed through the effects of the drug. Katherine hesitated, wondering if she should inject more or wait and see if he settled back under its influence. They'd found a seat on a boulder atop one of the cliffs. Forty feet below was rocky rubble, dead grass, and parched olive trees that stretched across the ravine and up the other side toward the Old City. Occasionally they could hear the cheers and roar of the crowd from the Temple Mount that was about a mile and a half away.

She glanced at her son. His eyes were already growing heavy and starting to close. "Eric?"

They opened.

"If you continue with Heylel, you'll be responsible for more people dying, maybe even more than Scorpion."

"Tha's their problem," he mumbled.

"Eric?"

He woke more. "If they get in the way, tha's their problem."

The coldness of the statement hit Katherine hard. Even in his half-asleep stupor, he knew what he wanted . . . and the consequences. And at that moment Katherine knew he would not change, he would never change. He would hold to the decision he'd made so many months before. He would follow Heylel, he would always follow him, and there was nothing she could say or do to change his mind. Regardless of the millions that had died in the recent past or that may soon die in the future, her son had made his decision.

Numbly, Katherine Lyon reached into her purse.

Memories of Eric flooded in—his sweetness, his kindness, his tearstained face when he'd caught his first fish and saw it struggling for breath on the riverbank. But other images came as well . . . the bloody carnage of the birds atop that rock in Nepal. The death of his friend, Deepak. *Momma, I made his heart stop!* The murder of the officer on the airport tarmac.

An unbearable ache spread through her chest, making it impossible to breathe as she pulled the first vial from her purse, followed by the syringe. She looked at her son. He was dozing peacefully. How was it possible? How could this child, this flesh of her flesh, this soul of her soul, be the murderer of millions?

She took a ragged breath, then pulled out the syringe. She removed the protective tip she had placed back over the needle. With trembling hands she inserted it into the first vial and drew out the remaining eight cc's of the clear liquid. She hesitated a moment, unsure, then reached back into her purse to pull out the new vial. She inserted the needle, and though it was difficult to see through the tears, she drew out the full ten cc's.

Another wave of cheers wafted across the valley.

Eric stirred and she watched him. So tender, so innocent . . . and yet a murderer, a mass murderer. Her heart screamed in agony, and she bit her lip so the words would not escape. *Dear God, dear God, please don't make me do this!*

But of course there was no God. At least for her. And, even if there was, he would not answer.

She reached back into her purse and pulled out a narrow cloth belt, the one that went with her green floral dress. Everything was blurring. She could see only the syringe, the belt, her shaking hands.

For God so loved the world that he gave his only begotten Son . . .

The phrase surprised her. It was a Bible verse, the one printed over the door of her father's church. She hadn't thought of it in years. Once again it echoed in her head.

For God so loved the world . . .

"God's love," the same words her father had preached, that Michael had preached, that Sarah had preached. Words. That's all they had to offer. That's all anyone had to offer except . . . except, perhaps . . . God.

. . . that he gave his only begotten Son . . .

Giving up his only Son . . . Well, at least maybe he knew a little of what she was going through.

She reached down to Eric's arm. It was tan and the hair was just starting to thicken from manhood. She looked down at his hand, the one that had clutched hers at the state fair during his first ride on the Octopus.

Momma, I'm scared!

Just hang on to me, baby. It'll be okay, just hang on . . .

She reached down and lifted the hand to her lips, then tenderly kissed its open palm.

For God so loved the world that he gave his only begotten Son . . .

Was this what God had felt? This impossible grief, when he'd given up *his* Son?

She pushed up Eric's sleeve, then wrapped the belt around his arm, pulling it tight until the veins began to bulge.

He stirred, opening his eyes. "Whar you doin'?"

"It's okay, baby . . ." It was all she could do to force out the words. "This will make you better . . . This will make everything better."

She searched her lap for the syringe. It was difficult to see it through the tears.

For God so loved the world . . .

If this was the type of pain he'd gone through . . . for the world . . . then maybe she'd been wrong, maybe he did have some love in him . . .

She found the syringe and lifted it up. Sarah had explained the need to tap up the bubbles and squirt them out, but her vision wasn't clear enough to see them. Not that it mattered, not with eighteen cc's. She lay his arm in her lap. For the briefest moment she lowered her head and rested it against his shoulder, unable to continue. She turned and kissed his neck. A sob escaped. This was her child, her cooing, gurgling, laughing baby.

He would also be the murderer of millions.

She raised her head from his shoulder. She tightened her legs around his arm to hold it in place, wiped the tears from her eyes, and searched for the largest vein.

That's when she heard Heylel's voice. *"What do you think you're doing?"*

Her words came out choking but determined. "I'm stopping you. You'll not use my son to kill anymore."

Suddenly Eric's body came alive. He tried to twist, to pull away his arm. *"Stop it!"* Heylel bellowed. *"Stop it!"*

But he didn't have a chance. Despite the movement, Katherine held his arm firmly between her legs. She brought the needle toward a puffy blue vein. It pressed into the skin, starting to pierce the flesh, when she heard—

"Momma . . ." It was the voice of her baby boy, of little Eric. "Momma, I'm scared."

And it burst her heart. She was overcome. She could not do it. She could not kill her only son.

That's when Heylel made his move. He jerked Eric's arm out of her lap. The movement startled her and before she could react, he grabbed the hand with the syringe and tore it from her grip. Then, with one swift move, he raised it into the air and plunged it deep into her chest.

"Eric . . ."

She caught a glimpse of his eyes but Eric wasn't there. Only Heylel.

She raised her hands to her chest, trying to pull out the syringe, which gave Heylel opportunity to scoot away from her, letting her tumble off the rock. As she fell, he slid down to join her, using her momentum to kick her the rest of the way . . . until she rolled over the edge of the cliff.

"Eric . . . !"

She hit one rock and sailed through the air. Then she hit another and another—falling, flying, flailing. Time slowed. She could hear Heylel's laughter high above, but she felt no betrayal or anger. Instead, her mind focused, growing amazingly sharp. She couldn't do it. She loved her son too much to kill him. And yet God's love was greater than that—because he *had* gone through with it. He *had* killed his Son . . . for the world . . . *for her!* Was such a thing possible? As much as she loved Eric, was it possible that God loved her even more?

The answer was vividly clear . . . not in words, but in action. He *had* killed his Son for her, he *had* gone through the agony that she could not endure . . . for *her*, to save *her*, because he loved *her!*

. . . that whosoever believe in him shall not perish but have everlasting life.

Suddenly it made sense. Suddenly she understood. Katherine had no idea how long she fell. The concept of time was gone. All she knew was that now, at last, she finally understood the fullness of God's love. And for the first time since her childhood, she asked that he would once again hold her in his arms.

Katherine Lyon's prayer was answered before she hit the ground.

As Sarah watched the video, she noticed the theme had begun to change. Instead of dealing with Brandon's "anger" and "hypocrisy" it began drawing connections between his statements and the world catastrophes. Using portions of Tanya's old broadcast, it discussed the worldwide drought, the consequent famine, the earthquakes, the volcanoes, even the outbreak of Scorpion, while cutting back and forth to Brandon on the L.A. stage, shouting the passages from Jeremiah.

"My anger and my fury will be poured out on this place ..." The scene was followed by various shots of eruptions, blasting plumes of smoke and ash. "On man ..." Next came portraits of suffering humanity, dying men and women, living skeletons, a starving child trying to nurse from his dead mother. "And beast ..." Malnourished cattle, a thousand chickens dead from heat prostration. "On the trees of the field ..." Pacific Northwest forests igniting in flames from fiery lava. "And on the fruit of the ground ..." Shriveled crops, desert farmlands. "And it will burn and not be quenched!"

The narrator resumed: "Perhaps this is all just coincidence ..."

Back to the video of Brandon onstage, shouting: "Be astonished oh heavens at this and be horribly afraid." Next a shot of him and Sarah pelted by rotten eggs. Back to Brandon. "Be very desolate, says the Lord ..."

The narrator continued. "Then again, perhaps it is not."

Sarah watched the screen in amazement. Heylel's fear and hatred was even greater than she had imagined. He was working the crowd into a frenzy. Many were shouting, swearing, shaking their fists as if they had finally found the source of their torment.

And still the images continued, recapping the most horrific moments as the narrator concluded: "Could one man really be responsible for all of this turmoil? It is doubtful. And yet we must ask ourselves, could these natural disasters be a death knell? Could they be, as he insists, the final act of a jealous God—a divine temper tantrum thrown by a desperate deity who knows he has lost control, who knows that we as a people will no longer endure his tyranny? Interesting questions and ones that may never be answered. And yet as we join together to face this new era, these are questions that we must all begin to ask."

Sarah couldn't believe her ears. In less than two minutes, he had started making the transition from blaming Brandon to blaming God. She suspected it would only be the beginning. Over the next few months, perhaps years, it would continue. The pride and hatred she had experienced last night up in Heylel's room would grow and spread until he persuaded the whole earth to attempt what a third of heaven had failed to do . . . to rebel and overthrow God.

Now she understood more than ever why Brandon had to speak today, why it was important the people be warned and the facts presented. Each and every individual would have to make a choice. If not now, then soon—very, very soon.

The music swelled to an ominous ending as the video freeze-framed on Brandon shouting. The image remained on screen several seconds before it slowly faded. But the crowd's anger did not. It continued to grow, feeding upon itself. And, the louder it grew, the more solid the serpent's head above the stage became. To Sarah it no longer appeared as a thick mist. It had become a tangible flesh-and-blood entity.

Lucas Ponte began to speak. "Please . . ." he shouted, "please . . ." He motioned for the crowd to quiet. "Please . . . I told you the video could be provocative, and I must apologize for its bias. Surely, not all of these facts could be true. Some must be exaggerated."

The crowd disagreed.

"Please . . . regardless of what we think of him, or his religion, he is allowed his opinion. Please." Again Lucas held out his hands. "Please, we must show restraint. Allow him to explain. We must allow him to justify his actions and his God. Please . . ."

Gradually the crowd began to quiet.

"Good . . . good." Then, scanning the Mount, he called out, "Brandon . . . Brandon Martus, are you out there? Mr.

Martus, please come forward and share with us your views. Mr. Martus . . ."

Sarah turned to her husband. He was as white as a sheet . . . and trembling.

"Mr. Martus, I know you are out there."

She wrapped an arm around him. Now was the time. All that they'd been through, all that they'd learned, it was for this one single moment. He took a shaky breath and looked at her. For the briefest second she thought he was too frightened to continue. "Be strong and courageous," she shouted over the crowd.

He swallowed hard and nodded. Then he shouted back, "What can they do to a dead man?" He tried giving his killer grin, but it would not come. She smiled anyway, hoping he didn't see the concern on her own face.

Wiping the sweat from his forehead with his sleeve, he took her hand and they started forward. The crowd in front of them began to part . . . not without grumbling, shouting occasional oaths, and spitting on the ground before them.

But they continued.

Sarah looked up ahead to the stage. The serpent's head began opening its mouth, as if preparing to devour them. Maybe it would. She knew Brandon saw it, probably more clearly than she. But she also knew he had faced its gaping mouth before and had survived.

She prayed he could do it again.

CHAPTER 21

I HAVE WAITED A LONG TIME FOR THIS."

Brandon recognized the voice instantly. He looked up at the serpent's head, which hovered twenty yards before them over the stage. Its jaw had opened wide enough for Brandon to see into the throat. But it was not the throat of a snake. Instead it was the swirling vortex of screaming, fiery faces, the anguished specters whose mouths twisted and shrieked in unearthly wails.

He glanced at Sarah. She saw them, too.

"YOU ARE MINE."

Although the voice came from the head, the mouth did not move. Just below the apparition stood Ponte, looking kindly down upon them as they approached the stage. They were fifteen yards away when a young man lunged toward them, screaming a curse in French. He was intercepted by security and immediately swept away.

For Brandon everything was turning ethereal, as in a dream, as in the dozen nightmares he'd had since his encounter in the church. They were ten yards from the stage now. He was so frightened he barely had feeling in his legs. In fact he was surprised he could even walk. But he continued forward, one foot after another.

The jaw unhinged, opening even wider. It was no longer possible to see the eyes or snout—only the fangs, the flicking tongue, and the twisting, screaming faces of fire. More memories rushed in. How he'd been sucked into that very throat—how he'd felt the fire searing his waist, his chest, his neck, and finally his face until . . . until . . .

"Don't look," Sarah shouted. "Think about the Lord."

Yes. That's what he'd done before. At the church. He'd kept his attention fixed on the Lord. Back then it had been on the vision of a nail-pierced hand. But this was not the church; there was no hand. And he could not look away. As he stared, the swirling faces began taking on forms of those he knew— first his little sister, then his father, then others who had passed away. Each cried out to him, beckoning for him to join them. He knew it was a trick, another deception.

But they looked so real.

"The Lord!" Sarah shouted. "Think of the Lord!"

Brandon barely heard. This was the mouth that had devoured him, that had nearly destroyed him. And now he was walking directly into it. Of his own free will! He wanted to bolt, to run away. But where do you run when you're surrounded by a quarter million people? You don't. The machine had been set in motion, and there was nothing he could do to escape it.

They arrived at the stairs leading up to the stage. He hesitated, unable to continue.

"Please . . ." He looked up to see Ponte spreading open his arms. "There is nothing to fear. We are all friends."

He glanced at Sarah. She was pale and almost as frightened as he. Still, somehow, she managed to give him the slightest of nods. And that was all he needed. He gripped her hand tighter, and the two of them started up the steps. As they did, the crowd's displeasure grew even louder.

"Please . . ." Ponte addressed the audience again. "Please . . . this will only take a few moments. Please . . ." But the crowd was far less gracious. "Please, if you do not give him an opportunity to speak, then that makes us no better than he. Please, now . . ."

The crowd settled slightly as Brandon and Sarah arrived at the top of the steps and started the long trek toward Ponte . . . and the open throat of fiery faces just above him. But as they forced themselves to continue walking in obedience and in faith, a most unusual thing happened . . . the apparition began to retreat.

"Brandon . . ." Sarah whispered.

"I see it."

It continued pulling back, maintaining the exact same distance from them until it was hovering over the dignitaries at the rear of the stage.

"It's afraid of us," Brandon said.

"Not just us." Sarah nodded toward the audience.

Brandon turned and caught his breath. Interspersed throughout the crowd, every twenty yards or so, were what appeared to be giant towering men. They were a good three to four feet taller than any men around them, and they were wrapped in robes of dazzling brightness.

He turned to Sarah in astonishment.

"That's not all." She motioned toward the hills surrounding them.

He turned to look. On every hill, as far as the eye could see, stood thousands of the same creatures . . . all glowing, all watching.

He knew who they were. And with that realization came the understanding that he and Sarah were not alone. Regardless of what would happen, they were not alone. As he stood there, before the host of heaven, he felt a confidence and a faith begin to swell inside of him. And with that faith came the warmth of the fire. It started in his belly, then slowly rose into his chest.

Ponte greeted them as they arrived. "Thank you both for joining us. I can imagine it is not easy to appear before such a large audience—not only in front of the hundreds of thousands of people here in Jerusalem, but before the billions of people watching on television around the world. To appear in front of so many people must be very intimidating, very intimidating, indeed."

Brandon knew what Ponte was doing. He could feel the terror at the edge of his mind eager to rush in. And it would take so little effort to allow it. A tiny choice of his will. But he also knew that was where the battle was being fought. Regardless of the odds, regardless of the outcome, the real battle was being waged within his will.

Keeping that in mind, Brandon chose not to look out at the audience, nor back to the serpent head. Instead of caving in and obeying his fears, he did as Sarah had suggested and looked upon the Lord. Quietly, in his heart, he began to worship him. And, as he worshiped, the fire grew hotter.

"Dr. Weintraub." Ponte smiled warmly. "It's so good to see you again."

Brandon watched as the man focused his gaze upon her. He could only guess what doubts and feelings of unworthiness he was stirring inside her mind. She took an unsteady breath, and for a moment Brandon thought she might crumble. But as she exhaled he saw her lips begin to move, almost imperceptibly. She was also praying.

"So tell us, Mr. Martus . . ." Ponte continued to speak as he gave Brandon a microphone which a stagehand had passed up to him. "As briefly as possible, have we in any way misrepresented your beliefs? Is there anything you'd like to clarify for us?"

There was another surge of panic. Brandon still had no idea what he was to say. Judgment of the world or warning to the bride? Which? But before he allowed the fear to take hold, he forced himself to blurt out an answer. "Yes!"

Instantly, the clouds of confusion parted, as if this act of faith alone had cleared his mind.

"Well," Ponte said, "we're waiting."

Realizations poured in. Now, Brandon understood why he'd been unable to decide which of the two topics he was to speak on. He was to talk about them both. He wasn't sure how, but that wasn't his concern. He turned to Ponte. And, in another act of faith, he opened his mouth. The words began to come. "The Lord would say two things to you."

"Two things?" Ponte asked.

Brandon nodded. "The Word of his mouth is a double-edged sword." The fire had risen to his throat now, emboldening him until he could look out into the audience. "One edge will protect and instruct the righteous ... the other will cut down and destroy the evil."

"I see." Ponte pretended to chuckle. "Sort of good news, bad news."

Amusement rippled through the audience.

"Please"—Ponte motioned to him—"share with us. Tell us what more we can expect from this God of yours."

The fire burst from Brandon's mouth. Words barely came to mind before he spoke them. And the more he spoke, the hotter they grew. "Who will have pity on you, O Jerusalem? Who will mourn for you? Who will stop to ask how you are?"

Ponte turned his back and walked a few steps away, obviously distancing himself from what was being said.

"You have rejected me, declares the Lord. You keep on backsliding. So I will lay hands on you and destroy you; I can no longer show compassion. I will winnow them with a winnowing fork at the city gates of the land. I will bring bereavement and destruction on my people, for they have not changed their ways."

Once again the audience began to voice their displeasure. But the broiling intensity inside Brandon could not be contained.

"I will make their widows more numerous than the sand of the sea. At midday I will bring a destroyer against the mothers of their young men; suddenly I will bring down on them anguish and terror."

Boos and catcalls began, but Brandon would not be stopped. He started focusing upon specific faces in the crowd, pleading with them, begging them to see.

"The mother of seven will grow faint and breathe her last. Her sun will set while it is still day; she will be disgraced and humiliated. I will put the survivors to the sword before their enemies, declares the—"

"Yes, well, I think you've made your point, Mr. Martus."

"But—"

Ponte approached. "Once again you've proven to us that your God knows nothing of love. He cares only for his own interests and nothing for ours. And, as far as I can tell, that's anything but love."

"But it is." Sarah leaned over and spoke into Brandon's microphone. There was a brief squeal of feedback. Brandon handed it over to her and she continued. "It's a deeper love. It's a greater love."

A flicker of concern crossed Ponte's face. He was not expecting this.

Sarah continued. "It's a love that tells us what we need to hear, not what we want to hear. It's a love that cares more for our lives than our feelings."

Brandon looked at her, marveling. She glanced at him, as pleased with her performance as he was. Obviously, the same fire had ignited her soul. She turned back to the audience. "Don't you see? God loves us so much that he'll sacrifice anything to save us ... even our love toward him. If it means disciplining us, he'll discipline us ... even if it means our hating him."

"Please, Dr. Weintraub," Ponte interrupted, "it makes no difference how you try to spin it, the truth of the matter is—"

"He loves us so much that he destroyed his own Son . . . for us."

"Dr.—"

"And"—she turned directly on him—"he will destroy anyone who tries to cut off that love."

"Love?" Ponte was no longer able to hide his scorn. "How can anyone describe what we saw up on the screen as love? Human suffering, indescribable agony, unspeakable sorrow? That's not love. The writhings, screamings, the ignored cries for mercy? How can you call that love?"

The audience applauded in agreement, and Ponte turned to them. "The intolerable bondage we, the human family, have been under all of these centuries . . . that is not love!"

Cheers of agreement followed.

Ponte grew more agitated . . . which had the desired effect upon the audience, giving them permission to vent even more anger. Brandon looked back out at the shouting faces . . . and that's when he spotted him. Just a few rows back, moving toward the stage. Salman Kilyos.

As Ponte worked up the crowd, Salman took advantage of the distraction, moving closer and closer. He was holding a sweater. Brandon's mind raced. Why was anyone carrying a sweater on such a hot day? Unless they were hiding something underneath. Unless they were——

Instantly, Brandon understood.

Ponte continued to rail. "You talk about a self-sacrificing love. An interesting theory . . . but where is the proof? I ask you, where is the truth to validate such claims?"

Brandon watched Salman, praying that someone would stop him before he got himself hurt or killed. He was in the second row now, working his way through the agitated crowd. Surely the dozens of security personnel around the stage would spot him. But they didn't. They saw nothing, almost as if they were blinded.

"Real love is based upon action. Like stopping the deadly Scorpion virus."

The audience broke into cheers.

"Like uniting every person, tribe, and nation."

The cheering grew louder.

"Like ushering in an age of peace and prosperity such as the world has never known!"

The Mount roared in approval. They were ecstatic—shouting, stomping their feet, waving their arms.

Salman made his move. He pulled the large black revolver from his sweater and lunged toward the stage.

"No!" Brandon shouted. But he couldn't be heard over the crowd.

Ponte stood less than six feet from the edge of the stage when he glanced down and saw Salman taking aim. Everything turned to slow motion as he began to turn, as he began to shout.

Brandon started toward him. He could not stop Salman, but he could knock Ponte out of the way.

Salman prepared to fire.

Brandon leaped toward Ponte, once again shouting. "Nooo . . ."

Salman pulled the trigger.

Brandon slammed into Ponte, wrapping his arms around him and pulling him to the ground . . . just as Salman fired once, twice, three times.

The first bullet went wide, the second shattered Brandon's clavicle, and the third pierced his lung and pulmonary artery. The impacts were so powerful that he didn't feel himself hitting the stage . . . though he did hear a multitude of shots fired and knew security had finally discovered Salman.

"Brandon!"

Lying on the stage, he saw Sarah's approach. He wanted to yell at her to stay back, that they'd misunderstand. But he could not move. Instead, he watched in numb horror as a half-dozen red laser dots found her body and a half-dozen hollow-point bullets tore into her flesh.

She landed inches from his face.

Security swarmed the stage. All Brandon saw were rushing feet and legs. What had gone wrong? Why had he only been allowed to deliver one-half of the message, the judgment? What about the other, the message to the bride?

Reality began disintegrating, strobing bits and pieces flashed at unexpected moments. He saw Ponte rising. Heard him shouting. He knew the man wasn't happy. He knew Ponte was all too aware of how Brandon's self-sacrifice would be construed. He'd been double-crossed. He'd been out-loved. "No," Ponte was shouting. "This isn't right! This isn't how it's supposed to be!"

"What's he doing?" the technical director cried.

Ryan Holton shook his head as he watched Ponte rant and rave over the monitors. "It's not right!" the chairman was shouting. "It isn't fair. You tricked me, you tricked me!"

"He's lost it," Ryan answered.

"We got to get off him. Cut to something else!"

Ryan nodded and quickly spoke into his headset. "VTR ... give me a segment."

"What do you—"

"Anything. I don't care what you have, just give me something, now!"

"Stand by."

Ryan watched the monitors in amazement as Ponte's anger continued. The man was definitely out of control. He was standing on the stage, seeming to shout at no one in particular. "It's not fair, you promised, it's not fair—"

"Tape ready," came the response through the headset.

"Roll tape," Ryan ordered.

"Tape rolling."

The VTR monitor before him came up. It was another segment on Brandon Martus. Only now he was standing in what looked like ancient ruins. Behind him were broken arches and stone rubble and beyond that was what looked like the remains of an ancient stadium. The kid turned to face the camera. Tears were streaming down his face as he began to speak.

"Where'd that come from?" the technical director demanded.

Ryan shook his head and leaned forward to listen.

"When I shut up the heavens so that there is no rain, or command locusts to devour the land or send a plague among my people . . ."

"Punch it up," Ryan ordered.

"But we don't know what it—"

"Punch it up. We've got to dump Ponte, punch it up!"

The technical director reached down to the board in front of him and hit one of the dozens of illuminated buttons. Suddenly Brandon Martus was on the main monitor. Suddenly he was up on the two Jumbotron screens. And suddenly he was being broadcast around the world.

"If my people, who are called by my name, will humble themselves . . ."

The technical director turned to Ryan. "Do we really need more of this guy?"

Ryan watched the screen. "Let's see where it goes . . ."

"My children!" Brandon cried, "my bride! I have chosen you from before the beginning of the world. You carry my name, yet you do not live my life. Though I have given you power, you have not used it to pursue my holiness. Hear my plea. Heed my warning. Quit seeking your desires, quit seeking your kingdom. Humble yourselves and receive mine. Receive all that I am."

Brandon heard his voice echoing through the Mount. Consciousness came in fits and starts. For a moment he thought he might be hallucinating . . . until he heard the familiar verse . . . until he realized the other edge of the sword was now being wielded.

"If my people will pray and seek my face . . ."

He looked over at Sarah. She lay in an expanding pool of blood staring at him. She was struggling to breathe, every gasp a torturous ordeal. But she heard his voice, too. And, for

the briefest instant, a smile broke through the pain and flickered across her face.

He returned it.

His voice continued. "I am eternal. All else you pursue
will burn."

Then he saw her hand. It was outstretched, just inches
from his. To touch it, to hold it these last remaining moments
suddenly became the most important thing in Brandon's
world. He struggled to move his hand toward hers. The effort
was excruciating, but it was something he had to do.

Ryan continued to watch the monitor.

"You fast in vain. You pray and plead and beg, but your
efforts are futile. Look into my eyes and know what is eternal.
Only when you behold my glory will your desires conform to
mine. Only when you know me can you pray in my name."

The technical director cleared his throat. "I don't like
this. I'm not sure what he's doing."

Ryan said nothing. He was looking at the love and compassion in the boy's eyes, and he was thinking about his last
conversation with Tanya . . .

He really got to you, didn't he?

Yeah, he really got to me.

"Let's cut to something. Ryan?"

He thought of the message she'd left on his service, the
report he'd been given of her trying to break in, and of the
"accidental shooting" by the guard . . .

"Ryan? Ryan, do you hear me?"

. . . and he thought of his own ever-present emptiness.

"VTR," the technical director spoke into the intercom.
"Give us something else. Maybe a—"

"No." Ryan cut in firmly. "Keep it."

"But—"

"Keep the tape rolling."

The technical director gave him a look, but Ryan had
made up his mind. And, as he settled back into his seat,

crossing his arms to watch, he half-whispered, half-prayed, "This one's for you, kiddo. This one's for you . . ."

Brandon's voice continued to reverberate across the Temple Mount.

"Repent! Turn! I have given you the power to overcome. All you need to do is choose: your wickedness or my holiness . . . your death or my life. For without repentance there is no forgiveness. And without forgiveness we have no fellowship."

But, lying on the stage, Brandon barely heard. He was using all of his concentration and strength to reach for Sarah's hand. He no longer felt pain. And he knew by the blurring and spinning that he'd be losing consciousness any second. If he could just get to her hand, if he could just move his hand those last fractions of an inch—there! He had it! His heart swelled with gratitude as he glanced back to her face. But her eyes were already closed.

No! his mind cried. *Please, God, not yet!*

But he was also going. He could feel it. He'd fought the fight and he'd won. He'd delivered the message. How it would be received was not his responsibility. His task was over. He gave Sarah's hand a tender squeeze, a gentle good-bye. Sights and sounds slipped away. He could no longer see, he could barely hear. And then, to his surprise, he felt Sarah's hand respond. It was weak, no doubt using the very last of her strength. But there it was, two distinct squeezes answering his one.

Then she was gone.

And, smiling faintly, Brandon followed.

"Humble yourselves! Seek my face! Turn! Then will I hear from heaven and will forgive your sin and will heal your land. My bride . . . my precious bride. How my heart yearns for you. How I love and adore you . . . more than I did my very life. How I long for this time of suffering to end, and for the cup of my wrath to be emptied. But you will not have it."

In Washington State, Beth O'Brien woke her husband, Dr. Philip O'Brien, and their two girls to watch the great Chairman Ponte speak. It was an important moment in history and one she felt they shouldn't miss. She'd even fixed coffee and hot chocolate to coax them out of bed. But as the family sat on the sofa watching TV, Beth began to think. It had been several years since she'd given God any serious thought, and longer than that since she'd attended church. And yet, watching and listening to this young man, she wondered if maybe, just maybe, it wouldn't hurt to expose the children to what she once believed in so strongly. Maybe it wouldn't hurt at all.

"You try to stop evil by changing others. Yet you do not cease from your own evil. Repent. Repent and turn your heart toward me. Repent and see if there is anything I would withhold from you. My arms are opened wide. Turn from your adultery."

Frank shook his head sadly. He'd just returned from a late-night, full-on party, and despite the booze and beer, he stood before his TV set stone sober. That had once been his friend on the screen there, a fellow "townie"—before he'd gotten religion, before he'd turned fanatic. Of course Frank had tried to get him to see reason, and they'd had more than their fair share of shouting matches. After all, it was one thing to believe in something, but to let it take over your life like that? No way. Yet Brandon refused to see reason. Even when the people had shut down the clinic. Even when he made a total fool of himself in L.A.

And now this . . .

Again Frank shook his head. This was a perfect example of the old order that Chairman Ponte was talking about—a perfect example of what happens when someone lets himself get too carried away with all that God stuff. Frank crossed over to the sofa and rummaged through the dirty clothes and magazines until he found the remote. He pointed it toward the TV and shut it off. He could not, he would not watch anymore.

Tisha Youngman could not stop the tears as she watched the broadcast from the Motel 6 room. Her friend for the night, some guy whose name she'd already forgotten, but who had more than enough access to the smack she'd fallen in love with so many months before, lay beside her, snoring, sweating, naked—sprawled out like some giant beached whale. But she didn't notice. Her mind was a thousand miles away. Back home, back when she was a little girl, back when she was sitting with her momma and daddy in church . . .

"Let my love break your grip on inequity. Let my love strip you of your sin. Turn and run into my arms that I may hold you as I once did. Come to me that we may again share the intimacies of husband and wife. That we may again be one."

Brandon's picture and voice continued to be broadcast in homes and countries all around the world. As the speech drew to its conclusion, those who felt drawn to him listened thoughtfully while those who disagreed counted him even more of a lunatic.

"For when we are one . . . when you are lost in my arms and when our hearts are intertwined, all of creation watches in awe. When we are one, delighting in each other's pleasure, there is nothing, absolutely nothing you can withhold from me, and nothing I will withhold from you."

On the TV screen, the taped Brandon Martus finally lowered his head. His message had concluded. And viewers all around the globe were forming opinions. There was no longer room for feigned impartialities, there was no longer an excuse for wavering indecision. The time had come. Now, everyone would have to make a choice. One way or the other, they would all have to decide.

EPILOGUE

William Zimmerman hated the assignment. Standing in the oppressive heat at four hours a shift, eyes burning from the smoke. He knew it was strictly disciplinary and he certainly had no one to blame but himself. Truth be told, it was a small price to pay for the astonishing lapse of judgment his security team had displayed over at the King David as well as here on the Mount. How they had let someone like Salman Kilyos slip past them was beyond him. But that was three days ago. And, as always, the brilliant Lucus Ponte had managed to take an ugly chain of events and turn it into something positive. Hence the two glass caskets to Zimmerman's immediate right . . . and their unspoken warning to any who had similar ideas of opposing the new regime.

Carefully, Zimmerman scrutinized each member in the passing line. From dawn to dusk they came, enduring the sweltering heat, sometimes breathing through handkerchiefs because of the smoke . . . every age, every race, every nationality. They'd already passed through security and the metal detectors—a requirement for anyone now visiting the Temple Mount—but emotions still ran high. Any one of them could break past the ropes, race across the fifteen feet of stone pavement, and attack the two coffins. In fact, this morning alone there had been two such attempts. Not that he could blame them. In record time these two corpses, resting under the white nylon canopy, had become the symbol for all that was wrong and oppressive with the old world order.

That's why Ponte, at the Cartel's insistence, had agreed to put their bullet-riddled bodies on display—here, less than a hundred yards away from the construction of the new temple. It was a riveting symbol of new versus old. The giant beams of steel, the powerful cranes, the raw vitality, the hustle, bustle, and camaraderie of building the new . . . versus the silence, the decaying remains, and the inevitable destruction of the old.

In line, one or two people had started to look up. At first Zimmerman paid little attention, until more and more began tilting back their heads and shading their eyes. Finally he stepped out from under the canopy to see for himself. It was only a cloud. White and puffy, no different from any other cloud. Except it was the only one in the sky . . . and it was growing. At least that's what he first thought. But the longer he watched, the more he realized that the cloud wasn't growing . . . it was approaching.

By now all of the crowd was murmuring and staring. And for good reason. Not only was the cloud approaching, but as it drew closer it was possible to see some sort of glow radiating from inside. Even in the bright midmorning sun, light was clearly visible. It was a remarkable phenomenon. Unfortunately, Zimmerman had become so engrossed in it that he did not see who had sneaked up to the coffins and suddenly struck both of their glass tops.

But somebody had. That was the only explanation for their simultaneous shattering as they broke into a thousand spiderwebs that crumpled and rained down on top of the bodies inside. The crowd gasped. Some cried out in surprise.

Zimmerman raced the five or six paces back to the coffins, preparing to apprehend the culprit. But he could find no one. He glanced over to his partner, who was searching the other side with the same lack of success. And then he saw it . . . the shifting of broken glass inside the casket. A little at first and then more and more. Something was moving. The corpse's arm. Both of the arms. No, it was the entire body. It was sitting up!

Zimmerman held his fear in check. He'd heard stories of corpses doing similar things. Sometimes when the tendons dry, they contract the larger muscles, literally moving the body or, in extreme cases, causing it to sit up. That's all this was. He glanced over to the other casket, the woman's. Her body was doing the same thing. A remarkable coincidence. Still, that's all this was, a coincidence.

At least that's what he thought until the corpse raised its arms and began brushing the broken glass off of its face . . . then finally opened its eyes. Now, Zimmerman could only stare in astonishment as the body put both of its hands on the edge of the casket and eased itself up and out of the container.

Beyond the ropes, the crowd panicked—shouting, running for protection. Zimmerman was unsure what to do. Yell out orders for them to stop? Demand that they stay calm? And what about the corpse? Should he order it to get back into its casket?

By now the body was standing. It was still in its blood-stained clothes, the bullet holes clearly visible. Then to Zimmerman's greater astonishment, the head slowly turned toward him. It was all the guard could do to hold his ground. But the gaze was not zombielike or unseeing. This person was now alive. Fully. In fact, he was looking deeper into Zimmerman than he had ever been looked into before—searching him, probing his mind, his heart. An expression of pity slowly filled the face . . . as if what he'd seen greatly saddened him. Then, just as slowly, he turned and started toward the other coffin.

Zimmerman could not move. He stood frozen, dumbfounded, as Brandon Martus arrived at his wife's casket. Zimmerman threw a look to his partner who was undergoing equal shock and paralysis of action. Now Martus was reaching out to his wife, smiling warmly at her, helping her up and out of the coffin until she was standing at his side. Despite the matted hair and blood-smeared faces there was no missing the look of love between the two as they gazed into each other's eyes. Then Martus reached out to his wife's hand. She took it. And they turned and strolled out from under the canopy.

By now, the crowd had scattered . . . at least those who could move had scattered. A handful had fainted. A few lay prostrate on the ground. It was definitely time to act. Time to override his fear and move into action. But to do what? As Zimmerman frantically weighed the possibilities, a voice boomed from overhead, clapping like thunder.

"COME UP HERE!"

He stepped out from under the canopy and looked back up to the cloud. It loomed fifty feet above them. And, although Zimmerman's logic dictated the sound came from the cloud, most likely thunder, it also came from everything surrounding him—from the stone pavement at his feet, the fabric of the canopy, its poles, even the remains of the caskets. It was as if every molecule vibrated with the terrifying voice.

He looked back at the couple. A wind had started to surround them. It came from nowhere, whipping and whirling about them. But neither appeared concerned. Instead, they moved closer to each other, facing one another, he wrapping his arms around her waist, she resting her hands upon his neck. Then the most remarkable thing happened. Ever so gently, the two began to rise up off the ground. Slowly, but steadily, they rose, higher and higher. But they barely noticed. As the wind continued to surround them and as they continued to rise, they directed their attention from each other and up to the cloud. The same love and adoration filled their faces, only now it was directed toward the cloud. The expressions were that of total awe and abandonment. The look of two people completely immersed in love.

As they continued rising, their features became more difficult to distinguish against the cloud's blinding brilliance. Eventually, the bottom wisps of the cloud began to wrap around the couple, enveloping them . . . until, finally, they disappeared altogether.

Then Zimmerman heard it. A deep, throaty rumble that grew until it was a deafening roar, until the ground beneath his feet suddenly turned liquid. Shifting, pitching, writhing. Wave after wave of earth and pavement rolling like the ocean. He opened his mouth but could not hear himself scream as he was thrown to the ground. And still the earth heaved and buckled.

From the pavement he caught glimpses of the buildings surrounding the Mount. They were falling, crumbling like toys. He turned to the Dome of the Rock. It, too, was disintegrating . . . as if it were made of sand, as if it were nothing but dust. It was as if the entire area, the entire city—all of man's finest and grandest creations—as if it was all being reduced to nothing but dust.

If you liked *Fire of Heaven*, you'll love these other books by Bill Myers!

Blood of Heaven

Mysterious blood has been found on the remains of an ancient religious artifact. Some believe it is the blood of Christ. And experiments with specific genes from the blood have brought surprising findings. Now it's time to introduce those genes into a human.

Enter Michael Coleman: multiple killer, death-row resident . . . and, if he is willing, human guinea pig.

Follow Michael through the pages of this carefully researched science and psychological thriller that looks deep into the heart of man and meet for the first time Katherine and Eric Lyon, the spellbinding characters from *Fire of Heaven*.

Blood of Heaven
Softcover 0-310-20119-5
Audio Pages 0-310-21053-4

Threshold

Some say Brandon Martus has a mysterious ability to see into the future, to experience what scientists refer to as a "higher dimension." Others insist he is simply a troubled Generation-X member plagued by the accidental death of his little sister. It isn't until he teams up with Sarah Weintraub, the ambitious neurobiologist, that a far deeper secret unfolds.

Utilizing the latest discoveries in brain research and quantum physics, the two carefully wind their way through a treacherous maze of human greed and supernatural encounters that are both legitimate and counterfeit—until they finally discover the astonishing truth about Brandon Martus.

This book takes you from the mountains of Nepal to the heartland of America, through the deceptions of hell and into the hands of Jesus Christ, in a carefully researched, thought-provoking, and thoroughly electrifying journey.

Threshold
Softcover 0-310-20120-9
Audio Pages 0-310-21571-4

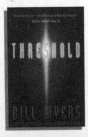